Racing to Armageddon

J. V. Robson

authorHOUSE®

AuthorHouse™ UK Ltd.
500 Avebury Boulevard
Central Milton Keynes, MK9 2BE
www.authorhouse.co.uk
Phone: 08001974150

© 2010 J. V. Robson. All rights reserved.

No part of this book may be reproduced, stored in a retrieval system, or transmitted by any means without the written permission of the author.

First published by AuthorHouse 1/7/2010

ISBN: 978-1-4490-5095-5 (e)
ISBN: 978-1-4389-2060-3 (sc)

This book is printed on acid-free paper.

Table of Contents

Chapter 1
    The Weapons Officer — 1

Chapter 2
    Channels of Information — 33

Chapter 3
    The Men for the Job — 98

Chapter 4
    Opening Game — 173

Chapter 5
    Rapid Response — 224

Chapter 6
    Improvised Journeys — 292

Chapter 7
    Alpine Interlude — 332

Chapter 8
    Fast Train to Berlin — 451

Epilogue — 522

To my mother and father

Chapter 1

The Weapons Officer

HE WAS WAITING. STILL WAITING. The plane was ninety minutes late, and every second increased the chances of discovery. He looked around the freezing cold waiting room, along the hard wooden bench where he sat, towards the groundcrew's quarters. They were clustered playing cards, obviously expecting nothing for some time yet. Then to the glass-partitioned office of the airfield commander, who had darted more than one suspicious glance at him. Then to the doorway which led to the tarmac, straining to see some sign of the Dakota transport that would be his salvation.

And last of all to the main doorway. That was where they would come. It had happened to so many, including some of his closest friends. Why should he be any different? He imagined the crash of the door being thrown back on its hinges, the tramp of booted feet towards him, the official voice challenging him with his real name.

He knew that his escape was full of risks, but there had been no alternative. They were on to him. The Tsarists and the British were getting impatient. To linger would have been suicide. But it all hinged on them buying the story of his illness and leaving him in peace at the dacha. And, of course, on nobody noticing the resemblance between Dr Dimitri Vlasenin, Nobel Prize-winning scientist and Hero of the Revolution, and Yuri Lermontov, weapons officer with the Red Army's Ordnance Corps.

For the fiftieth time he looked at his watch. Five to midnight, on Monday November 16th, 1942. Nearly two hours late now. Almost early for this time of year, but a lifetime for him. He looked to the commander's office again. Then he rose from the bench and began to walk forward. He had no conscious thought of what he would say, and his brain screamed at him to stay put even as he walked. But he could stand it no longer.

Just then a low humming noise was heard, faint on the midnight air. Immediately he halted and turned towards the runway, trying not to make his relief too obvious. He listened hard and, yes, there it was. The noise of aircraft engines, unmistakeable even to his untrained ear. The groundcrew were beginning to stir themselves too, rushing out of their quarters and opening the door to the runway. An icy November blast scoured him but he walked towards it as to a lover's embrace, following the groundcrew out on to the tarmac and watching as the Dakota descended.

It seemed like another eternity before it taxied to a halt and the weapons from Cyprus were unloaded. Then, as the groundcrew began loading the boxes of old rifles and faulty landmines donated by Comrade Stalin to Mr

Churchill in return, Vlasenin climbed the ladder up to the cockpit and showed his papers to the young RAF officer in the pilot's seat. The Englishman acknowledged them quickly, then his co-pilot indicated the passenger section, a long double row of metal bucket seats. Both men seemed tense and eager to set off again as soon as possible. Vlasenin could understand that. They were just ordinary flyers doing a job which broke all the rules. And if they were discovered... as Vlasenin moved to take his seat the pilot turned and gave him a nervous smile, making a thumbs-up gesture in the awkward manner of one trying to communicate with a simpleton.

As he turned back to perform his pre-takeoff checks Vlasenin sat down on the seat nearest to the cockpit. It was hard, cold and uncomfortable but he could not have relaxed even if it had been twin to the most comfortable leather armchair back at the dacha. Still he hardly dared to believe it might happen. Still he looked with anxious eyes to the airfield building. But at last the engines roared back into life. The Dakota taxied round on the runway, gathering speed, then launched itself into the air. And for the first time in twenty years Dr Dimitri Vlasenin felt free.

In the relative warmth and comfort of his office Captain Nikolai Danko heard the engine noise recede. He never bothered to inspect the cargoes now. It was always the same. The British (or, as Lieutenant Kaminksi called them, those stinking capitalist-imperialists) sent their rubbish across the mountains and got some Soviet rubbish in return. That way the glorious alliance was maintained while each side left the other to stew in its own juice. And the Motherland was stewing harder, as always, no matter what the newsreels said. This billet was quieter than most, but the Fritzies were still too close for his liking. He'd been a hero to the cause already, and look where it had got him. Now he just tried to stay out of trouble and stay alive.

That was why he hadn't questioned the weapons officer too closely. The poor little bastard was on the run, of course. That much was plain to anyone with eyes. He had made himself known to Nikolai late that afternoon, arriving in a plain black staff car which drove off as soon as its passenger got out. He was huddled in an Army greatcoat a size too big and all Nikolai had seen of him was a pale, pinched face and a pair of hunted eyes below a huge Cossack-style fur cap. The plane wasn't due for hours but he didn't seem to mind. He had briefly inspected the cargo, checked it against a list on a clipboard, taken a seat, and waited – and waited, getting more nervous by the minute.

Yes, on the run, all right. One of the dozens of black marketeers who had found rich pickings trading between the Middle East and the arsehole of the Soviet Union. Nikolai didn't blame him. Christ, it was the only way if you wanted to live like a human being. But there were plenty of risks. Nikolai knew that from experience and his escape route, should the worst ever come to the worst, would involve a lot more than simply hopping on the first plane out and hoping everyone looked the other way.

But, to be fair to the man, he'd got this far and Nikolai certainly wasn't going to be the one to turn him in. It was rare for a weapons officer to accompany these flights, but not unknown. His papers looked in order and it wasn't Nikolai's job to interrogate every passenger who crossed his path. Doubtless the Party has dealt this one the same shitty hand it deals everyone else, me included.

Nikolai had volunteered for the Air Corps after school and Komsomol in his dreary little hometown near Minsk because they'd told him that everyone had to fight to preserve the new order. Plus he didn't want to be a farmboy all his life, and he'd heard it paid better than the Army. Ah well, anyone can be wrong. Within a month of finishing his training he was in Spain, dogfighting with Messerschmitts in those fucking Rata orange boxes. Then Mongolia, at war with the Japanese to help the Chinese. He'd never quite fathomed that one out – all he knew was he flew eighteen hours a day around some butcher's yard named Khalkim-Gol for five months until his luck finally ran out. Shot down, captured, and... no, even now he didn't want to remember what they had done to him.

When some treaty or other released him, he was unfit to fly – unfit to walk without a stick or sleep with the light off for the first six months, in fact. So a suitably obscure desk job for a wounded hero was the inevitable next step and he was not too upset. At the start of 1940 this little corner of Georgia – halfway between Tbilisi and the Black Sea coast, tucked in between two sets of mountains – looked a long way from where any action was ever likely to be.

But then the Germans came. And all of a sudden there wasn't a place in Russia that wasn't near the action. They'd nearly taken Moscow last year and they might yet. Stalingrad too. And every day he could hear the guns on the other side of the Caucasus Mountains, getting closer. And if they got to the oilfields, brother, well... it didn't matter what the half-humans out east said; they had

Russia, they had the Soviet Union and they had victory. And Nikolai's little empire would go down in the rush. He'd heard what the Germans did to the *untermensch* and if the Party hadn't abolished God he would have said it was definitely better the Devil you knew. At least you could always bribe the commissars.

Yes, trouble would come along, anyway. No point in seeking it out. He had other things to worry about. Chief among them tonight, as on every night from mid-October onwards, was how to keep warm in his fucking icebox of an office. Winter had come early in 1942.

His thoughts were suddenly interrupted as Lieutenant Kaminski burst through the side door linking their offices. He hadn't even bothered to knock and Nikolai was about to deliver a mild rebuke when he saw Kaminski's face. He was a young, handsome, fair-haired Ukrainian, a genuine hero from the fighting around Moscow last year; 20 kills notched up when he was finally shot down, then captured by the SS. Zhukov's counter-offensive had liberated him before he could be shipped to a POW camp but not before the Germans had done to him what the Japs had done to Nikolai.

So he had joined the other invalids down here and despite an irritating, inexplicable loyalty to the Party Nikolai liked him. This was mainly because he was cool, sharp and disciplined enough to basically run the place. At least, that had usually been the case. But now his face was white with anxiety and uncertainty. It was the first time Nikolai had seen either emotion visit Kaminski, though they were regular guests in his own heart. And they'd just arrived again.

"What is it, Comrade Lieutenant?" he asked as calmly

as he could.

"A... er... a disturbance outside, Comrade Captain. I think you should come and see."

"What kind of disturbance, Mikhail? And tell me slowly and clearly, please. I can't go rushing around on every trivial errand here, you know." Nikolai adopted his tone of friendly, paternal authority to calm the situation. It didn't work.

"It's... it's the guards, Comrade Captain. They... they... I really think you should come outside at once."

"Very well." Nikolai was already making for the doorway. He chivvied Kaminski through, then across the waiting room to the main door. As soon as Kaminski opened it the icy chill hit them, but it was not that which stopped Nikolai dead in his tracks.

The guards were huddled ten yards to his right, in the doorway of their wooden barracks hut. They had never looked quite so unfit to be in uniform as they did then. Old, cold, thin, wasted, frightened men; coats and helmets far too big, weapons held like poisonous snakes. But they were not the only troops there.

Nikolai could see more, many more, vague shapes in the shadows, standing guard over his men, coming in from left and right to cover Kaminski and himself. A terrible memory of Mongolia darted across his brain, but a sense of surreal puzzlement replaced it just as quickly. Faces. That was all he could see. Only their faces were visible. Dozens of them, moving in on him. No bodies, no uniforms, no guns. Only the faces and they were all he needed to see. Hard, grim faces that seemed not to notice the cold around them or the dread they inspired. Looking at those faces Nikolai's eyes saw trouble, and his bowels began a wedding dance.

The faces moved nearer, one standing taller, leading them. It was only in the last few yards that Nikolai saw the men clearly and then he knew why he had seen only faces before. They were dressed in the same basic uniform as the regular army – round helmets, plain smock tunics, breeches and low, heavy boots. But where the ordinary soldiers' uniforms were the dull brown of Russia's earth, these were black.

Everything. Even the gloves on their hands and the submachine-guns now trained on the Air Corps men were jet black. The only flash of colour was one which to the average Russian was even more sinister. Green shoulder flashes, green on the cuffs of the tall officer now standing before them, a green star on his sidecap. The green of the NKVD. The Tchekists. The Organs of State Control. Beria's boys.

Nikolai forced himself to look the officer in the eye and hoped his terror wouldn't show. You didn't send this lot out to arrest a black marketeer. The weapons officer had been a big fish. And Nikolai had let him go. He knew now that to ask what they were doing here and why they had taken his guards from their posts and why hadn't someone had the courtesy to tell him about it would be a waste of time. They asked the questions and if the answers were not satisfactory he and all his men were dead.

"Captain Nikolai Danko?" the officer barked suddenly. Nikolai almost jumped out of his skin before stuttering a nervous "yes".

"You have a flight leaving here for Cyprus tonight. Has it taken off yet?"

"Yes, Comrade..." Nikolai trailed off as he realised

there was no mark of rank on the uniform. Only the sidecap and the air of complete authority marked him out from the rest of the cold-faced, black-clad killers. He didn't know this man's rank and probably never would. So he merely repeated stupidly: "yes, comrade."

The NKVD officer gave a savage curse and looked Nikolai in the eyes. "And there was a passenger on board?"

Nikolai forced himself to hold the officer's gaze despite his terror. "Yes, comrade. A weapons officer. His papers were in order," he added hopefully, but the NKVD man shook his head.

"Forgeries. Excellent ones, but forgeries none the less. You have had training in their detection, no?"

Nikolai nodded dumbly. Oh, of course he had – half an hour in a smoky room on an airless summer's day when he first came here, with some drunken Georgian pederast who kept getting his name wrong. A little book that had lain in his desk unopened ever since, a few slides nobody paid any attention to – and two years later you don't notice when some poxy runaway waves a forgery in front of you.

So this is how it ends. Well, just make it quick and don't kill the rest. They did their duty. Strangely, he felt almost calm; at least the lies and deceit of a rapidly declining life were over. A pathetic end, no doubt, but who got a glorious one these days? Still holding the officer's gaze, he said calmly: "I have had such training, comrade, and there is no excuse for my failure."

The officer saw his expression and gave a wintry smile. "You know the penalty for such negligence?" Nikolai nodded, but the officer seemed to have lost interest in him for the moment, turning to a burly man at his side. "They'll be over the border now, sergeant. We'll have to bring the others in. Get on the radio to Istanbul at once." The sergeant saluted and doubled back to a fleet of trucks parked at the main gate. Nikolai had only just noticed them. They were exchange too; American Dodge trucks, still with the white stars on the bonnet. And with machine-guns mounted above the drivers' cabs, trained on him and his men.

The NKVD officer turned back and looked on both Air Corps men but his words were aimed solely at Nikolai. "Yes, you know the penalty. But you are not the only one this man has deceived. Many more, some much higher than you... or I," he added, almost to himself. "Remember, Comrade Captain, not a word of this, or your negligence may be investigated a little more closely than I have the time or inclination to now. We place a high price on secrecy – and silence."

And then he was gone. His men moved back quietly and efficiently with him and then, with a roaring blast of petrol fumes and volleyed orders, the convoy was gone into the night. The airfield was dark without their headlights, quiet as their engines faded. Just the howl of the wind from the mountains broke the silence, sounding even more desolate now. As Nikolai's knees almost buckled with relief Kaminski asked: "What the hell was that, Nikolai Andreievich?"

His commander seemed not to notice the unusual tone or Kaminski's first ever use of his first name. He smiled a humourless smile as he replied: "You mean you don't know, Mikhail Grigorivich? That was the guardians of victory, freedom and prosperity protecting the safety of honest, decent Soviet citizens – and issuing us with a death threat." He turned and walked back inside.

∽

Vlasenin woke to the sound of the co-pilot talking softly over the cockpit radio. But only the last few words were audible. "Understood. Over and out." He turned to the pilot. "What do you think?"

"Well, it's an unusual request. And that wasn't the group captain's voice, though he did say the notification of final route would come from London. And they used that code word we were given."

The co-pilot looked uncertain. "Go to Turkey, though? That's bloody strange. Why not Iraq, or Syria?"

"This whole op's bloody strange. But it's the closest of the three to Cyprus. Syria's suffering bad weather too, so he said. Iraq's in the wrong direction, and they had trouble with the locals last year."

"Don't the Turks have a problem with our boys setting down in their territory, though? I heard they were interning RAF crews that had to make forced landings."

"They're a bit more lenient with us than they are with the Huns. Besides, this place is different. That Secret Service bod who briefed me says the commander there isn't averse to sheltering a few fledglings and saying no more about it if you grease his palm sufficiently. They're obviously very keen to keep this fellow in one piece. If they think it's safer to take him on by land and leave us as guests of the Turkish Air Force until the weather clears, I say fair enough. Their coffee's better."

"Should we radio the group captain?"

"He said to maintain radio silence; only transmission to be final confirmation of route from London. Sounds to me like that was it."

The co-pilot laughed and gave a shrug. "No skin off our nose, is it? I'll get navigating, then."

Vlasenin was listening intently now. His English was good enough to follow the gist of the conversation, and it sent a spasm of fear through his stomach. He walked towards the cockpit and, as the RAF men turned towards him, said: "Excuse me, what is the problem?"

"Bad weather in Cyprus. We cannot get there." The pilot addressed him like a backward child once again. "We have to land at an airfield in Turkey. Our people will be waiting for you. They will take you on to the coast by road, and a boat will be waiting to take you to Cyprus."

"No, that is not possible. I must get to Cyprus as quickly as possible. It is arranged. This could be a trap."

"They used a recognised code word," the pilot replied. "If the weather is bad, this will be safer."

"Cyprus by tomorrow morning – that was the agreement," Vlasenin persisted. "You must take me there."

"It is not safe. We cannot land if the weather is bad. We may fly off-course, or crash," the pilot said with growing impatience. "And might I remind you that you are not in command here. Now please return to your seat."

Vlasenin saw that further protest would be useless. So he did as he was told and sweated out the half-hour it took them to find the Turkish airfield. He tried to reassure himself that this was simply a minor complication, that it was safer not to risk flying over the sea in bad weather.

But still the slimy eel of fear that had hatched inside his stomach slithered and twisted.

He felt the plane descend through the blackness, toward a row of lights, then level out and bump to a halt. The pilot switched off the engine and rose from his seat, the co-pilot doing likewise. "Right – they said they'd be outside. So let's get him off." He indicated to Vlasenin to follow them. Then he opened the door.

There was a blast of cold air and a soft click. "Oh, shit," the pilot said softly, backing away as three men in civilian clothes climbed into the cockpit. Two were big, thick-set bruisers holding Tokarev automatic pistols on the RAF men. The third was smaller and slighter, but obviously the leader. He held nothing but a large handkerchief. "A small change of plan, Comrade Doctor," he said in Russian. "The British are not to have the pleasure of your company just yet."

Before Vlasenin could resist he had clamped the handkerchief over his mouth and nose. The sickly odour of chloroform was the last thing Vlasenin remembered before he went under.

∞

"Thank you, Flight Lieutenant Carter. That will be all." Group Captain Roderick Anson watched as Carter rose to his feet and left the office. He looked as shaken as the co-pilot, Dawson, had been. Hardly surprising. The daily routine of an RAF pilot in these parts did not usually consist of receiving coded messages, making emergency landings at airfields in neutral countries and being threatened at gunpoint by Bolshevik thugs straight from the pages of Sapper.

But such things all fell within Group Captain Anson's remit. As the RAF attaché at the British Consulate, and even more so as the local representative of the British Special Intelligence Service, he had become very used to shepherding various bits of flotsam and jetsam across both sides of the Bosphorus in his two years in Istanbul.

Much of this work had been done without the knowledge or approval of his Soviet opposite numbers. This was only to be expected. Spies never told each other any more than they had to, no matter what the official protocols said. But this job was different. This was the smuggling out – some might even say kidnapping – of a senior scientist working for a country allied to Britain. He'd not heard anything like it in all his time in SIS. But the orders from London were crystal clear. Co-operate with the Tsarist underground network in getting this Doctor Vlasenin to Cyprus. Then make sure the boys down there get every available serviceman on Aphrodite's Island to watch over him until he could be smuggled out to England. Any protests from anyone to be referred all the way upstairs. His station chief, Harold Gibson, had delegated the job to Anson because of his RAF contacts, and also because the Russian-born Gibson was well-known to Soviet intelligence in the city and closely watched at all times.

Very big. And very worrying. Delicate enough if it had all gone smoothly. But now... he looked at the other two men who had heard every word of the RAF crew's testimony, seated on either side of his desk. On the left was Colonel Richard Forster, the SIS link man from London. Anson had not really taken to him but he had to admit he got things done. Even as they spoke hundreds of troops were still on standby in Cyprus (and Iraq, Palestine, Syria and the British-occupied zone of Persia) ready to guard the new arrival. Had he in fact arrived at any of these destinations, of course. And every spy and informer in the region had their ears to the ground for any information that might have influenced or assisted the mission. It was clear that Forster saw his role as bringing some much-needed discipline to Anson's free and easy backwater. This latest development had made his naturally mournful, ascetic face look even more cadaverous.

The man sitting across from him could hardly have looked more different. Lev Vrushkov, the local head of the Tsarist underground, looked like a Cossack huntsman from a Russian folk tale. Big, red-faced and hearty, with a bristling moustache and a booming laugh, he had shared many a convivial evening with Anson over the years. But now he too looked grave and troubled.

"Well, gentlemen, you heard what they said. It was definitely the Russians. They were waiting for him."

"Of course they were." Forster sniffed. "Once that faked transmission was made to the plane all they had to do was get to the airfield before our men and enrich the local commander even more. Since all our dealings with him are unofficial we can hardly complain when he takes someone else's money."

"The question is: who made the transmission in the first place?" Anson asked. Forster glared at him.

"I was hoping you might be able to furnish us with that information, group captain – since the security failing was obviously at this end of the operation."

Anson squirmed inwardly. "Well, that's not necessarily so. I mean…"

"Oh, please, group captain. That code word was devised by you and Mr Vrushkov here. Whoever found it out must either have been one of your contacts. Or," he turned a frosty eye on Vrushkov, "one of yours."

"Impossible!" Vrushkov bristled with indignation. "I can vouch for every man involved in this operation. They are White Russians to the core."

"With all due respect," Forster replied, his tone indicating clearly how much respect he felt was due, "there have been several Tsarist underground cells which have been infiltrated by Soviet agents over the years. I was reluctant to involve your organisation from the start. And it would seem I have been proved right."

"You have no proof it was my men." Vrushkov controlled himself with visible difficulty. "Who was it who first heard of his desire to defect? We sheltered him, we organised his escape from Russia. We could have informed the NKVD at any time. But we did not. Are those the actions of double agents? No, Colonel Forster, we know what life is like under Stalin. We know how many wish to escape, and we try to help them all. But there are many people in England who still think Stalin is a hero, that Soviet Russia is the future for the world. How do you know some of them do not work in your organisation?"

Forster started to reply, his indignation as plain as the Russian's, but Anson gave a diplomatic cough. "Perhaps a more pressing concern is to find out where Vlasenin is," he said. "And to begin to think of rescuing him."

"Indeed." Forster's eyes, locked with Vrushkov's, now

switched back to Anson. "Well, I think we can be fairly sure that they will remain in Turkey for the time being – thanks to the foresight of Vlasenin himself."

"Ah, yes, the briefcase," Anson replied. "Thank God he didn't take that with him. But you say that no-one knows where it is hidden?"

Forster nodded. "He was most adamant about that. He feared if he entrusted anyone else with its fate there would be the risk of betrayal." He looked across at Vrushkov again. "All we know is that it was smuggled out some time ago, through his links with the scientific community, not the Tsarists. He would not give any names, or tell us where the briefcase is, except that it is somewhere in Turkey. As you know, he was to have revealed the precise location upon his arrival in Cyprus. But now... the Soviets will be well aware that he would leave no trace of his new findings behind. They will try to extract his secret from him."

"And they have many ways of doing so." Vrushkov's voice was bleak.

"Indeed. But they will not wish to return without both pieces of the jigsaw, as it were." Forster got up and walked over to a large map of central Istanbul on the wall. "I am sure they will have him in the Soviet Consulate even now."

He stabbed a finger into the centre of the map and traced a line along Istiklal Boulevard, the elegant street that wound its way down the hill from Galatasary to the bridges that spanned the Golden Horn and gave passage from modern Istanbul to the teeming, bazaar and mosque-studded labyrinth of the old city. The Soviet Consulate was located half-way along Istiklal, less than a mile from its British counterpart but for their purposes as inaccessible as the back of the moon.

"As you gentlemen are no doubt aware," Forster continued, "it is sovereign Soviet territory. For us to attempt to get inside without official permission would be regarded as at best a diplomatic insult, at worst an act of war. But we believe it also contains some, er... equipment designed to make people talk. Essentially, gentlemen, we have to rescue him before he can reveal the whereabouts of his papers. We must assume that will occur in a matter of days. If not hours."

"But at the same time we cannot spark an international incident," Anson said. "And we cannot afford to let whoever betrayed us last night find out anything more of our plans."

"Precisely." Forster turned back from the map. "I believe, in that case, that we must relinquish our role in this matter." He sighed. "And enlist the help of the SOE."

"SOE?" Anson's nose wrinkled in distaste. "The sabotage squad? They're just a bunch of cowboys."

"Indeed." For the first time in their acquaintance a glacial smile appeared on Forster's face. "But, after all, we are asking them to go into Indian country."

∽

The room was cold and damp and bleak and bare. Vlasenin had been in there for what seemed like hours – ever since he had woken to find himself dragged from the boot of a car through a doorway and down a flight of steps to his new quarters. Without his coat or cap the plain Army uniform had long since given up the fight to keep any of the chill out. He hugged himself, blew freezing breath on frozen knuckles, jumped up and paced around for the fiftieth time, walking around the metal and canvas chair by the metal table, circuiting all four walls before collapsing on the filthy mattress that covered the metal and wire-spring bed.

He felt as though he would freeze to death, but he knew they wouldn't let that happen. They had plenty of other things to do to him yet and once all that began he would look back on this period as fondly as a childhood holiday. He gave a shiver that was more than the cold.

So close, damn it. He had known his superiors were getting suspicious of his continuing lack of results, knew that this was the moment when action had to be taken. So he had contacted the Tsarists. The first directly treasonable action of his life, but one which he knew would put him beyond the pale at a stroke. Everyone knew the Whites were still active, some inside Russia, others scattered to the four corners of Europe. The names of the contacts, the locations of the dead letter drops, the code words which could gain you an audience... they were not hard to reach. But in reaching for them you put your head on the block – and quite a few other parts of your anatomy.

He smiled grimly despite himself. No other organisation was hunted quite so fiercely by the NKVD. That was why he had chosen a small group, near to where he worked, with few contacts in the wider reaches of the underground. They had fallen over themselves to help, and so had the British. The plan was arranged quickly – too quickly. He knew that now. But they had insisted that even a minute longer than necessary spent in Russia could be fatal.

And like a coward he had let himself be swayed. To what avail? He had still been taken. That meant the network had been blown and had betrayed him. So they would all be prisoners or in hiding now. Were there any left in Turkey to retrieve the briefcase? Thank God he had told no-one where it was hidden, otherwise it would all be up by now. But equally no-one from the other side could find it and make it safe. Only he knew the secret. And soon the finest torturers in the world would come through that door and make him reveal that secret.

If only... ah, why run over it all again? There were always so many alternatives – half a life lived as a scientist had taught him that much at least. Better to concentrate on staying alive and staying strong. The longer you hold out the more chance there is of another chance coming along. Hope and despair. He had lived with both for most of his life and sometimes it was harder to know which drained the spirit most. Perhaps neither mattered now. All that mattered was that he say nothing, agree to nothing. Whatever defences he could marshal from his mind and body and spirit were all he had left.

There was the sound of a key in a lock, then the door opened. Vlasenin sat up and turned, to see the man from the plane walk in, dismissing the guards who flanked him with a casual wave. He moved to the centre of the room with a quick, graceful step and drew up the chair, turning it to face the prisoner on the bed as he sat down. Vlasenin got a good look at him for the first time. He was a dark-haired, well-built man of medium height, with dark green eyes set deep in an angular face. He wore uniform now

– the uniform of an Army major, not the green and black of the NKVD. His face was lined and hard, but the eyes sparkled with intelligence. He didn't look menacing but then the real bastards never did. When he spoke his voice was educated, calm, almost indolent. It was the voice of a sophisticated Moscow bureaucrat. "So, Doctor Vlasenin, do you think we might have some explanation of your recent movements?"

"My name is Lieutenant Yuri Lermontov, and I..."

"Please don't." The voice was not angry, not even raised, but the force behind it stopped Vlasenin dead. "There really is no point in bothering with that any longer. We know exactly who you are and what you were planning to do. All we need to know is why. And you will tell us – quickly, I hope. So please do not waste my time and yours."

"If I give you my true name, you will have the advantage of me," Vlasenin said with as much dignity as he could muster. It was all a game; why not give them some of their own bullshit back? The visitor smiled.

"How terribly bourgeois. I was told excessive formality was one of your more irritating character traits, Comrade Doctor. But, since you insist, my name is Amarazov – Major Yevgeny Amarazov, of Military Intelligence, at your service. Now we know at least one of us has been open and honest. Perhaps we can improve on that."

Vlasenin shrugged. "Very well; I am Doctor Dimitri Vlasenin. And if you want an explanation of my recent movements, I can tell you that too." He was getting angry, he realised, the words were coming out fast and careless. He hesitated, taking a deep breath. Amarazov noticed and pulled a gold cigarette case from his breast pocket.

"Would one of these help? A civilised aid to conversation – and your favourites, Balkan Sobranie. Better than that *machorka* rubbish, eh?"

Vlasenin leaned forward, putting the cigarette in his mouth and inclining his head to catch the flame from Amarazov's gold lighter. "*Spassibo*. As I was saying," Vlasenin continued, sitting back, "my recent movements were an attempt to escape from the Soviet Union. I see no point in denying it. And since you know so much about me, you must be aware of my reasons."

"Oh, yes." Amarazov nodded, drawing on his own cigarette. "You have been a somewhat vocal critic of... certain aspects of the regime in the past. Nothing absolutely seditious or treasonous, of course, and your support of The Great Patriotic War was well received. But we forget nothing, Comrade Doctor, and we have been watching.

"You seem to be very dissatisfied with a system which has afforded you an unusually high place in its ranks. Party Commissar, Member of the Soviet Academy of Sciences, holder of the Order of Lenin. This country you obviously despise so much," Vlasenin made to protest but Amarazov silenced him with a raised hand, "has given you your own research centre; time, money and resources to achieve discoveries in your field which have benefited all mankind. You have a worldwide reputation, a generous budget, and a Nobel Prize – the highest honour science can bestow." His voice hardened. "The Soviet Union has given you all this. Your repayment is to betray her in her hour of greatest need."

"I did not take this decision lightly..."

"That makes us all feel so much better, Comrade

Doctor."

"Hear me out, damn you!" Vlasenin shouted, goaded by the intelligence man's sarcasm. "I love my country. I have worked for her, fought for her, all my life. But for too long she has been ruled by a highly questionable system, using highly questionable methods to sustain itself."

"Questionable?" Amarazov seemed to savour the word on his lips. "An interesting word to use. You have questions, Comrade Doctor – what scientist does not? Why not ask them?"

"Because it is not permitted."

"Your previous criticisms were allowed. Noted, but not acted upon. Is that the action of a tyranny?"

"You chose to allow them because you wanted something from me."

"We want something from every Soviet citizen – their best efforts to preserve the Motherland which has sheltered and rewarded them. Is that such a hard bargain?"

"This system is corrupt, inefficient..." Vlasenin changed tack, momentarily at a loss to counter Amarazov's reasonable and forgiving tone, stung by his own sense of guilt.

"You have complaints about your facilities, your funding; complaints about local bureaucrats? We help you as much and as quickly as we can, but if..."

"This system is evil! Ruled by a madman with blood on his hands. Rotten to the core. Brutal, repressive and... evil!" Vlasenin cried it out, half-angry at the passion goaded from him, half-glad to speak his mind at last.

Amarazov waited until he had caught his breath again, then said with a note of sorrow: "So you have turned against the Soviet system. So you choose to deny it your talents. You make this decision on behalf of everyone in this system. The soldiers who battle the invader. The families in the occupied territories who groan under the weight of an oppression far worse than any you could imagine. The workers giving ten times more than you to the cause of victory for a hundredth of the reward. All the good men and women fighting to defend the finest political philosophy ever imagined, the most humane conception of social order – I know you still believe that, Comrade Doctor. While the whole world prays they can conveniently destroy themselves in destroying Hitler. Comrade Doctor, I too hope you did not take this decision lightly."

"If you're trying to make me feel guilty, it won't work," Vlasenin said with more force than he felt.

"I do not wish to make you feel anything." Amarazov showed impatience for the first time. "All I want you to do is tell me all you know. What secret of yours was too vital to keep in Russia? And how can we use it to defeat our invaders?"

"As if you've ever used anything so efficiently." Vlasenin gave a scornful laugh, some of his spirit returning. "Besides, all my latest research has been well documented. It's highly theoretical, still at an early stage and I don't see how it can help you."

Amarazov shook his head. "You're being very stupid again, Doctor. I warn you, don't. For some years now, you have been concealing a large part of your work from us. You scientists," he gave a light, contemptuous laugh, "do you think you're the only people with brains? That we ignorant *moujiks* swallow everything you choose to tell us?

"All your scientific career has been obsessed with concentrated forms of energy. Your first major work was with Kulik's team in 1921, analysing the Tunguska blast. The paper that you wrote on your discoveries there was praised by Einstein himself. You won your Nobel Prize for work on atomic power. And deserved it, because you were years ahead of your time. When Otto Hahn proved the atom could be split in 1938, he named you as his main inspiration. Hahn and Heisenberg are working on the explosive power of nuclear fission in Germany at this moment. So is Fermi with the Americans, Frisch and Peierls in Britain, and many of our other best scientists. But they all look to you, to Vlasenin. And you tell us that your research has reached a blind alley; that practical applications will not be possible for years, if not decades. At the same time you start to privately criticise the Five Year Plans, the purges, our policy in Spain... really, Comrade Doctor, do you think us imbeciles? Your precious principles are denying us the fruits of your genius. We know they are rich fruits. Share them."

"And if I will not?"

Amarazov laughed again. "Well, at least you admit there is something to share. And I would answer your question, Comrade Doctor, were it not based on an unsound premise, as you scientists would say." His voice hardened. "For you will tell us. Be under no illusions. You can tell us now, saving myself a great deal of time and yourself a great deal of pain. Or you can have your secrets drawn from you by force.

"Please believe me when I say we can and will do it. I've never seen a man last more than a few hours. I had hoped to spare you this. If the NKVD had had their way they would be working on you now. We managed to gain control of your interrogation, not only because we see this as more a military matter – and, because of the regrettable British involvement, an external security one – but because we want you to come to as little harm as possible. And to continue to serve the Soviet Union in the future. Once you have told us your secret, you'll find it's easier to live with the loss than you think. You will be a better person. A better Soviet citizen. But first you must tell us."

"I will not. You can't make me."

"Yes, we can."

"I'll die first."

"You will die if and when we decide it is time for you to die. Not a second before. And not before you have told us everything."

"Even if I did," Vlasenin said grudgingly, laying heavy stress on the 'if', "you can't expect me to trot out all my findings just like that. It would be a garbled mess."

Amarazov gave that laugh again; Vlasenin was beginning to hate it. "I'm sorry, Comrade Doctor. We have become so sidetracked in this interesting discussion I forgot to mention our prime purpose. We know you have all the findings you wished to withhold from us documented somewhere. And you have sent them out of Russia.

"We suspected this for some time and now the counter-revolutionaries who were misguided enough to connive in your escape have confirmed it. Incidentally," he gave a lazy smile, "you may be interested to know that all the White Russian networks, both here and abroad, have been almost entirely infiltrated by Military Intelligence agents. Some are even completely run by us.

"A pity you did not choose one of those. In fact, had you approached the underground at a higher level you would have been immediately apprehended. As it was, we could not act until this network told higher authority of their prize. And if they had not been swayed by the British and acted without official clearance you would not have come as close as you did to freedom. It must be very hard," he continued cruelly, "to have your hopes raised and then dashed, to find the organisation you placed your trust in built on sand. Still, if one allies oneself to the Tsarists..."

"I did not. They were a means to an end. I have no sympathies with Tsarists."

"Of course; we have already seen how fastidious you are when it comes to your allegiances. But we stray from the point – that you have documents hidden detailing all your findings. Our contacts have told us that they are somewhere in Turkey. Perhaps here in Istanbul? Or Ankara? Or any one of a hundred places? No matter. You will tell us. The Tsarists do not know where, or we would have found out. The British do not, or they would have made a move for them. And, as you have no doubt realised, everything the British do we know of also. So only you hold the secret. And you are here. So you will tell us and we will recover them. We are looking now, anyway. And we are the only ones who are looking. The Tsarist agents in Turkey not under our control are a leaderless rabble. The British have disowned you to preserve our 'precious alliance'. This building in which you are held is Soviet territory. None of your erstwhile rescuers would dare to touch us here. You are alone. We are your only hope. Save us time. Tell us."

"Never."

"Do you understand what I am offering you? More than the NKVD would, I assure you. Tell us and we will let you live." Amarazov was trying hard to control his temper. "Once we have the papers, you are expendable. Our loyal scientists could take over your work. We could put a bullet in your head that very moment. After all, one less Fascist traitor..."

"I am no Fascist! Do you think I wish to see them win?"

"No Fascist, no Tsarist, no Communist – what exactly are you, Doctor Vlasenin?" Amarazov was genuinely angry now, but his raised voice also held a note of righteous triumph. "You do not wish Germany to win, but you do not wish us to, either. Is there no limit to your arrogance? Will you personally award the victory to whichever country you choose?

"You must be a wise man to make such a decision, Comrade Doctor. Wise, or proud. So you choose the British – a crumbling empire run by decadent aristocrats who grow fat while their workers live in rat hovels, but so much better than us. Or are they merely a convenient intermediary? Is it America where your heart is set, the money-grabbing gangster government? Are your high principles to be bought by the almighty dollar?"

"Nobody buys me!" Vlasenin was angry too, angry that Amarazov should cheapen the hardest, most courageous decision he had ever made. "I know the western allies are not perfect, but I'd sooner see them victorious than you. I know the power I hold," he continued softly. "It is greater than you could imagine. To deliver it into the hands of you and the people you work for would mean the whole world could be run as Russia is now. I will work to stop that. And if it means my country must stand alone and suffer more while the war is won elsewhere, then so be it. I will answer for my actions to God and no-one else."

"You sad, conceited fool. As if you still believe in a God. As if you can, you who lived through the last war. You renounced Him when you joined the Party. Admit you acted for your own selfish, arrogant motives, not to become some tarnished but forgiven saint.

"And if Cyprus had been invaded the day you arrived? If your plane were shot down on the way to England? What then? Neither we nor the western allies would prevail. We would have to fight on. Risk the Germans finding the secret, and seeing a tyranny worse than any ever known in history conquering the world. But still, at least we would be comforted as we died by the fact that Doctor Dimitri Vlasenin had not betrayed his sacred principles. You talk of answering to God – I think you seek to become Him."

Vlasenin started to speak and Amarazov slapped him back-handed across the face. "Say nothing! I wish to hear no more excuses, no petty self-justifying. Individuals and their voices and their principles are unimportant except in what they can give the State. You can give the State victory and you will!"

He took a deep breath, then smiled crookedly. "Come, now – I am sorry, truly." He produced a silk handkerchief from his trouser pocket and dabbed at the thin trickle of blood on Vlasenin's right cheek. "But you must not treat me like some ignorant jailer, or one of those NKVD apes. I truly believe we are not so far apart as you think. We are both seekers after secrets, knowledge – truth if you will. We both believe in a victory for what we think is right. We both hate Fascism. We have simply chosen slightly differing paths. The Soviet Union does not seek to rule the world as Hitler does. We merely wish to defeat him. If we do that our system can live on, prosper, perhaps change. You can be a part of that, using your power and your reputation. I can help you. I have influence. Save your country, Dimitri. Save it with us. It is the best way."

Vlasenin's head reeled from the blow, from the cold, from their arguments and from Amarazov's sudden compassion. He seemed so reasonable, the seeds of doubt were sown again. He does want the Germans defeated. So do I. There are risks in working for the west. They are not perfect either. There is so much good in Russia and her people that could be saved, should be saved. I could save it. He looked up, beginning to speak – and his mind saw a burning farmhouse, oily black smoke rising above. Pigs and goats screaming. Shrill animal terror. The stench of roasting flesh on the air. Human flesh. He spat blood at Amarazov's feet. "I'd sooner work with the Evil One – bastard."

Amarazov showed not a flicker of emotion. He simply sighed, rose from the chair, walked to the door and slammed his palm against it twice. Within seconds it was opened and the two guards walked in, followed by two other men, also in army uniform. They carried a small rectangular object, about the size of a briefcase. Two large engine batteries were screwed to the base. Several switches studded its surface and a voltmeter at the top formed a crown. Two wires attached to the batteries rested on top of the box, crocodile clips at their ends.

"Get up," Amarazov said. Vlasenin swallowed hard, but did as he was told. The torturers were placing the battery box on the table. A switch was flicked, a red light throbbed. Vlasenin saw that the voltmeter went up to ten thousand as Amarazov vacated the seat by the table and the guards sat him down. Amarazov spoke, to the torturers: "On the arms first; five hundred volts." As the torturers grabbed the wires he turned to Vlasenin. "You can stop it now, or at any time during the interrogation. All you have to do is tell me where the documents are."

Vlasenin shook his head dumbly, not trusting himself to speak. *I must say nothing, I am right to resist. Any state which can do this does not deserve victory. I must...*

"One last chance, Comrade Doctor. When it is over, we can talk of systems and principles and victory and defeat and right and wrong, for as long as we wish. But first you must tell me where the documents are."

Vlasenin shook his head again... *to resist. Any state which can do this...*

Amarazov shrugged. "Begin."

∾

At that same moment another bleak, bare, cold, damp and filthy cell, in a building in the centre of Toulouse, was found empty by a medical orderly from the army of the Vichy French Republic. Within seconds sirens wailed, searchlights flashed and booted feet rang on stone floors. Within minutes soldiers, gendarmes, *Milice* and the few German troops who had so recently joined the interrogation team were searching every house in the city.

And at the edge of the city, in a dark, remote railway yard, three more medical orderlies' uniforms were burning in a watchman's brazier as the lock was picked on a goods train truck ready to roll from its isolated siding. A sharp click, a whispered command from one of the three men clustered by the door and a fourth emerged from the shadows. He wore old, ill-fitting clothes hastily put on. There were new papers in the jacket pocket and new dressings on the multiple wounds that three days of torture had put on him. His square, firm-jawed face might once have been handsome and might be again. But new scars had speckled it, the skin was pale and tight, the grey eyes dead and the long broad nose broken and crooked.

Yet still he moved with speed and grace, lifting himself into the truck unaided. One of the rescuers gripped his hand briefly. "Good luck, my friend. And don't worry – the bastards who put you in there..." he made a quick throat-slitting gesture.

"Just keep your heads down," the fourth man replied. "Plenty of time for that when we're winning again. We'll get there yet." He jumped inside, the door slammed and he added under his breath: "And if pigs had wings they'd be eagles. Jesus, what a shambles." The wheels screeched as the train began to move. "It'll be a long time yet before the return match, boys – and I'm damn sure I'll be coaching from the touchline." Major Alexander Rawlings lay back on a bag of grain and lit a Gauloise in cupped hands. Then, for the hundredth time in the war and the thousandth in his career, he said softly: "I need a rest from this bloody game."

Chapter 2

Channels of Information

THOUGHTS OF A SIMILAR NATURE ran through the mind of Group Captain Anson as he flicked the switch on the radio, cutting out the static that had been drilling into his ears for the last minute. Another washout. Was there any Tsarist group in Turkey responding to broadcasts at the moment?

He looked up and across the tiny office, windowless and lit only by a bare light bulb, at Forster and Vrushkov. Their expressions mirrored his. They had been clustered in the tiny space, no more than an anteroom behind a secret door in Anson's main office, for hours. But no-one among all the Tsarist contacts was at home this morning. Anson had been disinclined to share Forster's gloomy assessment of the Soviets' infiltration, but he had to admit this did not bode well. He took off the headphones and rubbed his eyes.

"Well, that's all the main active groups outside Istanbul. No reply from any of them."

"That is impossible!" Vrushkov's blustering certainty was beginning to sound somewhat forced now. "We told them to be on the alert. They knew the package had been sent to Turkey. They must be there."

"If they were, they would have replied." Anson tried to keep his patience. "I can only conclude from this continuing silence that Colonel Forster was right and the Reds have been playing us for fools with dummy networks all along. Either that or the networks are genuine but they are under such close surveillance that they daren't reply to our transmissions."

"Whichever it is, gentlemen," Forster's mournful tones cut in, "it is placing the mission in great jeopardy."

"Do we have to use them, though?" Anson asked, ignoring Vrushkov's accusing look. "After all, we know where Vlasenin is. The SOE have some Russian émigrés on their payroll, and plenty of fluent Russian speakers. Surely that's all we need?"

Forster shrugged. "SOE in London and Cairo both seem to think that the raiding party needs to work with a group on the ground who have knowledge and experience of working and travelling in Turkey, but one not connected too closely with Mr Vrushkov's operation. And they have a point. All the Tsarists in Istanbul are being watched twice as closely now. It's going to be a long journey from Istanbul to any suitable air or sea rendezvous – the port and the airfields near the city itself will be watched too damn closely – and they'll have a lot of people on their tail. A large, well-organised group with good local knowledge to shepherd them across the country would be most useful. And since we are, in effect, asking SOE to do our job for us, we must give some credence to their opinions."

He sniffed. "It's my view that they are being too high-handed, as usual. After all, it was our men who confirmed that Vlasenin is being held in the consulate. But this de Chastelain fellow has had some success in setting up an effective network here – especially given the delicate situation with the Turks..."

He tailed off. All three men knew the problems of operating in Turkey. At the beginning of the war it had seemed ideal territory. A treaty of alliance had been signed with France and Britain in 1939 and Istanbul, a centre of intrigue since the Byzantine era, was the summer retreat of the entire diplomatic corps when Ankara became a scorched dustbowl. But two years of *blitzkrieg* had seen France defeated, Britain besieged and Turkey's old enemy, Russia, almost destroyed. A treaty of friendship had been signed with Germany in 1941 and since then all espionage activity had been constrained by that Balkan rarity – an efficient and almost incorruptible police force. They were backed by the security and intelligence service Emniyet, which had won an outstanding reputation in the espionage world considering its mother country, the modern Turkey created by Ataturk's vision, military skill and sheer bloody-mindedness, was barely two decades old.

The upshot was that, despite a city teeming with spies, no intelligence agency had anything like the penetration that they enjoyed in other neutral countries. SIS had done diligent work but resources were needed elsewhere. And SOE's involvement, once the Russian front had stabilised and the threat of German occupation of the Middle East receded, had been scaled down. Added to that, Russian émigrés in Turkey were habitually regarded with suspicion. It made the task facing the Istanbul triumvirate far from simple.

"But we must find someone," Vrushkov said at last. "They will break him soon. And then they will find the papers."

"Well, there is the other list." Anson put down his main codebook, fished around in his desk drawer, and produced another, much more worn and well-thumbed. "These are the contacts that were established early on. Most of them haven't been used for over a year. I don't even know if they're still alive. But if we must make some contact..."

He saw Forster's expression. A 'by the book' intelligence man, the idea of cold-calling second string agents and risking the consequences was clearly anathema to him. Even Vrushkov looked uncertain. Still, if this man was that important... ours not to reason why. He flicked the radio back on.

༄

Anson was still hunched over the radio, anger and frustration growing as he barked call signs into empty ether, at 11 am that morning, Tuesday November 17th, 1942. In Moscow it was an hour earlier, the clocks striking ten as Lieutenant-General Bogdan Renkovich emerged from the conference room in the deepest depths of the Kremlin, his naturally pale face looking as though it had just lost a pint of blood.

Within minutes the car had taken him back to his office near Red Square. His hand trembled as it turned the ornate brass door handle. He steadied himself briefly, wiping sweat from his brow with his free hand. Stay calm, he told himself. It is too soon and too close for a sign of weakness. That's all the wolves will need to go for your throat. They've just made that very clear. He gave a quick glance round but the corridor was empty and when he turned back to the door his hand was steady enough to open it.

Renkovich's office was considerably larger and better appointed than Group Captain Anson's but that was only natural for the acting head of Military Intelligence, one of the ten or twelve most powerful official positions in the State at any time and automatically elevated to the top five or six in time of war. The huge desk was solid oak, with three antique finish telephones within easy reach. The pen-holder was solid gold, like the frames of the photographs which jostled for position around its edges. Most prominent was the one showing his wife and twin daughters, now far away from Moscow and the fighting and intrigues. Next to it the one of a young man who now seemed almost a stranger; cap set at a rakish angle, wavy dark hair spilling from under it, hammer and sickle armband worn proudly with the crossed ammunition bandoliers as he and his comrades from the "cavalry of special assignments" posed in front of the burnt-out White Russian HQ. And finally the middle-aged grandee in full uniform, shaking hands with Comrade Stalin himself, both smiling broadly, surrounded by the ghosts of men long since betrayed, denounced and purged.

Renkovich's gaze lingered on each of them. They told the life story of a man who had reached the heights of his profession, then spent every waking hour plotting and lying and betraying his ideals to refine the one quality he shared with his leader; the ability to survive.

The Revolution had been the making of Renkovich. When all had been cast down, those who accepted it and fashioned themselves anew reaped rich rewards. Not all could accept their 'former lives' were gone. But for young Bogdan 'former life' meant only two things: a harsh, unloving military family who had sent him from his childhood on the shores of Lake Ladoga to the military academy at Petrograd with indecent haste; and iron discipline in the service of a regime he had grown to despise.

When the mutinies began he was one of the first to pledge himself to the cause. And such was the loyalty he had earned in three years of war that his regiment went with him (well, not 'his' regiment, exactly; he had earned the colonelcy his parents had dreamed of by shooting his predecessor in the back and sharing out the old bastard's hoard of vodka). That regiment was soon joined by others, to become a division which he presented like a dowry to his new bride – Bolshevism.

He had stormed the Winter Palace. He had guarded Lenin and Trotsky. He had fought the Whites (and the Greens, the traitorous Mensheviks who had proved the worse threat in the end), with the courage of a bear, the cunning of a fox and the savagery of a wolf. All these qualities won him the notice of his peers. Especially Trotsky, who wanted an army and wanted men like Renkovich at its head. Soon young Bogdan found himself leading a picked squadron of his men in the "cavalry of special assignments", the Praetorian Guard of the Red Army, the force that was to become *Spetsnaz*. They rode to and fro across the vast battlefield of Russia in its civil war, gathering vital intelligence and using it in savage lightning raids. Renkovich loved the excitement, the challenge, the sense of fulfilment. This was to be his life.

But away from the fighting, the new order was beginning to quarrel amongst itself and the target for the rumours and hatred was Trotsky. To Renkovich this was unthinkable. Trotsky had taken him from the ranks, raised him up. When the Department of Military Intelligence, the GRU, was set up in October 1918, it was as much Bogdan's child as Leon's. Because both saw the need for a balance to the other war dog on the leash – Tcheka, the State Security Organs, created within days of the Revolution by Felix Dzerzhinsky, the Polish nobleman who had made it a force to strike terror into every Russian (and, if you believed the legends, had run drunkenly through the Winter Palace on the last night of 1917 crying: "God forgive me, what have I done?"). Trotsky had warned him to fear the Tchekists then. Now, a quarter of a century later, he did still. For they had killed the teacher and now they wanted the pupil.

All that was far away as Renkovich rose steadily in the GRU, and even when Trotsky was exiled his opponents could find no fault in his work. He had denounced his former mentor as loudly as the rest – there was no other way – then acquiesced as Tchekist after Tchekist took the throne of the organisation he had helped to create. He remained a humble secret agent, and had proved himself a brilliant one. His knowledge of the Baltic states had helped reverse the GRU's early failures there. Then he had engineered the "special enterprises", the establishment of shops and factories throughout Europe and North America which had served as profitable fronts for spy networks. He had been abroad on this work when intelligence setbacks during the war with Poland prompted a purge of the GRU. It was the first of his many strokes of luck.

In the 1930s he gradually took a less active role, becoming instead an administrator and co-ordinator. He chose his subordinates well. Chief among them were Anatoly Grigorin, a handsome, narcissistic and totally ruthless Navy lieutenant from the Crimea; and Yevgeny Amarazov, an aristocratic Muscovite who had worked as ADC to a White Russian general for three years, then betrayed his entire command. They became known as the 'Unholy Trinity' of the GRU. Renkovich came up with the ideas, Grigorin turned them into meticulously detailed reality and Amarazov carried them out. Together they stole documents, tortured traitors, recruited friends and executed enemies in all four corners of the capitalist world.

By the middle of the decade the GRU's budget was several times that of the OGPU, as the Tchekists now called themselves. It was the favoured child of the monstrous twins, so Comrade Stalin chose it for a special task. He had become convinced (with a little help from Reinhard Heydrich of SS Intelligence, the only opponent Renkovich had ever feared) that his general staff must be purged. The OGPU were chosen to do this, but like Caesar's wife they must be above suspicion when they did so. Therefore they must be purged first, and who better for such a task than the GRU?

Their chief at the time, Berzin, jumped at the chance but realised that Moscow would be a dangerous place when the killing began. So when the work was set in motion he offered to step down. As his successor Uritski took office he held a meeting with the 'Unholy Trinity' and offered them the chance to carry out special work for Military Intelligence in the spies' playground that was Civil War Spain, making very clear the dangers of remaining.

So they went and won new laurels infiltrating the POUM and the CNT and every other organisation on the Republican side. Amarazov even joined a company of White Russians fighting with Franco and replayed his finest hour. Meanwhile the OGPU was destroyed, but was born again under Yezhov, the "bloody dwarf" of the Central Committee. It performed its great task of purging the generals and then, as natural reward and revenge, wiped out the GRU from Uritski to the lavatory cleaners.

But the heroes of Spain were left untouched. They returned to plaudits and promotions, and Renkovich was taken aside and told the price of survival. He and his protégés would die unless they denounced Berzin. They were not so important, but he was a chief and no chiefs survived the purges. So Renkovich did the one action that had ever shamed him. He betrayed a comrade in arms, a commanding officer and a friend. To survive. And he did. Berzin died and Yezhov became head of both the GRU and OGPU until Comrade Stalin realised the unfitness of this and the dangers of two intelligence agencies with no reason to hate and mistrust each other. So Yezhov died in turn. Logic at its purest.

While all this was being played out the capitalists too had decided to make war on each other. But Russia did not stand by. Unfortunately, killing all save a handful of her best agents had impaired her intelligence network somewhat, as the Winter War with Finland proved. The OGPU was renamed the NKVD and 'Lavratka' Beria, an all too natural heir to Yezhov, took up its bloody reins.

At the GRU Renkovich continued a strong right hand to its leaders (it had been made clear he had too tainted a record and too many enemies to ever hold the highest rank). The first of these was Golikov, the crafty fighter who wormed secrets from the British and the Americans while charming their women. But after the disgrace of Barbarossa he went back to the army and the GRU was then split into two sections: the Directorate of the Supreme High Command, answerable to Stalin himself and mainly concerned with work in Soviet embassies and consulates; and the Directorate of the General Staff, with a vacancy for leadership.

At last Renkovich had his command, even if only a *de facto* one – and it was the command of an organisation divided and in turmoil, asked to operate throughout the world against ally and enemy alike, with instant success taken for granted and the slightest failure punishable by death. And now, with the Vlasenin business, he really had caught the wolf by the tail.

To begin with, they had taken the operation from the NKVD – that had been the crux of the latest meeting and several more before it. When Vlasenin had disappeared from sight it had been due to a lapse in the NKVD surveillance. And when he had resurfaced it had only come to their attention again because the GRU had infiltrated the Tsarists so completely – what Amarazov told Vlasenin had (for once) been no less than the truth.

So, a double triumph for Renkovich, a double blow for Beria – and a chance to establish the ascendancy of the GRU once and for all.

It was the biggest gamble Renkovich had ever taken but he knew that wresting the operation from the NKVD completely and delivering Vlasenin and his documents to Moscow would be the crowning glory. The GRU would give Stalin ultimate victory and in return it would have ultimate power. And the man who engineered that victory would, of course, be offered full leadership of it. Of course it would never free Renkovich from the danger of denouncers or rumour-mongers completely. That was not the way that power worked in the Soviet Union. But his position would certainly be stronger, almost on a par with that of the Georgian seminarist himself.

The Politburo had agreed to give Renkovich full control of the operation – on condition that he deliver results immediately. And here Amarazov had let him down. His inveigling brand of questioning had failed, and so far the torture had also. Vlasenin had proved far more resilient than anyone could have guessed. What should have been a matter of hours now looked like taking days. The Politburo had not been impressed and at that last meeting Beria had used all his powers to win back the prize. He had almost succeeded, but Renkovich had promised results very soon. It was a promise that depended on how his subordinates performed. And if they failed…

The ormolu clock on his desk chimed the half hour. Renkovich forced his mind out of its reverie, cursed himself for daydreaming, and pressed a switch on the intercom. Within a matter of seconds there was a polite tap on the door connecting his office to Commander Grigorin's. "Enter!" Renkovich shouted and took a deep breath.

He had known Anatoly Grigorin for almost fifteen years now and there had not been one second in that time when his feeling towards his closest subordinate had been anything other than intense dislike. This had not affected their working relationship. Few people in the higher echelons of Soviet Russia liked or respected their close colleagues; to become too intimate was positively dangerous and concealing true feelings was a necessary survival skill. But, all the same, Renkovich wished there was one aspect of Grigorin's character which did not irritate him.

It was not that he was incompetent. If he had been he would not have lasted fifteen minutes in the GRU. Nor was it because he was ambitious. Renkovich knew Grigorin wanted his job and would do anything to get it. This was natural and laudable. He had felt the same at that age. He had fought the old stagers who knew his ambition and the better man had won, the way of the world. And, of course, it was not because Grigorin was totally lacking in any human virtue except courage. That was what made a good spy; to reproach him for that was to reproach the maestro tenor for having a high voice.

No, Renkovich disliked Grigorin because he was too perfect, and he was man enough to admit his dislike came from envy. Just to look at him now, as he marched to the desk with the same fluid grace that some men danced the waltz; or as he stood to attention looking down at his superior from six feet five of perfectly proportioned, immaculately uniformed splendour, feet the regulation distance apart, hands pressed to the seam of his trousers; or as he barked out: "At your service, Comrade Lieutenant-General" in parade ground tones. It all made Renkovich feel an old, bent, ugly man.

He resented that. And he knew Grigorin knew of his resentment and played on it, knowing his boss could make no rational criticism. That face, which could have graced the cover of a cheap Romanov novel, with its corn-coloured hair, square even features, smooth tanned skin and the piercing blue eyes which seemed to dissect all of Renkovich's imperfections with every look, radiated a happy knowledge of the superiority that would soon put its owner behind that desk.

Grigorin did his duty like a robot, with no emotion, no sense of triumph or disappointment, frustration or elation; no sense even that he believed the Party slogans which riddled his conversation. Amarazov was an amoral bastard of the deepest dye and Renkovich trusted him less than he would the Evil One. But his faults were human ones and you could talk to him as a human, sometimes even about things outside the dirty world they had made their own. Grigorin was a blank, a pillar of insolent perfection. And one of the few pleasures left in Renkovich's life was to pierce his armour, make him feel afraid and unsure. This was a useful controlling tool with any subordinate. But with this one it was a pleasure also.

He had let Grigorin stand, puzzled, while all this ran through his mind, and now he waited for him to break the uneasy silence – uneasy for Grigorin, at least. "A fruitful meeting, Comrade Lieutenant-General?" he asked at last.

"No," Renkovich replied. "The Politburo is very

displeased with us, Anatoly Ivanovich."

"The Vlasenin business?" Grigorin replied, neutrally as usual.

"What else?" Renkovich snapped. "Why isn't he here now? Why is he still in Istanbul? What happens if the Germans learn of his presence and try a rescue mission? Or the British? Why has Amarazov not made him talk? The same questions from everyone, especially Beria." He looked hard at his subordinate. "And I found it hard to give a satisfactory answer to any of them."

"Surely they can appreciate our position," Grigorin replied calmly, with just a trace of impatience. "Vlasenin can lead us straight to these documents. To bring him to Moscow without them being found first is too great a risk."

"Exactly what I said. But the fact remains that Vlasenin is in a neutral country, which has no love for us, many miles from Soviet territory. If the Germans hear of this, they will stop at nothing to get him."

"There's no indication they have found anything out..."

"Thankfully, no – and we must do everything to ensure this remains so. But every moment Vlasenin remains in Istanbul increases the risk." He shook his head. "Comrade Major Amarazov is playing a dangerous game."

"The comrade major is a fine operative. I personally recommended his recruitment to the GRU..."

"Yes, you did, Anatoly Ivanovich," Renkovich said.

"... and I have every confidence he will soon achieve results."

"He has not achieved them yet." Renkovich looked

intently at his subordinate and Grigorin fidgeted. It was almost imperceptible but he fidgeted and for the first time that day Renkovich felt pleased. "Vlasenin is still refusing to say where the papers are hidden. They could be anywhere in Turkey. The Tsarists have some networks we have not penetrated. They may find out something, or try a rescue themselves."

Grigorin permitted himself a contemptuous smirk. "They're nothing. Of the ones who aren't in our pocket half are under observation by the Turks and the other half too scared to show their faces." He laughed out loud, then saw Renkovich's face and wished he hadn't.

"Do not underestimate the Whites. I have fought them. You have not. At the moment they may be demoralised, but they will not be so for long. It is in their nature. Time is of the absolute essence here, Anatoly Ivanovich. I agree there are advantages to keeping Vlasenin in Istanbul. That is why I let you persuade me to follow this course of action." He paused to let Grigorin savour every nuance of that latest twisting of the truth, then continued. "But the NKVD is waiting to pounce. And many others apart from Beria would like to see us fail. Even the new directorate is complaining at us using the consulate building.

"If much more time passes – and I talk of hours, not days – they will want the man brought to Moscow, at least. If it comes to that Amarazov will be allowed to continue his interrogation. I'll see to it. And our people in Turkey will remain on full alert. Then when he cracks they can retrieve the papers immediately."

"So what action for now, Comrade Lieutenant-General?"

Grigorin had never referred to him in any other way for 15 years and Renkovich's reply was just as formal. "We, or rather you, Comrade Commander, will get on the radio to Amarazov and tell him that the traitor's tongue must be loosened – quickly!"

∾

"...so then I told the old fool that if Amarazov doesn't have the little scum talking within twenty-four hours, then I chose the wrong man and I chose the wrong job!" It was eleven o'clock that evening and once again Anatoly Grigorin was feeling very pleased with himself. He had a good meal and half a bottle of champagne inside him. For the first time in days he was lying in a bed, not the metal and canvas cot in his office. And Petar was on top of him.

The pale, slim body was tucked between Grigorin's open thighs, his mane of jet black hair spread right across Grigorin's stomach, his fingers tracing patterns in the luxuriant curling mass of chest hair above. As the diatribe ended Petar raised his dark eyes, bright as diamonds in that pale, sharp face, like the cat goddess on an Egyptian frieze, and drank in the power of Grigorin's presence with adoring passion.

Tonight had been Grigorin's first visit to Petar since the Vlasenin business had sprung up. Really he should not have been away from the office at all. But he would be back first thing in the morning. He doubted if Renkovich even knew of his nights away from office and home. Besides, the old goat never stopped bleating about the need to relax occasionally. And Grigorin always followed the Comrade Lieutenant-General's advice.

Added to that, of course, was the thrill of beating the surveillance – from the Tchekists and his own department and all the rest of the prying eyes, escaping to this little sanctuary in a side street barely a mile from the Kremlin itself, a haven of comfort and pleasure which he had taken great pains to keep secret from everyone else in Mother Russia.

But most of all he wanted Petar again, this exquisite little black sable with the devil's eyes. Petar could touch him as no other man, or woman, had before. The very first day he had seen him, queuing for food with all the other workers from the ministry, he had wanted him. And what Anatoly Grigorin wanted he took. It had taken a little while, granted – the time it took to arrange a discreet private meeting through his friend at the ministry. And to set up this flat through his underworld connections. And to negotiate the bribes to the half a dozen key people who each played their part in the deception.

At last it was all arranged to his satisfaction. The flat was behind a hidden door at the top of a warehouse, once used by the Ukrainian 'mafia' in Moscow to entertain their contacts in the higher reaches of government. He had paid them well to change the venue for their little games and they had rewarded him by promising to whisper a few revelations if any snoopers became too curious about the new occupant. No, his landlords would not betray him because he was too good a customer. And he had plenty of dirt on them too. Almost as much as he had on his chauffeur, his friend at the ministry, his secretary and the rather pretty little Jewboy who he had soon discovered was his NKVD 'shadow'. They would never dare to tell. In the society which observed its members more closely than any in the world, he had created an oasis of absolute privacy. It had been an accomplishment he suspected only a handful of men in the world could have matched. That was probably another reason why Petar adored him.

For there was no doubt about that. If he had not he would have tried to escape or made some indiscretion which might have compromised them (though Grigorin would, of course, have eliminated all concerned before anyone with any authority heard of it). But Petar had never been careless, never showed the slightest hesitation when summoned. He cleaned Grigorin's uniform, massaged his tired body, cooked like a French chef and did everything demanded of him in bed like the licentious little Sybarite he was.

And afterwards he listened attentively as Grigorin talked. Talked as he could to no-one else, of his struggles and victories inside that inferno of plotters and fools. Like now. "I had to tell him straight. Renkovich is a good man, but he's getting old and over-cautious. As soon as... the prisoner first went on the run I told him to get the operation out of the hands of those Tchekist *duraks*. That was why our men went... down there. And it worked. Now all we have to do is get him to tell us where these papers are."

"Why not bring him straight back? I was just about to tell you; have patience. Because it's untidy otherwise. What's the good of having one half of the equation if someone from the other side stumbles across the other? But Renkovich prattles on about incurring the Politburo's displeasure and having him safe in Moscow. It's leaving a job half-done, I told him. No, of course I didn't use those precise words, you stupid bitch. He's got to be handled carefully, like all the rest. Now he's bleating like a gelded ram and of course it's all my fault – mine and my man's. I tell you, fast action and pay no heed to the politicians – that's what's going to win this war. Then the Politburo will forget they ever doubted us. And I won him over." He paused and gave a smug smile. "Again."

"But what if... your man can't make this prisoner talk, darling?" Petar asked mischievously.

"Don't talk of things you know nothing about." Grigorin's reply was cold. "I've yet to see the prisoner my man couldn't break. He'll succeed soon. I admit Vlasenin is proving to be a little more stubborn than most. But when he breaks we'll have something that could give us the power of victory. And I don't just mean victory over the Fritzies, either. Think about that for a moment." He stroked a stray strand of hair away from Petar's face. "And then think of the man who made it all happen."

Petar narrowed his cat's eyes and moved his fingers lower. "I am," he said softly. And Grigorin decided he'd had enough of talking for the night.

∾

Grigorin left for his office just before dawn and Petar kissed him lovingly in the hallway as he left, tongue working deep inside Grigorin's mouth. And when the secret door had long since closed and the sound of the car was lost in the still morning air, Petar ran a hot bath and washed every bit of the bastard's filth from his body.

God, it had been hard this time. Feigning passion and

submission, obeying his bizarre demands and listening to the endless litany of complaint which even the moment of climax barely halted. All the while struggling to conceal his glee at finally breaking the guard. For the first time Grigorin had mentioned a name. A solid piece of information, not just anonymous figures in unnamed locations. Something Petar's masters could use, something to justify their faith in him and his many sacrifices. Grigorin probably didn't even remember his lapse. And if he did he would never dream that Petar would betray it. No, because Petar was the Comrade Commander's little slave; his hidden, forbidden fruit. And Petar's past life, apart from his unnatural deviancy of course, had become an irreproachable one. But it was not Petar's true life. That was gone forever. Destroyed by scum like Grigorin.

Petar was thirty years old, and he had been born into a different world just as it died. His family were prosperous grain merchants from Kharkov; childhood was a huge house surrounded by a wooded estate, a house full of servants and pretty things, visited by friends as rich as they for evenings of laughter.

Reality entered this enchanted world when Petar was five years old. It came as a truckload of hard-faced, cold-voiced men from the city, dressed in workers' clothes, drab and dirty save for the shiny red stars in their caps. They were armed, they had the new government on their side and they brooked no argument. They took Petar's house "for the people" and threw out those who had made it a home.

They walked all the way to the city. Petar remembered his two elder brothers crying, his mother carrying him in one arm while she held a suitcase in the other. Papa carried two valises, all the men from the city had let them keep, looking ahead with the look of a man who has seen the sun rise at midnight. From time to time he whispered softly, but with absolute certainty: "They cannot do this."

Ah, but they could, and more besides. Petar's family began lodging with relatives in Leningrad, as it was now known, and Papa tried to carry on trading. Only now all the talk was of state quotas and ministry licences and blockades and essential supplies only. Petar understood none of it. He knew only that there was no grain to trade. And then there was no bread to eat.

His parents began to quarrel, and never more fiercely than when Papa said he was going off to fight "the Reds". Petar knew that they must be the men from the city. The men who had taken their home away. He was pleased Papa was going to kill them. But Mama wept when he left, taking Petar's eldest brother Sergei too. Sergei was barely sixteen but keen as his father to fight. Within three months the news came back. Papa and Sergei were dead. The Reds had killed them. Petar's seventh birthday was still some way off when he learned to hate and found a goal in life. To make them pay.

But first his family had some paying to do. Papa's actions had rendered the family outcasts, no matter how much Mama protested innocence. They were thrown out of the apartment and moved from city to city. Mama took what work she could, as a seamstress, a cook or even scrubbing floors. By night she taught the two babies she had left to read and write. And hate. The Reds. The Party. The Bolsheviks. They had taken everything. They were evil. They had to pay.

But always the hate was kept inside. Petar had seen what the alternative was. So the hate was never spoken, never written, kept alive by memory only. The Reds could take everything else but as long as the hate remained hidden they had no victory.

Poor Levka could never understand that. He could not keep his hate in. So he spoke it out loud. Only once, and to a close friend. It was enough. The Tchekists came and that was the last they saw of him. 'The *teplushka* joyride' they called it; 'joining the Ministry of Labour'; 'wintering in Siberia'. Petar learnt well that this was the punishment for talking out of turn in the world that had been built with his family's blood and money. That was why he kept quiet and did as he was told, like Mama, even though the pain of losing Levka sent her to an early grave. Her last words to Petar were: "We are not Red cattle. We are Tsarists. We are White Russians and no matter what they do to us we will never surrender in our hearts." And she spoke those words as one adult to another.

Now Petar had no kinfolk, but he had an address for some old family friends who had gone to live in Moscow. And it was there that he learnt there was a way to hit back. His new guardians hated what the Bolsheviks had done as much as Petar did but they had learnt that the way to prosper was to let the Reds think they had seen the error of their ways. To renounce your old life, to spit on your memories, made you twice as dear to their hearts as the hundred who had never deviated from the true path. That was the way to win power and favour. That was the way to beat them. White uniforms only made better targets.

Petar was a bright boy. He saw the sense in this, and

besides these were his elders. So he joined the Komsomol. He publicly confessed the sins of his bourgeois upbringing, burnt his precious possessions and spat on the Tsar's picture. Inside he cried but his face, growing to young manhood with his mother's vivid green eyes and his father's thick shock of dark hair, revealed nothing.

It worked. After Komsomol he was given a good job in the Food Ministry and he worked his way up quickly. His mother had found time in all her struggles to begin educating her youngest boy herself, and then his new guardians had sent him to a good Bolshevik school. He had a particular gift for languages, which won him a job working with the embassies of those countries who traded with the Soviet Union. That was when his guardians first broached the subject of working for the Germans.

They had been passing information for years. It was easy, they told him, and it was a chance at last to really do something to help bring down the Reds. Hitler was getting ready to liberate them all from Bolshevism and bring back the old order. Any information which might weaken the system from the inside could be vital.

Petar agreed at once. At first it had been only routine scraps, passed on to his contact, a half-Finnish official at the Swedish Embassy with a radio link to German Intelligence, the Abwehr. They had been duly noted and he had been modestly rewarded. It became as much a routine as queuing for food, drinking vodka with the other workers in the canteen or making love to women – and later men, when a feeling he had felt since early childhood became impossible to deny. But all his lovers were nothing but a source of brief and muted pleasure. True love with a Red was an absurd idea. They merely fulfilled a physical desire and were then forgotten. Working for the Germans was his only true passion.

Even when Stalin and Hitler signed the Non-Aggression Pact and divided Poland between them his faith did not falter. It was part of the grand design, his elders said, and Barbarossa proved them right. Petar could hardly contain his excitement then, even though the Luftwaffe pounded his home city to rubble and nothing was said of bringing back the old order. It truly seemed the Reds might at last be vanquished and there was a new message for the embassy every day.

And then, one morning in January of 1942, his section controller had told him to report to the Interview Room at four that afternoon. His first reaction was blind panic. They had found out. When he went in the NKVD would be waiting and he would go the same way as Levka. And the Reds would truly have won because his family would be no more.

But there was no escape. So he had remained outwardly calm and on the stroke of four he knocked on the door of the Interview Room. A voice he did not recognise bade him enter. Inside he saw only one man; a tall, blond, handsome man in naval uniform seated at the desk. As soon as he had closed the door the man rose from his chair, crossed the room in three strides and kissed Petar savagely.

Petar was still recovering from the shock and fear and repulsion as Grigorin told him who he was and what he had ordained for him. Petar's surprise soon faded. The man was very senior and he wanted his own private catamite. It happened a lot to boys as pretty as him and he knew better than to even hesitate before accepting. In any case, here was a real chance to hit back at the Reds. Only let this Grigorin's guard slip once, Petar thought as the GRU man kissed him again, gave him the keys to the apartment, straightened his naval uniform back to perfection and left the Interview Room. Nobody ever mentioned the incident – though Petar's section controller was noticeably more polite to him from then on.

His guardians could hardly believe the news. Neither could the Abwehr. Within twenty-four hours Petar had new instructions. He was to cease all his routine message duties, but keep in touch with his embassy contact. He must do exactly what Grigorin instructed, be available for him whenever he desired and do nothing to rouse any suspicion or displeasure. And if Grigorin ever mentioned a name from a list of people and places regularly transmitted to Petar's guardians in code he must inform the Abwehr and then use the escape route they had devised.

Only those names. Nothing else, even if he felt it to be important. But for months he could give them nothing, because Grigorin brought the practices of concealment into every aspect of his life. He always spoke of "the latest subject", "my usual man", "our place in the south". Too vague to be of use. Until now.

As Petar stepped out of the bath and dressed himself, as he stepped outside the warehouse for the last time – that in itself was a glorious feeling – and walked to work, he could barely keep from jumping for joy. Within hours he would take his allotted lunch break and walk into the embassy, walking out again with false papers for a flight out of Soviet Russia that afternoon. By evening he would be in Stockholm, and in Germany the next morning.

He felt none of the stigma of spy or traitor, nor did

he think of the possibility that he might never see his homeland again. When the Germans won the victory he had helped to secure, he would return and live the life to which he had been born. As he turned from the narrow alleyway onto the busy street and joined the crowds running to catch a tram, it occurred to him that for the first time in his adult life he felt truly happy.

∾

At noon that same day, Wednesday November 18th, 1942, as Petar was anxiously counting the minutes until his trip to the embassy, the minister's secretary finally made his decision. It should have been made long ago, as soon as the Politburo meeting had ended yesterday. But instead he had hesitated, stricken by doubt, staring at the four walls of his office, listening to the sounds of marching and barked orders in Red Square below. He had worked all evening, or tried to, then slept on the camp bed in his office. Then all this morning too, turning the issue over in his mind when the course of action was clear.

They had Vlasenin. They wanted information from him and they would stop at nothing to get it. He had seen it before, too many times and no matter how much he saw his heart always cried out pity. The heart he thought had died when he left home to join that glorious tide which had swept away the old privileges, injustices and cruelties. The pity he had forced himself to crush when he fought and killed and betrayed all he had once held sacred. The small voice which he had ignored as he climbed the ranks of the Party and persuaded himself that all the bloodshed and pain imposed by the authority he represented was for the greater good. That voice was often silent, sometimes for months on end. But then it would scream for action and it screamed now.

And then he acted, with all the decisive speed and calm thoroughness which had won him a place at the shoulders of the great men, the few words of advice before they began their great meetings. Like the one yesterday, perhaps none greater. He pressed the intercom on his desk and informed his assistant that he would be lunching early at home that day. Next he pulled a piece of plain white unheaded notepaper from a drawer, pulled a pen from the ornate holder (only slightly less ornate than Renkovich's) and wrote in plain Cyrillic script: "Black king's knight to king's pawn four. White queen taken." He studied it briefly. Good enough. Perfectly innocent to anyone's eyes, even an NKVD or GRU codebreaker. But Vladimir would know what it meant.

They had worked out the system together years ago, when they had both decided that the Soviet Union needed pressure for moderation from outside and that in such cases the news needed to be spread a little more quickly than Tass or *Pravda* were inclined to. That was in the Thirties, of course, when protest and outrage seemed almost meaningless in the face of that tide of suffering. But there was always the chance, so always they tried. And of course, if the forces arrayed against Soviet Russia should prove victorious, contributions such as theirs could mean the difference between life (even power) and certain death.

So they had devised the chess game. They would communicate the moves to each other by notes left at the café not half a mile from the Kremlin. The board was set up in Vladimir's house and for months on end they would play a regular game, occasionally taking a little longer over the moves, occasionally meeting at each other's houses to play face to face. They never established too much of a pattern, because patterns were suspicious. No, this was simply two senior members of the hierarchy with not much time to spare, indulging in a little relaxing mental stimulation.

But whenever a situation arose that needed immediate action they would meet, play a game to its conclusion, then begin another with all the people involved allocated a piece. These roles were always different, memorised by both players and never written down. Anything that showed the game to be more than just that must never fall into the wrong hands. They had started the game as soon as Vlasenin had dropped out of sight and he had become the white queen – the most powerful piece but not the most vital. Renkovich was the black king, Grigorin and Amarazov his knights. They had begun the opening gambit and the activities of the Tsarists and the British had been incorporated into the game.

It was the only way Vladimir could be kept informed. He was senior in the hierarchy but outside of the Politburo's counsels. He had risen swiftly in the GRU after the purges and now his position in the new Directorate of the Supreme High Command gave him vital access to information about the secret activities in Soviet embassies and consulates around the world. But he was not at the decision-making level. He could disseminate the information but it had to be provided first, and the most vital matters were always kept to as few men as possible. Hence the game. An innocent game between friends who had known each other since childhood and no-one could prove any different.

These thoughts ran through the mind of the minister's secretary as he left the office and walked towards the café. He was followed, of course, but all he did when he reached the café was give the note to the barman in plain sight of all the customers (and his shadow) then proceed on his way home to lunch. Sometimes he stayed at the café, but not today. He had done it too often lately; too close to a pattern.

And some time later (it always varied) Vladimir would come in and receive the note. And when he returned home that evening he would move the pieces accordingly. But in between the message would find its way into the daily round of instructions fed to 'Rodrigo', the GRU's contact in the Vatican.

For years the Holy See had been the most fertile ground for Soviet efforts to undermine White Russian émigré groups and their links with the western intelligence agencies. There were dozens of GRU and NKVD agents in Rome and the Vatican City, all conspiring with and against the Germans, the Italians, the British, the Japanese… all virtuosos in the 'Red Orchestra', all virtually ignorant of the other's existence. That was the way Stalin liked it. And it suited the chess players too.

They had chosen the Vatican as their conduit because they remembered the famines of the Twenties, and the food parcels labelled 'a gift to the children of Russia from the Pope'. Of course there had been ulterior motives for the aid. Stalin wished to build a diplomatic presence in the west and the Vatican saw in the new Russia a chance to gain a foothold again, breaking the power of the

Orthodox Church.

It was an unnatural and fragile alliance, doomed to fail very quickly. But in the meantime those caring young priests with their food parcels had saved many lives – two in particular. That was why Rome was chosen. Neither of the chess players felt anything but hatred for Germany and in any case they knew the Abwehr's much-prized 'Max' network which claimed to reach into the Kremlin was a Trojan horse, kept on a very tight rein. Britain and America were allies now, but in the Thirties they had wanted Russia to collapse. They could not be trusted. No, it had to be Rome.

'Rodrigo' was trusted, had been for years. He did both his regular and extra-curricular espionage efficiently and discreetly in a Vatican dominated by Pius XII's hatred of Communism. It was always a risk that the dual role of 'Rodrigo' would be unmasked. But if this latest message could help Vlasenin, it would be worth the risk. A dangerous game, but both men could play it better than chess.

ow

The bells of St. Peter's were chiming six that evening when 'Rodrigo' received Vladimir's message. In Istanbul Amarazov was pulling hard at a cigarette in his quarters, knowing the next session must begin soon and that it must be decisive. And in Moscow Grigorin was preparing to leave for the flat again, not knowing that Petar was currently aboard an Aeroflot plane bound for Stockholm, forged papers authorising his passage out of the Soviet Union and instructing him to report to the German

Embassy on arrival.

But 'Rodrigo' was still hard at work. His little office in the Soviet branch of the communications section in the Secretariat For Foreign Affairs, the Vatican intelligence service in all but name, buzzed with radio messages, coded and plain, from all corners of the world night and day. But this one jerked him out of the half-doze he had been in for the last hour. And when he had noted it down he used one of his codebooks to double-check it twice, making sure it said exactly what he thought it said. And then he realised that this was what his real masters had been waiting for.

'Rodrigo' had worked at the Secretariat for six years now, ever since his local bishop in eastern Lombardy had decided that his untiring parish work should be rewarded. A highly-educated mind, fluency in many languages and Slavic ancestry on his mother's side had made him a natural for work in the Russian section. He had been there for almost five years now. All but one of them had been spent on Vladimir's payroll. Many of the Catholic and Orthodox priests who had fled the new Russia were not all they seemed and even in the capital of Il Duce's Italy twenty years on the Communist Party was still active underground. Any new recruit to the Russian section was discreetly tested and 'Rodrigo' was soon found to be more worldly in his worship than most, and perfectly willing to devote himself to the "secular religion" for a price.

His task was to keep GRU informed of the latest developments in Pius XII's ongoing crusade against the Bolshevik monster, as well as helping to disseminate false information about the few Orthodox priests who were left in the Soviet Union, designed to dampen enthusiasm for any new attempts to reverse the 900-year schism and build a religious power base in the godless empire. His reward was a fat monthly fee in a numbered Swiss bank account, plus guarantees of a favourable mention when Il Duce's New Roman Empire collapsed and reckoning was made of the Vatican's role in propping it up.

He had set to work with a will, supplying the right sort of information quickly yet carefully, doing nothing to arouse the suspicions of his ever-alert superiors. So good was his work, in fact, that after nearly two years he was summoned to an audience with Vladimir himself, at a safe house in Rijeka. He knew it must be important and leave was easily arranged on the pretext of visiting his mother's relatives.

But the meeting was not for a special reward or a more complex task, as these things usually were, nor even to sever the link in the most final sense, over some real or imagined transgression. He had feared it might be that; so much so that he had left documents with his will designed to set a fox into several hen-roosts if there was any danger of his weak flesh being granted passage to the next world.

No, for once it was something he had truly not expected; the revelation of Vladimir's secret sympathies and his desire to have a team member who could occasionally receive special information "for the greater good". 'Rodrigo' had been chosen because of his rising position in the Vatican, his constant good work and Vladimir's assessment that money rather than ideology was his main motivation. Naturally this would mean extra payment and also a hedging of his bets. If Soviet Russia did destroy itself in destroying Hitler he could be said to have aided in the downfall of two ungodly tyrannies. What could be more proper for a man of the Church?

'Rodrigo' agreed at once. Of course he would do what his paymaster told him, no matter how quixotic. And not only because Vladimir made the consequences of refusing or informing anyone else of the offer abundantly clear. Because now 'Rodrigo' was at last in the perfect position that Colonel Ciarelli had been steering him towards for all these years; trusted intimately by the Kremlin and the Vatican, channelling the secrets of both to Il Duce.

He had been recruited years ago, long before the move to Rome. In the early years of Fascism, a local Blackshirt official had noted the zeal with which 'Rodrigo' informed the Carabinieri of which parishioners seemed to be neglecting Mother Church for the insidious attractions of Communism. 'Rodrigo' had always known which was the winning team. It was the only way to get on. He had been a boy of sixteen in 1922, a tenant farmer's son with no future but the same round of back-breaking labour that had reduced his parents to pain-racked husks, with no option but to continue their toil.

But they had raised a clever boy and his priest knew it. With his encouragement overriding any objections, it was easy for young 'Rodrigo' to make sure his father managed to set aside enough money to send him to the seminary. There he could learn enough to make a life that did not involve sweating in the fields; a life that brought a place to live, easy work and the chance to win favour with those who mattered.

Faith never entered into it. Of course he knew there was nothing above or below this world. He had done since he was a boy. No God could have ignored so completely such devoted servants as his parents. But the young priest could tell his flock that the life beyond was the only one that mattered and that the Holy See was the one true path to it, as well as anyone. He still had plenty of time to lay up treasures on earth without any trace of guilt. Money was what you needed. With it you bought power and those were the two things a man needed most in this imperfect world, and the particularly imperfect corner of it ruled by Il Duce.

He had not been surprised when he was approached by the OVRA, secret police of the Blackshirts, early in 1930. Many of his colleagues were critical of the regime and were apt to be more vocal to a brother of the cloth. It was all noted down and passed on. Soon after a scandal would be engineered and the dissenter stripped of his robes, posted to some Mafia-run hell hole or even charged with treason.

All very subtle, nothing that could be directly linked to 'Rodrigo'. And when that stupid bastard of a bishop had recommended him for the Secretariat his masters were ecstatic. It was 1936 and Mussolini's adventures in Spain and Abyssinia were in full swing. 'Rodrigo' was transferred to the payroll of the SIM, the Italian Army's intelligence service, and placed under the personal control of the legendary Ciarelli. He provided a mine of information on those few acres of holy ground which were a separate state from the rest of Italy and home to diplomats, intriguers and refugees from all nations.

When the first Soviet offer came along SIM jumped at the chance of a double agent working for a country from which they had much to fear but barely understood. And when the second offer came Ciarelli kissed 'Rodrigo' on both cheeks and doubled his salary on the spot. At last the deepest secrets of the Kremlin could be known. For Ciarelli it was a great coup; even greater than his part in the murder of King Alexander of Yugoslavia or the infiltration of the Garibaldi Brigade in Spain. Because this was a link the Germans knew nothing about. Like all the rest they had to rely on the low-level clerks and translators burrowing around in the Vatican archives, pathetically proud of the titbits and gossip they supplied. Ciarelli had more. He had a priest rising through the hierarchy and for once the 'senior partners' in the Axis could come to him for the scraps of his table. There had been many, but none so juicy as the one which 'Rodrigo' gave him at 7.30 on the evening of November 18th at the meeting place reserved for face to face conversations, a private dining room in a restaurant near Villa Borghese. After he had finished speaking Ciarelli, a bluff, burly Tuscan normally given to almost comic opera confidence and volubility, sat silent and open-mouthed. "Jesus Christ," he said at last. "Are you sure?"

"Perfectly, Signor Colonel. The message came through on a channel specially reserved for such communications and it was in the same code as the other messages on the Vlasenin situation. You remember that period when he dropped out of sight and Vladimir first thought he might attempt to escape."

"He wasn't the only one. I knew the bastard was ready to try something. But he bungled it, as he would if he trusted the English and the Tsarists. Amateurs! If he wanted to leave, we could have sprung him easily. Even the *Tedeschi* could have managed that," he added grudgingly. "But, no, he has to trust to amateurs. And where does it get him? Into the hands of Amarazov."

"It is very grave news, Signor Colonel." 'Rodrigo' adopted the pious, mournful, tone he had once employed with the grieving relatives of rich businessmen. But for once Ciarelli's response was unexpected. "What do you mean, grave news? This is the best news we could possibly have. At last we know exactly where he is." His burly frame shook with laughter and the florid, moustachioed face broke into a beaming smile. "More important, the Reds don't know we know."

"But surely they will be torturing him now. How long can he hold out?"

"Not long," Ciarelli admitted. "But long enough, I think. I've learned a lot about Vlasenin lately. He strikes me as a man of strong will and plenty of hate for his jailers. And they need to make him talk, remember, not just break him for being a traitor. They go on about these new truth drugs, but all I've heard is that they take days to work and you either get a stream of nonsense or nothing at all.

"So they'll keep doing it the old way, but play it safe for a few days." He chuckled. "Safer than they would if they knew that we know where he is. We have time – but still not much. I'll talk to General Ame tonight, get the Duce's approval for a rescue attempt. You get back to the Vatican.

"Keep that radio channel open whenever you're around. Close it down completely when you are not. Keep passing on all your regular messages from the radio work, and keep in contact with your legitimate Red paymasters as well. We don't want suspicions aroused too much. When I tell you, you can pass this message on to your Monsignor Tardini also, and His Holiness can make an official denunciation of Vlasenin's imprisonment. But not before the rescue's completed. They've got under our feet too often in the past. This way we look like the heroes. We'll get Vlasenin to make some statement of thanks once we've persuaded him to work for us.

"If anything changes, contact me by radio or on the private telephone numbers I gave you. If I'm not available on any of them go straight to General Ame. By then the only thing you'll be able to give me of any use will be the last rites."

'Rodrigo' gave an uncertain smile. "Do you really think there's a risk of that? Who else could find out what we know so quickly?"

Ciarelli shrugged. "Probably no-one. But I'm a Tuscan. We always fear the worst. That way everything is a bonus." He paused. "And we do not forget those who help us. You have my gratitude for this news; mine and all of Italy's."

"I'd prefer something a little more concrete, Signor Colonel."

Ciarelli joined in his laughter. "You ought to be in charge of the Vatican Bank. But for this I expect an extra half a million lire could find its way into your Swiss account by tomorrow morning."

"You are most kind, Signor Colonel."

"I know. Now get the hell out of here and save some souls." He paused again. "I suppose you could light a candle or recite a novena to bless our mission. It seems appropriate."

'Rodrigo' was half-way to the door but he turned with a beatific smile. "God's light always shines on the righteous. Didn't you know?"

∽

By nine the next morning Ciarelli was beginning to have very strong doubts about that. He was in General Ame's office and his superior had just told him the result of his meeting with Mussolini. And once again the great barrier that blocked all their efforts to make the SIM the world's finest intelligence and espionage service had been slammed down again.

Eduardo Ciarelli was a Tuscan, a soldier and a patriot. Nothing else, and in that order. His loyalties were all to the land that had raised him, the army he had made his life and the country he served thereby. Politics and international relations were irrelevant except in how they impinged on his sacred duties. He had joined the army at sixteen, soon after his country had joined the Great War. The terrible battles in the mountains of Caporetto, where the artillery blasts turned the shards of limestone rock into shrapnel, had destroyed his youthful dreams of the glory of combat. But they had proved he had a talent for fighting, staying alive and leading others.

A battlefield commission soon arrived, and propelled him into a different world. One of middle-class intellectuals, pretentious aristocrats and pompous military academy-trained fools. Contempt was mutual, but he also made some friends. Men like him, who wished to see the flaccid constitutional monarchy swept away. And replaced with a strong government which would honour the true heroes of Italy's war, the workers and soldiers, not repay their sacrifice with scraps from the

Versailles table.

So the Fascisti were the natural choice. Eduardo joined the march on Rome in '22 and was rewarded with promotion and a posting to the colonies. Libya first, then Eritrea and Somaliland. His success against the guerrilla bands of tribesmen showed a flair for intelligence work as well as brutal action when necessary and with his colonelcy came a chance to work for the SIM.

It was a different world, but the foes were the same. The foreigners who wished to take what was Italy's by right, scorning her status on the world stage. And the even more dangerous enemy within; liberals, Bolsheviks, pacifists, freemasons, Jews. All those who denigrated the great traditions of the country that had nurtured them. The subtler nuances of Mussolini and Foreign Minister Ciano's foreign policy escaped him, but tell him the enemy's name and he applied a keen military mind to the task of destroying them.

At first it was minor operations at home, working with the OVRA against the underground Communist resistance of the Rosselli brothers and Luigi Longo. Then the relations with Yugoslavia turned sour as King Alexander began making demands on the territory around Trieste and flirting with the French. Working with the extreme elements of the Croat separatist movement, Ciarelli arranged for the king's asassination during a state visit to Marseilles in 1934.

The exploit won the attention of Il Duce himself and a move to Abyssinia, restricting the flow of arms to the rebels by ensuring that many a dealer's agent was "persuaded" to withhold his investment. Next was Spain, sending a steady flow of agents into the ranks of the Garibaldi Brigade. And when he returned to France with Emanuele and Navale to organise the murder of the Rosselli brothers in June 1937, Mussolini showered him with medals and honours.

Then it all started to go wrong, and for Ciarelli the cause of the trouble could be summed up in one word: Germany. He had even less time for the land of the *Tedeschi* than for any other country that was not Italy, but he knew, as every Italian did, of Il Duce's public and voluble admiration for Hitler. And he knew the admiration was not, and never would be, reciprocated.

The first inklings had come in Spain, when he was forced to share information with some streak of Prussian piss named Ziedler. From then it had got worse every day. Any news he discovered had to be passed on to them. No operation could be mounted without their permission. Would the Fuhrer approve? What would the Fuhrer do in such a situation? What he would do, and did, was shit on Italy at the drop of a hat. Every contact with the Germans made it quiet clear they regarded Italy as the junior partner in the Axis, a useful source of extra manpower but not to be trusted to do anything independently.

When the Germans had conquered Europe, Il Duce had to ape them. So war was declared on France. For the gain of a few miles of ground, they earned not one but two enemies in the Mediterranean, because war on France meant war on Britain. And before anyone knew it Abyssinia and the rest of East Africa were lost and Libya three-quarters occupied. Two years on, good men still fought and died for land that could have been preserved by a more cautious stance.

But that had been just the beginning. To make up for those defeats the already-occupied Albania was used as a base to invade Greece, a costly adventure serving only to increase the debt to Germany. Now British bombers laid waste to some of the finest cities in Europe, Rommel ran the North African campaign and twenty-five German divisions made Italy their own on the way out there. Because men with the power of emperors acted like children.

Ciarelli had tried. He kept his precious information as long as he could. He even won some autonomy in the joint missions, mainly thanks to Ame, the new SIM head, and Ciano, men with a firmer grasp of common sense than Mussolini. But it hurt to see his country abused and his work undermined. And now the 'Rodrigo' link, the one network he had fought successfully to keep Italy's own, had delivered the greatest intelligence prize of the war. And the prize was to be handed to the Germans again. What could he do? Protest, as he had done all throughout this breakfast meeting with Ame and Ciano. And when his tirade was over they looked at each other again and sighed.

"It's no use, Eduardo," Ame said patiently. With his spectacles and trim white beard he looked more like a mild-mannered university professor than a spymaster. But there was a sharp gleam in his eyes as he continued. "Il Duce is most adamant. This must be a joint operation."

"Surely he must realise this is a unique opportunity." Ciarelli's words came through clenched teeth. "All I need is a dozen good men, and no interference. This plan would work. Vlasenin has the knowledge that could win this war for us. And when Europe was divided up afterwards all would take what we give them and be grateful for it. Even the Germans."

"He feels we owe them too great a debt," Ciano said evenly, then held up a hand as Ciarelli snorted and made to speak. "Listen to me. Hitler can make much trouble for us. There are thousands of German troops inside our borders, moving to and fro as they wish with no heed for us. They command our forces in Libya, share our burden in Greece. If they hear that we have acted in this without consulting them... well, we could find ourselves facing a new enemy."

"They wouldn't dare!"

"Oh, indeed, Signor Colonel!" Ciano's handsome features creased in an ugly scowl. "Forgive me if I do not trust to your wisdom in matters diplomatic. I have talked to Hitler and all his inner circle for six years now and I am convinced that they would. Do you know where I have been these last few days? At a conference in Munich where Hitler told me he would occupy Vichy France – while the head of her government waited in a drawing room to be summoned.

"That is the man we are dealing with. Their intelligence services know of Vlasenin's work, they know his hatred of Stalin and I have recently been informed that they know he is taken. If we were to hide the fact that we know his precise location the repercussions would be serious enough. If we try to rescue him on our own, they will wait until we have him safe. Then they will lay siege to Rome until Il Duce gives him up. They will try to do so without a fight, but if that does not work they will go the extra mile."

"Let them! We are not cowards, for all they say, and

if it takes a matter like this to prove so..."

"Eduardo, be reasonable," Ame implored. "Even if we were strong enough for such an endeavour, Il Duce would not allow it. He would give in to Hitler and then dismiss us all. What profit is there in that?"

"Especially when there is more to be gained from co-operation," Ciano added slyly and both men were silent for a moment, as Il Duce's son-in-law, his voice and right hand, the most cunning fox of the whole Grand Council, lit a cigarette and rocked his immaculately-uniformed body back in his chair before continuing.

"Let us look at what we have to our advantage. We know exactly where Vlasenin is; the Germans do not. We can use this to our advantage. I have used it. It is the main reason why we have a joint operation. Believe me, they could have acted without us.

"But they realise this could lead to problems. So they have agreed to take us along and give us access to the papers. They know we have no scientists one-tenth as far advanced in these matters as theirs. At least, we do not now that Fermi has gone."

There was an uncomfortable silence. Enrico Fermi, the first man to split the atom, had escaped a regime he had grown to despise by simply flying to Sweden to collect his Nobel Prize in 1938 and never returning. Now he worked with the Americans. "Fucking traitor," Ciarelli said at last.

"Indeed," Ciano agreed, though inwardly he winced at Ciarelli's barrack-room language yet again. "But it does put us behind the Germans in these matters. So we make them think we are willing to defer to them completely. We say 'thank you for allowing us to join your expedition'.

You join it, Eduardo. You help in every way you can. And if you get any chance to spirit Vlasenin away, with or without his papers, you take it."

For a moment the two SIM men stared at him. Finally Ame asked: "Are you serious?"

Ciano nodded. "Indeed. Gentlemen, I share your opinion of the Germans, but for policy's sake I can say it out loud to few. Their subordination in this conflict would be an untold blessing for us. And this affords us the ideal opportunity. Not by swaggering and sulking and refusing to help them, but by playing along – in an enterprise where the unexpected is almost certain to happen. Create the unexpected, Eduardo. Work it to our advantage, and we can have Vlasenin and still preserve the Axis – a little strained, perhaps, but intact. With Italy as the dominant partner, yet leaving Germany with no reasonable grounds to protest at her actions."

"You have a plan?" Ciarelli asked eagerly, some of his old fire back now that he heard fighting words.

"Well, some ideas at least," Ciano replied with a wave of his hand. "I am not such an expert in these matters as you gentlemen. But we will, after all, be operating illegally in a neutral country. Some situation might arise where spiriting Vlasenin to Italy were absolutely essential. Either to avoid the Russians or the western allies apprehending him, or to prevent his internment by the Turks. This might well be a necessity if our German allies had been... incapacitated by the fortunes of war. Could you envisage such a scenario, Eduardo?"

Ciarelli gave a broad smile. "I could indeed, Galeazzo."

"Well, I can assure you of every assistance from our operatives in Turkey," Ame added. "And those of the

OVRA. But how much of all this will Il Duce know?"

Ciano waved a dismissive hand. "Il Duce has many problems to occupy his mind at the moment. The Vichy situation and its implications for our occupied territory in southern France. The American landings in Algeria, the Libyan campaign, the continuing problem of Malta... the list is almost endless. I try to shoulder as many of these burdens as possible, and I'm sure I can convince him such a complex matter is best left to me – or should I say us?"

All three men were smiling now. "No, he will be happy to await the final outcome, take all the credit and bask in the glory. And we shall let him, for we shall have won something much more important. In the meantime we shall not trouble him with petty details."

"Excellent." Ame nodded his satisfaction. "Eduardo, select your best men and leave for Berlin immediately."

"They are waiting." Ciarelli rose to leave, but Ciano motioned him to sit.

"One more thing, Eduardo. Failure in the slightest part of this plan will, of course, mean disaster for us all." He flicked his cigarette into the ashtray. "Please try to avoid it."

༄

The meeting broke up at 9.30 a.m on Thursday November 19th, 1942. At roughly the same time Hauptmann Gunter Muller was realising that he had the worst fucking job in the whole fucking Abwehr. Whatever you did was wrong, whatever news you passed on was bad. A few hours before he had engineered a coup which he thought was the ticket to a section leadership. Now, as he stood in the office of Admiral Canaris himself he felt as though he had just delivered a communiqué announcing that Russian paratroops had stormed Tempelhof airport – and that he had given their aircraft clearance to approach.

At first he thought the summons to the Admiral's inner sanctum was to congratulate him on the success of his 'Deep Sleeper' operation (a rather pithy title in view of the queer Petar's function; he had thought it up himself). The usual thing; coffee, cigars, a chat about promotion, possibly even a medal. But when he opened the door he found himself staring at four of the most powerful men in the Third Reich. The Admiral himself, head of the Abwehr, Germany's oldest and slyest spymaster. Next to him Heinrich Himmler, head of the SS and Gestapo. Then Brigadefuhrer Walter Schellenberg, his protégé, rising star of Sicherheitsdienst, the SS intelligence service. And last, but by no means least, Martin Bormann, head of the Party Chancellery, a man whose power was the most frightening because no-one truly knew how far it stretched. They were seated in easy chairs around Canaris' desk; they were in full Nuremberg regalia; and they were looking at Muller like four bishops discovering a young pastor emerging from a brothel.

"Good morning, Hauptmann Muller." Canaris spoke with his usual urbane politeness. "Thank you for seeing us so promptly. My colleagues are here to discuss the implications of the information you have received from Moscow. I should explain, gentlemen, that Hauptmann Muller is in charge of the Russian Department of Section One, which deals with espionage abroad, and..."

"We know all that," Himmler broke in, taking off his silver pince-nez and rubbing his eyes wearily. "Let us proceed to the point."

"Very well," Canaris continued. "As I have already informed you, Hauptmann Muller's department have been controlling an agent who has developed a... close attachment with a senior official in the GRU." He smiled approvingly and every man in the room wondered how much truth was in those rumours of his liaisons with Mata Hari in the last war.

"Last night this agent escaped from the Soviet Union and reached Berlin early today. He informs us that GRU agents have captured Dr Dimitri Vlasenin. I doubt he will be able to tell us much more. However, thanks to him we know that Vlasenin wishes to leave the Soviet Union. We can guess why this is. He has information in his... particular field, about which he does not wish Stalin to learn. We also know the GRU are now trying to extract this information from him by force. From our knowledge of Vlasenin's movements we can have some idea of where he is being held. A creditable performance, Herr Hauptmann."

Muller, his fears slightly diluted by the Admiral's honeyed words, was about to murmur some modest platitude when the killer punch came. "But how do you explain that the Italian SIM knew all this, plus his precise location, a full twelve hours before we did?"

Muller had not wet himself in fright since the age of nine. And he did not now, but it was a close thing. His brain whirled. He was dead, what would they do, the fucking Italians, how the hell did they... he knew that the worst thing in his line of work was to have no answer.

A confident reply, even if it was total bullshit, at least gave you time to think. But in front of those monstrous gazes his voice dried and he simply gaped like a landed fish.

The Admiral continued, reeling off facts as if to jog his memory into finding the simple explanation thatwould make everything all right. "They knew all this less than thirty-six hours after the Politburo meeting that decided to keep him in the Soviet Consulate in Istanbul. All this was being transmitted to them while your contact marked time at work waiting to visit the Swedish embassy, meet his contact and wait for the allotted hour to escape on a... scheduled flight."

"But Herr Admiral, we agreed upon that method long ago, when the Grigorin contact was first established." A simple sense of unfairness loosened Muller's tongue. It hadn't been his fault. "Because of the nature of his work, his movements would be closely observed. He could not make an independent rendezvous or set up a radio link without the NKVD becoming aware of it. And we had no way of knowing when he would come by such important information."

"A rather loose arrangement, *hein?*" Schellenberg spoke for the first time, in the oily, condescending tone of one (much superior) professional to another. It made the Admiral's steel and Himmler's bile seem positively benign. "He fulfilled the function he had been programmed for, and yet vital hours were lost because the Abwehr could think of no quicker way to channel information that could win or lose the war."

"Might I point out that no objection was raised when we made you aware of the arrangement," Canaris said frostily. He didn't want this turning into a general pillorying of the Abwehr. He'd crucified Muller in front of them. That should have been enough. "In fact, I seem to remember the Reichsfuhrer praising the fact that we had a free-standing alternative to the 'Max' network, despite their consistently good results."

He was referring to one of the Abwehr's triumphs; a radio transmitter inside the Kremlin itself, controlled from the Abwehr station in Sofia. But the regular flow of reports from Stalin's War Councils were distrusted by Himmler for one overriding reason and mention of the network brought the usual reaction.

"Quite right." The SS head's voice was harsh, a flash of colour in the normally pale cheeks. "We cannot trust the information of the controller, this half-Slav Jew Kauder. Why should he possibly want to work for us?"

Canaris shrugged. "Men have many motives for this type of work. I can only point to the fact that not ten days ago we received news of four new offensives decided by a War Council, within hours of it taking place." Without giving Himmler time to reply he continued. "I think we are becoming a little sidetracked – this situation would not be half so grave if the Italians had not been allowed to build up a contact in Moscow of almost equal strength."

He looked coldly at Muller who gulped and bit back an insane temptation to tell the truth for once. The Italians had been allowed to do it because we were all too damn soft and didn't dig too deeply into their operations for fear of offending that fat clown Mussolini. But nobody wanted that admitted in plain language. So he stayed quietly roasting on his spit while four pairs of cold eyes bored into him.

"Whatever the reasons," Himmler said, "the fact is that Hauptmann Muller's information is now out of date and we have to put up with the Italians as... partners."

"Not equal partners," Canaris said flatly. "I don't care what that Tuscan peasant Ciarelli thinks. They will do what we say and I will tell him so myself."

"I look forward to that." Himmler consulted his watch. "He should be here in a few hours' time. Arriving with a fully assembled team, a dossier of information and a plan of action – still at a much more advanced stage than we."

"This is our show." Canaris was angry now, goaded once again by Himmler's customary sardonic tone. "We will use whatever he has for our own ends and discard the rest. Germany will get Vlasenin out, Germany will use his knowledge and Italy will be content with the scraps we throw her."

"I'm glad you have finally grasped the essentials." Bormann spoke for the first time and as soon as he heard that deep yet cultured voice and its tone of absolute assurance Muller truly knew who was the most powerful man in the room. "We can discuss the apportioning of blame and the relative merits of our various networks until Doomsday. But the game has moved on. The fact remains that Vlasenin is held on Soviet territory in a neutral country under intensive interrogation. If we do not move quickly it will be neither Germany or Italy, but Russia, which takes the prize."

"*Naturlich*," Canaris agreed. "We need a team down there now – but with the Italians?"

"I think it's inevitable," Bormann said ruefully. "At least it is now." He looked at Muller with a resigned disappointment more terrifying than open hostility or contempt. "But this does not mean to say they take an active part or be allowed to find out anything we don't want them to. With the right man in charge and a good team behind him that shouldn't be too difficult."

"Hoffman." Himmler's voice was emphatic.

"Ziedler." Canaris matched it. There was a moment's silence then the Admiral turned to Bormann. "It has to be him, Herr Reichsleiter. He's good undercover and under pressure. You've seen for yourself the results he has given us in the past. Hoffman's just a policeman."

"The finest policeman in occupied Europe," Himmler replied acidly. "Might I remind the Herr Admiral that the reason neither of these men is with us at the moment is that they are chasing one of His Majesty's most senior agents around Vichy France – after Hoffman caught him and Ziedler let him escape."

"An interesting interpretation of events, Heinrich." Canaris kept his temper under control by a mighty effort. "I was under the impression that the French caught him on Abwehr information and that he escaped during Hoffman's unsuccessful interrogation."

Himmler started to reply but Bormann held up a hand and both were silent. "It doesn't matter. Each of you is right. They are the best men for a two-phase operation such as this. Ziedler will be in charge of Vlasenin's rescue and the retrieval of any necessary documents; Hoffman of his interrogation and safe conduct to Berlin. They will have a back-up team of officers drawn equally from the Abwehr, SD and Gestapo. Units of the Hermann Goering Division and the Brandenburgers will make up the assault force.

"Each officer will have a directive from the Fuhrer himself giving absolute authority over all military and civilian subjects of the Reich. The wheels have already been set in motion and will be completed by the time we have recalled Ziedler and Hoffman from this French assignment. One more thing..." he turned back to Muller. Himmler and Canaris looked too. It was clear they had forgotten he was there. Muller wished they hadn't remembered. "The man Petar – the contact? He is now in Berlin, yes?"

"Absolutely, Herr Reichsleiter, we had the escape route well worked out," Muller gushed, happy to impart some positive information.

"We want to see him. Any information on Grigorin and the rest of the Russian set-up could be vital. No formal debriefing, no rest. You can fetch him immediately, Herr Hauptmann?"

"*Jawohl,* Herr Reichsleiter," Muller replied promptly while he tried to remember where the hell they'd put the little ponce. "And what of his fate afterwards?" he added in an unctuous tone. "Usually such agents are given minor employment here at Tirpitz Ufer, since they are no longer of any use in their particular field. But if you prefer I can ensure there is... er... no chance of him passing on what he knows to the wrong people."

Bormann looked at him in genuine dismay. "I do not think that will be necessary, Herr Hauptmann. He has done valuable work and deserves some recognition. Our criticisms were of the organisation, not its members. After all, we are not gangsters, eh, gentlemen?" He gave an indulgent smile and the three others laughed thinly.

"No, just give him some job in your section where

his knowledge may be useful," Bormann continued. "But keep him away from any sensitive work. And maintain a close watch on him, of course. If he looks like changing his views on our destiny to rule his land or decides to tell anyone what his previous role was then naturally take the appropriate steps."

"No need to reward him too much," Himmler said, his dislike of sodomites and suchlike perverts plain for all to see. "The Slavs are a petty, vengeful race. And prone to decadence, as this case proves. I fear it was a personal grudge rather than a deep-seated idealism which motivated this one. Such people do not deserve too much trust."

Muller looked questioningly at Canaris, who merely nodded, satisfied with the general outcome of the meeting and not inclined to argue over details. Muller hesitated for a few moments, then realised he had been dismissed, gave a very punctilious Nazi salute and got out as fast as he could.

As the door closed behind him, Canaris sighed. "A good man up until now. But he should have known about the SIM network."

"Indeed," Himmler said. "Such a failing may cost us dear."

"Perhaps, perhaps not," Bormann said. "Anyway, his part is over now. More important matters demand our attention." He paused and turned to Canaris. "But if I might suggest, Herr Admiral, his obviously deficient knowledge of Russia and its people could be improved by a period of field work in a slightly lesser capacity."

"As you wish, Herr Reichsleiter."

"Good. Now, as to the operation itself..."

∞

As Muller was descending the stairs back to his office, silently cursing Canaris, Bormann, Himmler and the entire High Command and Nazi Party for good measure, life crackled through the static of the big radio transmitter in Group Captain Anson's cubby-hole and he jerked from a half-doze to (almost) complete readiness. Those few moments of blessed oblivion had been his longest period of rest in over two days. But now as he checked the call sign and heard it repeated at the regulation intervals it seemed his labours had not been in vain. He blinked the last traces of sleep from his eyes and flicked the 'receive' switch as the Russian-accented voice repeated again and again: "Borodino calling Austerlitz".

Anson replied: "Austerlitz calling Borodino. Are you receiving me?"

"Loud and clear," the voice replied. It sounded anything but, a ghost on the airwaves virtually drowned by the static, but Anson could just about make it out. "We need to send some visitors to you," he said. "Can you accommodate them?"

"Yes. But they must come soon." The voice was heavily-accented and Anson strained to make out the words. "We know that there is a special guest in the opposition's hotel. We think they will be leaving soon."

"We will send the visitors as soon as we can," Anson promised. Vrushkov had told him about the 'Borodino' group. They were a hardy bunch, mainly woodmen and farmers from the Ukraine, who had established a timber business in the forest country to the west of Istanbul. Most of the locals thought they were no more than that, which meant they could travel around widely without exciting too much suspicion. They were Whites to the core, but had chosen to work against the Communists while in exile rather than bleat and drown their sorrows and scheme against the other Tsarists, so they had little to do with the heavily infiltrated upper reaches of the underground. And when the Germans had made overtures to them they had invoked the spirit of Alexander Nevsky, sending back the message: "One oppressor for another is no fair trade."

All this endeared them to SOE, but their one drawback was lack of numbers and specialist training, as their own reply confirmed. "We need many. The hotel is well staffed and the concierge one of the finest. It may be hard to get the guest out quietly."

"I understand. Will transmit further instructions. Keep channel open at all times. Over and out."

He switched off. It was wise to never make these exchanges last too long. The Russians' monitoring equipment in Turkey was good, though limited, as it was in all neutral countries. He didn't think they'd broken any of the latest codes linking SOE with the few remaining trustworthy groups, but they were such devious bastards you could never be sure. That's how they'd caught dear old Sidney Reilly, after all.

The whole area of links with the Whites was very delicate ground. Officially, of course, there were none. Britain and Russia were allies, the best of chums, always had been and the government would never support any little fleas in the old bear's hide. But the Secret Service, MI6, SIS, the Foreign Section, whatever you wanted to call it, had helped put half the bloody fleas there in the first place.

The Russians knew it and we knew they knew it and it had probably been worth a few dozen extra Hurricanes to Murmansk or something for them not to kick up too much of a fuss about it. But both sides remembered Churchill's remark that the strangling of Bolshevism at birth would have been an untold blessing to the human race. And many men who now talked of unity and alliance had looked at each other along gunsights barely two decades before, when British forces had rode out with the Tsarists in a bitter, bloody campaign. Anson had met some of them – Christ, one of the top SOE bods, Gubbins, had got half his ideas from it – and he knew that 'unity' and 'alliance' were different words to 'friendship' or 'understanding'.

So an intricate gavotte was played out in neutral cities like Istanbul, where the British and Soviets used Czech exiles as intermediaries, each passing on the intelligence they deemed safe enough for the other to have at clandestine exchanges in the Blue Mosque and Aya Sofia, the sacred sites that dominated the centre of the old city. It worked well enough and the diplomatic facade was maintained while each side got on with the real job of maintaining their own separate anti-Axis networks and finding any dirt that could be thrown in the other's eyes if they should ever find themselves real enemies again.

Well, this came as close to that situation as Anson had ever known. But officially nothing had changed. That was why the station chief was to have no direct involvement in this operation, and not a single detail of it would ever go down on paper, that was for sure. But it was still fragile as hell. He wondered how far London would go to preserve the facade this time. And he wondered yet again, as he went to tell Forster the news, just how important this Vlasenin really was.

∞

He would have been in no doubt had he been present at the meeting which took place behind locked and guarded doors at the SOE headquarters in Baker Street that evening. Seated around the small conference table in the centre of the room were the four most powerful men in the entire organisation.

At the head of the table was Viscount Selborne, Minister for Economic Warfare, the department which had overall control of SOE. He had been in charge for just over eight months and was as different as any man could possibly be from his predecessor Hugh Dalton, the blunt, burly Durham miners' MP who had famously declared that his brainchild would set Europe ablaze and had burnt quite a few fingers in Whitehall proving it. With his grave, pale face and dark hair streaked back from a high, domed forehead, Selborne looked every inch the Empire Tory he was. But he had also been a passionate opponent of appeasement in the pre-war government. He had gained a reputation as a sharp political operator and, most importantly from SOE's point of view, he was a close friend of Churchill himself.

To his left sat Sir Charles Hambro, the SOE's chief executive. Like Selborne, he was a relative newcomer to the post but a veteran of many SOE operations, to which he had brought the combination of shrewd efficiency and go-getting spirit which had made him a director of the Bank of England at thirty. His face was stern and commanding, with clear, sharp eyes constantly darting from one face to the next.

Across the table from him was Brigadier Colin Gubbins, director of operations, the SOE's 'little Highland terrier'. A veteran of guerrilla conflicts as far apart as Ireland and Russia and author of definitive manuals on partisan warfare and covert operations, he had been a guiding light to the organisation from the start. Now he was leaning across the table eagerly, bushy eyebrows and toothbrush moustache seeming almost to bristle.

Like the two other members of that powerful triumvirate he was listening intently to the fourth man. He was small, with a shabby uniform and wispy, ill-disciplined red hair, the least physically striking of them all but in his own way the most important. Colonel Hugh Davies, originally of the South Wales Borderers, but for the past ten years an alumnus of military intelligence and covert action groups too numerous to mention. He was presently in charge of SOE's Section Z, the "odds and sods department".

Unlike the other sections, which concentrated on one particular country, Section Z recruited those men and women who had travelled widely in various capacities and used them in jobs which might involve the crossing of several national boundaries or dealing with neutral, and even allied, countries in "unusual circumstances". He was giving the other three a rundown of those in his section he felt best suited for a particularly delicate assignment.

When he had finished, Selborne nodded approvingly,

then looked up at the ceiling and rubbed his eyes as they travelled downwards again, a sure sign that the afternoon session at Number 10 had been a gruelling one. "Thank you, Colonel Davies, a most succinct and illuminating summary. So, gentlemen, we know we have the men for a hazardous and delicate operation. And that is exactly what the Vlasenin business will be. We know where he is being held; the Soviet consulate in Istanbul. In the middle of a huge city teeming with spies, in a neutral country currently inclining towards the Axis powers if anything, and a long way away from any sovereign British soil.

"He is heavily guarded and the Russians have their best men working on him, we presume to obtain the whereabouts of these papers he mentioned in his initial contacts with us. We must assume they will be successful in this very shortly. We also know that both Germany and Italy are aware of Vlasenin's whereabouts and are mounting a joint rescue operation. The Prime Minister has instructed me to tell you that we must get there first. Dr Vlasenin must be released from captivity, by force if necessary..."

Gubbins snorted. "If necessary? I doubt they'll be persuaded if we ask nicely!"

"Force is likely to be inevitable," Selborne said coldly. "Though other channels will be explored on an unofficial basis. However, should it come to a rescue operation, Vlasenin will be immediately brought to London by the shortest possible route, together with the relevant papers. That is a crucial point. These papers must not be left behind."

"That will render the operation a great deal more problematic," Hambro said.

"As if it was not so already," Gubbins added. "May I ask what the involvement of the other agencies is in all this? We might need a helping hand."

Selborne took a deep breath. "As you know SOE was brought in because the initial SIS operation to bring Vlasenin to Cyprus failed, due to infiltration. For that reason The Prime Minister feels that making this matter known to too many people would constitute an unacceptable security risk. Apart from the team in Istanbul, including the SOE station, no-one else knows our mission exists. The Prime Minister is keen to keep it that way. That is why the mission will be operated independently of the rest of the SIS network in Turkey. No contacts are to be made with them unless absolutely necessary.

"And of course it goes without saying that the nature of the prize will be kept secret from all but a select few. Even the men taking part will not be aware of why Vlasenin is so important. If we have to make any contacts with SIS, or the agencies of any friendly power in the course of the operation, they will be instructed to give us every assistance but on no account be told any details of the mission."

"They'll love us for that," Gubbins grunted.

"The Prime Minister is prepared to back us all the way," Selborne replied. "Ideally such contact will not be necessary. The same goes for agencies of any neutral country. And to answer the question I know you all wish to ask, Russia is to be treated as a hostile power." The other three men exchanged glances. "But every effort must be taken to conceal our involvement in Vlasenin's rescue until he is safe."

"In other words, we pretend it's the Tsarists acting alone," Hambro said. "And unless the Russians catch one of our men alive they must be content with that. Once Vlasenin is safe the diplomats can fight it out."

"Yes, indeed." Davies' dry, sanguine Welsh lilt was heard in the debate for the first time. "They'll say 'give him back'. And we'll say 'officially, we haven't got him; unofficially, if you want him come and get him like we did'."

"Precisely." Selborne gave one of his rare cadaverous smiles. "The Prime Minister is very clear on this one. Vlasenin wanted to come to us and we are to continue helping him in any way we can."

"And never mind the alliance?" Hambro looked doubtful. "If Russia decides to make things difficult it could seriously hamper the war effort all round."

"The Prime Minister thinks that unlikely," Selborne replied. "We know they will protest, make things a lot more difficult for our chaps over there – official or otherwise. But what else can they do? Pull out of the war completely?" He smiled again. "I hardly think Herr Hitler will let them at this stage.

"They have to keep fighting Germany, until one or the other is crushed. And they need the help of Britain and America for that. The Prime Minister believes they will be unwilling to risk losing that help, even for something as valuable as Vlasenin. In any case, we will make clear to them that the fruits of his knowledge will be available to all friendly powers and will only be used against the Tripartite Pact and their misguided allies." The three other men searched his face and voice for any hint of irony, but there was none.

"Frankly, gentlemen," he continued, "what happens after Vlasenin is rescued is none of our business. We must concern ourselves with the task in hand. Now, you have all been briefed on the operation so far and have read Group Captain Anson's report. Colonel Davies has given us an excellent round-up of some of our agents who might be suitable. I would welcome any further comments."

"I don't suppose you would welcome the most obvious comment," Davies said lugubriously. "It can't be done. Even if, by a small miracle, our men can get to him, they'll never bring him back."

He was conscious of the frowns from all round the table as Selborne replied: "I believe it can be done, colonel. The Prime Minister has told me that it must."

Davies took a deep breath. "In that case, I believe the only way is as I have indicated; a small force of men, a dozen or so, parachuting into the area south of Istanbul, making contact with this Tsarist group and then hitting the consulate. Vlasenin must be picked up by aircraft that same night and be on sovereign British territory – Cyprus first, then Egypt or Palestine, since Tehran is compromised by the Russian presence in Persia – ideally no more than six hours later. Any longer and the risk of detection or capture, the one thing we wish to avoid most of all, increases greatly. A larger group could not move around undetected; a smaller one could not take over the consulate."

"Agreed," said Selborne. "It seems feasible." He looked hard at Davies. "Yet you say it is impossible. Why?"

Davies sighed. "Because what I have just outlined involves operating further from a secure base than any SOE team has ever done. They must break into a consulate of a friendly power in a neutral country, essentially commit an illegal act. They must contend with a guarding force which will almost certainly outnumber them, how greatly we do not know. They must then smuggle Vlasenin out of the country undetected by Russian intelligence or the Turkish authorities. They must also contend with the best efforts of Axis intelligence in the area. And probably another… rescuing force, equally well-trained and possibly of greater size. They must do all this and ensure no-one is captured alive because it would precipitate a diplomatic and propaganda disaster." He shook his head. "I don't believe the Good Lord gave any man the kind of luck these boys will need to pull it off."

"But you think it could be done?" Selborne asked bluntly.

"My professional opinion is that it is theoretically possible. My personal one is that we will waste good men. And open a bloody big can of worms into the bargain."

"Surely you would not deny that this man's knowledge is worth it?" Hambro asked.

"From the reports, it certainly seems he could win us the war," Davies admitted. "And if the Russians use his knowledge he could still win us the war. He wouldn't be the first we've left to their tender mercies. However, I am well aware that this is about more than just who wins this war." He looked evenly at all of them. "Not that the men we send to almost certain death will know anything about that."

"War often demands the ultimate price – we are all well aware of that," Selborne said. "But harsh decisions must be made."

"Yes, I know," Davies said wearily. "But if this mission

is to succeed, the right leader is essential."

"I notice you did not suggest any of the men you mentioned earlier as a possible team leader," Gubbins said. "Despite the fact that Captain Curtis, for one, seemed to have the right qualifications."

"Curtis is a good man, but I don't think he has the experience. In my opinion, gentlemen, only one man could make a success of this mission." He took a deep breath. "Major Alexander Rawlings."

Selborne's deep frown made him look even more cadaverous. Hambro looked to the ceiling and Gubbins bit back a ripe Gaelic exclamation. "I think we are all aware of Major Rawlings' reputation," Selborne said at last. "Are you quite sure of this, Colonel Davies?"

"Perfectly, Minister." Davies became more formal, as always when justifying his most troublesome charge. "I, too, know of the major's reputation – for initiative and cool thinking under pressure, for fast action, for utter ruthlessness when necessary, for leading and inspiring men..."

"I was not thinking of that reputation." Selborne cut him off acidly. "But I admit he has had his successes in the past."

"His last operation could hardly be classed as such," Hambro said.

"With respect, sir, many factors contributed to our failure in that one," Davies replied.

"Perhaps a more salient fact about the mission is that, technically, it is not over," Gubbins pointed out. "Major Rawlings is still making his way to Spain and our contact with him has been irregular – as usual," he sniffed. "There is a chance he may not return in time."

"The rest of the team are still en route to Cairo,

where I shall be joining them. I still need to finalise the details of the operation," Davies said. "In any case, as I indicated the ideal time for the strike would be on the night of Saturday the 21st. There will be fewer staff in the consulate and Istanbul as a whole will be quieter because of the weekend. That gives us at least twenty-four hours before the team would need to fly to Turkey. I feel confident Major Rawlings will be back with us by then." He paused. "And if he is not, and we truly want this mission to succeed, I suggest we do our damnedest to find him."

Chapter 3

The Men for the Job

MAJOR ALEXANDER RAWLINGS WAS AT that precise moment up to his knees in a Pyrenean snowdrift. He was freezing cold despite the sweat that plastered his raven-dark hair to his forehead. His pale face was pinched in a grimace of pain and exertion. And his numb, tired limbs could barely be forced to wade ever onward, through the narrow ravine which he sincerely hoped would mark the last stage in this bloody nightmare of a journey.

Raoul, the guide, had been assuring him for the last two hours that the next stop was to be the last. Rawlings had never really believed him but he had never quite given up hoping either. He needed to rest more than anything in the world and his desire to finally reach the resting place was greater than fatigue or cold. For when they did rest he would be out of France. Over the last few weeks that had become the lodestar of his life.

He looked up and ahead at Raoul, many years older but still striding on, oblivious to the cold and clearly as much at home in these steep, trackless defiles as a cabbie on the streets of London. He was a short, squat man, like Rawlings swathed in a white hood, sheepskin coat and leggings. The same white as the covering on the shotguns slung from their shoulders. They were virtually invisible in the gloom shadows of the high peaks all around and the sepulchral light of snow in the early evening – the best time for their journey, Rawlings had been assured; after dark but with the moon still low. As far as Rawlings was concerned, the sooner he left France the better, and he knew better than to question Raoul's expertise. Only when Raoul turned to check that his charge was keeping up did any flash of colour break the white camouflage, and it was the deep brown all-year tan of the high country shepherd, with teeth of roughly the same hue flashing in a reassuring smile. The network had picked a good man for this last stage.

Unfortunately that was just about the only thing they had got right in this whole sorry escapade. When Rawlings had gone into Vichy three months previously SOE had been eagerly anticipating their first big success in the function for which they had been established – organising and directing large-scale resistance in enemy territory. Andre Girard, an artist living in Antibes, had persuaded Section F, which dealt with both Vichy and occupied France, that his 'Carte' network – a secret force nearly a quarter of a million-strong, many with military experience – was ready, willing and able to undertake large-scale sabotage throughout Petain's regime.

Early agents' reports had been favourable, and Section Z had been asked to lend a hand. It was hoped that links could be established with anti-Franco elements in northern Spain, to create an escape route for British PoWs and perhaps even exploit the simmering hatred for the newly triumphant *Caudillo*, so dangerously close to the Axis dictators politically and geographically. Rawlings – familiar with the territory, fluent in French and Spanish, and chafing at a desk after yet another brush with authority – was a natural choice.

He had landed by *felucca* from Gibraltar, established contact – and quickly realised that the whole thing was an illusion. Girard's 'army' was nothing more than a few scattered networks, most of them disorganised, inefficient and leaderless. The Vichy police, aided by Abwehr agents under an old enemy, Oberst Ulrich Ziedler, were steadily whittling away even those. Despite telling his masters as much he had been ordered to persevere. But while he was on a trip to one of the more northerly 'Carte' groups in Toulouse, the final blow had been dealt. One of Girard's couriers, Andre Marsac, fell asleep on a train from Marseilles to Paris and his briefcase, containing what amounted to a payroll of almost the entire movement, plus details of their British link men, was stolen by an Abwehr agent.

Rawlings was one of the first they picked up, and he received special treatment. Another old enemy, Hoffman of the Gestapo, arrived from Berlin. His brief was to discover everything about Section Z and 'turn' one of its star operatives. He was armed with a formidable talent for torture and a burning hatred for his prisoner. The three worst days of Rawlings' life had ensued and if the survivors of the Toulouse network had not rescued him he would have given in or died within hours.

Instead he ran, south through Vichy France, one step

ahead of the gendarmes, *Milice* and German soldiers who had only just arrived in the country as a result of the dramatic meeting witnessed by Ciano. There had been few from the remnants of the networks willing to help him, but for these last three days they had been enough, shuffling him from safe house to safe house in stinking goods trains and farm lorries.

But now he was nearly at the border and his tortured body and mind were ready to rest. Tonight at last he could have a good night's sleep on neutral soil. Spain was not out of the woods by any means, but it was safer than France. And now as they reached the mouth of a narrow gulley he could see in the deep valley below a small wooden hut. Raoul pointed downwards and whispered "*Espana*". Rawlings' heart lifted. He forgot the cold and pain and fatigue, following his guide down quickly.

They reached the bottom of the valley, still hidden by the rocks from any prying eyes in the hut despite the fact that it was unlit and seemed utterly deserted. Raoul skirted forward, still using every scrap of cover, invisible, almost at the hut now. Then a quick crouching run, under the single window, to the doorway. He pulled his sawn-off shotgun from under its covering and, kicking the door open, darted inside. After a few seconds he whistled the 'all clear' signal. Rawlings ran forward, using the cover at first, then sprinting the last ten open yards. He panted to a halt as Raoul closed the door behind him – and realised he was caught.

He realised it before Raoul said softly: "I'm sorry, *mon ami*". Before the silenced Lugers were rammed against each temple. Before the strong arms grabbed him, pulling the shotgun from his shoulder and binding his wrists together. Before the door was slammed shut behind him. Before he was pushed roughly into the centre of the room. And before the match flared in the darkness, touching the wick of an oil lamp at a table, bathing the room in light. Directly in front of Rawlings, seated around the table, were four men in civilian clothes, Schmeissers and pistols trained on him. In the middle of them was a fifth man; Reichskommissar der Geheime Staatspolizei Klaus Hoffman.

His broad, scarred face was creased in a triumphant smirk, florid red in the lamplight, contrasting vividly with the black slouch hat above and black leather coat below. His right arm lay strangely crooked across his lap but his left held a Mauser pistol with the distinctive tulip bulb silencer, pointing straight and steady at Rawlings' heart.

He gestured wordlessly and the two Gestapo men with the silenced Lugers shoved Rawlings towards an empty chair. As he sat down he glanced over his shoulder. Four more; the two who had grabbed him and two standing by Raoul, covering him with Schmeisser machine pistols. Nine altogether. Not terribly good.

"So, Major Rawlings," Hoffman said with a wolfish smile, English heavily overlaid with the distinctive accent of the Hamburg waterfront. "Good to see you again. Enjoy your 72-hour leave, did you?"

"Nothing like a spot of mountain air to restore the spirits," Rawlings replied lightly, cutting across the sycophantic laughter of the other Gestapo. He didn't feel much like joking – in fact, he felt sick with fear – but he wouldn't give the bastard the satisfaction of knowing that.

"It seems to have loosened your tongue," Hoffman sneered, displeased at the glib response which had undercut his triumph. His men were looking at the Englishman with a hint of admiration, especially the plain clothes French *Milice* who had been drafted in to help his interrogation team. "So, you feel like telling me anything more?"

"I think I already told you my name, rank and serial number."

Hoffman gave a scornful laugh. "Don't talk to me like a soldier. You come to France as a terrorist and try to leave like a criminal. You know, under the Geneva Convention I could shoot you right now."

"If you'd wanted to do that, you could have done it before I reached the door." Rawlings called the bluff. "But you want to do more than kill me quickly – or see me beg first. And that's got nothing to do with the Carte network." He jerked his head towards Raoul, standing nervously between his guards, tanned face now grey with fear. "He's just proved how well you've won that one."

Hoffman smiled again. "Yes, we have. And for a very small price."

Raoul moved forward uncertainly. "My family, Herr Hoffman? You promised they would be safe if I did as you asked."

"*D'accord.*" Hoffman switched to the same Basque French, again heavy with the Hamburg accent. "They are as safe as you yourself." He smiled winningly, then shot Raoul in the head.

There was virtually no noise from the pistol and none at all from the guide, even though the impact flung him against the wall of the hut. For an instant he was still. His eyes rolled up in his head, as though seeking to look at the bloody hole above them. Then his knees buckled and he fell to the floor.

"Poor bastard," Rawlings said. "You always did favour the best bribe of all, eh, Klaus?" He looked at Hoffman, whose Mauser had flicked back to cover him as quickly as it had flicked away, and his pretence of urbane detachment gave way to pure contempt. "He was a good man."

Hoffman nodded in agreement. "He wouldn't have been much use for anything else. One of our own will be better for this section of the route. Besides," he added almost absently, "with all his family dead he wouldn't have much to live for."

"I could have told him you'd kill them the minute you picked them up."

"But you didn't. Still, that's hardly the first mistake you've made on this assignment."

"And finding and capturing them – and him – is what took you three days? I can't see why you didn't just pick me up on the French side?"

Hoffman smirked. "I wanted you to think you'd got away. It might help lower your resistance when I get back to work, knowing that you fucked up all along the line."

"It won't." Rawlings shook his head. "Though I admit I should have been more careful. If I'd had any sense I'd have told him to take a different route to the usual one."

Hoffman smiled. "Another mistake. You must be getting tired of making them on this mission. Still, we can talk all about that soon enough. Now move!" He barked the order, gesturing toward the door with his pistol. Two of his men pulled it open, two more grabbed Rawlings and pushed him into the doorway. Hoffman rose and grabbed the lamp, the rest of the Gestapo and *Milice* rising with him.

"That's right, Klaus," Rawlings said, pausing in the doorway. "Don't want the Spaniards to find a few foreign nationals illegally loitering in their territory."

Hoffman smiled, making no effort to extinguish the lamp as he pushed Rawlings out into the freezing night. "The guards around here are no problem. Another reason why I thought it would be more entertaining to wait until you thought you were safe. Half the men on this border post have sons in the Blue Division. The others can be bought. No, there's no hurry to get out of Spain, Rawlings." He held the lamp up close to put it out and his face was bathed in yellow fire. "I just want to get back to work on you soon as I can." A second later there was darkness and Rawlings was grabbed and pulled into it.

As his eyes regained their night vision he was aware of a low rise beyond the hut, to which his guards frogmarched him. Once across it and out of the valley there was a steep descent along a worn, narrow shepherd's track to one of the few open roads through the mountain passes, worn smoother by the recent flood of refugees from Franco.

Parked by the side of the road were three large black Mercedes saloons. At a shout from Hoffman three more men emerged from cover and got behind the wheels. Another command and two more men clambered down from the slopes to their left and right. Like the rest of the Gestapo they were dressed in civilian clothes, but wore thick climbing boots and fur-lined jackets. Mauser infantry rifles were slung on their shoulders. Obviously the lookouts, or a second line if Rawlings and Raoul had evaded the trap. Hoffman had left nothing to chance.

Unfortunately, leaving nothing to chance was Hoffman's business and he had become extremely good at it, Rawlings reflected as the riflemen pushed their way into the cars, five men in each now plus the prisoner, who now had a Luger at his temple and a Schmeisser at his stomach. He guessed half of his captors were *Milice*, the Vichy's paramilitary police force composed of Nazi sympathisers. He had found in the past few days that they made just as efficient jailers, and torturers, as Hoffman's Gestapo veterans. As the cars drove off, the one containing Rawlings and Hoffman in the middle, he realised there was no chance of escape – and that was rapidly becoming another Hoffman trademark.

SOE and every other anti-Nazi organisation in occupied Europe had learnt to fear Klaus Hoffman since the start of the war. But in Germany his notoriety stretched back even further. One of the most outstanding officers in the Hamburg police department, he had become a detective at the age of 28 in 1930. His intimate knowledge of the Reeperbahn and the Sankt Pauli underworld, plus his heavy-handed interrogation methods, had ruffled a few feathers in the department. But when he caught a notorious sex killer known as 'The Nightwatchman' in November 1932 he became a national celebrity.

This brought him to the attention of the Nazi Party, who saw the advantages of having good policemen and recognised public figures in its ranks. Hoffman had already joined the Party, mainly because of his hatred and distrust of the foreign dregs who polluted his waterfront and the Jewboy get-rich-quick merchants who traded around it, growing wealthy on the sweat of good German workers like his father and brothers. But he also had a detective's nose for who was becoming the rising power in the land. Now they offered him work and a chance for revenge.

At that time, Hitler was not in power, but his bodyguard, the SS, was beginning to take on a half-military, half-governmental structure. This included an intelligence department, the Sicherheitsdienst, or SD, headed by Reinhard Heydrich, the naval officer who had begun his career in the Abwehr but moved on to greater things under the patronage of Himmler. He was anxious to carve a reputation and one of his first coups was gathering a mass of intelligence on police officers who might not be sympathetic to the New Order. Inspector Hoffman was one of Heydrich's most diligent informers and when the great day came he and his cronies moved up into the offices of the men who had underestimated them so badly.

After that he never looked back. Joining the Gestapo in 1936 was a doorway to another world, a chance to root out the real criminals in Germany – the Jews, the queers, the Communists, all the enemies of good Germans like him. And no-one to question his methods. His results were excellent and after the *blitzkrieg* he was sent in to extend his own brand of policing to the occupied territories, the special rank of Reichskommissar giving him equivalent power to a governor; he used it to build up tight security networks, staffing them with his protégés before moving on.

He had succeeded everywhere – except Norway, where the Resistance had been active from the start and SOE had been well-placed geographically to help them. One Major Rawlings had been a regular passenger on the

'Shetland Bus' and a particular thorn in Hoffman's side. Even when Hoffman had cornered him at a farmhouse near Bergen in December 1941, Rawlings had shot his way to safety, wounding Hoffman in the right arm. By the time the Gestapo man reached hospital they were unable to save it.

He returned to Germany an invalid consumed with hatred for the Englishman, but after several months' recuperation and learning to shoot as straight with his left hand, he resumed work with the Gestapo. And one of his first assignments was to help the French break up a little network in Vichy. God was kind sometimes. He had finally caught Rawlings and only Ziedler's plan, to keep such a prized SOE agent fit enough to carry on working if he could be 'turned', had prevented Hoffman from crippling him in return.

But now he's got me again. Rawlings' musings ended with that stark fact, and at the same moment the convoy slowed down. They were approaching a tiny border post, no more than one wooden barrier next to a barracks hut. Four Spanish soldiers raised the barrier and waved them through, happy in the knowledge that they had just earned the equivalent of a month's pay. And then the cars were crossing a rickety bridge spanning the high gorge above a river it had taken Rawlings and Raoul thirty freezing minutes to ford earlier that evening.

The convoy braked to a halt at an identical border post on the far side. But here the garrison was much more than a handful of pliable reservists. Well over a hundred troops were spread across the clearing which led to another mountain pass. Vichy gendarmes and uniformed *Milice* mainly, but with at least a platoon of

German soldiers among them. They were all armed to the teeth and moved to cover the convoy efficiently as soon as it approached. Behind them, a knot of senior officers stood beside an impressive row of staff cars, Kubelwagen scout vehicles and trucks. In their midst was another well-remembered face.

Whenever he looked at Colonel Ulrich Ziedler, Rawlings could not help thinking that the Abwehr's gain was Hollywood's loss. At six feet four, he topped the other officers by a head, but his body was so perfectly proportioned that such height did not look ungainly or unnatural. Broad shoulders and chest tapered to a slim waist and the long, powerful legs of the champion runner he had once been. He wore the uniform of the Wehrmacht's Transport Corps, a handy device to explain one's (often fleeting) presence anywhere in the Reich. A plain, travel-worn uniform, but on him it looked like the pride of Savile Row.

As soon as he saw Rawlings being pushed unceremoniously from the car the impossibly handsome face beneath the peaked cap broke into a smile. High intelligent forehead fringed by thick chestnut hair perfectly combed; sparkling grey eyes, clear skin and strong cheekbones; full lips stretching over even white teeth above a firm jawline. Yes, if you'd put him on the Warner Brothers soundstage in the Thirties Errol Flynn could have whistled for his dinner – and I'd have been spared a lot of grief over the years.

Ziedler had begun his espionage work during the Weimar days, a second lieutenant on the General Staff in Berlin. He was fresh from the Prussian Military Academy, an outstanding student and a star of the athletics team with little to do in an army heavily circumscribed by the Treaty of Versailles. But his work brought him to the attention of the nascent Abwehr, which needed bright young talents.

His first assignment was helping to boost the rearmament programme, with a few secret visits to the Skoda works under cover of official business. He had used his family's Czech background to secure pledges of good faith and constantly eluded the British and French agents detailed to keep tabs on him.

After the Nazis came to power Ziedler adjusted to the new regime smoothly, becoming a Party member without qualm or question, though there continued to be some doubts about his true loyalties. His family were Sudeten German shopkeepers who had lived in Czechoslovakia for generations but had come to experience increasing hostility from the Czech majority in their district. Finally they had left, arriving in Plauen early in 1905, just before Ulrich was born. They found a better life in Germany, determined that their only son should have the best this new country offered – and never cease to love and respect it.

They saved to send him to the best schools, then the academy. When he married Ilse, a true Prussian aristocrat he had met soon after his posting to Berlin, they were overjoyed. He had absorbed and accepted their teaching completely and it had given him the intense patriotism so often found in second-generation nationals, much more respectful and uncritical than the disgruntled, almost grudging, variety of the natives. This was all to the good in Hitler's Germany yet some of his superiors still wondered if this was greater than his loyalty to the higher ideals of National Socialism.

But his work spoke for itself. He had been dispatched to London in 1934 on the staff of the military attaché, to delicately sound out Britain's opinions on the new chap in the Chancellery and establish contacts with Mosley's Blackshirts. An edict from Hitler, keen to foster an Anglo-Saxon *entente*, that no direct espionage work was to be undertaken against Britain curtailed his work there. But his success was noted, his store of languages increased and a taste for Dickens and Shakespeare added to his love of Goethe and Schiller. On his return to Berlin the new Abwehr head, Admiral Canaris, took him under his wing.

A similar spell in Washington followed, where Melville, Twain and Fitzgerald were added to the bookshelves while the Seversky plant in Long Island was raided for blueprints of the new pursuit planes and Scout bombers. Then in 1937 he helped Ritter and Lang obtain the plans for the Norden bombsight and even the Fuhrer himself began to take notice.

He was chosen to infiltrate the Thaelmann Brigade of German Communists fighting in Spain, running a network of agents from Barcelona and establishing an efficient link-up with Ciarelli, despite their personal feelings never rising above cordial dislike. Spain was also where he had first come into the orbit of Rawlings. The Englishman's suspicions of the passionate left-wing German exile Dieter Kuhlmans, who seemed to bear a strong resemblance to a low-ranking staff officer who had been seen around London a few years earlier, were aroused. Ziedler was for once thwarted.

But he had laid the ground for some useful work to

be done. In any case more important tasks were at hand. Hitler was out to reshape central Europe in his own image and the first stepping stone was Austria. Ziedler, posing as an itinerant journalist, helped to strengthen the Austrian Nazi Party and find out more about the country's defences. The success of the *Anschluss* was due to him in no small part, as the Fuhrer said many times when pinning the Iron Cross on his chest. Czechoslovakia was next, for him and his parents an even prouder time, helping the misguided Czechs back into the fold by planting information to help the British and French diplomats to reconsider their opinions of that Hitler fellow.

Despite his success there, Poland proved the straw that broke the camel's back and war loomed. It was now felt that Ziedler might be better employed as a spycatcher, helping to keep his country's ever-increasing borders safe. He had made the move from Abwehr I to III smoothly, helping the upstart Schellenberg to secure the capture of the two British agents at Venlo in November 1939. The fact that the SD man won all the credit only confirmed a growing suspicion throughout the Abwehr that the Fuhrer would divert more trust and resources to SS Intelligence in the future.

But Ziedler had continued assiduously breaking up networks of spies and terrorists from Holland to the Ukraine. And, of course, Vichy France. He had helped to catch Rawlings while gauging the lie of the land for the takeover which had occurred just a few days ago. But the situation was still delicate, as the French officers had made very clear to him when they agreed to co-operate in hunting down a man who should never have escaped from German custody in the first place. So perhaps this was why the smile was a little less brilliant and the impeccable English slightly bitter in tone as he stood before Rawlings and Hoffmann.

"Hardly the right time for a hiking holiday, Major Rawlings."

"I felt I was getting a bit cooped up – you know how it is?" Rawlings smiled and Ziedler could not help but smile back.

"A little too fresh out of doors, though." Ziedler pulled a flask of schnapps from his greatcoat and gestured for one of his aides to untie Rawlings' wrists. "For the journey," he said with a strange note in his voice which Rawlings did not immediately recognise.

The Englishman drank deeply and gratefully as Ziedler pulled Hoffman to one side. "Well done – did everything go according to plan?"

"He's here, isn't he?" Hoffman replied impatiently. He always found this bantering attitude of Ziedler's with enemy agents inexplicable and irritating. "Now can we get him back quick?"

"You never were much of a countryman, were you, Klaus? But that's not the way we play it any more. Orders from Berlin. Something big's come up – very big. They want us both on it and they don't want to risk a top SOE man getting away and getting involved. So we take a drive to the nearest airfield – and Rawlings dies. Here and now."

Hoffman's face was a picture of conflicting emotions, the pleasure of a kill like this vying with frustration. "I could turn him in one more session; get all he knows at least. He's ready to crack. We could do it here..."

He was almost pleading but Ziedler silenced him

with an imperious wave of the hand. "There isn't time." He gestured towards the guard hut: "Behind there. One bullet."

"Why not out here – in front of everyone?"

Ziedler's brow wrinkled in distaste and he looked down on Hoffman from a fair height. "What do you want him to do – beg for mercy? This isn't a show. And I doubt very much if he'd oblige you, anyway. Besides, in case you didn't notice, we're in a minority here. These French troops seem solid enough, but we've just taken over their country and they might get unduly sentimental over public executions."

Hoffman started to protest but Ziedler cut him off again. "We can't afford the risk. One bullet, silenced, well out of sight, then on the trucks before they've time to think." Hoffman still hesitated and Ziedler really laid it on. "As quickly as you like – Inspector!"

The Gestapo man looked murderous, as he always did when Ziedler used his old police rank. Then he turned on his heel and strode toward the guard hut. "Two men – bring him!" he barked as he stamped past his team, not bothering to see who responded. They had stood slightly apart as Rawlings and Ziedler had talked but now two of the *Milice* sprang forward eagerly. The first was the one they had called Gerard, a big, blond bruiser. He was closely followed by a pale, hard-eyed ferret of a man named Leon, who had been one of the most enthusiastic assistants at the interrogations. They grabbed Rawlings and pushed him roughly in their master's wake. A few of the French soldiers' heads turned but nothing more.

Behind the barrack hut was a small patch of ground, perhaps ten or fifteen yards square, ending in an unfenced drop to the river below. "Afterwards he goes over the edge," Hoffman said to the guards as he turned round and walked up to Rawlings. "This is the end at last, you bastard. One bullet – I couldn't deny myself that pleasure – then the long drop. How do you feel?"

"Bored," Rawlings replied, then very carefully spat in his face. Hoffman recoiled, raised his metal hand, then abruptly lowered it again and stepped behind Rawlings. "On his knees," he said to Gerard and Leon. As they pushed Rawlings down he drew the Mauser from his leather coat, silencer still on. The guards stood impassive, one hand on each of Rawlings' shoulders – until Gerard's came up and out, lashing straight into Leon's throat. The *Milice* gave a choking grunt and fell back dead. Hoffman looked round in shocked surprise, Mauser coming up – and found himself staring down the barrel of a silenced Luger.

"Call for help and you're dead." It's hard to make a whisper sound commanding but Gerard managed it well enough. "Drop the pistol, then stand back," he said in the same flat, emotionless French. "Any tricks when we walk back round the corner and you're dead." As Hoffman obeyed like a man in a dream, covered all the way by the Luger, and Rawlings scrambled to his feet and pulled on Leon's hat and jacket, Gerard said in English: "Sorry I couldn't spring you in the car. We could have avoided all this."

"No problem, lieutenant," Rawlings replied amicably as he gathered up Hoffman's Mauser. "You didn't have too many opportunities. I'm just grateful you took no notice when they told you never to volunteer for anything. Now, give Ziedler a shot just in case he's listening ever so hard, then we'll be on our way."

Gerard nodded, checked that Rawlings was covering Hoffman, then put a bullet dead centre in Leon's chest. There was a soft thudding sound, audible perhaps ten yards away. Leon's corpse jerked, then was still again. As Gerard turned back and moved towards the corner of the hut Rawlings searched Hoffman's coat pockets, unearthing a large wad of notes and two spare magazines for the Mauser, all of which he pocketed with a smile. Then he held the pistol in front of Hoffman's face. "Been wanting one of these for ages. They're rarer than hen's teeth in the department. I don't suppose you're going to tell me which side it favours? No? Ah, well, I'll find out soon enough."

"They recommended him." Hoffman spoke like a man on novocaine. "Two years in the paramilitaries. One of their best men."

"Of course he is," Rawlings said sympathetically. "We don't just send anyone in. If he hadn't been so good they wouldn't have recommended him. And then I'd really have been up the Swanee. Probably never have escaped in the first place. He gave the Resistance the layout of the prison, of course. And if he hadn't been telling us about Vichy interrogation methods in detail for so long I'd probably not have lasted long enough to be rescued. Yes," he added ruefully, "it's a shame the cover's blown now. Still, if you can't help a brother officer, where are you?"

"As you English say, all in a good cause," Gerard replied. "But we still have the soldiers to get past."

"Oh, I think we've got something to smooth our passage." Rawlings prodded Hoffman in the back with the Mauser. "Start walking."

The Gestapo man glared but did as he was told. Within a few seconds they were out in the open again. Ziedler moved forward briskly when he saw the three figures re-emerge, on the point of remonstrating with Hoffman for taking so long. Then he recognised Rawlings. For a fraction of a second he stopped dead, then raised one arm. The officers behind him barked a volley of orders and a hundred weapons were aimed and cocked. In the still mountain air the noise as safety catches were slid back, breeches opened and bolts engaged echoed like the wings of some great flock of birds disturbed at roost.

An unnatural silence followed, then Ziedler drew his pistol and shouted: "No further, Major Rawlings. I don't know what you think you're doing, but..."

"I'm escaping," Rawlings cut in. "And you're going to let me." He surveyed the ranks of French and German soldiers, every one still covering him. "You've got this lot very well trained, Ulrich. I'm sure when you tell them to lower their weapons and let us through they'll be just as obedient."

Ziedler smiled and shook his head. "No deal, major. One more step and you will die, I assure you."

"So will Hoffman. Do you want that, Ulrich? He's a valuable partner – even if he is a bit careless who he trusts sometimes. Let us go and you can keep him."

"Two for one, eh? That's nobody's idea of a fair trade."

"A man's entitled to a reasonable profit. Besides, you're way ahead on this deal. The network's blown. You'll be picking up our men and theirs from now until next Christmas with the information you've got. And despite what Klaus here might think I'll die before I tell you any more, let alone work for you. Why kill one of Berlin's blue-eyed boys, just to stop me skulking back to London?"

Ziedler thought hard. All he had to do was give the order and all three would die. Even if Rawlings didn't pull the trigger himself few of the Germans and even fewer of the French would worry if a Gestapo man died in the fusillade. For himself, he would shed few tears at Hoffman's demise. But he did have his uses. And Berlin would be furious. Himmler wanted him on the team for this next mission, obviously. Best not to antagonise him, as the Admiral always said. The messy end to this mission was bad enough.

And Rawlings? He was dangerous. They might well meet again. And soon if SOE got involved in this business. But he was no threat now. As he said, he had been beaten. Thoroughly. And by me. If they send him, that knowledge will give me an edge. If they don't, whether he dies here or not makes no difference.

And there was his contingency plan, too, of course. If that played out as he anticipated Rawlings would be dead within minutes anyway. "All right, major." Ziedler spoke with the air of a proud father indulging a precocious child. "How do you want to play it?"

Rawlings smiled, trying not to let his profound relief show. "Now you're talking. Let's have all guns down for a start." He waited until every bolt and breech was disengaged, every barrel pointing to the ground. "Now we'll have two men raise the barriers across the bridge," he continued as he pushed Hoffman towards the nearest Mercedes, Gerard shadowing them. "And that includes the shark's teeth." Ziedler gave a rueful smile and gestured to the officers. At a barked command two French soldiers raised the metal pole barring the road onto the bridge while two more pulled away the spiked chain, almost invisible against the tarmac. Gerard was at the wheel of the Mercedes now, Hoffman and Rawlings in the rear.

The engine roared into life and the car moved forward slowly, the ranks of troops parting to make way for it. As it passed close to Ziedler and the other officers Rawlings signalled for Gerard to stop and wound down the window. "We'll get rid of Hoffman once we're on the Spanish side. He walks back across the bridge with a gun on him all the way. Any tricks and he dies. Once he's back on your side we all go home."

"Home's a long way, major. And Spain can be a dangerous place for foreigners, so they tell me."

"Especially Germans." Rawlings smiled back. "I think I'll make it all right."

"Until next we meet, then." Ziedler held out his hand, palm up. Rawlings laughed, pulled the hip flask from his pocket and threw it to him, then signalled to Gerard. The Mercedes moved off and up into second, past the barrier, onto the bridge. Rawlings searched Hoffman's pockets again, more thoroughly this time. "Don't look at me like that, Klaus," he said in a reproving tone. "I just saved your life, and... hello!" A tiny hidden pocket had yielded Hoffman's wallet, with more money and various Gestapo identity papers. Rawlings held them up. "Never put all your valuables in one place, so my mother always said. A real treat for the forgery department, this lot – and the money should keep Franco's crusaders happy."

They were almost across the bridge now. "Well,

thanks for everything," Rawlings said, then yanked the car door open and hit Hoffman across the face with the Mauser. Hoffman fell from the moving car like a sack of grain, hitting the tarmac and slamming against the bridge parapet. After a few seconds he raised himself up stiffly and groaned. Looking around in a daze, he saw the Mercedes was driving to the end of the bridge, now just in front of the Spanish border post. Rawlings was leaning out of the rear window, Mauser trained on him. Hoffman turned slowly and walked back. Rawlings kept the pistol on him and with his free hand passed the wad of notes to Gerard. "Give it to those guards. Coming up left and right."

Gerard looked up. He had not noticed, but there they were, coming out of the cover around the road. Two on each side, rifles raised. Two more had them covered from the barracks hut. Gerard gave a reassuring smile and threw the money to the nearest. A second later all four broke into broad smiles and rushed back to raise the barrier. "Drive on – slowly," Rawlings said and the Mercedes inched onto Spanish soil at the exact moment that Hoffman re-entered Vichy France. Rawlings shouted: "Open her up, lieutenant," and ducked back in his seat as Gerard slipped the Mercedes straight into fourth, speeding past the waving Spanish guards.

"Must have been about a year's wages for each of them, judging by the speed they got the barrier up," Rawlings said as he waved back. "Still, I'm sure Hoffman can afford it."

"Yes, sir," Gerard replied, then added: "But why not shoot him on the bridge back there? We could still have got across the border before they had time to do anything.

And we both know how dangerous he is."

"Indeed, lieutenant. Believe me, there's nothing I'd enjoy more than putting a bullet into Klaus Hoffman – were it not for the fact that Ziedler had a sniper above the bridge. Spotted him coming in. If I'd killed Hoffman we'd have been dead half a second later. And if I hadn't told you to hit the gas just then he could have nailed us before we got among the Spaniards."

Gerard blushed. For the first time he looked what he was – a young man picked to do a long and dangerous job, which had ended in a burst of unexpected activity. "I didn't see him. Or those Spanish guards. I could have got us both killed."

"Capers like this are a little different to sleeper work." Rawlings gave him a weary smile. "You've done a hell of a job for the last two years, son – SIS are going to be furious at me for blowing your cover, I guarantee. And back there was as tough a spot as I've ever been in. If it weren't for you I'd have died in the cells, anyway. I reckon you can go back to the Free French feeling pretty proud of yourself. Providing you get this little baby to Barcelona as quick as is humanly possible, of course."

"Yes, sir." Lieutenant Gerard Dubois, late of the Chasseurs Alpins and the French Section of SIS, hit the accelerator and Rawlings stretched himself out for the blessed oblivion of sleep.

And back at the border post Ziedler's flask of schnapps was out again. Hoffman finished a long swig and gingerly touched the field dressing on his forehead. His face was unusually pale but his eyes blazed. "Next time – next time," he said softly.

"*Ja*, next time," Ziedler repeated. "And if this thing's

as big as they say, I don't think that time will be long in coming."

∽

The Germans' return home was considerably quicker and simpler than that of Rawlings and Dubois. They were back in Berlin by eleven that evening – to be summoned straight to Tirpitz Ufer for a meeting with the same quartet that had so discomfited Hauptmann Muller. By midnight they had been fully briefed and introduced to their team, and Ziedler was listening with feigned politeness to Colonel Ciarelli's rescue plan.

At about the same time the citizenry of Barcelona were treated to the sight of an expensive but travel-stained Mercedes driving through their streets with two disreputable looking civilians inside. Rawlings had decided that a secretive approach would have taken too long. The usual precautions of blending in with the surroundings, even in a neutral country, were outweighed by the danger. Ziedler was right; Spain was a dangerous place for spies, especially ones well-known but not popular with Franco's intelligence agencies. So he and Dubois had driven all evening to throw themselves on the mercies of the SIS Barcelona station.

They were as reluctant to assist SOE as ever, but the presence of Dubois helped and by the early hours of Friday November 20th, 1942, the Frenchman had been placed as supercargo on a Portuguese air freighter bound for London via Lisbon. And Rawlings had been put on another for Malta, with instructions to report to the SOE liaison officer there upon arrival. In fact, the liaison officer reported to him, an irascible Scots RN Commander who chivvied Rawlings on to a plane for Cairo, thrust a folder marked 'Most Secret' into his hands and informed him with some glee that Colonel Davies expected to see him as soon as he arrived.

By the time he had read the folder Rawlings had time to catch a few hours sleep before landing in Cairo and being driven straight to SOE HQ. It was eleven o' clock in the morning. Rawlings had travelled almost two thousand miles in twelve hours. He knew he would soon be on the move again, on a mission that would require his body and mind to be on full alert constantly. And his main worry was whether he would be able to stay awake through this first meeting with Hugh.

Davies had hardly been idle since the summit in Baker Street. He had flown to Cairo and assembled all the men, equipment and information within SOE's resources for what would undoubtedly be its biggest mission so far. Now everything was ready except the most important element – the leader. As he waited for Rawlings to arrive, and read his file over and over again, the more Davies was convinced there was no-one as suitable for the job. And the more he wished to God that there had been.

Alexander Rawlings had been born near Otterburn, Northumberland, in January 1900, the first son of a family of gentleman farmers. He had grown up in the starkly beautiful border country where once the reivers had roamed (and some in the village said that was how the Rawlings family had acquired their fair stock of money and land); a boy as wild as any in that wild country, alternately frustrating and delighting the masters of the local grammar school.

He had excelled at all sports, especially rugby. But he was equally adept at English, History, languages of any kind – and getting into trouble. Truancy, fights and cheeking the teachers, that had been young Alex's stock in trade. Many senior men in the SOE believed it still was.

After a series of long talks with the headmaster, Alex's parents had decided to send him to live with his uncle and aunt in Durham and attend the new Durham Johnston School, an establishment already acquiring a good name in the area. Formed from the bequest of a Durham University professor, it had grown from an evening establishment offering technical education to a full-scale secondary school with an impressive languages department and a good rugby team. The fees were a full £1.10s a term but his parents could afford it and thought the change might calm Alex down a bit.

In fact the reverse happened. Alex came to Durham in the autumn of 1914 and found a beautiful, bustling city where the war was much more real than in the country. His fellow pupils were boys on scholarships or whose families had scraped the money together. They came from many parts of the north-east and many backgrounds, all keen to make something of themselves through learning. But they were even keener to join up as soon as they could. Alex saw soldiers everywhere, heard their talk of Flanders and Mons, Mesopotamia and Palestine. He heard the distant thunder as Von Hipper's warships pounded the east coast ports in the December of that first year, and the guns scared him but excited him too.

He began playing truant to follow the soldiers around and one morning in February 1915 his desk was empty and a very young-looking volunteer was walking towards the headquarters of the 5th Battalion of the Durham Light Infantry. The recruiting sergeant was suspicious, but Alex was bigger than some of them had been and he was on the point of becoming a soldier when his housemaster arrived.

He narrowly missed expulsion and school increasingly took a back seat as he continued to follow the war intently, but he still passed his exams with flying colours and captained the school rugby team. Even after the Armistice, he remained restless. There was a world outside and he wanted to see it. He returned to the farm briefly but ran off again to join the Black and Tans when the Irish Troubles broke out. His aunt and uncle caught him at Durham station, about to sneak on to the London train.

Soon after, with his parents' encouragement, he enrolled at Durham University to study Agriculture and Business. A few of the brighter Rawlings boys had done that over the years. Get some letters after your name, sow a few wild oats then come back home for the real business of life – to farm the family land, turn out for the local rugby side at weekends, marry some suitable girl and raise the next generation. Perhaps his parents saw it as the last chance to put him back on the right lines and snuff out the spark of adventure.

Instead he became friendly with a fellow student whose brother was serving in the Peshawar Police on the North-West Frontier. A few autumn nights in the pubs on the rain-washed old streets between the cathedral and the castle, with tales of bandit hunting in a beautiful wild country populated by spies, informers, *badmashes* and *nautch* dancers, ensured that Alex would never be a farmer. At the end of his first term he packed his bags, wrote a long letter to his parents, and left his college rooms. Then he set off for India.

It took a long time – the best part of seven years, in fact. The money from a term's worth of weekends at the races got him as far as Paris, but his gift for languages landed him a job as a café bartender and his charm landed him a place to stay – with a German artist, whose embracing of Vorticism had not immured her to the beauty of the male nude. Soon after young Alex passed through what Frank Harris had called 'the gateway to life' he was a waiter at Maxime's and a very junior member of the Montparnasse café set of struggling yet glamorous writers and artists.

But much to Anna's dismay his heart was still set on India. In 1922 he moved on, but his time in Paris had left him with a taste for the high life. The Riviera took his money, but six months as a stevedore in Marseilles reacquainted him with reality, particularly in a brush with the Corsican underworld over paying protection money along with his union dues. He acquitted himself well when the enforcers arrived but still ended up in hospital. His only visitors were the police, who urged him to "travel south for the good of your health".

He left France as a deckhand on a Mediterranean freighter, moving through Italy and Greece to arrive in Egypt early in 1925. A spell as a tour guide followed. Then, on a whim, he fell in with a motley group of war veterans, explorers and Arab scholars who had determined to cross from Cairo to Muscat unaided and unguided.

They mapped out a new route, caught every disease known to the Near East, skirmished and traded with both sides in the civil war that created the kingdom of

Saudi Arabia, and learnt the true meaning of thirst – but they made it. Davies smiled. The English between the wars had given a new meaning to the word eccentricity. But they had had guts by the truckload too. Many of the men on that trip worked in SOE now and all agreed their success had been due in no small part to the farmer's boy from Otterburn.

But when they reached Muscat Alex was alone and penniless again, just one journey away from the jewelled continent. He took passage as a deckhand once more, and two months later he saw Bombay through the sea mist of a summer's morning in 1926. At last he had arrived – and almost immediately he got into trouble again.

Exotic maidens had not been the least of India's attractions in Alex's vivid imagination and his months with Anna had sharpened his anticipation. There had been others along the way but after eight months in the desert and two at sea, he later told Davies, he wouldn't have turned down the ninety-year-old, betel-chewing *begum* who ran the waterfront hotel where he spent his first night.

But instead a fickle Providence provided Naima, a young and beautiful but very naïve girl whose father was strict, vengeful and politically powerful. For both it was forbidden fruit and Alex soon revisited the gateway. But Naima's three brothers reminded him of the baser world. The last of his hard-earned money went on hospital bills.

He might have been forgiven for going back then, but the years between Durham and Bombay had changed the daydreaming northern lad. He pawned his grandfather's watch for stake money and a bespoke, but distinctly back-street, dinner suit, then went to the casino at the Taj Mahal Hotel and won £5,000 in one night. Soon after one brother was set upon by a gang of bazaar-wallahs. Then another had his left leg and hip broken when the brakes on his Rolls failed mysteriously on a downhill bend. And the third was clinically beaten up by an unknown assailant. The authorities never got to the bottom of the matter, but Naima's father was in no doubt. Alex was advised to relocate himself several hundred miles north by the local commissioner, who privately wrote to a friend in the Peshawar Police that this young Rawlings might have the makings of a bandit-hunter.

His advice was heeded and in November 1926, Alex was commissioned a lieutenant. Within six months he was a captain. He proved excellent at both painstaking intelligence work and lightning strikes on villages and mountain hideouts. His results were impressive but his methods questionable. Too many prisoners slipped on the stairs, too many deals were struck with lesser villains to catch greater. After five years of unrivalled success but not a hint of further promotion he was becoming disaffected. The offer from a former comrade who had been recruited to the SIS came at just the right time.

Alex said goodbye to India with some regret, but work in London with the 'Home Section' proved a welcome change and added to a growing reputation. He helped to crush an attempted resurgence of violence by the IRA, working on both sides of the water, and did much to ensure that Ziedler's operations in London never achieved their full potential. But in the course of his work one of the more notorious Blackshirt leaders died in mysterious circumstances. Press speculation was rife and much pressure was put on the Home Section to bring one of its wilder cards into line. It was agreed that a move to the Foreign Section was in order, at least until the fuss had died down.

Davies smiled. They should have known better. Rawlings' talent for upsetting the wrong people surfaced again in Abyssinia. He had orders to slow down Ciarelli's campaign against the arms dealers (especially the British ones) supplying to the tribesmen and many an SIM operative met a sticky end in the dark alleys of Djibouti and Dar es Salaam. But he continually complained that his hands were tied, that more should be done to stop Ciarelli and even to get Mussolini's army out. Such remarks were completely above his station and were not forgotten. Which was why he never got above major and stayed out 'in the field'.

He didn't mind. He loved the adrenalin charge of field work. A desk job would have been anathema. He proved that with his work in Spain: keeping an eye on the Britons fighting for both camps; organising the infiltration by agents with an Irish background of O'Duffy's Franco-supporting, Fascist-influenced Blue Brigade to mark out who might be potential troublemakers on the wider stage; and generally thwarting the efforts of Germany and Italy to learn too much from the army of volunteers, journalists, exiles and adventurers in Barcelona.

He had renewed his acquaintance with Ciarelli, kept an eye on Renkovich's team (meeting and forming a professional respect and personal dislike for Amarazov) and once again offended the higher-ups with his comments about the Nationalists, especially when it had become clear they would be the victors. Just as efforts were being made to improve relations with Franco one of Rawlings' Spanish contacts was killed by Nationalist agents who wrongly believed him to be collaborating with the Soviets. Rawlings was ordered to take no direct reprisals, and he obeyed. But within six hours Amarazov knew of the whereabouts of the agents responsible. Within twelve hours they had been tortured to death.

Rawlings returned early in 1939, under a distinct cloud, to cool his heels at a desk in Whitehall. But before the year was out came the flood. The gloves were off, Rawlings' special talents were in demand and he never seemed to stop working. He provided 'security' for the SIS mission to Poland which brought back the Enigma secrets. He liberated gold from Belgian banks, diamonds from Amsterdam dealers and platinum from the Courtaulds factory in Calais, always staying one step ahead of the advancing Wehrmacht. He was equally adept at procuring people, notably several members of the Norwegian Royal Family, which was where he had first crossed Hoffman's path.

But none of this stopped the Germans reaching the Channel with virtually all of Europe under their belts. The nascent SOE, formed in July 1940, seemed to offer the only way of keeping the struggle active and he was a natural choice. There were rumours that SIS were only too pleased to get rid of him, but he found a natural home in a motley band of adventurers, internationalists and eccentrics. There were also rumours that Dalton, still a Durham MP, had personally asked for him because he wanted "a good local lad on the team". Whatever the circumstances, Rawlings had proved his worth. Davies had seen to that. They knew each other from the SIS Foreign Section and he set Rawlings to work "down among the Z men".

He had been involved in the abortive attempts to sabotage the Romanian oilfields and the bid to prepare a defence network in Spain if Franco should ever allow the Axis safe conduct to hit Gibraltar and North Africa. Officially no action was ever taken, but Alex still made a few night trips from Gib to renew old acquaintances – and settle old scores. One of these trips left a rather bloody and public corpse and he returned to Baker Street in disgrace.

The German invasion of Greece in the spring of 1941 led to a very secret mission to sound out the possibilities for resistance when it became apparent the Axis would triumph – and to keep him out of the news for a while. Davies felt a twinge of guilt at that. There had been a sort of unspoken hope that Rawlings might provide the information then very conveniently get himself killed. But he had returned with knowledge that had proved invaluable in their recent efforts.

A return to Norway was next, one of SOE's most fertile hunting grounds. Yet again he courted controversy. One raid ended in betrayal and the capture of several SOE agents and Norwegian Resistance fighters. The remainder were ordered to lie low. Instead Rawlings organised a jailbreak from Gestapo HQ in Bergen. The operation became legendary in Resistance circles but it had been done without any authorisation and resulted in heavy casualties. Rawlings' response – that there was no point making a secret war so secret that the enemy never knew about it – went down like the proverbial lead balloon. So when he returned, fresh from the gun battle with Hoffman, a lengthy desk job analysing the possibilities of concerted action in Central Europe was considered a suitable purgatory.

After months of trying to be diplomatic with members of SIS, the Foreign Office and the various governments in exile he begged to return to action and play by the rules this time. The new target in the spring of 1942 was France, at Gubbins' insistence. Rawlings had made valuable inroads, helping to co-ordinate the first fact-finding visits trying to mould the dozens of disparate groups and the massive but unfocused groundswell of hatred for the occupiers into a fighting force. But still he chafed for action. The Vichy operation had seemed ideal all round.

Ah, well. Davies sighed as he put down the folder. Anyone can make mistakes. But in wartime they can be costly. Alex had undoubtedly made the best of a bad job – again.

Davies looked down at the bulky file. A remarkable life. A remarkable career, with far more on the credit side than the debit. It painted a picture of a man with uncommon courage, toughness, cunning, intelligence, leadership and survival ability. Not forgetting a lucky streak a mile wide.

It also portrayed someone with little or no respect for authority and a positive delight in unorthodox action. If he had stayed a little longer in Paris he might now be one of those rather precious intellectuals safely encamped in America. He was well-read, wrote a little in his spare time and unlike most men Davies knew his wit went beyond regurgitated Noël Coward. Everyone who knew Alex had not been too surprised when he courted and married Angela Holden, an exquisitely beautiful gossip magazine writer who dabbled on the fringes of the London literati, during his time in the Home Section. But the divorce had been no great surprise, either.

And if he had been able to curb his tongue a little more he could have been on the General Staff or a senior commissioner in India by now. Instead he had ploughed his own furrow – and his country had benefited from it immensely. That was the bottom line. That was why Davies had been sending him into the field, with SIS and SOE, for eight years now; thanking God he was out there and apologising because he wasn't reporting back regularly. There could be no other man for the job. He had examined and rejected all the other candidates. He honestly didn't think anyone but Rawlings could do it. But he would do it in a way no-one could predict. And someone would have a hell of a job explaining it all afterwards.

There was a knock at the door. "Enter," Davies called and Rawlings stepped in. He was freshly bathed and shaved, and someone had managed to find him a major's uniform that fitted. He looked tired, no doubt, but the salute was immaculate and he took the proffered seat at Davies' desk with no stiffness or stagger, removing the mission folder from under his arm and placing it to one side.

After a brief pause Davies spoke. "You had a chance to study the file?"

"Yes, sir. Read through it on the plane." He made no further comment, simply looked straight ahead, so that after a few seconds Davies said with some asperity: "Well, what do you think?"

"About what, sir?" Rawlings spoke politely and evenly, but there was a world of weariness in his voice. "About the fact that we've got to do what no British combat or intelligence unit has ever done before? About the fact that we have to take hostile action against an ally? About the fact that hardly any of these men, myself included, knows anything about Turkey? Or can speak Turkish? Or Russian, for that matter? About the fact that the Italians and Germans will be sniffing round too, and they all know my face in the crowd? Or about the fact that I need a month in a sanatorium, preferably on a Caribbean island, after that French fiasco?"

He sighed deeply and went on without waiting for a reply. "Well, we could bat all those imponderables back and forth till Doomsday, couldn't we, Hugh? But you and I both know we've got to make do with the resources available and this plan." He gestured towards the folder. "It looks plausible on paper, I'll admit – though what happens in the field could well end up looking like its forty-second cousin twice removed and I hope everyone's aware of that. But honestly, Hugh, do you really think I'm the man to take charge? Frankly, I'm bloody knackered."

Davies was slightly nonplussed; even after eight years he was still not used to such directness from a subordinate. But he knew better than to give him a dressing down. "I know it's rough, Alex, but I can't think of a better operative than you for this one. You're tough, cunning, resourceful, a born leader..."

"They'll never get all that on the tombstone, you know."

"...you're also one of the most insubordinate,

undisciplined bastards I've ever met, in uniform or out! But I'd still pick you above anyone else for a job like this. And back you to the hilt afterwards."

"Well, I'm glad to hear that, sir," Rawlings said with a fair helping of irony, "because there'll be times on this trip when we won't be operating according to the manual. And I don't want the high-ups breathing down my neck telling me how to run a mission."

"They won't," Davies replied soothingly, then added: "But they will want to keep a close eye on how things are going. You can't blame them on a mission like this. And they are entitled to."

"Yes – but they're not entitled to make me do something that could get me or my men killed, and I hope they don't try." He clicked his tongue and studied the ceiling. "Selborne, Hambro, the lot of them – they're only interested in guarding their little empires. Playing it straight so they don't offend anybody in Whitehall. Haven't a bloody clue what it's like at the sharp end any more. Even old Gubbins, and he used to…"

"I know, I know – it was better in Dalton's day, he meant business, can't set Europe ablaze without any matches…" Davies pursed his lips. "That sounds like a cracked record, Alex, and you know it. They've given you a free rein often enough."

"And when I took it up, they pulled me in, ticked me off and put me behind a desk trying to get all the bloody lower slobbovians to agree how they're going to liberate Central Europe. Thanks very much. And that's another thing – if I hear one word about not provoking a diplomatic incident with our Russian allies…"

"Oh, come off it." Davies was angry too now. "You

know that's all being handled higher up. As far as you're concerned they're the opposition."

"That's what you said before Abyssinia, and Spain – both times. 'Treat them like the enemy, old chap, let the diplomats sort out the mess'. Next thing I know I'm being threatened with recall, swimming in official bullshit and being told not to play so rough.

"If I'm going to do this job, I need room to manouevre. Any problems with the Russians, any dealings we might have with our official set-up in Turkey or elsewhere, any help we might need from SIS – I bet they'll try to muck things up, just to make us look bad – I need backing all the way to Number 10. If Selborne's not happy with that, tell him to send someone else. Someone not so dog-tired and knocked about."

"You're fit as a fiddle." Davies was anxious to change the subject. "Damn sight better shape than me, that's for sure."

"I know," Rawlings countered brutally, casting his eye around the office, with a huge fan keeping out the heat and a well-stocked drinks cabinet by Davies' desk. "Glad to see they can still keep you in the style to which you're accustomed on the wrong side of Suez. I'm sure I could sit at that desk making telephone calls and sorting files all day. My trivial round and common task is a little more demanding – sir."

Davies ignored the sarcasm. "I've read the report from the doctor who examined you on arrival. Apart from the broken nose, which seems to have fully set, all you suffered was severe bruising and localised burns. That and fatigue. He said that a few more hours sleep would be ideal, but barring that you're back to operational fitness."

"Oh, that's all right, then. Here was me thinking Hoffman and his boys half-killed me and nearly drove me mad into the bargain." He shook his head. "You should send that doctor out to Turkey, Hugh. He's a tough old bugger and no mistake. In fact …"

"Shut up!" Davies spat the words out so sharply that Rawlings sat up a little straighter despite himself. "There's no time for this. You're going because I say so. And I say so because I think rescuing this man is the most important task any SOE agent has ever had to achieve. And I think you can do it. But if you go out with a chip on your shoulder, sulking and whining to nurse your precious ego, then we damn well will find someone else."

"No. You're right, Hugh. There isn't time, and all this is just pissing against the wind." Rawlings was calm and sober now, his eyes looking straight into Davies'. "I'll get this boy out or die trying. Count on me."

"I am counting on you." Davies was equally sober. "And so is everyone who took the right side in this war."

"That must include the Andrews Sisters, then," Rawlings returned to his old manner and Davies was almost relieved. "Can't let them down. So what's the drill now?"

"The plane leaves here at 1800 hours. Your team are ready and waiting. They've been told as much as they need to. Operational details only; who they're springing but not why he's so important. The car will take you to the airfield at noon. That'll give you a chance to have a word with your lieutenants, go over the details of the strike and so on. Then a briefing for the whole team and off you go."

He reached under the desk and passed a small but

obviously tightly-packed briefcase across to Rawlings. Attached to the handle was a sheet of plain paper. "This contains everything we think might be of use to you; money, spare ID papers, lists of all SOE, SIS or other intelligence operatives who might be able to help in unforeseen circumstances. Naturally you'll memorise and destroy those before you leave. The sheet of paper is the combination. If anyone tries to open it any other way half a pound of plastic explosive wired to a mercury switch will persuade them otherwise. So for God's sake don't forget that either."

Rawlings raised an eyebrow. "I won't."

Davies sat back. "Well, that's it, unless you have any questions – sensible ones, that is."

"Just one, sir – very sensible. What about the Americans?"

Davies looked up sharply, but his tone was neutral: "What about them?"

"Well, have they been told, for a start?" Rawlings said impatiently. "If Vlasenin is so important, do they know he wants to work for us, that the Russians won't let him? They're our closest allies – more so than ever now. And if they do know, why aren't they taking part in this operation?"

"The situation is quite simple, major." Oh, rank only, eh: methinks I spy an official line on the horizon. "Washington has been aware of Vlasenin's work and its importance for some time. As soon as this new development emerged, we passed the information on to them. We also stressed that we felt SOE was in the best position to mount a rescue operation, given our greater experience in the... Balkan theatre. And, very sensibly, they agreed." He permitted himself a patronising smile. "After all, Mr Donovan – or 'Wild Bill' as he likes to be called – has done a good job in short time with the OSS, but in these matters the Americans are hardly as advanced as us."

"You know it's funny, sir." Rawlings face and voice suggested it was anything but. "People like you have been telling me that about the Americans ever since I started in this game. And everywhere I've gone there's been some fellow slapping me on the back, swearing blind he's just here to have a look round for the guys at the embassy. The ones in uniform said they'd far rather be taking their boys on the firing range or steering the old tub back to the Pacific; the other ones were just businessmen doing an old Harvard pal a favour. Every one of them said they'd be mighty grateful if we could show him the ropes. Every one of them was plotting deeper than damnation. Half the time they got the goods before any of us Old European master spies – and more than once they left a few bodies behind."

Davies looked at him coldly. "What exactly are you saying, major?"

"Just passing on my observations, colonel. And I'm sure I don't need to remind you that they are beginning to establish a presence in the Balkans; that they virtually took over the intelligence element for the Operation Torch landings in Algeria; and that we agreed an exchange of information in all theatres, at all levels, back in February – told you I was paying attention when you had me confined to barracks. But if you say they've agreed to play it our way, then fine. And what happens when we get Vlasenin back? If his secret's so important, who gets to keep it, may I ask?"

"No, you may not." Davies reply was firm, but there was an uneasy edge to his voice. "Your job is simply to get him back. However, if it makes you feel better, and because I trust you, the official line is one of co-operation. Both sides will have equal access to Vlasenin, but it is far simpler to bring him back to Britain. His initial acclimatisation and his preliminary work will also be done here. That's logical. He will feel more comfortable and our... facilities are as good as theirs. After that it's up to the politicians. Our job is to get him back. Nothing more."

"Oh, naturally, sir," Rawlings said lightly, but added in a tone of pure steel: "I just want to know whether we'll be seeing any wild cards on the table again. You say not. Very well. But the only reason I'm here is because either SIS or the Tsarists became compromised. As far as I'm concerned, apart from my team and any contacts I'm one hundred per cent sure of, everyone else is the opposition. And if they get in my way, or try to take Vlasenin or his papers – for any reason at all – I'll cut them down and I don't care whose flag they're flying."

"Who's arguing, Alex? That's standard practice. Don't even see why you're making such a fuss about it."

Rawlings almost laughed at the tone of aggrieved innocence in his lilting Welsh brogue. "No-one's arguing, Hugh – not yet. But it hasn't come to the sticking place yet. This man's already wrecked one beautiful friendship and he might do the same again. Just don't try to hand me the butcher's bill when it's all over."

Davies' curt dismissal and his belated "good luck" were still half-running through Rawlings' brain nearly seven hours later, as he stood behind the main desk in the RAF briefing room, his team ranged before him. He should have been a little less hard on the old bugger. Davies had always played as square with him as the peculiar circumstances of their relationship allowed. He should have accepted that. Once or twice at their final meeting, just before the car came to take him to the airfield, he had tried to apologise. But there had been too much to do – going over radio call signs, the details of the journey, the plan for the strike itself – and their parting had been brisk and businesslike.

Still, no point in dwelling on that now. The main task in hand was addressing his men, getting their working relationship off on the right foot and at the same time gauging their readiness, and willingness, to do the job. And the thought uppermost in his mind was: they may be willing, but they're not ready.

He had read their dossiers on the plane from Malta and again on the way to the airfield. He knew every detail of their wildly differing careers, their specialities, their proven strengths and possible weaknesses. He had lost count of the number of times words like "courageous", "ruthless" and "resourceful" had sprung out of the page at him.

Their pedigrees were impeccable – active service with an intelligence unit, a raiding force or a resistance organisation, sometimes all three. In addition nearly all of them had visited both SOE training schools, at Arisaig and Beaulieu. But the acid test was to see them in a group, minutes away from zero hour. There had to be supreme confidence, a sense of total acceptance and familiarity with the roles they were about to play. But there wasn't.

The fifteen men were ranged across the front row of canvas seats in front of him, dressed in the rough motley of Turkish farm workers and labourers; heavy quilted jackets; rough cotton and denim shirts; thick corduroy or canvas breeches; low sturdy boots on their feet, cloth or knitted wool caps and battered slouch hats on their heads.

But they still looked like soldiers. They tried not to, some more successfully than others; not one convinced Rawlings fully. They should have looked like a group of Turkish workers suddenly transported to an RAF briefing room, able to convince anybody that was exactly what they were.

It was not just that they didn't look particularly Turkish, with two notable exceptions. There were plenty of refugees and exiles from western Europe in there at the moment, as there were in every neutral country. And since the mission was only due to take one day and night the problem of them standing out in a crowd was not too acute. But that was part of it. They clearly felt uncomfortable with this particular dissemblance and that feeling was almost palpable.

Rawlings tried not to think of the fact that only three of them had any experience of the country or spoke the language, and only two could pass for natives. It was even worse with the 'Russian' element. One fluent speaker and traveller, two academic scholars. Rawlings himself had picked up enough Russian to get by during his stay in the Montparnasse melting pot and later in Spain. He did not count it one of his strong languages – but he was still far ahead of most of the team. His Turkish was not much better.

There was the great weakness of the mission, as he had pointed out to Davies on more than one occasion. It was new territory for SOE. All these men, he knew, would have been perfectly comfortable in German and Italian, or the languages of the occupied countries. But Turkey, a neutral country and Russia, a friendly power... the real deep cover espionage there was being done by SIS and they were out of the loop. SOE's Turkish section was mainly a clearing house and a listening post, not a combat facility. The Russian section did not officially exist and it only numbered a handful of agents, maintaining links with the underground groups from London or Cairo. By the nature of their work, few of them had seen direct action. So the bulk of the team were men who had, but knew virtually nothing of the country in which they had to operate and the people they would encounter. Jack Sprat and his wife; between them they would lick the platter clean, that was the way the high-ups saw it.

On paper that had a certain logic. This would be an in and out job, Davies had told Rawlings that *ad nauseam*. Once Vlasenin was in British hands he would give the location of his papers and SOE's Turkish network would take over. As far as Rawlings' team was concerned, they had a day to make contact and size up the target, the strike to be made that night and out of Turkey before dawn. Minimal contact with the indigenous population. All well and good, but it still left maximum exposure on the day, in a teeming city which would be hard to escape quickly, or in open country where any new faces were immediately noticed.

And what if there were unexpected snags, if the day and night turned into days, or weeks? Rawlings had known that happen. It had been made very clear that they were not to approach SIS, or any other British organisation, in Istanbul unless absolutely necessary. What if they had to find their own way out? Then you needed a team who could live their roles, who felt confident and comfortable with them – and each other.

These men were trying their best, he could tell, but they needed time, to get to know the country they were to work in, the equipment they were to use, and the men they were to work with. Rawlings could only hope their proven talents would compensate for that. Allied to his inspiring leadership, of course.

So he looked again at his team in those few moments before he spoke, matching the file to the face, the body, the human being. First he looked at Captain Jonathan Curtis, his second-in-command. A lean, aesthetic looking young man of twenty-one summers. With his clear blue eyes, wispy blond hair and pale, aristocratic face he would have been an ideal leading man for a provincial repertory company.

Three years ago that was exactly what he had been. But not for long. His talent had been spotted by the legendary Tyrone Guthrie and soon he was treading the London boards, sharing the limelight with Olivier, Gielgud and Ashcroft and winning a fair reputation for Shakespearean roles. Benvolio and Laertes rather than Romeo or The Dane, but that was held to be just a matter of time. Even some talk of Hollywood, until the storm broke. Curtis had joined up before September 3rd was out. His action had certainly shielded him from the occasional accusations of cowardice levelled at those of his theatrical brethren who had decamped to America or fought the war from an Ealing soundstage. And it had pleased his father, a pillar of the City not enamoured of Jonny's career choice. But the real reason for his decision was that his mother's family were German Jews, who had simply disappeared in the days of terror after *Kristallnacht*.

Curtis vividly remembered his mother's grief and the guilt that followed it; guilt that she had left them to marry Edward, that she had not helped them enough, that she had not made them leave Germany when the danger became apparent. The guilt had stayed until her death in 1939, just after his West End debut, and slowly Curtis had learned to hate the people whose language he spoke like a native.

He had volunteered for intelligence work after kicking his heels on garrison duty in Palestine and had performed wonders for SIS in operations amongst the wasps' nest of spies and Nazi sympathisers in the Levant. Heydrich's early attempts to exploit the situation in Iraq had been regularly thwarted by the pale young intellectual who had turned out to be a natural marksman with any kind of handgun. SOE Cairo had managed to attract him with promotion and promises of even more direct action. He had won further laurels with Wingate's column in Abyssinia, then leading the second wave of missions into occupied Greece.

The Vlasenin business had cropped up between visits and he had been a natural choice for second-in-command (even leader had Rawlings not made it back). In addition to all his other qualities he could even boast a smattering of Russian and Turkish picked up on SIS duties.

But the real Russian expert was Captain Chalmers. He was a tall, broad, brown-haired, square-featured man, Curtis' opposite in every way. A career soldier and diplomat, who had actually spent time in the Soviet Union in the Thirties, taking himself off on highly unofficial sightseeing trips to Tashkent, Samarkand and Vladivostok, acquiring a wide variety of NKVD shadows along the way. He was recalled just before the outbreak of war and selected for SOE's Russian section. He had read Russian History at Oxford, spoke the language fluently and most importantly (as his perambulations had occasionally had cause to show) could pass as a native.

He would lead the deception element of the strike, along with the Tsarist group and the two other Section R operatives in the squad, Second-Lieutenants Emerson and Mitchell. They had known each other since their days as Russian Literature students at St Andrews, and they still looked like undergraduates; clear-eyed and pale-cheeked, constantly pushing back unruly fringes of dark hair. But the two young subalterns had seen their share of action. Separated from the rest of their Highland unit during the French campaign they had managed to lead a motley group of fellow strays to Dunkirk, avoiding the St Valery surrender. Soon after returning to Britain they had volunteered for SOE and been seconded straight to Section R.

Rawlings had spoken to them, as well as Curtis and Chalmers, just before the main briefing. Their knowledge of Russia and its people was certainly impressive – if a little encyclopaedic. Knowledge was one thing, but understanding was another. The empathy one developed with another nation or race or culture by living and working and fighting with a cross-section of its people was a difficult thing to learn but it was crucial to any deception operation. Even one with such a short action span as this. He sincerely hoped they (and Chalmers for that matter) had it, as the Americans would say, in spades.

Then there were the senior NCOs, the front row of his rugby team; Sergeant-Major Mayhew, and Colour-Sergeants Rowley and Sanderson. Mayhew had been recruited from the Grenadier Guards into the Commandos after the fall of France and his performance in the early raids had led him into SOE's own squad of Channel hoppers; the Small Scale Raiding Force, formed by Gus March-Phillips, the broken-nosed poet-mariner who had sailed to Lagos and brought back the *Duchessa D'Aosta*, richest maritime prize of the war.

His death in September had cut short their work and most of the force had been transferred to the new Special Boat Service, but a few had been retained by SOE for its shooting missions – like Mayhew, who had traded in parade-ground proficiency for a war of patience, stealth and cunning and proved a natural. Rowley and Sanderson (seconded from the Welsh and Scots Guards respectively) had been with him all the way, accumulating hard-won experience, the knack of inspiring the men under them and a drawerful of medals. They would form the backbone of the actual rescue mission and they certainly looked the part; all were big, barrel-chested men with florid, good-humoured faces. The same went for the three other 'squaddies', all privates: Jones, Pearson and Garside.

But what of Corporal Walters? He was not an espionage man, nor strictly speaking a raider, nor even from the Russian Section. He had in fact only just joined SOE and his voice and manner proclaimed his true origins: the Sydney dockyards. He had spent all his early life there – until the jail term for assault and inciting public disturbance. That, and an active presence in the stevedores' union movement, had made work hard to come by. So he had taken himself off to Spain and developed a talent for killing Fascists while staying alive himself. Captured outside Madrid, he had escaped from a prison camp near Burgos and travelled in disguise across several hundred miles of Nationalist-held territory to rejoin his unit.

His return to Circular Quay after the International Brigades were disbanded had been marked by three days of drinking, whoring and fighting which had seen him up in court again. He was offered the choice of enlisting in the Army instead of jail and reluctantly agreed, having seen enough of prisons to last him a lifetime. Posted to Malaya, he was cut off from his comrades during the lightning Japanese advance and had again proved his talent for improvised travel. Just as the survivors of his regiment were going into the bag at Singapore he turned up at Darwin in a fishing junk.

He was fêted as a national hero – until he broke a military policeman's jaw in a bar-room brawl. The authorities were unsure of what to do with such an embarrassment, but SOE came to their aid. A training school for Far East operations had been founded in Victoria by Spencer Chapman, the Arctic explorer and Gordonstoun teacher, whose own school achievements had included asking a fellow pupil to repeatedly hit him with a cricket bat to see how much pain he could take. He was keen to have Walters on his team, and the Australian military were happy to oblige.

Walters had revisited Malaya several times to deadly effect after that, but was in between ops when a party led by Chapman was captured and the old man himself was listed as missing. The training school's work foundered for a time and Walters was sent to work with the LRDG in Libya. But they had found out, like others before them, that Walters' idea of recreation between ops was constant drinking, brawling and womanising. And that he regarded the British and Commonwealth governments as only marginally less repellent and hostile to the working man than those of Hitler, Mussolini and Hirohito.

The latest stage in his 'pass-the-parcel' career had been return to SOE Cairo, where he had accompanied Curtis on the first Greek missions. Despite Walters' hatred of (in descending order) Poms, officers, toffs and intellectuals they had worked together well. It was Curtis who had recommended he be seconded for the Vlasenin operation. He had picked up some Russian in Spain, he had a proven ability to stay alive and free in enemy territory – and he was good at killing people. Looking at the stocky, well-built figure slouching in his seat, the hard eyes embedded in a face which seemed to have been carved from granite with a particularly blunt chisel, Rawlings could well believe all the stories. But this job might need a few killers in the ranks.

He wasn't sure if Corporal O'Hare, the team's explosives and communications expert, fitted into that category or not. Rawlings had worked with him in Ireland, later in London and Spain, and he had shown the necessary ability to lay low and adopt an undercover role without cracking. His skill with explosives and Unionist background had made him a natural to fulfil the Home Section's very secret instructions to give the Sinn Feiners "a taste of their own medicine" after the bombing campaign of 1939. But the Fenians had got wind of the men tearing holes in their ranks and O'Hare had been forced to leave the land of his birth, possibly for good. But his talents had been used in many places since then, including every corner of occupied Europe. He could rig up a bomb, a booby-trap or a radio set from virtually nothing, a technician without equal. Perhaps this was what had kept him from more senior rank; the snobbery in certain quarters, even within SOE. Rawlings had felt it himself and he knew it must be worse for Conor. Spies were gentlemen, after all, romantic adventurers. What was Corporal O'Hare but a glorified mechanic – and an Ulster hooligan to boot?

If any of that bothered Conor he never showed it. In all the years Rawlings had known him a broad smile had rarely been far from the gypsy-dark face framed by the ebony curls. But this was part of the reason for Rawlings' disquiet. All Conor's killing had been done long-range. He had never been on a mission like this, where he might literally have to throw a bomb at a man's feet, or shoot one in cold blood. He wondered if, even with his background, he was up to that sort of work.

If all went to plan, he would not have to find out. His duties were to lay a few loud and noisy, but harmless, diversions to hamper any pursuit (be it by consulate guards or Turkish police), staying out of sight while the military men did the rescue, then keep the radio link open to London as they escaped. Rawlings hoped that was just how it would work out. Conor was a friend. If anyone deserved to survive this thing, he did.

The last specialist was Private Hawkins, and he remained a private only because he had constantly refused promotion through three years of distinguished service. A racing driver and sports car enthusiast before the war, he had spent his time with the Transport Corps, and latterly SOE, riding, driving, sailing or piloting every kind of land, sea and air craft known to man, from a German dispatch rider's bike (which took him from a temporary prison camp near Arras to Dunkirk in what would probably have been a record had anybody been around to time it) to a Greek fishing *caique*. More importantly, he could repair them all, too, with basic tools and at very short notice. That and a talent for staying alive proved in several ops, most recently in Greece, had brought him here.

It was also the provenance of the final two men in the briefing room: Privates Costas and Stavrakis, the 'local knowledge'. They had volunteered to work with SOE when the first missions had encountered them, leading resistance in the mountains of Macedonia. But they had been fighting and killing Germans, Italians and Bulgarians for a long time before that – all through the Albanian campaign and the heroic defence of Greece itself. Their units had been destroyed but they had made new ones from the men who were still willing to fight. So impressive had their efforts been that they had been brought back to Cairo, via Turkey, for special training. While there, the Vlasenin business had cropped up and they had been selected.

There were many Greek fighters on SOE Cairo's

books but none with the unique qualifications of these two. They had been born in Turkey, two among the nearly one and a half million Greeks forcibly exchanged for Turkish citizens in Greece under the 1923 Treaty of Lausanne. They had no love for the Turks who had driven them from their homes and little for the British who had brokered the treaty. But they hated Fascists and invaders of all stripes and working with the British forces in the Greek campaign, then later with Curtis and the other SOE infiltrators, had modified their opinions. They could speak Turkish fluently and blend in with the natives. They would help with the driving and the talking during the brief period of travel between the Tsarists' safe house and the target.

That was the team; very strong on paper, but facing their first match together and looking a little uncertain at the prospect. Well, that was his job and any doubts stayed private. He took a deep breath and began to speak. "You all know why you've been brought here. You know it's a very important mission. A very delicate mission, a mission you've had virtually no time to prepare for. Well, I can assure you you're not the only ones."

A thin ripple of polite laughter. Ah well, I never said I was George Formby. Wonder if they realise I'm really not joking. "But you know the destination and the objective. Much more than that I can't tell you, except that this man and his knowledge are absolutely vital, to all of us, to everyone in this war. We have to get him out, and soon.

"It's unfamiliar territory, I know, but you've all done quick rescue missions before. Here the only difference is the opposition — and you must remember that's exactly what they are. Never mind the official position. They're the enemy and I don't want anyone getting misguided ideas. As you've probably guessed, this isn't just about who wins the war. It's about what sort of world we have afterwards. We wouldn't be doing this if we didn't think it had to be done." Christ, you can't half come out with some bullshit sometimes. "You may have worked alongside Russians before, and we don't want this op to turn into a butcher's yard, but they're in our way. It's your duty to get them out of our way and I don't want to see any hesitation. Clear?"

They all nodded. Only Walters looked a little uneasy, but he kept silent. "Good. Now, the details. We head for Cyprus first in an RAF transport ostensibly on a routine run. Then switch to a Dakota with the markings of a Turkish transport company, which SOE... acquired recently.

"The drop zone is here," he pointed to a large-scale map of European Turkey pinned to the wall behind him, "in the hills near Esenyurt, and the underground group should be waiting for us. The Jerries haven't got much in the air or sea around this area at present, and the Turkish Air Force presence is minimal. If we're unlucky and run into anything we'll have to rely on the skills of our gallant pilot." Morton, the lean, lugubrious flight lieutenant from Squadron 138, SOE's air arm, raised his hand in ironic salute.

There was another ripple of laughter, but Rawlings raised a hand and took a deep breath. "If we hit trouble on the ground, from whatever side... just try to get out alive and then regroup. If myself or the other officers are killed, carry on. Mayhew will take command, then the sergeants, then the corporals. Then," he smiled humourlessly, "it's up to you; elect a leader, go by length of service. Form a spies' co-operative if you like. But whatever you do, don't abort the mission. You all know the plan. And it must go ahead, even if there are only a handful of you left. Use the underground to make up the numbers. You can postpone it for one night, but that's the limit. After that they're almost certain to move him. If Colonel Davies can get replacements out in time, well and good. If not, you do it yourself."

He paused for breath, and to see how they were taking it. These were unusual orders. Under normal circumstances, caution was the watchword. If the odds looked too heavy, or any initial trouble was encountered an op was called off, and rightly so. But these were hardly normal circumstances. The team had been chosen because of their ability to work independently, but who wants to be reminded of their own mortality?

They were taking it well, no expressions of surprise, or worse, apprehension. Good lads. "I'm not trying to scare you or be a prophet of doom or sound like some tough old super-bastard, but this isn't like other missions. Once we start this one it's a fight to the death. And we're like the old Spartans – come back with your shield or on it. OK, let's get aboard."

They rose like robots, at attention. Rawlings jumped down from the platform and scowled at them. "What the fuck's that for, comrades? It's an easy life on guard duty." He called their parentage and biological origins into question in the same half-remembered Russian, then swept by. After a few yards he stole a glance over his shoulder and was relieved to see that they were ambling along in small groups, chatting amongst themselves. Walters produced one of several packs of Russian cigarettes which they had been issued with before the briefing and passed them around. There was a chorus of raw coughs a few seconds after they lit up and by the time Chalmers passed a pack to Curtis and Rawlings the pungent aroma filled the air.

"They take a little getting used to, Comrade Major," he said in fluent, perfectly-accented Russian. "But they keep the cold out."

"*Spassibo.*" Rawlings took one and inclined his head as Curtis offered a light. He took a deep puff and his lungs blasted the thick, raw taste straight back out. "*Kazana*," he gasped. "Thank the Holy Virgin we won't be out there long enough to get used to this stuff." If Chalmers had any reservations about his commander's command of Russian he kept them to himself – largely because he seemed to be coughing up his insides too.

Just before they reached the door of the briefing room there were two long trestle tables, one on each side of the door, piled high with the equipment they would be taking. First the weapons. Half standard SOE equipment, half Russian – the guns that the 'deception group' would be using. There were four PPSH41 submachine-guns, looking like a child's copy of a Thompson Gun with their long butts and drum magazines, but capable of firing smoothly all day in any temperature after a double dose of rough handling.

The three bolt-action Moisin Nagants were equally basic and equally reliable. But pride of place went to the SVT-40 snipers' rifle, the very latest from Stalin's armouries, not given as a goodwill gesture like the rest of the Russian weapons on one of the flights from Captain Danko's airbase but acquired via the international arms black market. It was a marksman's dream and Rowley, the team's sharpshooter, looked at it slowly and lovingly before running his hand along its whole length.

It was far from standard issue for a consulate guard, but it had been reasoned that for this sort of work a few extras could make all the difference. That was why they were taking the two Mark IIS silenced Sten guns. They would be dismantled, kept out of sight and ditched in any search, as Rawlings patiently explained to Walters, the other designated user, who was examining it with a professional eye, remarking that the silencer tube looked like a worn-out bog brush. Even in the British Army, few knew of their existence and they would look totally out of place if carried in broad daylight where they were going. But they could fire a full magazine in almost total silence and that outweighed the risk. There were two ordinary Stens too, as well as three Lee-Enfield rifles, each with a telescopic sight.

The pistols were similarly varied, one for each man plus the little extra. Rawlings had already got to know the intricacies and eccentricities of Hoffman's Mauser and didn't intend for it to leave his person until the job was over. It was still a fairly common sight among the armies and police forces of a dozen nations, even though it had first been fired by the Kaiser's African police and Boer cavalrymen at the turn of the century. The model modified to take a silencer was a little more recent and much rarer, however, only issued to senior officers and intelligence operatives. He wondered if Hoffman had managed to get a replacement.

The rest of the handguns were more prosaic. Four Tokarev automatics and four heavy Nagant revolvers were designated for the deception group. Curtis and Walters had already seized two of the Nagants, and were now busily spinning cylinders and testing barrel balance. As handgun experts they knew where the real stopping power lay. There were also two Webley revolvers, two Browning automatics, two Lugers and one of the new Walther P38s. It was all commonplace SOE hardware, fired more than once by every man there. The same went for the tiny Lilliput automatic, but unlike the others that could be hidden from even an expert body search. Rawlings took charge of that for the time being.

There were also a few stabbing and throwing knives, mainly the Fairbairn models invented by the ex-Shanghai policeman turned SOE instructor who had taught most of the team all they knew about the dirtier aspects of close combat. They were the best in the business, but of a sufficiently international appearance not too attract too much attention.

The same went for O' Hare's bag of explosive tricks. But some of the more ingenious SOE charges from Station IX at Welwyn were included, as well as the new time pencil detonators developed there. Plus dynamite and gelignite, of course, with a wide range of fuses and even an old-fashioned plunger detonator. O'Hare had worked with cruder materials, but it made for a heavy handgrip. And he also had to carry the radio receiver and transmitter, a new 1500 series designed for long-distance missions, in his backpack.

Then there were binoculars, field dressings, emergency rations, water canteens, flare pistols, spare clothing. And of course the Russian army uniforms. All to be crammed into the backpacks – half Russian army issue, the rest Turkish army surplus. Davies had left nothing to chance. The team shouldered them, groaning at the weight, and headed for the blackness of the runway and the waiting RAF Dakota. The crew were already on board, completing the last of the flight checks.

"Once more unto the breach, dear friends," Curtis whispered as he and Rawlings led the team to the doorway.

"Captain Curtis," Rawlings said gravely, "if we're to have a Shakespearean quote for every occasion, I'll shoot you here and now." Curtis looked at him for a moment, then caught the half-smile as he continued: "Besides, on a job like this I think 'hunt the badger by owl-light' is a little more appropriate, even if it was written by a second-rater."

"Webster? Oh, he had his moments, sir. 'Tis a deed of darkness'," he completed the line and tried to smile, but it didn't quite come off. "That's true enough. Hope we don't have the same mortality rate as one of his cast lists, though."

"Me too," Rawlings said with some feeling, and opened the door into the night.

∽

At exactly the same moment that the Dakota took off a Messerschmitt 323 'Gigant' transport plane was coming in to land at a supply base in the German-occupied sector of Thrace. Colonel Walter Unterbrecht saw the huge aircraft screech to a halt as he stood stiffly to attention with his staff, a few guards and the commanders of the seemingly endless stream of German, Italian and Bulgarian units who had been pouring into the base and the surrounding area for almost two days now.

He hadn't a clue what all this was about and realised it was unlikely he ever would. All he knew was that his superiors had been instructed by the High Command to instruct him to turn the base into a fortress and make ready for a very special party from Berlin, all the while making sure that no prying eyes spotted what he was up to.

Well, at least that hadn't been too difficult. The base had originally been built in the last war by the Greeks for the Salonika campaign, and extended over the years – especially in the few months since the Turkish border had become a magnet for refugees and spies that Germany was keen to police thoroughly. It was in the middle of the Dhadhia Forest, well located to serve all the garrison towns along the border, but remote enough to discourage casual looting. No-one who did not have official business had any reason to be anywhere near it, making Unterbrecht's regular job, and this special assignment, so much easier.

And its evolution had rendered it capable of withstanding any but the most determined large-scale assault. The trees had been cleared for five hundred yards in every direction, a killing ground for any enemy attack. It was big – the perimeter covered almost two square miles – but compact, with a network of wooden storerooms, barracks and offices, connected by long natural corridors, covering almost every inch. There was even a new landing field with runway, hangars and control tower at the eastern edge to accommodate the transports that flew in from the main German HQ at Salonika itself. Twenty feet of barbed wire fence, liberally sprinkled with machine-gun towers, covered the entire perimeter and the wooden-gated main entrance at the south end was heavily guarded. Unterbrecht had to admit that, from a supplies soldier's point of view, it was virtually perfect.

And another element of the supplies soldier's lot was catering for emergencies at short notice. He had all the experience of it that a fifteen-year military career could garner. But he had to admit that finding room for all the soldiers who had converged on his camp – from barely-trained Bulgarian recruits to SS partisan hunters – and still keep the day-to-day business running had been something of a headache. And now another planeload was disembarking. And a big one. The 323 was a much rarer beast than the Junkers 52 workhorses that normally served bases like this. Usually you only encountered them in big offensives – or special missions.

And as soon as Unterbrecht saw the first man he knew they were trouble. Of course, High Command didn't make this sort of fuss over just anyone. But when he saw the tall, brown-haired, impossibly handsome officer emerge from the lowered main ramp and walk towards him he realised just how big this thing was. He was a dirty tricks specialist, and a pretty high-up one too, never mind the Transport Corps uniform. You could smell them a mile off and they always smelt of trouble.

Behind him were two other officers, lieutenants, also in Transport Corps uniform. Then three men in camouflage jackets, but with uniform breeches and jackboots. Their SS shoulder flashes showed them to be a Hauptsturmfuhrer, Obersturmfuhrer and Untersturmfuhrer – a captain with a first and second-lieutenant in plain language. They wore sidecaps at a rakish angle, and the latest model Walther automatics rode high on their hips. They were followed by an Italian colonel in *Bersaglieri* rig, then two black-uniformed Gestapo captains flanking a big, red-faced tough in civilian clothes. Unterbrecht tried not to gulp too noticeably. But at the same moment the lead officer reached him, flashed a dazzling smile despite his tired eyes and held out his leather-gloved hand. "Oberst Unterbrecht? Ziedler. Glad to meet you – and glad to see you're ready for us."

"It's an honour, Herr Oberst," Unterbrecht stammered, suddenly feeling much smaller and shabbier for some reason. "May I introduce Major Raumann, my adjutant, and…"

"Yes, yes, I know," Ziedler raised a hand and gave an engaging but impatient smile. "Could we save all that, by any chance, Herr Oberst? It's rather important these men get inside as quickly as possible. I'm sure your security is excellent but it never pays to advertise one's presence, *hein*?"

"Damn right," the Gestapo man said. "This isn't a fucking victory parade."

"Not yet," Ziedler agreed calmly. Unterbrecht waited a few seconds to see if he would elaborate, but was not surprised when silence reigned. "Of course, Herr Oberst, your quarters," he continued hastily. "This way." The officers trotted towards the main administration block, a group of huts which doubled as offices and living quarters, but Unterbrecht glanced behind at the main body of troops disembarking from the plane and his fears redoubled.

Filing in behind the Gestapo officers were a dozen black-uniformed privates with slung Schmeissers. Behind them was an Italian captain leading a dozen troops in *Bersaglieri* uniforms. Then came the real horror. Two platoons of infantry, the first in ordinary uniform but with the shoulder flashes of the Abwehr's elite 'Brandenburg' unit, the second dressed as paratroopers, but with the insignia of the Hermann Goering Division – one of the world's first airborne units, the men who had dropped in on the strongholds of the Berlin Communists back in 1933. Unterbrecht had never seen either of those units in the flesh before but they looked as mean and dangerous as all the rumours suggested. And they were at his base.

Several of them were behind the wheels of some unfamiliar-looking vehicles. But as he strained to identify their transport he realised that the Gestapo man's basilisk eyes had been on him all the while. He gulped and turned back, quickening his pace to draw level with his officers again.

Ziedler was deep in conversation with them. "...I want the motorised patrols increased from a twenty to a thirty-mile radius and I want more of them. Plus search and destroy missions against all known partisan units in the area. I trust I can leave that to our Gruppenfuhrer Strasser?" The leathery Waffen SS colonel nodded curtly. He, like all the others, seemed to be finding no difficulty in taking orders from a Transport Corps man.

"Is there anything I can help you with, Herr Oberst?" Unterbrecht asked with some irony. "I'd be only too happy."

"Not necessary," Ziedler smiled back; Unterbrecht's mother had warned him never to trust anyone who smiled all the time. "It's really only a matter of keeping the security tight but not too obvious. Tomorrow I shall be taking these troops," his gesture took in the Germans but not the *Bersaglieri*, which caused the Italian officers to look up sharply, "on a mission into Turkish territory. We will bring back a prisoner and, after a brief period, another mission will be undertaken of a similar nature. After that we return to Berlin, you get back to your normal routine – and forget any of this ever happened." He produced a document from his tunic pocket. "This explains everything."

It certainly did. It was a directive ordering everyone in the Third Reich and its allies to offer Ziedler and his team whatever assistance they required. It was signed by the Fuhrer himself, as well as lesser luminaries like Bormann, Himmler and Canaris. Unterbrecht swallowed hard. "My command is entirely at your disposal, Herr Oberst. I trust you will find the facilities adequate."

"I'm sure we will – is that the men's barracks over there? Splendid." Ziedler was all charm again, calling the procession to a halt and turning to the sergeant in charge of the Brandenburg platoon. "Kobal, get your men settled down. Same for the others. Full briefing in an hour." The Germans peeled off to the barracks hut and at a nod from their officers the *Bersaglieri* followed. "These are my offices, Herr Oberst." Unterbrecht gestured to a one-storey wooden building in front of them. "*Danke,*" Ziedler said and led his officers up the wooden steps. He opened the door and ushered them in, then closed it in Unterbrecht's face.

The supplies colonel stood there nonplussed for a few moments, then said decisively: "I shall be using your office and quarters for the time being, Major Raumann," and strode off to the next hut in the administration block. The rest of the officers took their cue and disappeared.

Had Unterbrecht surrendered what was left of his dignity and succumbed to an insane temptation to listen at the keyhole his apprehension about this whole business would not merely have doubled again, but increased by a power known only to pure mathematicians. The men who had taken over his camp and stood poised to execute the mission which would bring about the final Axis victory were having a furious argument.

Ciarelli's face was crimson with rage as he hissed at Ziedler in his halting, forced German: "Why aren't we going along, dammit? This is supposed to be a joint operation and this is my plan! I demand that my men form part of the assault group."

"No." Ziedler had automatically seated himself at Unterbrecht's desk, commanding the ten officers ranged in front of him, and was smiling blandly at Ciarelli, whose face was a matter of inches from his own. His voice was calm but firm. "I thought we had discussed all this in Berlin, Signor Colonel. I really don't see any point in taking the matter further."

"I thought you might be more co-operative without Bormann and Himmler at your shoulder."

"You were mistaken – and you left out Canaris, my commanding officer. I said it there and I say it now. I am in command here. Your presence is a valued one in this operation, but for the rescue attempt itself you and your men would be a liability. One of the most important elements is the ability of the assault force to look like Englishmen." He sighed. "If you wanted your unit to play a part, Signor Colonel, why did you select men who seem to have been recruited from a Sicilian sheep farm? They look as Anglo-Saxon as Arabian camel-traders."

"They all speak English – and those Russian apes wouldn't know the difference. Especially in pitch darkness, wearing camouflage cream." Ciarelli slammed his fists on the desk. "That excuse sounds more feeble every time."

"Very well, here's another." Ziedler's urbane manner was beginning to slip. "Those Brandenburgers and I have worked together on half a dozen missions like this. Their discipline and cohesion is a byword. All the men in that unit know and trust me, as they trust Leutnants Dressler and Weiss." He gestured at the other 'Transport Corps' officers, then turned to the Gestapo contingent. "That is why none of Hoffman's men are coming, either. Not because I don't trust them or I'm determined to keep them in the dark, but because of simple military logic. And I notice they haven't made any protests."

"We know damn well what reply we'd get," Hoffman grunted.

"Exactly." Ziedler seemed pleased beyond all mortal bounds by his words. "The same one I'm giving you, I'm afraid. A decision has been made and any misgivings should be directed to higher authority."

"They will be." Ciarelli's voice was calmer now, but his eyes still burned. "And you'll be mentioned plenty in the report."

"Then I suggest you go and begin writing it while it's still fresh in your mind. I'm sure Unterbrecht can find you a typewriter. There's nothing further we have to discuss."

Ciarelli turned on his heel and stamped out, followed

by the other officer, a Captain Riva. Ziedler rocked back in his chair and selected a cigarette from the gold case on the desk, tutting irritably. Leutnant Dressler, who had worked with him for two years now and realised that for Ziedler this was the equivalent of shouting out loud and kicking his chair across the room, proferred a light.

Ziedler accepted it gratefully. In the twenty-four hours since saying farewell to Rawlings at the border post he had flown across Europe on just a few hours' sleep and managed only one telephone call home. Manfred had asked why Papa had to be a soldier again so soon. And Ilse had been as sharp, accusing and anxious to hang up as ever. Now all this. But that was his job and he managed a thin smile as he addressed the officers. "The Italians, gentlemen – when will they learn that their empire crumbled a thousand years ago? And that largely thanks to the Germans."

Even Hoffman laughed at that, adding: "We knew they'd be trouble. Just didn't expect they'd start so soon. Well, you know what they said in Berlin. If they get too difficult we ditch them."

"We will," Ziedler said airily. "If they become sufficient a nuisance to warrant such action. I doubt it will come to that. What we have just seen is a typical display of Latin petulance. Ciarelli will cool off and realise that there are good reasons for my decision. He will also realise that to keep close to Vlasenin after the rescue it would be politic to be on better terms with us. No, I expect him back here full of apologies within the hour." He stubbed the cigarette out, as if to put a seal on the matter. "In the meantime, are there any other questions?"

"Only one, Herr Oberst." Dorsch, the SS

Hauptsturmfuhrer, spoke up in a languid, professional manner. Ziedler had already marked him as one to beware of. He remembered Schellenberg from the Venlo raid, and his talent for pricking under the skin in such a manner that no direct reproach could be levelled. It had gone hand in hand with a diligence in reporting back to his superiors everything that reflected well on him and lowered the reputation of the Abwehr. The combination of those two qualities had raised Schellenberg very high very fast and Ziedler had soon realised this young sprig was cut from the same cloth.

But he listened attentively as Dorsch continued: "It seems somewhat unusual to divide our force, Herr Oberst. I can deal with the British with half a platoon. That would leave you fifteen men as replacements for any casualties, or even a shadow force should the Turkish authorities intercept you."

Very good, my boy, Ziedler thought, but I can delve a yard below your mines. "I take your point, Herr Hauptmann." He used the army rank deliberately to emphasise that Dorsch was two promotions below him. "But, if you will permit me, the information we have received indicates a substantial force, when the SOE agents are combined with the Tsarist partisans. And we know that Major Rawlings is in command. Kommissar Hoffman and I can both attest to his expertise. In addition, it is precisely because there is a danger of apprehension from the Turks that I wish your men to be completely separate from mine tomorrow. If we are taken, then there will still be a platoon of highly-trained men to execute the strike – as I am sure you will have wiped out the British by then. I hope those reasons satisfy you."

"Of course." Dorsch's gossamer-light inflection of irony matched Ziedler's. "I was merely thinking aloud."

"Indeed," Ziedler said. "Now, as to the question of transport..."

And outside Ciarelli and Riva walked towards the barracks where their men were billeted with the Germans. But halfway there they ducked into one of the alleys in between the storerooms, out of sight of the many guards. "So – a success, Signor Colonel?" Riva asked.

"Partly." Ciarelli's big, even teeth gleamed in the darkness. "As long as they're convinced when we go back in to apologise in... let me see, half an hour should do it. Let us allow them to think we are merely blustering malcontents who have accepted our station. We will be on our best behaviour until Vlasenin is rescued. They'll be off their guard after that. Did you put that call in before we left Berlin?"

"Yes, Signor Colonel. The *Tedeschi* still think my travelling case is just that. But the planes will be at our disposal inside Turkey for the next seven days."

"Good." Ciarelli lit a Toscani, a sure sign of satisfaction. "All we need to do is stay in character for a while. Then we show Ziedler and his bunch that they have underestimated us once too often."

༷

Ninety miles to the east, Doctor Dimitri Vlasenin fell headfirst to the floor of the interrogation cell for the hundredth time. He scarcely felt the pain. For the past four days they had torn at his body and mind using every conceivable means. Individual shocks and blows had merged into one vast dark lake of agony a thousand miles wide and he was floating in the centre.

He was vaguely aware that two more teeth broke off in the impact, but he'd lost count of how many he'd lost now. They'd pulled out three for sure. Now two more. He couldn't tell which ones they were straight away because of the suffocating black bag which covered his eyes and half-filled his mouth. They rattled around inside it like two bloody dice, as the guards hauled him to his feet and propped him up against the wall again, then fell to the heavy fold where the rope pulled the bag taut around his neck. He couldn't see them. He could hardly even remember whether his eyes were open or not and they were so badly bruised from the beatings it scarcely mattered.

The bag had been on for hours now, or so it seemed. He could hardly breathe. What air there was tasted stale and bloody. Colours flashed in his brain like the electric shocks. Ghosts of the past trooped before him in half-waking nightmares. Soon he would slide into unconsciousness again and a guard's rifle butt or club – he couldn't tell which, it was hard and heavy, that was all he knew – would jolt him awake. But this time they would untie the bag, surely. And there would be Amarazov, kind and reasonable as ever, asking him where the papers were.

Kind? What the hell are you thinking of? Amarazov is the biggest bastard of the lot and when he has the information, then I'm dead. But he had never raised his voice since that first night. Through the electric shocks, the cold-water treatment, the blanks fired at his face and now the no-senses, no-sleep trick. Amarazov was always there, when it started, when it reached its climax and in the brief rest period before some new horror began. Always just that one question. And sometimes it had been so tempting to give in and drift into sweet oblivion. Sweet, sweet...

The guard hit him, just under the ribs as always. Vlasenin was hauled upright again. But this time there was another pair of hands untying the bag, plucking it away. Pure white light, slowly, so very slowly, becoming a desk lamp on the cell's steel table, beaming straight at him. Amarazov was at his side, holding the bag in one hand, smiling kindly as ever. Oh, tell him this time, anything to stop the light and the pain.

"Where are the papers, Comrade Doctor?"

But this time there was something different. Perhaps... yes, definitely. A hint of urgency and impatience in Amarazov's normally level, neutral voice. Vlasenin was amazed he could detect it, but it was there. And so was the image of the burning dacha. "Go to Hell – bastard."

"This is stupid, Comrade Doctor. Very stupid. What do you hope to gain?" He was definitely agitated; normally he simply asked the guards to begin again. "Any more of this and we'll have to transfer you to Moscow and the NKVD, you know. And I warn you, they'll not be so reasonable."

Amazing even himself, Vlasenin actually laughed. Then he said, in a slurred, half-human croak: "What the hell does it matter – Moscow or here? Same cell, same torture. And I'll still die before I tell you a fucking thing."

"No, you won't." Amarazov said it with absolute certainty, then threw the bag to one of the guards. "Carry on." Vlasenin saw him turn and walk towards the door before the darkness came again and his defiance vanished like a cup of water poured into a desert. He'd lost his only chance. He had spat into a face that offered an end to the pain. He wanted to call Amarazov back, call on him for forgiveness and tell him what he wanted to know. But the truth was he had not the strength to speak.

Amarazov walked through the open cell doorway and walked away briskly. His temporary office was only a few yards down the dimly-lit corridor. Inside he sat down at a large radio set and began to transmit on the special frequency reserved for communications with Grigorin. The expression on his face would have done Vlasenin as much good as eight hours sleep and a hot meal.

It wasn't working. He couldn't believe it. All done by the book, almost guaranteed to have a man confessing everything within forty-eight hours. This had gone on for twice that time, a situation Amarazov had only encountered a few times and always with much younger, stronger subjects, not this weak middle-aged man. Of course, he would go soon, very soon. But Moscow wanted results now. Tempting to try some of these new drugs, but the tests so far had been inconclusive. And the old methods should be working, as they had worked so many times before. So close. Vlasenin and the papers. His reputation would be made if he delivered both, the sort of hero no-one could ever touch. Instead it looked like being broken, another nameless functionary paying the price for failure. All because of that runty, pasty-faced, little Jewish-looking bastard.

"Amarazov calling," he said curtly; it was time for Anatoly to start helping out a little. "Are you receiving?"

"Renkovich here. What have you to report?"

Amarazov almost had a seizure. His face would have been worth an injection of painkillers to Vlasenin now. "Comrade Lieutenant-General, this is an unexpected honour. Normally Comrade Gri..."

"Grigorin has been arrested for betrayal of state secrets. I am taking personal charge of the operation. What have you to report?"

Amarazov composed himself with some difficulty. "He is still proving stubborn, Comrade Lieutenant-General. But he is close to cracking. I just need a little more time."

"You have twenty-four hours. The Germans know Vlasenin is being held. We do not think they are in a position to mount a rescue yet, but time is even more short now. If he has not been broken, and those papers found, within twenty-four hours, bring him to Moscow. Lose him and you die."

The radio went silent.

Chapter 4

Opening Game

THE SAVAGE WIND BLASTED INTO Rawlings' face and straight through his body as he pulled back the door of the plane. Snowflakes danced before his eyes and melted on his jump overalls, forming a thin, moist film. The howl of the wind, coupled with the deafening hum of the aero engines, almost drowned out his voice as he shouted "ready – go!" His team tumbled out into the darkness, parachute cords clicking on the static line as they went. Curtis first, smooth and expert, then the rest; no hesitation from anyone, even those like Costas and Stavrakis, whose only experience had been a training course.

Walters was last, then Rawlings clipped the line and launched himself out, braced for the jerk back and up as his parachute opened. Then the slow, free-floating sensation that still thrilled him even after all these times. He looked downwards. The fifteen parachutes were drifting like pale water lilies on a dark lake, towards the vague outline of lights on the ground. Two rows of ten lanterns equally spaced, just as had been arranged. But that was no guarantee of a warm reception in itself and as the descent suddenly speeded up Rawlings turned every sense up to maximum alertness for danger. As soon as he hit the ground and sprang to his feet to unclip the 'chute, his hand snaked to the Mauser inside his jump suit. "Archangel," he shouted into the darkness.

"Murmansk," came a heavy-accented reply from his left as three figures loomed in the shadows. But even then Rawlings stayed alert until Chalmers appeared on his right and shone a torch at the central figure. The light illuminated a tall, broad-shouldered man with a lean, bearded face, a long scar running from left eye to jaw. Chalmers gave a shout of joyful recognition. The two men met and embraced, the big Russian kissing Chalmers on both cheeks, then walked towards Rawlings, arms round each other's shoulders. "Major, this is Vasily Stolnikov," Chalmers said proudly. "Best man in the whole underground. I made a few fact-finding trips with him to Armenia back when the world was young. Vasily – Major Alexander Rawlings."

"I am honoured, *Gospodin*." The Russian held out a hand. As Rawlings took it Vasily gestured to the two figures flanking him. One was as big and broad-shouldered as the leader, but the other was unusually short and slim. "These are my lieutenants," Vasily said in the same formal, heavily-accented English. "Yuri Konstantin and Yelena Artova."

They both stepped into the torchlight, but Rawlings only noticed Yelena. She was indeed slight, and no more than five feet five. But she carried herself with pride and moved with the speed and grace of an athlete. She was wearing a canvas jacket, corduroy breeches and knee-length boots, the same shapeless homespun as the rest of the group. Even that could not disguise how perfectly proportioned her body was.

But it was her face that held Rawlings' attention, and continued to do so as she formally introduced herself then stood back while Yuri did the same. Her hair was jet black, pulled tightly back across her temples. It contrasted perfectly with the pale skin and framed the high slanting cheekbones, long straight nose and firm jaw. It was a face that could have been cold and forbidding, were it not for the eyes. They were vivid green, bright and kind. There was sadness in them, pain and loss, but a spirit that overcame all those things, that retained hope and humanity. They were like votive candles lit against the suffering of the world. In all the time Rawlings knew her their light never dimmed. And when she smiled, as she did at that first meeting, they changed her face to that of a happy and mischievous young girl.

It was an effort to stop himself from staring dumbly at her, but the perfect excuse was provided by Mayhew trotting up at the double. "All present and correct, sir, and all in one piece, bar a few bumps and bruises."

"Thank you, Sarn't-Major. Right – your men ready to go, Vasily? All we need to do now is bury our 'chutes."

"It is done – see." Rawlings looked around as two men appeared on his left, grabbed his discarded parachute and carried it off into the darkness, where the sound of industrious digging could faintly be heard. It was only then Rawlings noticed that the lanterns had already been extinguished and the only lights on the drop zone now were a couple of hooded torch beams. "It is never wise to linger too long." Vasily switched to Russian to issue a volley of orders to his men, six in all, who converged on their leader, work done, leading Rawlings' team with them. Another order sent them away, two moving to the head of the party, two slipping behind and one moving to either flank.

Rawlings was impressed, and equally pleased to see that his men had formed naturally into column of twos, ready for the off, weapons to hand, eyes constantly scanning the darkness. Well, so far, so good. "Right, let's move out. No talking unless absolutely necessary and then only in Turkish. If you don't know any, keep quiet. If we hit trouble, do as the guides tell you, but try to regroup as quickly as possible. OK – forward!"

The path sloped upwards, out of the small valley where they had landed, and continued to rise for half a mile or so before levelling out and leading them through thick forest. The darkness became almost pitch black as the huge pines threw their shadows, branches so thick they even blocked out the falling snow. There was an eerie stillness to it all and Rawlings half expected to see a goblins' lair or gingerbread cottage at the end of their journey. Instead the trees abruptly gave way to another small valley, surrounded on all sides by the forest but with rocky slopes and clear ground around the wooden farmhouse and outbuildings.

As the group walked down the single path into the valley, Rawlings saw that what he had taken for a farm was in fact a lumber yard. Piles of logs, beams and fence posts lay all around and a small sawmill stood to the left of the large, one-storey house. A small square building, like the bunkhouse on a Western ranch, lay to the right. Three elderly trucks and a large pre-war saloon car were parked beside it. "This is my business," Vasily said. "It makes it easy to travel round, and because I hire more workers when I need to, new men don't look so out of place. Most of my work is helping those who flee from the Reds get across the borders. There used to be many, coming across Turkey, heading for Greece and Bulgaria. Now the Fascists are in control there, not so many. But I still travel around a lot. Good way to pick up information."

"Doesn't that attract some suspicion? I thought the Turks weren't too keen on Russians."

Vasily shrugged. "We've been here a long time. I set the business up with money from the underground. Some of the people we helped to smuggle out stayed to help with our work. They sleep in that building over there," he indicated the bunkhouse. "There are many like us in this part of Turkey. We keep to ourselves but we stay friendly with all the villages. We never break the law. I give the police a sack of logs for their stoves once in a while and they leave me alone. I'm a good Russian," he said solemnly, then shouted with laughter.

Rawlings laughed with him, warming to the man. But it was not merely professional curiosity that made him ask next: "Are you and Yelena…"

He tailed off, uncertain as to how the Russian might take such a question. But Vasily merely gave an equable shake of the head. "We live under the same roof – it helps the cover. But for the rest…" he hesitated before continuing, and when he did it was in a whisper. "Yelena came when the purges began. She was married to a young colonel on the general staff. A brave man, and a good Communist. But Stalin butchered him, as he butchers everyone. She only just escaped. Now she hates the Reds more than any of us. She has fought them a dozen times when we have gone back in to rescue refugees, or do work for your government. Chalmers knows her; he can tell you. She is the best fighter I have ever known." Vasily paused and looked Rawlings in the eye. "But she will not love a man again, I think."

Vasily obviously considered that an end of the matter, and in any case they were now at the door of the farmhouse. Two more men were at the doorway to usher them in quickly, then take up station as the night sentries, along with two of the party from the drop zone. All four carried rifles slung over their shoulders. "Isn't that unusual for a timber merchant?" Rawlings asked. "Armed sentries? We don't want to attract attention."

Vasily shrugged again. "There are many bandits round these parts. They rob farms and places like this sometimes. We do not always take the trouble, but for one night – better safe than sorry, no?"

He was still smiling, but in a somewhat strained fashion and Rawlings decided not to pursue the matter, instead following Yelena and Yuri inside. The rest of Vasily's men moved towards the bunkhouse as Rawlings' team filed in behind him and made themselves comfortable inside the main living room. Vasily had laid out bedrolls for all of them but there was still plenty of room for a large table and a pair of benches plus several other chairs, all made from the same age-dark pine as the rough-hewn beams in the roof, blackened by the constant roaring of the huge open fire at the far end. Walters immediately took his boots and socks off to toast his bare feet, complaining loudly of chilblains. When Rawlings made no protest, the others decided not to stand on ceremony and followed suit.

Vasily disappeared into the kitchen to their left and within a few minutes they were all seated at or around the table, enjoying a late supper of *borsch* and black bread, washed down with Turkish coffee. Afterwards Rawlings pulled a large map from his case and the team gathered round, some in chairs, some standing or squatting, lighting *machorka*s or taking pulls from the half-dozen vodka bottles Vasily had put into circulation, but all alert, studying Rawlings and the map intensely.

"This is the target – the Soviet Consulate in Istanbul. It's right in the heart of the city, on a busy main boulevard. But we'll be hitting it late at night, it's the weekend and it's a long way away from the fleshpots in the old city."

"Shame," Walters observed. Rawlings waited until the laughter had died down before continuing. "That means it should be fairly quiet. We set off at nine tomorrow morning with Vasily and two of his boys in two of the trucks. Our cover is that we're going to pick up some supplies in the city. Most of us will be in one truck, with just a driver for the other, so it all looks natural. Both drivers will be Vasily's men. Yuri, together with Curtis, Mayhew, Walters, Jones and Costas will take the car into the city by a different route. That means that if anything happens to one group there's a reserve force to carry out the strike.

"The rest of Vasily's team, with Ye… I mean, Miss Artova in charge, will stay here until the strike's over then head for the rendezvous in the third truck to make sure it's not been blown and provide security when we arrive.

"Once we're in the middle of the city we rendezvous

and park the vehicles in a garage run by a contact of Vasily's. Inside is a brand-new Soviet staff car which we'll be using to get to the main gate undetected. We spend the rest of the day split into small groups, scouting the target. We don't want to attract any attention but by the time the sun goes down I need all of you to know everything there is to know about that building. How many guards, what the patrol routines are, what are the strong and weak points defensively, are there any escape routes in an emergency? Then when the sun goes down, we keep looking – to see how well-lit the streets around it are, how much cover there is for an escape, whether there are Turkish police patrols nearby and, if so, how often? That continues right up until thirty minutes before the strike time. Any questions?"

There were a few murmurs, but only Walters spoke up. "Beg pardon, sir, but why all this monkeyin' around? No-one's twigged us yet. There can't be a whole army in a building that size. Why not just steam in there, break a few heads to get the Ruskis to tell us where our boy is then hightail it out before anyone knows what's hit them? Fire a few rounds in the air to scare the Turks off; what's the bother, we ain't comin' back. Seems to me all this pussyfooting around's just asking to get ourselves spotted."

Mayhew looked ready to deliver a thunderous rebuke, but Rawlings held up a hand. "You're right, corporal, no-one's 'twigged' us yet. And no-one will – provided we refrain from the Australian habit of complaining loudly about every bloody thing under the sun. In English."

Some of the men laughed, but the laughter died when they saw Rawlings' face. "As I said, this is one of the most difficult – and delicate – operations SOE or anyone else has ever mounted. Officially it will never exist. And we absolutely cannot afford to have a man go down or get left behind. Anything that the Russians can use as evidence that Britain is involved in the rescue will turn this into the biggest political hot potato of all time.

"Believe me, corporal, there's nothing I'd like better than to just… steam in. But afterwards we've got to get clear away from one of the world's biggest cities. It's the best part of three miles before we even hit the suburbs and the streets are a maze for most of that. Vasily and his men know their way around pretty well but the last thing we need is to have to navigate it with the police on our tail and a pile of corpses behind us.

"So by the time we make the strike we know every possible way in and out of that building. And while we're finding that out we keep our heads down and don't attract suspicion. Talking to be kept to a minimum and nothing in English, at all. It only takes one officious policeman to decide he wants to have a word with any one of us and our cover's blown. The mission's going to be hard enough without that. So we play it my way. Clear?"

"Yes, sir." Walters looked chagrined, but mollified as well. Rawlings nodded. "I'll give you more details just before the operation begins. For now all you need to know is that the plane which brought us to Turkey will be waiting at a small commercial airfield here," his finger stabbed down on a circled map reference half-way between Esenyurt and Istanbul, "at 0300 hours on Sunday morning. If we get separated after the strike try to make for it. Well, that's all. O'Hare and I have got a broadcast to Cairo to make, but I suggest the rest of you get some sleep."

O' Hare unpacked the transmitter and hauled it away, Rawlings, Chalmers and Vasily following as arranged. Curtis settled down like all the rest but Mayhew, in the bedroll next to him, noticed as he turned round to get more comfortable, that Curtis' eyes were still open.

"Everything all right, sir?" he asked.

Curtis seemed not to have heard him at first, then looked round and gave an uncertain smile. "What – oh, yes, Sarn't-Major. It always takes three nights to get used to a strange bedroom, my mother always said. And they don't come much stranger than this one. I've never perfected the art of instant sleep, unlike some of my Middle East colleagues.

"And all of this lot, to judge by the snoring. Well, goodnight, sir."

"Goodnight, Mayhew," Curtis replied. Mayhew closed his eyes, but the noise of the coded message being transmitted kept him awake. He opened his eyes again, and noticed that when O'Hare left to bed down Rawlings continued talking with Chalmers and Vasily for what seemed a long time. Their low, whispered tones were his last memory before sleep claimed him. That and the sight of Curtis, still awake and listening intently.

༄

The morning of Saturday, November 21st, 1942, dawned crisp, clear and cold but few of the team even noticed. Rawlings had set 7.30 for their "wake-up call", giving them six solid hours' rest. It wasn't long, yet he knew they'd all performed wonders on less before and he trusted Vasily's men to keep watch. But the British soldier's inbuilt alarm clock was hard to switch off. Most of the men began to stir at around six and never really settled down afterwards. By 7.30 most of them had wolfed down a breakfast of bread and honey with more coffee and immediately afterwards began cleaning and checking their weapons or going over the maps and plans of the target. Yuri and Yelena stayed inside with them, keeping watch at the windows, together with Mayhew and Hawkins. Four more Russians stood sentry in the hills above.

Rawlings took four men outside to help Vasily and the rest of his men load the trucks and otherwise keep up the impression of a normal day's work at the sawmill; Chalmers because he could interpret any sudden commands, Rowley and Garside because they would be useful in a firefight and Walters because he had politely but steadfastly insisted that he need a bit of fresh air, begging the major's pardon.

It certainly seemed to cheer him up. He set to work with a will, carrying the plain boxes which now held their equipment to the trucks and throwing them inside, whistling 'The Wild Colonial Boy' as he always did when in a good mood. As he turned to fetch a second load, Rawlings walked over from the sawmill, stepped close as if to start a conversation – and whispered: "Let's have a good old Turkish work song or nothing at all, eh, corporal? Sound travels in these parts."

Walters stiffened. "Ah, come off it; nobody could have heard me – sir."

"Not here, maybe – but on the middle of Istiklal Boulevard… get yourself into character or you're on the back-up team – cobber."

Walters considered arguing the point, but saw the look in Rawlings' eyes, then turned and walked away. Around him, everyone had continued working but as he reached the farmhouse Garside passed him on the way with his own load and said: "I nearly did the same meself, mate – just about to give you all a chorus of 'Run, Adolf, Run' when I caught his beady eyes on me. It could have been any of us."

"Yeah – but he enjoyed it more with me."

"Maybe." Garside, a small, dark Yorkshireman with a mischievous glint in his eye, gave a half-smile. "We have a hard time trusting ex-convicts." Walters bristled, but then Garside produced a cigarette, gave him the rest of the smile, and they both laughed. "Relax, mate. He's not a bad officer – O'Hare reckons he's the best of the lot and I've known worse. Stop trying to rub him up the wrong way and you might start getting along."

From the hillside above Viktor, one of the four men Vasily had as sentries, watched the scene from his camouflaged trench with mild interest. But he still kept half an eye and both ears open for any strange sights or sounds. He was used to that. Watching out for trouble had been second nature since even before the war, when Vasily had recruited him to fight the Reds. He had escaped to Turkey by his own efforts, but with an Ukrainian background and half his family in labour camps it had not been too difficult a decision to join the underground.

And now he, and all Vasily's men, had the chance to make a real difference. That was why it was so important to stay alert. For the twentieth time that morning he raised the binoculars to his eyes and checked that the other three were still there, covering their quadrants. Each one was hidden in a trench like Viktor, invisible to all but those who knew where to look. Good. Viktor was lowering the binoculars when he heard it. A slight rustling amongst the bracken in the trees behind him. Just the kind of noise a forest animal might make. Except all forest animals slept by day.

He knew exactly where it had come from. Twenty yards back, where the hillside sloped gently upwards. Instantly he crawled out of his trench and back into the trees, still using every scrap of cover, approaching the spot from a right angle and five yards to the right. For the final approach he half-crawled through the bushes to the patch of bracken in the small clearing before standing up, rifle cocked.

Nothing. No footprints, no stems broken, no earth kicked up, not even animal sign. Well, it never hurt to be too cautious, Vasily always said, and the forest was never completely silent. Viktor turned round – quicker than expected, so the Luger bullet meant for the back of his head took him between the eyes.

The silencer was a more standard model than that of Rawlings' Mauser but it was still inaudible past ten yards. It made less sound than Viktor's body falling into the bracken and hitting the leaf-strewn earth. His killer stepped out from cover, approached the body and checked for any signs of life. As usual, there were none. He straightened up, then motioned the rest of his men forward.

"Weren't you a little hard on him, sir?" Chalmers asked cautiously as the two of them checked the engine on the truck furthest from the house, lined in a row with its two brothers and the car. "It's an easy mistake to make on your first undercover trip."

"Mistakes like that can be fatal," Rawlings replied. "I don't want to see a member of what's supposed to be the finest SOE team ever assembled making them. I know Walters is probably thinking there was no need for it, that he couldn't have been overheard and we're not in the danger zone yet… but let that pass once and it happens again – where you don't get second chances. Walters should know that."

"Well, I'm sure he does now," Chalmers said hastily. "I mean, you're right of course, sir. It's just that he's not had quite the same kind of experience as us. After all," he gave an ironic laugh, "chasing a few little yellow men through a mangrove swamp is hardly…"

A rifle shot rang out. Chalmers' head bulged out of shape for half a second, then exploded. Blood and brains spattered across Rawlings' face as he dived for cover under the truck's axle, just as the wild staccato crackle of a dozen rifles and submachine-guns ripped the still morning air. As he rolled clear of the truck's underside and stood up he could see the whole lumber yard, now turned into a killing ground. Two of Vasily's men were down already, one almost in front of him, shot in a dozen places. Another going down to the left, blood gouting from chest and back. Explosive bullet; sniper's issue, like the one that had taken Chalmers. They went in one side, came out the other and took whatever was in between with them. Whoever was up there knew their business.

Rowley had been at the trucks too, but he had dived towards the house and was firing his Sten from behind an upturned bench on the porch. Walters and Garside were taking cover behind one of the piles of lumber, the remaining Russian behind the other. The piles of lumber that were steadily being whittled to matchwood as a dozen or more men swarmed down the slopes, firing their weapons on the run, using every scrap of cover. They were wearing civilian clothes but Rawlings could see they carried Schmeisser machine pistols and Mauser infantry rifles. There was at least one heavy machine-gun supporting them from up in the trees, as well as more rifles and Schmeissers set at various heights. A perfect enfilade.

The only hope of survival was to get back in the house, quick. Where was Vasily? He had been in the cab of the truck and had ducked down a split second before a Mauser bullet shattered the windscreen. Now he joined Rawlings behind the body of the truck, firing his Nagant revolver wildly. A volley of shots shrieked against the elderly metal of the truck, and one man used the cover to get close enough to throw a grenade.

"Move!" Rawlings shouted. The Russian needed no second bidding. They had just cleared the rear axle when the grenade exploded, tearing the truck apart and blasting them the few yards to the next one. They took cover behind the body, taking station at opposite ends. This truck was partly shielded by one of the lumber piles about ten yards in front of it, but offered a clear field of fire to right and left.

And there was no shortage of targets. Their attackers had reached the piles of timber offcuts at the edge of the yard and were using them as firing positions while their comrades moved up on either flank, throwing grenades and firing from the hip. They had not lost a man so far, but now Rawlings and Vasily opened fire, taking one man apiece. The attackers dropped prone and fired back, forcing them to duck behind the bonnet for cover. Costas had sprinted out to another bench at the opposite end of the porch, only yards from the lumber piles, trying to give the men behind them covering fire with one of the Russian submachine-guns. Curtis and Emerson were at the doorway firing pistols, oblivious to the bullets that came in return. Every window at the front of the house was a firing post, but still that terrible hail razored down the piles of lumber where the three men lay helpless, knowing that to run for the door or try to fire back would be suicide.

Then the Russian put his submachine-gun to his shoulder and leapt from behind the timber with a savage cry. Walters and Garside took their cue and sprang for the doorway as he ran in front of them, firing wildly. Within seconds he went down, hit by a dozen bullets. But he had bought the SOE men time to reach safety. Two attackers raced forward wildly to stop them, but shots from Rawlings and Vasily put them down. A fusillade was immediately directed at the trucks, forcing them into cover again. More men sprang out – and Walters and Garside turned, firing from the hip. Three attackers fell, the rest dived for cover again. Garside turned and sprinted through the doorway, but Walters fell back firing, seemingly oblivious to the danger. "Come out, you bastards," he yelled, then Rowley ran to pull him inside, joining him a second later. Curtis and Emerson were still at the doorway and Costas was covering the near side of the porch, frantically signalling Rawlings and Vasily to make a run for it.

As Rawlings looked back from the house, another grenadier burst into view, aiming for the second truck. Vasily shot him in the heart, then both men turned to run – and the world turned white-hot as gas stench, smoke and red fire blasted into their vision. They dived for the third truck just as the flamethrower burst engulfed the second. Choking, half-blinded, Vasily tripped and fell. Rawlings turned to pick him up and they staggered past the truck and the car to the doorway, Emerson coming to meet them, covering them, helping to drag the winded Vasily along. Bullets cracked around them; one hit Emerson in the shoulder and all three went down.

The flamethrower man ran out from cover, zeroing in on them – and Curtis shot him in the heart as he ran to help the three on the ground, Costas following. Mayhew was behind them, covering from the doorway with his Sten. Just as Curtis reached Rawlings he dived to the ground as the flames hit the second truck's petrol tank and a huge blast engulfed trucks and car. But the smoke hid them from their attackers and the men at the windows poured fire into the yard, keeping all heads down for the few seconds it took Rawlings and Curtis to grab a man apiece and run for the doorway, Costas running and firing with them.

Mayhew kept covering them until the last moment then ducked inside as they reached safety. All five fell to the ground as Mayhew slammed the door, then rolled aside as a firestorm from outside almost blasted it off its hinges. Walters looked at Vasily as they squirmed into better cover and said fervently: "Jesus, mate, you need to stop short-changing your customers."

The big room reeked of cordite and blood. Every man in the team, and Yelena, was at the windows. A bench had been upended to barricade the back door, which was equally pock-marked with bullets. Hawkins and O'Hare covered the windows at either side of it – and the body of Yuri lay before it. "Both exits blocked?" Rawlings asked needlessly, gasping for breath.

"Yessir," Mayhew replied crisply. "There's a machine-gun and a couple of sharpshooters in the trees at least. Nailed that Ruski sharp as ninepence when he took a look outside."

"That 'Ruski' had a name!" Vladimir shouted.

Rawlings rounded on him. "Yes – and I can think of a few for his leader, too! How the hell did they know we were here? If that's a bunch of bandits, then they bought their weapons from some SS partisan hunters. I tell you, if any of your men decided that working with the Krauts is the best way to bring down Stalin, then…"

"My men would never do that!" Vasily was equally angry now. "You would not be in here if one of them had not sacrificed himself. Is that the action of a traitor?"

"What about the men on the hill? Any one of them could have let…" Rawlings broke off. He could see the pain as well as the fury in Vasily's eyes. All but one of his group were dead and now the people he had risked them to help were questioning the one thing even more precious to him – his honour. "Anyway," Rawlings muttered, "someone brought them here."

"Yeah, and I think they want to come in," Walters said suddenly. Rawlings and Vasily jumped up and ran to the window. The firing had intensified, carving up the wooden frames and tearing through the walls as everyone inside relearned the lesson that wood is little protection from a bullet at close range. At the enemy positions reinforcements were moving in from the trees, small groups peeling off to left and right.

"They're going for a rush," Rawlings predicted and as if in response another grenadier, flanked by two men with Schmeissers and two with rifles, burst from cover. A rifle shot took him in the head before he could throw but his comrades reached one of the piles of lumber close to the doorway. Three seconds later a grenade came soaring onto the porch and blasted half a wall section away. Then a man carrying an anti-tank rifle sprinted for the burning wreckage of the vehicles, but the heavy weapon slowed him down and Rawlings shot him in the heart. "I make that eleven down so far," he shouted to Curtis.

"Yes, sir," Curtis replied. "Seven or eight of them dead, I reckon."

"Still twenty-plus up there, I'd say." Mayhew's voice was almost apologetic.

Rawlings nodded. "Platoon strength. And probably the cream of the crop, for a job like this."

"Why the hell rush us, then?" Walters' tone of complaint had been replaced by one of bewilderment. "That many, with the hardware they've got, could shoot this place to buggery – and us with it."

"If they're who I think they are, then they don't want to hang around in Turkey any more than we do. They might be dressed as civilians, but…" the rest of his words were drowned by a deafening whine. Then a thunderbolt hit the door full on, blasting it half off its hinges. Redoubled firing crackled through the gap. "What the fuck was that?" Walters yelped as he sought a safer position.

"*Panzerschreck,*" Hawkins replied. "Nifty little portable rocket launcher. Brews up a tank if you hit the right spot. They don't have to worry about whittling the place down," the deep Cornish voice added lugubriously, "they'll just demolish it."

"Jesus – anything this lot haven't got?!"

"Pin him down." Rawlings' voice cut through the babble. A dozen guns zeroed in on the lumber pile and the protruding tip of the launcher vanished. But the enemy fusillade was still the stronger. The noise of bullets thudding against the woodwork and shell cases hitting the floor was almost deafening but Rawlings still caught Mitchell's voice as he yelled: "Right-hand side. Two o'clock. They're going for the sawmill."

Rawlings raced to one of the right-hand windows. It was true. Four or five ran from the trees on the far side and at the same time two riflemen raced from one lumber pile to the other. They reached it safely, deadly fire keeping the Britons' heads down. Then one ran on for the wreckage of the trucks while his comrade covered him. Walters leapt to the window and aimed his Nagant but just as he squeezed the trigger a Schmeisser burst hit the frame. Walters jerked back with a savage curse.

"You hit?" Rawlings cried.

"No – missed the kill," Walters replied angrily. And then the wounded man started to scream, a high, animal shriek of agony. "Gut shot," the Australian said grimly. "Wouldn't wish that on a dog." He moved back towards the window, pistol coming up. "I'll finish him."

"I'll do it!" Curtis said sharply and cocked his Nagant, moving in front of Walters. But Rawlings was there before either of them. "Leave him. He might say something useful." Curtis looked appalled, but saw the look in Rawlings' eyes and did as he was told.

The wounded soldier was still screaming, writhing in agony. He tried to crawl back into cover but his strength failed him. Then he turned to the farmhouse. "Help me, please. Have mercy." The voice was distorted by pain, but the words were in English and the accent German.

Curtis moved to the doorway but Rawlings held him back. "Come on, son, shout some more," he whispered softly. "Shout for your officer. Tell me who I'm up against."

A rifle shot rang out abruptly. The German slumped lifeless to the ground. Rawlings turned to his men in fury. "Who did that?!"

"None of us, chief," Walters said solemnly, and now Rawlings could see every weapon was lowered, fingers away from triggers. "It come from his own blokes."

Rawlings shrugged. "Figures. Damn shame, though. Maybe he'd have said something useful. OK, so we know they're German. But no ordinary squaddies. English speakers, special ops blokes. Still, I suppose they were never going to send the Westphalia Bicycle Battalion." His face darkened. "And if they know we're here, they know why. Still, we'll worry about that later. For now we have to sort this mess out."

"So what's the next move, chief?" Walters' eyes were glittering.

"Just what it would have been anyway, me old mate." Rawlings slammed a fresh magazine into the Mauser.

"Bury the bastards deep."

"How?" Curtis asked dumbly – then winced as a second *Panzerschreck* rocket hit the wall, blasting another huge hole. The ruined planks smouldered, then began to blaze. "Put that fire out for a start," Rawlings shouted and, as Mitchell threw his jacket over the blaze, turned to Vasily. "That tunnel you talked about – where is it?"

"Here." Vasily scuttled to the centre of the room and pulled a coarse rug aside. Beneath was a huge square door set into the floorboards, opened by one huge heave on a metal pull handle. A short flight of wooden steps led down a shaft shored up with wooden beams to an unlit floor. Curtis stared into it, dumfounded. "You never told us this was here," he said at last.

"I hoped there'd be no need, and the less you know the better. Anyway, here it is and I'm going down it – along with Vasily, Walters, Garside, Rowley and Sanderson. The passage ends up on the hillside, among the trees. Once we're there, Walters and I will take one MG, Vasily and Garside the other; Rowley and Sanderson will take care of any snipers – there's one out front at least and probably another opposite him. Hand me that flare pistol, Sarn't-Major, if you please. We'll fire it as a signal when we're ready. As soon as you see it, you do your stuff. O'Hare, I want two clusters of grenades ready to blow out those lumber piles and another of smoke and flares, get them confused. Once that's done five men come out shooting. The rest can give them covering fire. I don't want any of the men out in the yard left alive. We'll deal with the jokers on the hillside and take one for interrogation. Got all that, Curtis?"

"Yessir!"

"Repeat it." Curtis reeled off the instructions as the rest of the party clambered into the tunnel and Rawlings stuck the flare pistol into his belt. "Remember – wait for the signal. It should take us about ten minutes to make ready."

"What if the signal never comes, sir?" Curtis asked solemnly.

Rawlings gave him a lopsided grin. "Does SOE Cairo encourage its junior officers to doubt their superiors? If it never comes, young Jonny, then you really start to earn a captain's pay. But it will." Then he was gone.

"All right, men," Curtis turned back to them. "Keep returning fire. Don't want the bastards getting suspicious." He saw Yelena at one of the windows, submachine-gun still smoking in her hands, and blushed. "… er, would you do that too, Miss Artova, please?" He asked very slowly and carefully in Russian.

"You can call me Yelena, Captain Curtis," she replied in excellent English. "I think I am part of your team now."

"That's right, love," Pearson, a big, cheerful Mancunian, grinned as he reloaded his Sten. "And SOE teams do everything together. Fight, work, eat, tek a bath…"

Yelena gave a mischievous smile as a chorus of agreement broke out from the rest of the men. "Russian women never bathe. Don't you listen to Dr Goebbels' broadcasts?"

"Only when we can't get *ITMA*," said O'Hare. Yelena gave a puzzled look at the unfamiliar reference, but then Curtis broke in. "All right, back to it. Double return fire. Make it sound like we're all still here."

"Quite right," Hawkins agreed, surveying the wreckage of the farmhouse as he rammed the stock of his Lee-Enfield into his shoulder again. "And if we make it fierce enough they might surrender to us."

∞

Inside the tunnel all was dark, cramped and cold, the only light coming from a torchbeam held by Vasily in the lead. The six men crawled along on hands and knees through the oppressive gloom for what seemed an eternity, but was only a few minutes. The tunnel sloped steadily upwards, becoming quite steep, then abruptly Vasily scrambled up a small bank of earth and pushed hard on the tunnel roof with both hands. A small square piece of wood, covered in earth and leaf litter, came up and, as daylight flooded in, Vasily sprang up and out, the others following as quickly and quietly as they could.

They need not have worried about cover. The trapdoor was in the middle of the thickest part of the forest, away from the firing positions. A quick check to ensure no enemy were nearby, then a silent crouching run up to the brow of the hill, where a quick binocular sweep told Rawlings all he needed.

The main force was behind the two lumber piles and amongst the still-burning wreckage of the trucks, a dozen men in all. Further back, at the edge of the treeline, commanding the path his team had taken last night, was a rifleman and another with a Schmeisser machine pistol, providing the first level of cover. Twenty yards further up, among the trees, but in a clearing with a field of fire onto the path and the house, was a tripod-mounted MG42 manned by two men. A sniper was perched in a tall pine nearby, undoubtedly the man who had nailed Chalmers. Further off to the right two men surveyed operations from another clearing. They were obviously the officers, and one was obviously in charge; a tall, athletic-looking man with cropped blond hair. He gestured to the opposite side of the slope and his adjutant, a burly, dark-haired giant, raised his binoculars for a closer look. Rawlings looked too. The set-up there was exactly the same. It was a good containing formation, but vulnerable to attack from the rear.

"Right." He lowered the binoculars and turned to his men. "We take the snipers first. Rowley and Sanderson, that's your job; make it quiet." They nodded. Sanderson screwed the silencer onto his Luger pistol; Rowley already had his fitted to the Simonov rifle. "Vasily, you and Garside work round to take the other MG team. No prisoners – I'll get one of that lot down there alive." Garside nodded and drew his Fairbairn knife; Vasily merely flexed his bear claw hands. Walters had pulled a garotte from inside his jacket and was testing the tension. "Five minutes from now I fire the flare and you all open up. The men on the MGs take the sharpshooters below then zero in on the boys in front of the house. Rowley, try to nail both the officers. Sanderson, just shoot anyone who's not on our team. OK – go!"

They were out of the copse in seconds, veering off to their alloted targets. Rawlings and Walters moved too, quickly at first but once they were ten yards from the machine-gun they stopped, looked up to make sure Rowley had taken the sniper's place – the sound of the falling body had been drowned by the firing – and dropped to their bellies to begin the laborious crawl forward, inch by inch, in complete silence, until they were barely a yard away. The noise was deafening. Slowly they rose to their knees, still hidden by the trees at the edge of the clearing. Walters had the garotte ready; Rawlings drew the flare pistol from his belt, cartridge already in place. He looked at his watch. Thirty seconds.

The machine-gun stopped. Walters and Rawlings sank back to the floor as the gunner cleared the breech. "Let her cool off. That hovel's near to matchwood now, anyway. We'll be carrying them out soon. Got a light?" He was a Bavarian, eastern half, Rawlings guessed from the accent. But the MG loader did not reply. He looked across the valley, then stiffened. His finger pointed to the far side of the hill. "Hey, Hans, look. See over there…"

Rawlings rose up, fired the flare pistol, then lunged for the gunner. The German half-turned, and took the butt of the flare pistol in the middle of his forehead. His eyes rolled up and he fell to the ground. Rawlings pushed him well away from the MG and looked to his left. The loader was struggling desperately as Walters pulled the garrotte ever tighter. Then, abruptly, the resistance stopped. Walters pushed the body aside and began feeding ammo into the belt as Rawlings grabbed the trigger. At that moment all hell broke loose.

O' Hare and Curtis appeared in the doorway and threw the grenade clusters. Three seconds later the lumber piles blasted apart as the Germans ran for cover. Below Rawlings the two marksmen took aim. Rawlings squeezed the MG42's trigger. The clattering hammer filled his ears and Walters cursed as the cartridges streamed through his hands like a snapped cable. The first burst caught the

Schmeisser man full in the back. The rifleman turned with a look of utter amazement and caught the next burst in the chest.

Rawlings traversed down to the farmhouse. Curtis, O' Hare and four others – Emerson using a pistol in his good hand – were laying down a murderous field of fire. Two men had fallen to it but the *Panzerschreck* operator was out in the open, kneeling in front of them. The thunderbolt roar, the screaming whine and Curtis' men were diving for cover. Rawlings tracked left, seeking to eliminate the new danger, but now the air was alive with bullets as the ground force saw what had happened in the trees and strafed the MG position. Rawling and Walters ducked – then threw themselves left and right as a *Panzerschreck* rocket streamed towards them. It hit the MG42 full on then detonated, turning the gun into a lump of twisted metal and blowing it twenty yards away.

They rose to their knees, dazed, and dived behind tree cover. Rawlings took another look down. Curtis' group had been joined by Vasily and Garside and constant puffs of rifle smoke came from the far slope as Sanderson, the party's other sharpshooter, picked and dropped target after target, including the *Panzerschreck* operator. One of his comrades tried to pick the weapon up but Sanderson nailed him too. It lay abandoned, as now the Germans were pulling back – in good order, but they were pulling back.

Rawlings ran back to the gunner, checked he was still alive, then used his belt and the loader's to swiftly bind the German hand and foot. He looked up as Walters joined him. "The officers," he said simply and ran from the clearing, Mauser out. Walters drew his Nagant and followed him. As they neared the officers' position Rawlings called up to Rowley: "Did you get them?"

"One," came the reply. "The big one. Other bugger dived out of sight like a hot rivet. I reckon he's still close."

"Keep your eyes open," Rawlings replied, then motioned Walters to cover him as he moved cautiously into the copse. The dark-haired officer lay on his back, a bloody hole in the centre of his forehead. Rawlings searched his pockets quickly. Nothing but a Walther pistol and a set of papers proclaiming him to be Hamluk Irzin, a farm labourer from Edirne. He looked more like a Swabian blacksmith. Rawlings pocketed papers and pistol, then motioned Walters to join him. "I think the other one's our top man. I want him alive too. His tracks head down to the right. I'll get him, you cover me." Walters nodded and they moved off again. Rawlings stole a quick glance at his watch and was amazed to see that barely two minutes had elapsed since he had fired the flare.

The tracks were easy to follow. Their man was in a hurry to get away. Within a few seconds they saw him, crouched in a thicket of bracken just under the crest of the downward slope, a few yards from the road. He had a Walther in one hand, a small metallic object in the other. Rawlings motioned Walters to take up a covering position and wormed through the bracken to a bank just above and to the right of the German, moving a long way from his original position to reach his quarry's blind side. The German raised the metallic object to his mouth. Rawlings saw what it was and began to run. Too late. Three short whistle blasts and then the roar of truck engines split the morning air.

Rawlings jumped, hitting the officer square on as he turned at the noise from above. Rawlings' left arm smashed into his mouth, slamming the whistle back in, splitting lips and gums. His left leg hit the officer's right arm and the Walther spun away. Then they went down in a tangle of arms and legs, Rawlings on top, one hand on the neck.

The Mauser was in the other and he aimed a stunning blow to the German's head with it. But the German's left arm came up, hitting Rawlings' just below the elbow. Agony paralysed Rawlings' right arm and he dropped the Mauser. Then both the German's fists slammed into Rawlings' kidneys. Rawlings gasped and his hold loosened. The officer grabbed Rawlings' left hand and twisted it away savagely, weight fully behind him as he threw Rawlings off. Rawlings rolled back as the officer stood up; tall, broad and powerful, eyes cold below the ruffled blond hair. He aimed a kick under Rawlings' jaw and Rawlings turned away just in time. It connected with the neck and shoulder, not fatal but enough to send him flying back six feet, to hit the ground winded.

The officer grabbed his Walther – then dived headlong as Walters fired from the edge of the slope. He came up shooting back, three rapid shots forcing Walters to duck, two more at Rawlings diving into cover. Then he was gone. The roar of engines grew louder. Then around a bend in the road came three trucks, like Vasily's but with tarpaulin covers stretched over the rear. The officer ran out, firing wildly at his attackers and the first truck braked sharply to let him clamber into the cab, machine-guns in the rear of all three raking the trees as they sped away again.

As soon as they were out of sight Rawlings jumped up and started after them. Walters emerged from cover at the run too. "Where the hell were you?" Rawlings shouted. "I said cover me."

"How can I do that when I didn't know where you were, crawlin' out of position like that. Couldn't see you clearly 'til the bludger stood up. Don't try playing Tarzan next time."

Rawlings stopped and stared hard at him, then relaxed. "Yeah, I moved too far away. But I wanted to make sure I got the bastard alive. Still, spilt milk and all that. Time's a-wasting." He turned and ran up the road, then down into the valley, Walters pelting after him. As they started down the slope, Rowley appeared to their left, rifle smoking. Rawlings' Mauser came up, then lowered. "Get anything?"

Rowley shook his head. "No target with the tarpaulins up. They were moving too fast to get the drivers or the tyres, and ordinary bullets don't do much to the chassis. But that's not all this baby takes; I'm loaded for bear now."

Rawlings patted him on the shoulder and all three ran on for the camp. "Might still be some left in the cave, I reckon. I just hope Curtis has realised we need transport."

Curtis had. When the trucks screamed into the valley his men had been at the lumber piles and had ducked for cover when the MGs opened up. Two of the trucks had stopped to pick up the survivors while the third screened them. The tarpaulin was off this one now, and the machine-gunner and two men with Schmeissers in the back had a clear field of fire to keep the Britons' heads down. But by now Rowley was at the head of the path, a clear shot in front of him. The machine-gunner never even saw the bullet that blew the back of his head open. The two other men in the back turned round – to take the next two bullets in the heart. The two lead trucks accelerated away and Curtis seized his chance. Covering fire from O'Hare and Mayhew kept all heads down as he raced across the yard to the third truck. Nagant out, one bullet into the left side of the cab, driver down, onto the running board, door wrenched open with one hand, Nagant in the other, shooting the cab passenger as he tried to take the wheel. Then both hands on the wheel, turning it into the yard and braking to a stop.

The other two trucks were long gone, up the road into the far slopes of the valley, Britons pouring fire after them and only one or two survivors managing to return it. By the time Rowley, Walters and Rawlings reached the valley floor it was all over. The bodies of their attackers and Vasily's men lay all around. The house was an uninhabitable wreck and small fires burned everywhere. Curtis manoeuvred the truck into the centre of the yard as the rest of the team tended minor wounds or collected equipment from the corpses.

Rawlings simply said: "Good work, captain," then turned as Mayhew marched up to him, for all the world as though he were on the Pirbright parade ground, and saluted. "No more casualties, sir. Just the nine... Russians and Captain Chalmers, plus Second-Lieutenant Emerson wounded of course. Fifteen of their men down, plus any you accounted for. I estimate about a dozen got away, couple of them wounded."

"Yes, Sarn't-Major." Rawlings drew a grimy hand across his bloodstained forehead. "A few too many, I think we'll all agree. And their commander among them."

"Still more of them down than us, sir," Mayhew said diffidently. "And I don't think we'll see the rest around for a while."

"No, not for a while, Sarn't-Major. But we might one day – and if that day comes we'd better be a lot more prepared for them. Anyway, two men come with me."

He cut back into the trees abruptly, Hawkins and Mitchell following, equally tired and bruised but still alert for any danger. They reached what was left of the MG nest just as the gunner was trying to get up and realising his hands and feet were bound. He pulled himself to a kneeling position, then saw the three men advancing towards him. He shrugged his shoulders and waited for them to come on. His throat worked tensely, but he made no sound. "Good morning, Hans," Rawlings shouted in German. "Now, do you mind telling me why you're not busy throwing the *untermensch* out of Stalingrad." He took two quick steps forward and kicked the gunner in the face.

∾

When the gunner awoke he was in a clearing again but he knew it was far from the target. The pines were sparser, the slopes steeper and narrower all round. A stream was flowing nearby. The watery sun had moved further upwards in the pale grey sky. He guessed he had been out for about half an hour. His head hurt like hell.

He was lying in the centre of the clearing. There was

a gag in his mouth and his hands and feet had been tied properly now. The rope had been soaked in water but only just, the bonds did not really hurt yet. Any escape would have been impossible, he knew that, but just in case the enemy had a man standing over him, silenced pistol pointing to his head. The rest were ranged before him, standing, sitting or squatting in a rough semi-circle. The dark, broken-nosed bastard who was obviously in charge stood up and walked towards him slowly. "Put him up on his knees, Garside," he said and the guard obeyed quickly and efficiently. The leader kept walking, until he stood directly in front of the gunner.

"Welcome back to reality," he said amiably. "And the reality is that you're a long way from home with no-one to help you. We need some information and we're in a hurry. If you want to talk just nod twice and the gag comes off." The gunner made no move. Rawlings took half a step back and kicked him in the chest. The gunner was hurled six feet backwards by the impact, falling on his back, but a soft grunt of pain was the only sound he made, even when Rawlings stood over him and stamped on his stomach. "Sorry – didn't quite catch that."

Still no move. Rawlings kicked him again, in the face this time, then stamped down on his genitals. This time there was a high-pitched scream, muffled by the gag, and a thin trickle of blood from where the gunner had bitten his lips. But nothing more. Rawlings knelt beside him and said patiently: "Tell us who you are, who sent you, how you knew where to find us and whether there are any more of you in Turkey. Do all that and you might just live. Otherwise this will go on until you are dead. Your choice."

The gunner looked at him blankly, eyes devoid of any emotion. Rawlings clicked his tongue irritably and rose to his feet, turning towards Vasily, who stood at the outer edge of the group. "Chalmers told me you're a good man with a knife." In reply the Russian drew a long, razor-sharp blade with a serrated top edge. "Tickle him up a bit; show we really aren't mucking about. Leave the mouth and throat alone unless he changes his mind about talking. Apart from that, do as you like. You know the drill." He looked at his watch. "Time to call Cairo. If he decides to talk, get someone to fetch me. O'Hare, bring the transmitter."

The two men exited the clearing, moving through the pines to a tiny gulley next to the stream, away from the tall trees which would have interfered with reception, but affording excellent cover. As nine o'clock, the time selected for their first 'sked' broadcast that day, arrived O'Hare tuned in to the correct frequency, then transmitted the coded message that Rawlings had written out for him:

Lords calling Headingley. Grey team have entered the game. Opened the bowling 0800 hours. Chalmers out, and all the home team except the captain. Emerson injured. Request further details on grey team. And how they got news of fixture.

It took several minutes, but O'Hare was used to broadcasting quickly. It was standard procedure for agents on longer-term missions and Davies had decided to keep the same policy on this crucial day; the next 'sked' was due for five in the afternoon, after the preliminary reconnaissance. When he had finished he took off the headphones and lay flat on the bank. Rawlings knelt beside him and offered him a cigarette. O'Hare took a long and grateful pull at it. "Chasing shadows again, eh, Alex?"

"Indeed." Rawlings' brow was furrowed as he took a cigarette out and held it in cupped hands. "This was supposed to be a secret to everyone but us, Davies and the top three at SOE. How the hell could the Krauts have found out about it?"

"You don't think it's one of our boys, do you?"

Rawlings looked at him. "If it is, we're sunk. I don't want to believe it – all their records were checked closer than anyone's before they were selected. And there's never been a traitor in SOE."

"Not one that we've found, you mean," O'Hare replied. "And if they had got someone in they wouldn't want him to show his hand – until a really big job like this came up."

Rawlings nodded. "In that case, we don't have to look far for our prime suspect; Curtis."

O'Hare turned to look Rawlings in the eye, astonished. "You can't mean that, Alex? Jesus, his mother's family were Jews. The stormtroopers wiped them out."

"So Curtis says."

"And his mother. She's been in this country since the early Twenties."

"Yes, 1920 to be exact. The year the Abwehr was really beginning to get active. They had reports about it in the Home Section. Rumours of agents being sent in with impeccable backgrounds – phoney ones. Designed not to arouse suspicions, and with instructions to work their way into British society completely. Well, if Mrs

Curtis was one of them, she certainly did that. All the information on the German side of Curtis' life comes from her. I've seen the files too, Conor – and the photograph of her. You've never seen a less Jewish-looking woman in your life."

"Even so – turning your son into an agent too? Getting him to hide all that from his father?"

"Curtis was never close to his father – he's admitted that himself. And he spent every summer holiday up until 1938, the last one before *Kristallnacht*, in Germany. With his mother. Daddy never came, and Curtis never spoke much about it. What if those last few holidays were spent doing a bit more than cycling round the churches?"

"Ah, but look at all the work he's done for us since he joined up, in the Middle East and everything? He's a hero."

"Oh, yes – just the kind of shining young paladin we like. But I saw something else in his files. Six months ago he got into a fight in an officer's mess in Jerusalem. Had an argument with one of the Palestine Commando Battalion boys about Zionism. The other fellow started it, but when it got serious they had to pull Curtis off him – and half a dozen witnesses heard him say that talk like that was the curse of the race."

O'Hare shook his head. "That's thin gruel, Alex. Plenty of Jews don't side with the Zionists. Nor do our lads – especially when they get the lie of the land out there. Besides, look at what he did today, grabbing that truck for us and all."

"It was impressive, I'll give you that. But he did it when he knew the strike was blown. As if he was trying to get in my good books. Before that all he'd done was shot one man in the heat of the moment – and tried to kill another before he talked. All I'm saying is I'll watch him closely from now on, and you should too."

"For sure. But I hope you're wrong. I like the lad – and if he is on their payroll it sure as hell won't make the job any easier."

"Say that again and a third time in Gaelic," Rawlings said bitterly. "Something about it doesn't ring true, though. And I'm not saying that because I like the lad, too. If it was a traitor in SOE, Curtis or anyone else, why weren't the Krauts waiting for us the minute we arrived at the drop zone? There was plenty of time before we left to tip them off. And why not come at us with everything but the kitchen sink?"

"Fear of being discovered, sparking a diplomatic row with the Turks?"

Rawlings shook his head. "If Ziedler's running this show – and since he wanted to get out of France without letting Hoffman have another crack at me, I reckon he is – he likes to make sure of things. And he'll have more than a platoon at his disposal."

"Maybe the rest are all off rescuing Vlasenin?"

Rawlings nodded grimly. "There is that, of course. So do we steam in, as Corporal Walters so eloquently advised us, to make sure we're first? Or stick to the game plan and risk Ziedler getting in before us? Or put the whole thing off for a day to find the grey team and make sure they never take the field again?" He frowned suddenly. "It could even be the red team – if SOE has a traitor like SIS then they could be planting info to get us at each other's throats, give them more time to crack Vlasenin or get him away."

"I'd say Walters is prime suspect if that's what it is," O'Hare said with obvious reluctance. "So what would we do then?"

Rawlings gave a grim smile. "Go in hard, like he said. But I wouldn't be worrying about not hurting the consulate guards. The more shooting there is the more chance one of our boys goes down – the right one. Trouble is, I like the moaning Aussie even more than Curtis." He gave an exclamation that was half-sigh, half-laugh. "Jesus, Conor, how did we get into this line of work?"

"Our youths weren't misspent enough, I reckon. We grew up bad bastards who still believed in something good. So I think the Boy Upstairs decided to play a little joke on us."

"You could be right – though I've never heard Davies called that before."

They both laughed, then O' Hare said: "Not really much of an answer, is it?"

"Better than any I've ever come up with." As if on cue, the radio began to transmit Davies' reply. *Stick to original tour schedule. Will try to arrange reserve player. No information on grey team or their scout, but will keep looking.* "And no answers from Cairo on the really important question," Rawlings said with a wry smile. "But maybe Fast-Talking Freddie back there's started giving us some. Let's find out."

When they re-entered the clearing the rest of the team were looking much less impassive. Vasily had cut the gunner to ribbons. Rawlings knew the tricks to be used in these situations. He had even passed on a few learned from the Pathans. But some of his team obviously did not. Only Walters' face was still set in merciless indifference.

Curtis was shaking as he walked up to his commander. "Sir, is this... butchery really necessary?"

"Yes, if it helps keep us alive," Rawlings replied. "I've seen worse, captain, and done worse. And so will you if you stay in this game much longer. However, it doesn't seem to have been too effective so far. Still no sound?" He asked Vasily; the big Russian merely shook his head.

Rawlings shrugged: "OK, so we know they know we're in Turkey, and almost certainly they know why too. So we keep an eye out for the survivors of his bunch and any others who may be around. But now it's even more important we complete the mission as quickly as possible. That will mean a few adjustments." He looked at the torn, bleeding body of the gunner. "But none of that is for his ears, so..."

Vasily reached for the man's throat, but Rawlings held up a hand. "Walters, you do it. Use the garotte." The little Australian moved forward. Rawlings knelt down by the gunner, who had listened with a grim smile, and ripped off the gag. "You can still talk. Tell us where the rest of your party are, tell us what their plans are and we'll keep you safe until after we're done then hand you over to the Turks. They'll intern you and you'll be out of the war." His voice softened a little. "You deserve that after what we've done to you."

The gunner's ruined body shook softly as he spoke for the first time. His voice was cracked and slurred with pain but the English was clear and almost accentless. "Don't make me laugh, Major Rawlings. It hurts too damn much. You cut me to pieces then talk to me like a soldier. Fuck you all." His voice rose as he addressed the whole party. "You don't have any fucking idea how much we know. If you did you'd give up now. Keep going, and I'll see you all in Hell tomorrow." Then he spat at Rawlings' feet.

Rawlings stepped back and nodded as Walters stood over the gunner. "Here we go, mate," Walters said. "Up on your knees. No, back towards me. That's it. Just keep still and you won't feel... nothing."

Even before the gunner's body went limp the team were beginning to board the truck. As Walters hauled himself in Garside said bitterly: "Very concerned for his welfare there, weren't you?"

The Australian looked at him with eyes like flint. "He deserved it – after all that shit with the knife. Whoever he's working for or why, he did his duty and took his medicine. That's all most of us can hope for – and I wonder how many would have taken it as well."

Vasily started the engine and the truck roared out of the forest and turned onto the road for Istanbul.

∾

The sentry was dead before he even knew he was being attacked. The Fairbairn knife pierced the skin just behind the right ear and found the brain within a fraction of a second. As the body slumped to the ground, strong hands grabbed it, one pair lowering it to the ground almost gently and dragging it into the shadows while two others pulled away the cap and greatcoat. Within seconds the fourth man had taken them, and the rifle, recommencing the sentry's patrol around the consulate grounds. He was the same height and build as the sentry – hours of watching and comparing every member of the team had seen to that – but he still stole a quick glance at the sentry on the opposite side, alert for any sign of alarm. No problem. He had been given the same treatment. And the guards at the main gate had obviously heard nothing. Their eyes were still trained on the street beyond.

There was the noise of a car approaching. A Russian staff car. It braked to a halt just before the gate. The sentries were immediately alert but then they saw two senior army officers, flanked by two guards, get out and they hesitated before challenging them. They looked so purposeful, especially when one of them shouted: "Open the gates – now!" in fluent, Muscovite Russian. Everyone had heard the rumours that some top brass or NKVD would be coming to take the stubborn old bastard inside away to Moscow. They did not open the gates but they moved closer to check the visitors' ID papers. And that made the pistol shots easy.

The silenced Tokarevs coughed twice. As the gate guards' bodies dropped to the ground, the officers caught them and manoeuvred them back towards the gate. One of the officers fished inside a guard's tunic and found the keys to the gate. Within seconds it was open and they were through, dragging the guards towards the consulate's doorway. The guards who had accompanied them took up station at the main gate, waving the staff car through. It parked in front of the doorway, partially shielding the six men who had dealt with the sentries as they darted through the shadows, reached the door and pulled it open.

They burst in, submachine-guns at the ready. But the main reception area was empty. The few regular consulate staff on Saturday duty had long since left for their apartments nearby. Behind them came the two officers, throwing the dead guards' bodies to the ground as soon as they were inside. The eight men moved quickly through the reception area and down a long corridor. The officers took the lead. The rest were not in Russian uniform. That would have been too conspicuous as they scaled the walls into the grounds. But now it was imperative that they were not seen first.

At the end of the corridor was a metal door with a small glass window set high up in it. An intercom was set into the wall to its right. This was the entrance to the torture room and cells. They had studied copies of the official blueprints and contacts among the Turkish workers who cleaned and maintained the building had filled in the gaps. Inside was Vlasenin – and Amarazov.

One of the officers switched on the intercom. "Colonel Yugarin, GRU. From Moscow. We've come to take the prisoner away."

A sleepy, suspicious voice answered. "We've heard nothing about this."

The officer put just the right note of lordly impatience into his reply. "Did you expect an official motorcade? If we had told too many in advance the British might have heard of it. Now let us in!"

There was the sound of footsteps on the other side of the door. "Show yourself,'" the voice said. The officer pressed his face right against the window. The second officer was partly obscured, and the six men in camouflage uniforms with weapons at the ready were completely invisible. He held up the forged papers supporting his identity. That was all he had. If Renkovich or Amarazov had insisted on any other paperwork then it would have to be the grenades.

A face appeared on the other side of the window. A broad, brutal face but with a gleam of intelligence in the eyes. His tunic, hastily buttoned on, bore a sergeant's stripes. He looked at the papers, then spoke into the intercom again. "Very well – Comrade Colonel. Come through."

The door swung open and the officers walked through briskly. The sergeant, and a small, tired-looking private stood back at attention. As the first officer approached the sergeant, papers in one hand, he pulled the Tokarev from its holster with the other and hit the sergeant full on the temple with its butt. The sergeant dropped as if poleaxed as the second officer unleashed a lethal karate chop at the second guard's throat. Half a second later the six camouflage raiders burst through the doorway.

It was the main guardroom. Two more men were seated at a table playing cards. The rest were sleeping in bunks lined along each wall. The two at the card table rose to their feet – then sat down again as they found themselves staring down the barrels of two Tokarevs and six submachine-guns. The first officer pressed a finger to his lips in the universal gesture for silence and they obeyed, as did the men on the bunks as they woke up to find themselves dragged into the centre of the room.

While the camouflage raiders kept them covered the two officers moved to a door on the far side of the room. This one had no window but they knew now that beyond could only be Vlasenin's cell and Amarazov's quarters. The door was not locked. Beyond it was another corridor ending in another doorway. This one had two guards stationed outside. They looked up as they saw the two officers striding towards them. This time there was no challenge at all. The guards reasoned that anyone who had got this far into the secret section must be the Moscow big shots of which the rumours had spoken. Their killers were close enough to touch them when the silenced Tokarevs coughed again.

As the first officer motioned two of the camouflage raiders to join him the second moved to a doorway ten yards back along the corridor, on the right-hand side. He tried the door. It was locked. That made sense. Amarazov was very conscious of personal security. He kicked the door open and hit the light as he strode in. There was a table with a chair beside it and a radio transmitter on it, and a bed in the far corner. Amarazov was sitting bolt upright in it, one hand under the covers, the other shielding his eyes from the sudden light. The second officer raised his finger to his lips in the universal gesture again.

Vlasenin's first thought was the same as everyone's had been. They had finally come to take him to Moscow. An officer flanked by two guards, arriving in the middle of the night. The only puzzling thing was that the guards were in camouflage uniform, not standard infantry issue. It was of no consequence. He was doomed. So too was the rest of humanity. His only hope was that they never found the papers.

He made no effort to resist, merely staying slumped on the metal bed as they came to him. He barely even had the strength to speak now. Then he saw the looks of compassion on every face, the muted gasps of horror, the lowered weapons. A hope he had thought gone forever began to rise in him. "Are you…"

"Your delivering angels, Comrade Doctor," the first officer said. "Major Alexander Rawlings, Special Operations Executive. You speak some English, I believe?"

"Why, yes – I do. I spent some time in England in 1933, doing research work."

"That's right – the Clarendon Laboratory at Oxford University, as I recall from your file."

"No – it was the Cavendish Laboratory, in Cambridge. But it was…" he stopped as the officer gave a light, ironic laugh. An English laugh. It sounded so utterly alien in the torture room that Vlasenin wondered if he was going mad. Then Rawlings spoke again, smiling so widely that even the eyes joined in.

"Of course – just our way of making sure you really are who you say you are. Though I doubt even Amarazov would go to the trouble of half-killing an impostor. Right, shall we go, then?"

"You mean…" the hope was soaring now.

"You're free, Doctor Vlasenin," Rawlings said gently, then added with a touch of steel: "host's generosity permitting, of course. Which means we need to hurry."

"Yes, of course." Vlasenin tried to rise from the bed, but his legs failed him. The two camouflage raiders took an arm apiece and half-walked, half-dragged him out of the cell. Rawlings followed them. As they passed Amarazov's room he nodded to the second officer, who turned back to Amarazov and took aim very deliberately. "Tell me, Comrade Major," he said in English, "what's the Russian word for 'goodbye'"?

"*Dasvidanya,*" Amarazov said and shot him through the heart. Always a light sleeper, Amarazov had been rendered almost insomniac by the pressures of the last few days. He had heard the booted feet in the corridor and been immediately suspicious but had only just had time to grab the Tokarev from its habitual place under his pillow and cover it with the blanket.

This Tokarev was not silenced. The noise of the shot rang around the room and the corridor beyond as the second officer was slammed against the wall and slid to the floor, a look of astonishment on his face. By then Amarazov was already diving across the room. He fired round the corner of the doorway, lying prone, only his head and gun arm visible. Accurate aiming was impossible, but by chance he caught one of the camouflage raiders in the back. He cried out and fell, dragging Vlasenin and the other man down with him. Rawlings turned and squeezed off half a dozen shots, forcing Amarazov to duck back into his room once again. When the Russian poked his head round the corner again he saw a grenade rolling down the corridor towards him. He dived back inside, upending the table to shield him as the door was blown into the room.

The two rescuers burst through the door to the guardroom. Rawlings had hold of Vlasenin now, motioning two men to grab him as they moved to the connecting door. The surviving camouflage raider followed, submachine-gun still trained on the corridor beyond in case Amarazov should reappear. He threw another grenade in and then turned to follow the rest. The other four camouflage raiders backed towards the door, guns still trained on the guards. Rawlings turned and gave them a 'thumbs down' signal. "Hope your victims are waiting for you in Hell, comrades," one of them shouted in English. Then they all opened fire.

The screams of the guards echoed behind them as they followed the raiding party along the corridor, then sprinted through the reception area and to the main door. The two bogus sentries had moved back to the doorway and covered the raiding party left and right as they moved towards the car, which had turned and was pointing towards the main gate, engine revving. "Sure you made enough noise back there?" said one of the sentries to Rawlings as they emerged into the consulate courtyard.

"Couldn't be helped," he replied. "But – watch out!" He fired his pistol one-handed to the left just as firing broke out all around them. Six or seven Russian soldiers were moving up from a long low building to the left of the main consulate. One of the camouflage raiders went down, shot through the head. Another clutched at his leg and fell to the ground. "I thought you said you'd barricaded the door."

"Not well enough," the sentry said as they all swung round to return fire, forcing the soldiers into cover. "Where the hell's that truck?" Rawlings shouted. As if in reply a low-pitched roar added to the crackle of small arms fire and the distant wail of police sirens. A truck emerged from the shadows, turning broadside through the gates and screeching to a halt next to the staff car. As the officer bundled Vlasenin into the car the rest of the raiding party scrambled aboard the truck, firing wildly to keep the guards' heads down as they did. Two men tried to reach their wounded comrade but the intensity of the return fire drove them back. As they hauled themselves into the back the truck turned and roared through the gateway and across the boulevard to the warren of streets beyond.

The staff car followed but before it could clear the gateway a bullet shattered the rear window. Vlasenin turned, to see Amarazov at the main doorway, aiming straight at him. Rawlings pushed Vlasenin down in his seat and fired through the shattered glass, forcing Amarazov to dive for cover. The sight of the GRU man's face, contorted with anger and fear, was the last thing Vlasenin saw before he fainted.

Amarazov picked himself up and ran to the main gate. The wounded raider tried to reach for his weapon as he approached. Amarazov shot him in the head without breaking stride. As he reached the gate, the consulate guards ran to meet him, the captain in charge at their head. His hand and voice trembled as he saluted and said: "Comrade Major, I beg to report that we could do nothing. They locked us in and…"

"And you let them!" Amarazov's rage-contorted features were bathed in the yellow street lights. "If we are not all to be in Stalingrad by Monday, Comrade Captain, I suggest we get after those bastards."

He turned and ran to the gateway – only to be confronted by a barricade of police cars. At least twenty policemen were advancing through the gateway. At least half of them were armed. And all of them seemed strongly disinclined to let Amarazov's pursuit begin.

∞

Vlasenin woke from a troubled sleep to find that the convoy was stationary at last, parked in a wooded clearing surrounded by high mountains. The first grey streaks of dawn were appearing in the sky. As he looked around more he could see that truck and staff car were parked in an 'L' shape, with the car forming the lower stem. Behind the shelter of the two vehicles he could see his rescue party brewing coffee and talking. Sentries patrolled the edge of the clearing. Rawlings had a large map spread out next to the fire and was talking with two other men. Like all the rest he was now wearing civilian clothing.

Slowly the events of last night came back to Vlasenin. First the frantic dash through the streets of Istanbul, glimpsed as he recovered consciousness. His rescuers had changed out of their uniforms then, the drivers doing so even as they swung the wheels this way and that and the maze of streets gradually thinned out. Once they had encountered a police roadblock but the truck had simply bulldozed a way through while the men inside fired in the air to send the policemen diving for cover.

They had twisted and turned, doubling back on themselves more than once to find the quietest byroads out of the city. And once out they had continued to mask their trail, as they headed ever further out into the country. Vlasenin's knowledge of that part of Turkey was vague and he had long since lost all sense of direction. Eventually he had followed Rawlings' advice and got some sleep.

It had been a broken sort of sleep, disturbed by the rhythm of the car and the bumpy, untravelled country roads they had used. But it had done him some good. His body still ached, but his mind was rested and alert. And he knew there was something he must tell them very soon. With some difficulty he opened the car door and stepped out.

Rawlings saw him and immediately ran to help him, leading him to the fire and placing an enamel mug in his hand. "Not real coffee, I'm afraid, Doctor Vlasenin. Not even in Turkey." He laughed that laugh again. "But it should still perk you up."

"Thank you." Vlasenin took a mouthful as he sat down by the fire. "Where are we?"

"A long way from Istanbul, if that's what you're worried about. In the south-west corner of European Turkey. Not far from where a plane will be coming to pick us up tomorrow, the one that will fly you to Cyprus, then on to England. But, as I don't need to tell you, we need something else before we can leave."

"Ah, yes, my papers. Of course. In fact, I was coming to tell you where they are."

He leaned towards the map. At that moment firing broke out on the edge of the clearing. One of the sentries cried out and fell, rolling down the slope. The other ran behind the truck, firing behind him as the air was suddenly alive with bullets.

"Get down!" Rawlings shouted to Vlasenin as he ran to the natural barricade formed by the vehicles. But there was firing from behind them too. Suddenly there was a noise from the trees and two German soldiers broke from cover, charging towards the fire. One aimed his rifle at Vlasenin.

Rawlings whirled, pistol out, and shot them both in the head. Then he ran into the open, hands spread wide and shouted. "*Breslau! Breslau! Nicht schiessen! Wir sind die Brandenburgen!*"

The firing died down, then stopped altogether.

More German soldiers emerged, including a young man wearing a peaked cap. Rawlings strode across the clearing to berate him, pointing to Vlasenin several times. Vlasenin could not catch the words, but he was definitely speaking in German. Vlasenin moved towards Rawlings – then stopped as he saw that all his rescuers now had their weapons pointing at him.

Rawlings ended his tirade by pushing the young officer away and turning to walk towards Vlasenin. For the first time Vlasenin got a really good look at him. He was tall, well over six feet, with a shock of thick chestnut-coloured hair and vivid grey eyes. The same eyes that had smiled so vividly last night as he took him from his cell. But they were not smiling now, as he said: "Oberst Ulrich Ziedler of the Abwehr at your service, Doctor Vlasenin. I know you speak our language, too. Welcome to German-occupied Greece."

Chapter 5

Rapid Response

RAWLINGS HAD HAD SOME EXPERIENCE of prison cells in his career, and the Turkish variety compared well with some. But the time he had spent in this one had been the most frustrating twelve hours of his life.

He should have known that to approach Istanbul was to walk into danger. If the operation was so compromised as to allow a German raiding party to target their safe house within twelve hours of arrival, then it was more than likely that the Turkish authorities had been apprised of the SOE's presence, probably by Ziedler as a back-up in case of the raiding party's failure. But there had been little alternative. The emergence of the grey team had rendered time even more of the essence than before. Vlasenin had to be sprung before the Germans got in first – or the Russians made him talk.

But the group had still proceeded with caution. Firstly, a trip to a nearby village where Vasily knew the local garage owner had procured a back-up vehicle. The ancient Lancia saloon had clearly seen better days, but it was sufficient for the task of getting Yelena to the rendezvous. Fortunately both radios had survived the German fusillade; her job was to use the SOE transmitter to keep in touch with Cairo and with the Istanbul group during the vital hours of the strike and flight, broadcasting at the 'sked' times using the SOE code and keeping the channel open for any messages from the other end, especially those with information on how the Germans had known the group's location.

That had always been the plan, though originally it had been envisaged that four of Vasily's men would accompany her for extra security. For all her eagerness to help, and the undoubted fighting qualities she had displayed during the ambush, she would have been too conspicuous in the raiding party. In addition, she spoke better English even than Vasily. Rawlings was relieved – his desire to have her as far away from immediate danger as possible had doubled since he had first seen her.

Once she was on her way, the rest of the group, still crammed into the truck they had liberated from the Germans, had headed for Istanbul. Rawlings had decided against splitting the force as originally planned; if it came to another fight he would need all the men he had at his disposal.

They had kept to back roads as long as they could. But they had to get to the heart of the city, where the garage with the staff car was located. To do so it was necessary to either take the coast road in, use one of the Golden Horn bridges further north, or cross the Kagithane river and approach from the northern suburbs. Rawlings had decided the last option would be less busy and offer more potential escape routes.

He would never know if the Turks had positioned over a hundred police and soldiers on every bridge into Istanbul – but that was certainly what greeted the SOE party just after noon on Saturday, November 21st, 1942. They were not immediately visible of course, but as soon as the truck was half-way across they converged from a dozen hiding places. Vasily's efforts, aided by Costas and Stavrakis, to bluff a way through, came to nothing as soon as one of the officers challenged Garside to say exactly which village in Turkey he hailed from. Rawlings put his hands up and ordered his men to do the same, thankful that he had left the vital briefcase with Yelena but acutely aware that was the only thing he had got right so far.

Within minutes they were inside the walls of a large police station in the northern suburbs. There they were separated and taken to individual cells. Rawlings had waited, hoping to see the SOE's station head, de Chastelain, arrive soon – or at least a British Consulate official. Instead his only visitor was a small, dapper police inspector named Bahir who introduced himself in fluent English, then assured Rawlings that his best course of action was to confess everything about his gang's plan to rob the Topkapi Palace.

Rawlings had to hand it to Ziedler, if indeed he was in charge of all this. He had rendered the SOE team *hors de combat* but at the same time ensured that the Soviet Consulate did not become the focus of undue attention. And the tale that Bahir told him was undoubtedly inventive. Rawlings' men were prisoners of war who had escaped to Turkey, with two Greek bandits to guide them, fallen in with criminal elements among the Russian émigré population and decided to stage an audacious raid on the Imperial Treasury with the objective of stealing the Topkapi Dagger and other priceless items.

Inventive – but plausible also. Not every British PoW who found himself on neutral soil had made a beeline for the White Cliffs. And often the ones who lingered had joined the local criminal fraternity. No doubt the Abwehr had sufficiently embedded contacts in every sphere of Turkish life to ensure that news of Rawlings' arrival had seemed like nothing more than a straightforward police informant's tip-off. It exploited the resentment of the British that had lingered since Lloyd George's interference in the Twenties. It invoked the symbol of the Ottoman Empire's power and magnificence, to which many still looked back with nostalgia. And it made scapegoats of the Turks' two least favourite neighbours – the Greeks and the Russians.

All in all, quite a coup for Inspector Bahir. So he was naturally displeased when Rawlings told him that there was not an ounce of truth to the story, and urged him to contact the British Consulate and mount guard on the Soviet one as soon as possible. Bahir told Rawlings what he thought of his advice, advised him once again to confess, then left him alone in his cell.

And there he had stayed for the rest of the day, and long into the night. His admiration for Ziedler's ingenious yarn soon gave way to the cold realisation that it had placed Britain out of the game. Bahir would try to get the confession out of his prisoners before he involved any official channels, and he was clever enough to know that keeping them apart to sweat in their cells was a safer, neater and possibly quicker way of getting results than applying the tactics of a Hoffman or Amarazov. Solid police procedure – except that Rawlings and his men had nothing to confess. So the impasse would last at least all day and the following night; ample time for Ziedler to mount a rescue or for Amarazov's interrogation to finally bear fruit. By the time the SOE team was released their mission might no longer exist.

Rawlings tried not to let that thought eat away at him, but as the evening wore on – the only break in the monotony coming when an armed guard brought in some bread and meat, with a tin cup of water to wash it down – he could not help feeling that the mission seemed destined to go down as one of failure from start to finish. And he knew enough of what Vlasenin's secret was to realise what that might mean for the rest of the war, and the rest of the world.

Could he have handled it better? Had he been wrong to head straight for Istanbul? Why had he wasted time and inflicted torture on a man who had merely done his duty, an exercise that had yielded nothing anyway? Not for the first time he found himself wondering why he had ended up in this strange line of work – not quite a soldier, not quite a spy, able to move unseen through a dozen different countries but truly at home in none of them.

And of course thoughts like that led to thoughts of Angela. At first his job and his reputation had intrigued and attracted her. The more so because he could never tell their friends (hers more than his, truth be told) exactly what he did. In those two years he had been a junior Foreign Office employee whose work involved a fair amount of travel. This enabled Angela's exquisite literary dinner guests to patronise him unmercifully. He had accepted that, because it gave him access to a glittering world – parties in every corner of fashionable London, weekends away in country houses, at the races or Brooklands. One night they had walked home along the Embankment. It was a perfect English summer's evening, the darkness lit by the row of lights that seemed to make a necklace for their elegant, beautiful city. The scent of summer mingled with her perfume as he kissed her. A few memories like that were all he had left now. Even if he had wanted to he could not contact her again, as it might compromise his work.

It was the work that had begun that long, slow destruction. At first she complained about the amount of his time that the job demanded. Then she complained about the job itself. They grew apart, each determined not to give any ground. And then his talent for uncovering secrets came into play when he least wanted it to. It was a basic task, in intelligence terms. The initial information was gleefully related to him by Angela's friends. Routine surveillance and more checks from independent sources confirmed its veracity.

She did not bother to deny it. There was no glorious, tempestuous Rhett and Scarlett quarrel leading to a reconcilement at the bedroom door. Just two people realising their relationship was over. The separation had been amicable; there were no children, no arguments about property or possessions. It had all been handled in a very proper English fashion – and when it was over Rawlings felt that the centre of his life had been torn out. He had never filled the aching hollow that Angela had left. The few fleeting liaisons (begun while they were still married as an act of passionless revenge, and continued at increasingly irregular intervals since) had meant nothing. The only time he had felt anything that had held promise of filling the hollow had been last night – from a woman with whom he had nothing in common and who he might never see again. Perhaps Conor was right, and God had selected a pleasantly ironic punishment for someone involved in this line of work.

But it was the work that had saved him in those first few months after Angela left. Keeping him so busy that he had little time to think about her. But when he did her words rang in his brain, leaving a taste of gall and wormwood in his mouth. "Paid assassin for a flawed system"; "Professional meddler without a conscience"; "Pillar of a crumbling castle". What had he ever given to the world? He could not build countries or inspire people to noble ideals – only destroy those who did, if his masters told him to.

He had given as good as he got in those arguments, constantly reminding Angela that his work helped to preserve the things that she and her friends took for granted, pointing to the things he had done in Spain and Abyssinia and a dozen other places to give practical help to freedom fighters when most of the British intelligentsia were content to write articles warmly approving of their efforts. He had scored the points, but her words had lingered and sometimes they returned. He still loved his work, but not unquestioningly. And it had never replaced the hollow that Angela had cut inside him.

To question the mainspring of your life is bad for anyone; for someone in his line of work it could be fatal. He reminded himself time and again of the good he had done, the great evil he was fighting – or not, at the moment. Even his work looked doomed and hopeless now. So the images returned again – the gunner they had cut to pieces that morning leading a parade of the men he had killed and tortured. He tried to banish them from his mind. But all reality yielded was a Turkish prison cell where he sat helpless while the war was lost elsewhere.

And in the other cells his men sat too, trying to keep their darkest thoughts at bay. For Curtis the distance from his father that had only grown wider in the last few years. For Walters the lack of a father or mother from an age too early to be given a number until much later. For O'Hare the memory of family members killed or driven away by the riots of the Thirties. It was that which had spurred him to work for the British but it meant he could never return to the land of his birth. And it had caused him to turn from the only woman he had ever loved. For Vasily a family massacred by the Reds. For Mayhew a wife and child lost to the Blitz. For Costas and Stavrakis the newly opened wounds of returning to the country they knew as home but which had driven their people to exile. For all of them memories of mistakes or tragedies returning, with leisure to plague the mind and weaken the will, with nothing to set against them but the knowledge of imprisonment, the spectre of failure and the chance of death in turn.

༄

Rawlings was woken from a fitful sleep by a light burning his eyes as the bare bulb in his cell flared on. Two prison guards were standing over him. He looked at his watch; 8 a.m. Before he could do anything more the guards were escorting him down a corridor. There was none of the rough stuff they had experienced on arrival and as his brain began to work he wondered what this might signify. Before he could make any speculation they reached the end of the corridor and he was ushered into a large, plain office.

There were three men seated around a desk. The first, who sat behind it, was a tall, handsome man in an immaculate blue serge suit. Rawlings had never seen him before. But he recognised both the men who sat at either side. On the left was the SOE's deputy station head in Turkey, Henderson, who had been de Chastelain's right-hand man in his Romanian oil business and had joined him in the task of making the city the hub of SOE's Balkan operations. On the right was Amarazov.

Before Rawlings could recover from his astonishment, the man behind the desk strode forward and shook him by the hand. "Major Rawlings, allow me to introduce myself," he said in faultless English. "My name is Arif Battakan. I have taken over this investigation from Inspector Bahir, now that… certain information has come to light. Please take a seat."

He drew another chair from the corner of the room, then perched himself on the edge of his desk as Rawlings sat down. All three men were ranged in front of Rawlings now, regarding him intently. At length Battakan spoke: "It appears that you were telling the truth, Major Rawlings. A short time ago the Soviet Consulate was attacked by a raiding force who succeeded in escaping with…"

"Kidnapping," Amarazov broke in. But his gaze never left Rawlings' face.

"As you wish, Major Amarazov." Battakan's already cold and formal voice dropped a few degrees as he replied, "…kidnapping Dr Dimitri Vlasenin. It would appear that the raid was carried out by members of the Royal Marine Commandos."

"That's a damned lie!" Rawlings rose from his feet. "It was the Germans – I told you they were coming!"

"Sit down, major – please." Henderson's voice was the calm Eton and Sandhurst drawl that Rawlings remembered from the Romanian operation, but it had an edge of steel to it now. Rawlings glowered at him, then remembered the delicate position they were all in and sat down. Battakan gave a diplomatic clearing of his throat, then continued.

"Your previous statements to Inspector Bahir have been noted, Major Rawlings. But we now have evidence to substantiate Major Amarazov's assertion." He took a folder from the desk and passed it to Rawlings. Inside were several large black and white photographs. Rawlings' heart sank. They showed three dead bodies laid out in the consulate grounds. They were dressed in the camouflage pattern smocks and trousers common to many special forces units, but the shoulder flashes and the distinctive berets were indeed those of the Commandos.

He looked at Battakan and Amarazov in turn. "Well, they were in disguise, obviously. That's always been one of Ziedler's tricks. You wouldn't expect them to come dressed in full uniform." He looked to Henderson for support as he continued with a wounded air: "The Germans intended to sow seeds of doubt and suspicion between two close allies. Surely you can see that, Comrade Major?"

Amarazov gave a crooked smile at Rawlings' display of innocence, then stuck the knife in. "All I see is that a unit of the British Army has committed an act of war against a friendly power. On neutral territory. I can also show you photographs of another dead man who took part in this monstrous action; he was wearing Russian uniform. I do not know precisely which article of the Geneva Convention that violates; more than one, I suspect.

"If these photographs were to be published to the world at large it would create a scandal," the Russian continued, his flawless English delivered in the cruel, purring tone Rawlings had come to know and detest in Spain. "The international reputation of the United Kingdom and her Armed Forces would be dealt a most bitter blow. Your relations with Communist resistance networks in occupied Europe would be terminated. Your own Labour Party and trade union movement might well consider widespread protest. And," he concluded with a silky smile, "the Soviet Union would be entitled to reconsider the nature of its alliance."

So there it was. A threat pure and simple. Elegantly expressed, as always with Major Yevgeny Amarazov, but a threat nonetheless. Rawlings began to speak, but Henderson got in before him. "Major Amarazov is justifiably outraged at the attack upon the consulate, but I think we must also accept that Major Rawlings' theory is the more plausible. After all, why would we risk such an operation if other avenues could be explored? And if we were to mount an attack, would we really make our men so obviously identifiable?"

"And if you had no such plans why are fifteen of

your agents in Turkey?" Amarazov replied. "All I know is that…"

"And all I know is that once again the Great Powers have used my country as a battleground in their own secret wars," Battakan cut in, looking at all three men with contempt. "It is obvious to me that you both want this man Vlasenin, as do the Germans. That is no concern of ours. But men have died in my city tonight. It is only by great good fortune that none of them were Turkish. If they had been, then I assure you gentlemen that none of you would be leaving Istanbul for a very long time.

"As it is, my government has decided it would be better for all concerned if this regrettable incident is forgotten as soon as possible. Last night's disturbances will be attributed to an aborted raid on a bank vault. A formal announcement will be made denying any truth in the rumours which have been allowed to circulate." He sighed. "Inspector Bahir has already been reduced to the ranks. After which, all that remains," he looked intently at Rawlings, "is to arrange that you and your men leave Turkey as quickly as possible." His gaze swung to Amarazov. "And the same applies to you and your fellow… operatives, Comrade Major, if any of them are still left alive."

Now it was Amarazov's turn to spring to his feet, but Battakan rose from the desk and looked him in the eye. "Believe me, we know everything that has gone on inside your consulate over the past week. Were it not for my government's desire to remain on friendly terms with the Soviet Union you would undoubtedly find yourself facing criminal charges. And I can assure both you… gentlemen that if you are not out of Turkey within twelve hours, or if you attempt to return, you will be interned for the duration of the war.

"That is all I have to say. Mr Henderson has asked for a private interview with you both. Because of his standing within the Istanbul business community we have agreed to this. I shall return in five minutes with the necessary release documents. By then I expect your business to have concluded."

He gathered his papers from the desk, then swept the folder containing the photographs from Rawlings' hand and put it into his briefcase, ignoring Amarazov's protests. "Tough customer," Rawlings said as the sound of the door slammed behind him died away. "Emniyet, I presume?"

"One of their top men," Henderson nodded. "Took me a long time to get him to agree to all this. Gardyne would have done it quicker – but I'm bloody glad he's out of town; this will set our operation back years." He glared at Rawlings. "And you're damned lucky not to be breaking rocks on the far side of Lake Van right this minute, laddie. But now that the Germans have got Vlasenin, there's been a change of plan." He looked at the Russian. "You and Major Amarazov are to both go after him – together."

"Not a chance!" Rawlings shot Amarazov a glance of pure contempt. "He'll kill me and all my men the first opportunity he gets. Whose bright idea was that?"

"Davies' – after a lot of pressure from above on both sides. It's blown open now, Alex, and the best thing we can do is try to stick it back together. All friends again, eh?"

"And if we manage to get Vlasenin back, where does

he go?"

"Back to Russia – but we get a promise of co-operation on anything he…"

"What? You know what they'll do to him! I can't believe Davies agreed to that. Let us go after Vlasenin alone!"

"Do you know where he is, Rawlings?" Amarazov asked, his tone equally contemptuous. "We do. Our Greek partisan contacts saw him arriving at a supplies base just over the border at dawn today. There are at least two hundred troops guarding him, with more stationed close by. Do you think your fifteen men can free him from that? We have an army at our disposal – a Communist army – and I have a plan that can get him out. But we need your help. We will let him live afterwards. He is too valuable for us to do anything else. His condition will be no worse than it was before. And the great Anglo-Soviet alliance will be maintained."

He looked at both men. "I will be waiting for you and your team at the consulate, Rawlings. If you have not arrived within one hour I will go after Vlasenin alone – and news of a British attack on Soviet territory will be immediately relayed throughout the world."

Then he too was gone. Rawlings looked at Henderson. "He's got us over a barrel, hasn't he?"

"Afraid so, Alex. This is the only way. The Turks want us all out of their hair pronto. We can't make any official protest because this mission doesn't officially exist. It's been made very clear that if I even think about contacting the British Consulate, or the embassy in Ankara, or the SIS station, then SOE Turkey is out of business. I can't afford that – there's still work we can do here. We've got a nice little escape route from Greece building up down in Smyrna and the Turks are looking the other way for us there too. So bite the bullet, old son – it's all you can do."

"Something's not right – why does he need us? Why not just head straight after Vlasenin?"

"The Turks wouldn't let him, I guess. They've not been well inclined towards Uncle Joe's boys since that botched bid to kill the German ambassador in Ankara a few months back. Anyway, Davies said to do as you're told, co-operate fully until the mission is successfully completed, then sneak back here or contact our boys in Greece to arrange a passage home..." he lowered his voice. "...and try to get the jump on Amarazov any damn chance you get."

Rawlings gave a grim smile. "I would have, anyway. But tell him thanks for the unofficial backing."

∞

By the time Battakan's twelve-hour deadline had expired Rawlings, and all his men, were indeed out of Turkey. They were in a convoy of three trucks parked in a large clearing deep in a pine forest, several hundred yards back from, and out of sight of, a narrow track that lead back into Turkey and forward into the German-occupied sector of the province of Thrace. A steep bank to a river lay behind them.

They had arrived on the Turkish side of the border just over an hour ago, at the end of a long day. They had left the police station shortly after Battakan returned with their release papers, the truck from the previous day waiting for them outside. Rawlings had insisted on a detour to the garage which had been their intended destination the previous day. While the others had waited in the truck Vasily and Rawlings disappeared inside, eventually re-emerging with more weapons and ammunition, plus a bag of gold sovereigns as extra 'operating money'. A fast final run got them to the consulate just in time.

The drive from Istanbul had taken most of the day, Amarazov leading the convoy in a truck with half a dozen picked guards from the consulate, now in civilian clothes like him. The SOE team had followed, Costas and Stavrakis taking it in turns to drive. Rawlings' reasoning had been that they would be the least conspicuous if any Turkish policemen with their heads still full of rumours about the British gang aiming to rob Topkapi Palace decided to make a name for themselves.

The rest had stayed out of sight and under cover in the rear. Vasily in particular was looking very worried indeed, casting anxious glances at the Russian truck in front and shifting uncomfortably in his seat from time to time. But Amarazov had made no mention of his presence at the initial meeting at the consulate, nor at the halt when they rendezvoused with a small detachment of partisans in a third truck, who had crossed to the Turkish side. There they had waited until after sunset before crossing back in, using a secluded dirt track, well away from the official border posts and the many patrols of German and Bulgarian troops they had seen criss-crossing the main roads. There was much more enemy traffic than was normal in such a far-flung outpost of the Third Reich, but Rawlings grudgingly admitted to himself that this meant Amarazov's intelligence was sound. They were getting near Vlasenin,

He had expected Amarazov to push on towards the main partisan force, but instead he had ordered the convoy to turn and take shelter in the forest. Then he ordered everyone to disembark. As they did so Amarazov called Rawlings over. "So, here we are, Major Rawlings. I thought a short rest would be beneficial. And it gives an opportunity to explain my plan. I am sure you are keen to hear it."

"I've nearly wet myself with the excitement."

Amarazov gave a humourless smile in return, spreading a map on the cab of the nearest truck. "Vlasenin is being held at this supply base here. About fifteen kilometres south-west of where we are now. Once we have rendezvoused with my main force we will make our way there, covering the last few kilometres on foot. The surrounding forest is well patrolled but our scouts have identified a blind spot. If we eliminate the nearest patrols we can get to within a few hundred yards of the perimeter fence in complete concealment and we will have an action span of over a quarter of an hour to affect the rescue.

"Unfortunately the base is extremely well-defended. A frontal assault would simply end in us all being wiped out. Therefore I propose a diversionary attack, intended to seem like a full assault, while a secondary force gets inside and gets to Vlasenin. That will be you and your men."

"I see. And you think they'll just wave us through the front gate?"

The Russian gave a wolfish smile. "I do. Because, as you have seen, every German unit in this sector that can be spared is on its way to that camp, Major Rawlings. When the rest of my men arrive, they will bring with them German uniforms and an Opel army truck. They have proved useful in the past, but for this operation to succeed we also need men who can pass as Germans on close inspection, who know enough of the language to get to where Vlasenin is being hidden.

"And once we've got there, we just persuade them to let us take him, do we?"

Amarazov clicked his tongue in irritation. "This operation was never going to be an easy one. But we know the men in charge; Ziedler and Hoffman." Rawlings gave a rueful nod as Amarazov continued. "One of the guards got a good look at the leader last night; fortunately for a spy Oberst Ziedler is very recognisable. And the Greeks' reconnaissance earlier today saw a man in plain clothes giving orders. When they described him I knew at once. Mention their names and that should help you gain access to Vlasenin."

"Without written orders?" Rawlings looked doubtful.

"Persuade them, major. We all have a hard task ahead of us tonight. But to have any chance we need each other. I can get you inside; you must get Vlasenin out. That I leave to you. But once you board that truck you will have ten minutes before we launch our attack." He shrugged. "And not much longer after that. In the confusion you should be able to get back out with Vlasenin concealed in the truck. It will seem natural for vehicles to be going out to engage the enemy. And if anyone should chance to see Vlasenin it will seem even more natural for him to be removed for safety's sake.

"Frankly, major, I do not care how you do it. Just

get him and bring him back to this point. We will have Vlasenin back on neutral soil before daybreak. And I think that between us we can get him back to Russia – once he has told us where his papers are, of course; you will obtain that information from him before rendezvousing with me again – before Ziedler or that jumped-up civil servant Battakan can do anything."

Rawlings nodded. "It all seems plausible, though we'll need a lifetime's worth of luck to pull it off. But if we do, and I get Vlasenin free and clear, what's to stop me running out on you?"

Amarazov gave his wolf's smile again. "The fact that two of my men will be in the truck with you. They cannot speak German, of course, but they will pass in a crowd. And at the first sign of treachery they have orders to kill Vlasenin and as many of you as possible. So then no-one gets him and we all have to search for the papers blind. I'm sure that your superiors would not want you to initiate that most unfortunate scenario."

"Probably not," Rawlings replied. "You're not asking much, are you? Infiltrate the most closely-guarded camp in occupied Europe, find Vlasenin's cell, spring him from it, get him out of the camp and bring him back here while giving the slip to half a division of crack troops who might just want to get him back. And what's our reward? Third-class berths home on a Black Sea freighter? I think for our efforts we deserve a little more than that, Comrade Major."

Amarazov's smile slipped a little. "And what were you thinking of?"

"Vlasenin's papers."

Amarazov did not smile at that. Instead he laughed

out loud. "I have always admired the British sense of humour, Major Rawlings."

"I'm deadly serious. We'll get him to tell us their location. He won't trust anyone else. We know they're in Turkey somewhere. Once we're back across the border we'll hand him over to you. In return you let us find the papers and make our own way home. Those are my terms. And they're non-negotiable."

"You are not in a position to make terms," Amarazov snarled. "I could kill you all – now!"

"And then you'd really be in the shit, *tovaritch*." Rawlings put his face within an inch of the Russian's despite the raised weapons of guards and partisans. All Rawlings' team moved up behind him. "You've just admitted we're your only hope. Without us all you've got is a handful of ordinary Russian squaddies who were standing at the consulate gates getting bored this time yesterday. That and a bunch of Greek partisans who are only doing this because their leaders have decided Russia's a better bet to keep the king from coming back and running the show again when all this is over.

"And that's all you're going to get, isn't it? All this 'you're in my power, gentlemen', Fu Manchu bollocks doesn't hide the fact that you've failed all down the line. You couldn't make Vlasenin talk and you couldn't keep him safe. I bet Renkovich has told you to get him back before the Politburo even know he's gone. Quite a tall order – and Renkovich never allows three failures in a row. We're the answer to your prayers and if we're going to send that poor bugger back to a living hell we're getting something out of it. You don't like my terms, kill us all now. Then try to think of another way to get Vlasenin out."

There was a long pause. Rawlings could see Amarazov weighing up his options. At last he said: "Very well, major. On your terms." He pulled a hip flask from his tunic and raised it in ironic salute before taking a gulp. "To another fruitful Anglo-Soviet alliance." As he passed the flask to Rawlings he added, in an offhand manner: "But might I ask a small favour, as an earnest of your good faith?"

Rawlings paused, flask half-way to his mouth. "What favour might that be?"

"This scum," Amarazov suddenly pointed to Vasily, "must die." Rawlings' men instinctively closed ranks around the Russian as every gun turned to him. "We have known all along about your use of the Tsarists in this operation," Amarazov continued smugly, "and this man is known to us. Well, now that the rest of his group have been wiped out it will be a very simple matter to pluck another thorn from the flesh of Soviet Russia for good.

"I thought this would be an opportune moment to raise the issue. To have killed him in Turkey might have prompted an investigation, or come to the attention of the rest of that nest of plotters that festers across the border. But here – one more corpse in a country where the Germans have made thousands? I think it will do very nicely. And I would like you to do it for me, Major Rawlings. Otherwise my men will take him and kill him slowly. Surely you would not want a comrade in arms to suffer?"

Rawlings looked stricken. He turned to Vasily, who had broken from the knot of SOE men and was walking uncertainly towards Rawlings and Amarazov, a pleading look in his eyes. Then Rawlings said: "Very well", and reached for his Mauser.

Vasily's face drained of all colour. He began to move backwards, eyes still locked on Rawlings. Amarazov smiled and threw his silenced Tokarev to Rawlings. "Use mine," he said. "Those things have been known to fire blanks."

Rawlings caught the Russian's pistol, checked the balance and the action, flicked off the safety catch. Vasily was still staggering back, away from the trucks, towards the bank. Several of Rawlings' men moved forward, trying to get in front of their commander. "If they take one more step, I will tell my men to open fire, major," Amarazov said, "and you can go in to rescue Vlasenin alone."

"Stay back!" Rawlings shouted. "That's an order!"

They halted, but the looks of horror on their faces matched that of Vasily as Rawlings advanced towards him. He staggered back a few more steps, then broke, running for the steep bank and tree cover behind him. "Stop, or I'll shoot you in the back, Vasily," Rawlings shouted. "Do you want that?"

The Russian halted, almost at the lip of the bank. And when he turned round, he was standing upright, his eyes clear and calm. Rawlings moved to within ten yards of him, and took aim. Amarazov walked up to join him, eyes shining with pleasure. "What are you waiting for, major? One more killing after so many. Surely…"

Rawlings fired twice. Heart and chest, the classic SOE 'double tap' method. The impact gouged two gouts of blood from Vasily's body and hurled him off his feet and over the bank. Rawlings walked up and looked over the edge, Amarazov and two guards joining him. Vasily lay at the bottom, huddled and shapeless, half his body in the river. A trail of red stained the water.

"Shall we bring his body back, Comrade Major?" one of the guards asked.

Amarazov looked at him as if he were mad. "Why? To give him a decent burial?" He shook his head. "Such a death is all traitors like him deserve. Leave him for the wolves. Now we get moving again."

He turned to Rawlings, hand out. Both guards trained their guns on Rawlings as he walked up to Amarazov and handed him the Tokarev, butt first. "I'd get that looked at if I were you. I think it throws to the right a little." Then he walked back to the truck, ignoring the faces of his men, and climbed aboard.

༄

Vlasenin's new home was cleaner and drier than the cell at the consulate, but that did nothing to raise his spirits. It had been twelve hours since that bastard Ziedler had pulled off the blindfold and he had found himself in this Spartan anteroom. It was obviously part of an office complex. Filing cabinets lined the walls, and he was seated in front of a desk on a plain wooden chair. But the only thing on the desktop was a packet of Balkan Sobranie cigarettes. After Ziedler had left Vlasenin had methodically smoked the entire pack. When they had run out he tried to engage the two black-uniformed guards at the doorway in conversation, without success. And then he tried to think of how he could possibly stop himself from telling them everything once they got to work on him.

The door opened and Ziedler walked in, this time dressed in German uniform. He was flanked by two other army officers; Vlasenin thought he recognised them from the rescue last night, but he could not be sure. He did not recognise the other three men, but he could tell from the look of the big one in the leather coat and slouch hat that he would take up where Amarazov had left off. The last members of the party were a burly, swarthy man in a slate grey uniform and sidecap and a grey-haired nonentity in a white coat.

Ziedler pulled up a chair opposite the desk, smiling broadly. "All the cigarettes gone, I see. I thought you would enjoy them. I think we can probably organise a hot meal and some real coffee next. But first allow me to introduce…"

"Save the pleasantries, German. I'm not interested in who your Fuhrer has sent to break me. And I don't care for the company of a man who brought me from one prison to another under false pretences."

"Prison?" Ziedler looked puzzled. "Herr Doctor, you are free to go back to your own people any time you wish. But I don't think you really want that. It is for that reason that we rescued you. False pretences, you say? A little deception, I admit, but only because I felt you would be more co-operative if you thought we were British. You obviously regard them as your saviours." He shook his head. "A misguided view, Herr Doctor, if I may say so. They never trust any man, even a scientific genius, if he has the misfortune to be a foreigner. Our operation simply pre-empted theirs by a few hours. They would have been quite happy to betray an alliance and kill your countrymen in cold blood to achieve their ends. Then, when they had you safely back in England, they would have used you to advance their own experts' knowledge as far as yours – then discarded you. You would have no control over how the fruits of your genius were developed and utilised.

"But with us you can be at the forefront. We have gifted men – ach, why do I say this? You know it better than I. But they all look to you, to Vlasenin. You could guide them, help them – perhaps be helped by them in a small way. But you would be their equal. Not a tool, or a prisoner. Your gifts can give us the power to destroy something you have always hated, something every civilised human being hates – Stalinism. Germany wants your talents only for that, and to defend her historic borders.

"We do not seek to imprison you, but to liberate you." He was leaning across the desk now, voice low and intent, eyes shining. "Believe me, Herr Doctor, once you had told us where your papers were, I would have told you our true identity. And given you a free choice; come with us to liberation, or return to torture and death. You still have that choice. Work with us, and this war will be over in a matter of months. So much needless suffering will have been avoided. And you will be free to do as you wish."

Vlasenin sighed deeply, then said: "I almost wish I was back in Istanbul. At least Amarazov never fed me this bullshit. He was honest. He told me what he wanted – me and my papers, to do his master's bidding. Just like you. Nazi, Stalinist – the same set of state-sanctioned gangsters. And I reject you both."

"You are wrong, Herr Doctor." Ziedler's voice was still passionate. "We offer you something different to Amarazov and all he represents. I wish with all my heart you could see that, and spare yourself unnecessary suffering. It hurts me to see a great man exposed to pain for the sake of his nobility and genius."

Vlasenin looked in pure amazement at the handsome, intense giant in front of him and said softly: "Do you know, I truly pity you. More than anyone I have ever met. You truly cannot see the depths of your self-delusion. You have pledged your talents – remarkable ones – to a madman who will drown civilisation in blood. I would rather give the Devil dominion over this world than use my knowledge for your master's gain."

Ziedler's shoulders slumped. "Then that presents us with a problem, Herr Doctor. The evening draws on. I had hoped that before this night was out we would be on the way to retrieve your papers. For that to happen you must tell us where they are. If you do you will receive food and rest, and Doctor Fleischer here," he indicated the grey-haired man, "can take a look at you."

"All I will tell you is that I will tell you nothing. And if I were you I would get me to Berlin before letting your torturers loose. Amarazov waited too long. Look what happened to him."

"I am not Amarazov." Ziedler stood up. "Truly, Herr Doctor, I wish it did not have to be so. But you will tell us what we need to know very quickly and until then this camp will be your new home." He turned to Hoffman. "He is yours."

"About time too," Hoffman grunted and signalled to the guards. One moved forward quickly, gesturing with his Schmeisser for Vlasenin to rise. The other held the door open and the entire party moved out, Vlasenin and his guards in the lead with Hoffman close behind. Ziedler caught up to him and whispered urgently: "Remember – he's already been through a lot. Be careful."

Hoffman turned without breaking stride and laughed in his face. "Go teach your grandmother to suck eggs, Ziedler. I've kept them alive when God thought they were dead. Remember, you're not talking to Mr Ham-handed Ivan now. I'll have the location of those papers for you inside the hour." He laughed again. "The poor bastard's almost ready to give in now."

They had reached the end of the corridor. As well as offices, this building in Unterbrecht's complex even had a small cell, located just behind the main reception desk. A steel door loomed in front of Vlasenin. Two uniformed Gestapo officers stood beside it. He gulped, hesitating as one of them opened the door. Hoffman pushed him through, the officers following behind him. Hoffman turned, blocking the doorway, as the others made to follow. "Might as well get yourselves a meal, gentlemen. He'll be talking by the time you've finished."

For once Ziedler looked as dumbfounded as Ciarelli. "That was never part of the arrangement," Ziedler said. "I am to be present during the interrogation, as well as Doctor Fleischer."

"Really?" Hoffman gave a smug smile. "The Reichsfuhrer made it clear to me before we left that you weren't. I assumed you'd got the message too. This phase of the operation is to be handled by the Gestapo. I suggest you call Berlin to confirm that."

"This is disgraceful! I demand full access. Vlasenin

needs careful handling."

"Take it up with the Reichsfuhrer – or your precious Admiral. I'm sure the end result will be the same." Hoffman gave Ziedler a sorrowful look. "Consider it my reward for sitting in this shithole all day because you thought it would 'disorient' him, and then having to listen to that rubbish you spouted back there. You really still believe it, don't you?" He gave a cynical laugh. "Power, Ziedler. That's all that matters. That boy in there's got more than anyone in the world, so they say. But I've got the power to make him talk."

"I'm warning you…" Ziedler took a step forwards and the two Gestapo guards moved to flank Hoffman, Schmeissers coming up. "And I'm telling you," Hoffman said, "this interrogation is to be handled by the Gestapo." He turned and opened the door, but then turned round again. "I'll tell you another thing, Ziedler. You talk about politics, ideals, nobility, genius and all the rest of it. But only three things will make this boy talk – pain, pain and more pain."

He slammed the door shut.

ᘛ

"I want some answers and I want them now! That was cold-blooded murder!" Curtis' face worked with barely-suppressed fury, a red beacon even in the gloom of the blacked-out truck.

"Calm yourself, Captain Curtis," Rawlings said as he wiped the sprayed spittle from his cheek. "Our friends back there will get suspicious if we raise our voices."

"Your friends, maybe. After doing their executions

for them I expect you would be the best of pals." The expression of fury gave way to one of contempt. "And you were the one who kept saying 'they're the enemy now'. You've betrayed our mission – and killed a man who was trying to help us."

"If you'd just give me a chance to explain," Rawlings said with a touch of desperation. He was seated in the front of the truck with Curtis next to him and Hawkins at the wheel. They were half a mile from the German camp now, and it was just minutes before Amarazov was due to launch his diversionary attack. Though the truck was hidden by darkness and thick forest he was acutely aware of the high security all around. The area was crawling with troops, the rescue bid stood on a knife-edge – and Curtis had chosen their first moments out of Amarazov's sight to accuse his commanding officer of murder.

"What's there to explain?" he almost shouted. "I saw it with my own eyes – you killed Vasily."

"For a start, I didn't. With any luck, Vasily is in that camp right now – along with Yelena."

Curtis' jaw dropped. His mouth worked but he seemed incapable of speech. It was a golden opportunity and Rawlings seized it. "His death was staged. We planned it all beforehand. On the first night, and later when we stopped off at the garage this morning. I had a feeling we might have to end up working alongside the Russians if Ziedler made a move first. What happened yesterday confirmed it. Whoever tipped the Germans off let Amarazov know we were in Turkey too. How else could he have known we were sitting in a police station on the other side of the city? He knew we'd made contact with the Tsarists, he knew which group and he knew they'd been wiped out.

"But he didn't know Yelena was still a free agent. Nobody did. That was why I didn't want her in Istanbul. Then when we were told we had to work with Amarazov I knew they wouldn't tolerate Vasily staying alive. So if he's out of the picture with me pulling the trigger on him we're all comrades again, Amarazov's convinced I'm as big a bastard as he is – and Vasily's free to warn the Germans."

"Warn the Germans?" Curtis found his voice at last, but he sounded like someone speaking a foreign phrase for the first time. "Warn them of what?"

"Of the attack, idiot." Rawlings stole a sideways glance through the partition at the two Russians in the rear of the truck with the rest of the men, and tried to keep his own voice down. "With any luck, Ziedler's been convinced there'll be a partisan assault on the camp any minute now. What he won't know is that we're going to use it to spring Vlasenin." Curtis still looked utterly confused, so Rawlings went on patiently. "I knew this was the only chance we had of rescuing him before Hoffman made him talk.

"But I also knew there was no way in the world I was letting Amarazov get him, or the plans, afterwards. As soon as he's got both he'll kill us all. So when we stopped off at the garage I used the radio that Vasily's contact has there. Got in touch with Yelena and told her to watch the main road north out of Istanbul and get on our tail. I had a feeling Amarazov would want to kill Vasily as soon as we were out of Turkey. With any luck he didn't have to wait too long before she came and picked him up. Then they were to find the nearest German patrol, mention Vlasenin's name and get themselves inside the camp pronto." He gave a rueful smile. "Let's hope they managed it or we'll really have to improvise."

Curtis looked at his leader as though he were from another planet. "So they've told Ziedler about Amarazov's plan?"

"Yes – but not the most important part of it. It also means of course that we'll have to get them out too. But I've a few ideas on that score, as well."

Curtis nodded, but his expression was far from one of understanding. "What about the survivors from yesterday? If they recognise Yelena and Vasily they'll know they're working for us."

"That's the hardest part," Rawlings admitted. "They'll have to claim that we forced them to work with us. Luckily they didn't see Yelena at all, or Vasily in the close quarter work. Everything he did yesterday could have been pure self-defence. I think they'll act on their information – they'll be too worried to do anything else – but keep them on a tight rein. And, like I said, we've got some ideas on that score." He clapped Curtis on the shoulder. "We won't leave without them, Curtis – not unless there's no other way."

"And what about Amarazov's men?" Curtis jerked his head slightly towards the rear of the truck.

"Well, nothing's ever perfect in this most imperfect world. Let's hope that in the confusion we can get the drop on them. Jesus, if I can't outsmart a couple of Russian footsloggers who weren't good enough for anything but consulate guard duty, then Davies chose the wrong man for this job."

"No, I don't think he did," Curtis said. "So the

shooting – it was all rigged?"

"Worked like a dream." Rawlings gave a beautiful smile. "Body armour and blood bags. Even an Old Vic veteran like you didn't spot the difference. We rigged him up in the garage." He shook his head. "The Tsarists have got plenty of men in Istanbul, but it's a damn good job at least one of them's a butcher."

"You might have told us," Curtis protested.

"Yeah – all the blokes thought you'd gone mad." Hawkins, in the driver's seat next to them, spoke for the first time.

"Exactly. If I'd told you about it beforehand you wouldn't have looked so bloody convinced. Amarazov was watching you all afterwards and you did me proud."

"You cold-blooded bastard – sir." Curtis spoke half in admiration, half in disgust.

"Good job they didn't look too close at the body afterwards," Hawkins said.

"Damn right," Rawlings agreed. "Having that slope down to the river was a big stroke of luck, I must admit. But I knew Amarazov didn't want to hang around too long, and I reckoned he wouldn't care if a Tsarist got a proper burial or not. The main thing I was worried about was that he'd insist on a head shot."

"And what if he had, sir?" Curtis asked.

Rawlings looked him in the eye. "I'd have done it, Curtis. I can assure you Amarazov wasn't bluffing about killing the rest of you. And Yelena would have still been alive to carry the plan through. I would have done it, to keep in with Amarazov and keep this mission alive. I'd have done it and I might have to yet. That or something like it. So might any of you."

There was silence for a few moments. Then one of the Russians looked at his watch for the fiftieth time, and pushed his face up close to the partition. "We go," he barked in guttural, rehearsed English. "Now!"

Hawkins revved the engine. Curtis adjusted the peaked cap of his German major's uniform. Rawlings was dressed as a lieutenant. The rest were privates, except Hawkins, who sported a sergeant's stripes. All carried Mauser rifles or Schmeissers. There were pistols, knives and grenades at their belts and O'Hare still had his SOE bag of tricks, now packed in a standard issue Wehrmacht knapsack. Rawlings took a deep breath. "Right, lads – good luck. Curtis, you do the talking and for God's sake make it convincing. You've got to get us right to where Vlasenin's being held. Hawkins, once we're all back at this truck – and I mean all of us – get us out the main gate and don't stop until I tell you." He paused. "And if either of you see any of the others lining up to shoot me in the back, try to persuade them otherwise."

They both smiled. "Anything you say, sir," Hawkins said and swung the truck out onto the road.

༄

Amarazov trained his binoculars on the western perimeter of the camp. There was a machine-gun tower at each end of the fence, but the snipers would take care of them. Two sentries patrolled along the fence, but they would go down in the first fusillade from Captain Veloutis' men. There were over a hundred in all, part of one of the largest groups in Thrace, sufficient to make a good enough show for the Germans to devote most of their attention to wiping them out. They might even blow the wire and make some red work in the camp itself. But that was of little interest to Amarazov. As long as they drew attention from where Vlasenin was being held, and the main gate that Rawlings' team would have to get through.

Amarazov had told them to disperse and head back for safety once he gave the signal that Rawlings was clear. He doubted any of them would make it. But that was the way of the world. The footsoldiers had to die in order for those who really mattered to stay safe to make the important decisions. Comrade Lenin had understood this, and his successor even more so. Amarazov felt he had been quite generous in selecting two Greeks to follow him and the four remaining consulate guards back to the rendezvous. But they would be useful in finding the quickest route there, then over the border afterwards.

And of course two extra guns would make the task of wiping out the British easier. Vlasenin would have told them the location of the papers by then, because Rawlings would be looking for a way to slip his shadows and win both prizes for himself. But Amarazov trusted his two men in the truck to stay close, and in any case the pursuit would probably be too close for independent action until the rendezvous.

Yes, it would all work out nicely. *Rawlings will pay with his life for daring to haggle a deal and make me look a fool in front of these Greek peasants, and none of his men will be left alive to tell the tale. The British would have to accept that all their brave agents had perished in the rescue attempt. Given that this mission does not officially exist they will be in no position to make too* much of a fuss. And Vlasenin and his papers will be in Moscow before nightfall tomorrow, with a reasonable amount of luck. This will be the making of my career, not just the salvaging of it. A seat at Grigorin's empty desk for a start, at least.

Veloutis tapped his arm, jolting his from his private thoughts. He was a tall, lean man, a trade union organiser in the local tobacco industry before the war. He had been a Party member long before he had joined the army and his battlefield commission in the Albanian campaign had made him a natural to become military commander of one of the first and largest groups in the area.

Amarazov nodded curtly. The man seemed to be under some delusion as to who was in command here, but that was the fault of the group's overall commander, the *kapetan*, who had given Amarazov this detachment and his two principal subordinates for the mission. Farzalis, the political officer in the group, had proved a much more malleable subject. He was a minor-ranking civil servant, Turkish by birth, who had avenged the years of discrimination from Greek and Bulgar alike by embracing Party doctrine and energetically eliminating all enemies of the one true path since joining the *andartes*. He was pathetically eager to help anyone from Russia (especially when Amarazov let slip that he had met Comrade Stalin personally) and had persuaded Veloutis to commit the detachment's entire strength to the assault.

Of course his reward for that would be to suffer the same fate as Veloutis and all the rest; Amarazov had insisted that the officers lead from the front. Any revolution needed ignorant cannon fodder like this. Far better they died than real organisers like me – or good

Russians like the guards. They wanted to be martyrs to the cause and Amarazov was happy to help grant them their wish.

Veloutis gave a series of signals and the partisans began to move forward. All except the two with Amarazov, forming a circle round him with the four Russian guards. Amarazov had been impressed with these men from the consulate. They had been the most energetic during Ziedler's raid, and they had eliminated the German patrol guarding this sector of the approach to the camp completely silently in a matter of seconds. Just peasants like the Greeks, of course, but good Russian fighters. That was the difference. They would be rewarded if they survived. But now their task was to keep him alive and get him to the rendezvous. He gave a signal to his bodyguard and they began to move away from the battlefield.

The partisans were almost at the edge of the trees now. Amongst them was Spiro Levkas – or 'Achilles' as he preferred to be known. All new recruits to the *andartes* were encouraged to take a 'fighting name'. It marked out their new identity as crusaders against the Fascists. For Spiro the group had become his family. His old one had been forced from their land to the north when the Bulgarians had marched in last summer and set about replacing Greek families with their own settlers. The mass flight from the Bulgarian sector had claimed hundreds of lives, including those of his parents and young sister.

Spiro had hoped to find better treatment in the German sector but it had been worse; beatings, villages burned, summary executions. In the end he had fled to the mountains to look for the *andartes* and they had not been hard to find. Now at last he had a chance to do something worthwhile, to hit back at the Germans and all their stinking allies. Especially the Bulgars. He would do his duty tonight. Sergeant Evros – 'Vulture' as he proudly called himself, feasting on the corpses of the enemy – had told him what to do. Keep moving, keep shooting and get to the wire. That was vital. No matter what happened, no matter how many comrades died. Get to the wire. That was his duty, and Achilles would do it.

∾

Hoffman looked up at the sound of a knock on the cell door, instantly angry. He hated to be disturbed at his work. He pulled off the bloodstained leather gloves, moved back from the chair with Vlasenin's groaning body strapped to it and opened the door. Captain Brandt, his second-in-command, stood in the doorway, looking anxious.

"What do you want?" Hoffman barked.

"Oberst Ziedler is here, Herr Kommissar." Brandt sounded very unhappy. "He wants to come in. And he has authorisation from Berlin."

Hoffman cursed under his breath, and thought for a moment then said aloud: "Very well – let him in."

The key turned in the lock and Ziedler stepped in, flanked by Dressler and Weiss as usual, together with Fleischer. Ziedler looked at Vlasenin, then turned to Hoffman, white with anger. "What have you been doing to him?"

"Just the usual," Hoffman replied. "You know the drill as well as I do. What did you expect?"

Ziedler did not answer. Instead he pulled a signal

flimsy from his tunic pocket. "From Berlin. Bormann and Himmler have agreed to the Admiral's request. The Abwehr has full access to this interrogation."

"Fine." Hoffman shrugged. "Just try not to get in the way." He turned back to Vlasenin.

"Well, far be it from me to interfere with methods that have had so much success. How long have you been working on him? Longer than the time it takes to have a meal, for certain. And still not a word."

"He's a tough old bugger," Hoffman admitted. "But he's weakening. You said yourself you didn't want the doctor here pumping him full of scopolamine. Give me time."

"That's exactly what we haven't got. I didn't just come here to check on his wellbeing. One of the patrols has picked up a couple of prisoners. They say there's going to be a partisan attack any minute now."

Hoffman was thunderstruck. "What – they found out we were here? Damn it, I should never have trusted security to that jumped-up little supplies clerk. These Greek bandits would never raid a base this size unless they knew we had something valuable inside. It's the British behind this – or the Russians."

"According to our prisoners, both. It's quite a story, but it could be true. On the other hand, your... unique approach might rattle them if they're lying. Meanwhile I've laid on a little surprise for our Greek warriors. They won't get close, of course, but if they know where Vlasenin is, they could come again."

"Damn right." Hoffman looked worried. "We should move him."

"If he's fit enough," Ziedler snapped back. "And

Berlin wants the papers too. We know they're in Turkey somewhere. The farther we move from the border the harder that gets."

"In that case, we've got to make him talk." Hoffman looked at Fleischer with a thin smile. "Do you think he's in a fit state to be given scopolamine, Doctor Fleischer?"

"Absolutely not! "Fleischer replied. "And can I say..."

"There you are, then, Ziedler. Unless, of course, you want to try appealing to his better nature again."

Ziedler ignored the sarcasm. "Even so, he probably needs a rest before we start again. And it'll help if we have to move him. A few minutes while you talk to the prisoners won't make much difference."

Hoffman looked suspicious, but then abruptly turned to Brandt and the two guards. "Give him some food and water. A cigarette if he wants it, too. And let the doctor have a look at him. But no-one touches him until we get back. And no-one else comes in. Understood?"

The three "*Jawohl*"s came in unison. Hoffman nodded in satisfaction then turned and followed Ziedler and the two Abwehr lieutenants out. Past the two Gestapo guards manning the door to the complex, then out and left along the broad thoroughfare that split the base into two and led back to the main gate. Fifty yards along was a T-junction where the rows of storerooms gave way to the edge of the landing field. The junction's left turn led to the barrack complex, the right to Unterbrecht's recently-vacated office. Two of the Brandenburgers stood guard at the doorway. One held the door open and Ziedler walked briskly through, his lieutenants and Hoffman close behind. Inside, Dorsch and Ciarelli were seated behind Unterbrecht's desk. Before it, looking suitably cowed and servile, were Vasily and Yelena.

"So what's the story?" Hoffman said, striding to stand over them.

"They're from the Tsarist group that the British were using," Dorsch said. "The one we hit yesterday."

"The one that sent you back with your tails between your legs, you mean," Hoffman sneered. "So why are they still alive?" He turned to them with a look of contempt. "Anyone who works with the British needs to give me a damn good reason not to shoot them like dogs."

"They claim that they were coerced into helping them," Ziedler said. "And that they were supposed to be springing Vlasenin from the consulate the same night that we went in. Fortunately my contingency plan worked, and the police picked them up when they reached Istanbul." He shot a quick glance at Dorsch and was delighted to see the SS man colour and drop his eyes.

"So how come they're here?" Hoffman's voice and face were suspicion personified. "Why didn't the carpet-sellers imprison or intern the lot of them?"

"This is where it gets interesting," Ziedler replied. "They say that after our raid on the consulate, the Russians – led by our old friend Major Amarazov – came to the police station where they were being held and offered the Turks some kind of deal in return for allowing the British to leave Turkey. They needed them to join forces for a rescue attempt. These two were allowed to go free because they have Turkish citizenship. And, because of the deal with the Russians, the British washed their hands of them."

"It is true, *Gospodin*." Vasily turned to Hoffman, hands clasped in supplication, speaking in English but with his Russian accent thickened to the point of caricature. "They betrayed us, those British pigs. Our fellow Tsarists still in Russia helped get this man out, and the British said they would not need us any more. Then this Rawlings bursts into my home two nights ago, and says we must help them. Dress up as Russian troops and raid the consulate. What could I do? He threatened to tell the Reds all about us. And because I was too much of a coward to defy them my men died when this man came the next day." He pointed at Dorsch.

"What do you say to all this, Herr Hauptman?" Ziedler asked in a neutral tone. "It was SD information that named this man's group as the SOE's link with the Tsarists in Turkey – and also said that they were pro-British to the core."

"That is not true!" Yelena spoke for the first time. "We use anyone who wants to see the Reds defeated. But we had not heard from the British in months before they… kidnapped us."

"It seems your source was misinformed, Herr Hauptmann." Ziedler's tone was a little less neutral this time.

Dorsch bristled. "We have used him many times in the past, and he has never been wrong, Herr Oberst. Might I point out that he gave us the exact location and disposition of the British force. For the rest of it, we have only the word of – these people."

Ziedler nodded in reluctant acknowledgment, adding: "And, as I recall, this group disdained an offer of employment from the Abwehr a year or two ago."

"And he and all his men fought back just as hard as the British yesterday," Dorsch added. "I didn't see the girl, but she must have been there too."

Ziedler turned a piercing gaze on the two captives. Yelena held it but Vasily spread his hands wide. "What can I say, *Gospodin*? We were betrayed. They told us that this man Vlasenin was too important to stay with the Reds. And we fought yesterday because we had to, and because we wanted to help fight the Reds. When we were attacked at first, we thought your men were the Reds. All the rest of our group died for the British. Now they want to give Vlasenin back. Why should we help them again? Why should we not work with you? We were fools to refuse you before." He hung his head. "I know that now."

"So you followed them all the way here, just to get even with them?" Hoffman said. "Tracked them across the border, and to here. A likely story. Why not just telephone or radio sector HQ to put the finger on them?"

Vasily spread his hands wide and risked a derisive laugh. "Would they have believed us? And what could we tell them? That a joint British and Russian force were headed for... somewhere across the border? We had to find out where exactly they were headed. So we used our contacts in Istanbul to get a car, and tracked them. We knew they would not suspect anything like that from a couple of Russian peasants."

"Maybe." Hoffman looked hard at both Russians. "Or maybe they wanted you to get caught."

"I can hardly imagine what purpose that would serve," Ziedler demurred. "This is what puzzles me. If they are still working with the British, why betray their plan to us? It's true that there is a large force approaching the edge of the camp. I've arranged an ambush. There's no way any of them can escape."

Hoffman clicked his tongue. "There'll be some stinking plot going on. Rawlings and Amarazov are both clever bastards. Get them together and the Devil himself couldn't second-guess them." He turned to Vasily. "If you're lying, I'll shoot the girl. Not you, just her. In the stomach. When this attack is over, we'll see if Rawlings is among the dead. If he isn't…" he turned to Ziedler. "Meanwhile I reckon we should keep them under guard – and move Vlasenin just in case this attack is a feint for infiltrators."

"I agree." Ziedler turned to Leutnant Dressler. "Bring the guards in. They can take these two to one of the barrack huts – and watch them like hawks."

"Can we not go free, *Gospodin*?" Vasily pleaded. "We have told the truth. If the Reds or the British find us they will kill us."

"As they might if they encounter you outside the camp," Ziedler replied. "It will not be safe out there for some time yet. You will not be ill-treated. And if we find you have told the truth, we will let you go."

Vasily saw from the German's eyes that further protest would be dangerous, and any attempt to dissuade them from moving Vlasenin would be suicidal. So he allowed the two guards to prod them out of the office at gunpoint and off in the direction of the barracks. Behind them came all five officers, walking briskly from Unterbrecht's office back down the road to Vlasenin's cell. Hoffman was just behind Ziedler, so he was the first to see him stiffen, look in the direction of the main gate, then draw his pistol.

∞

The tension inside the truck had been growing by the minute. Every man's nerves had been taut as a highwire from the moment they had approached the main gate. But Curtis had given their explanation – a patrol operating out from Soufli which had been in a firefight with a large concentration of partisans earlier in the day and had a wounded man who needed attention at the nearest German base – in such a commanding tone that they had been waved through.

Costas, Stavrakis and the Russians had kept their heads down in the back of the truck – Rawlings had ordered the tarpaulin taken down as it would look less suspicious and give a clear field of fire when the time came – and the sight of the conveniently injured Emerson added weight to their story. When the firing began, the gate guards would be ready to believe that all the partisans in Thrace were attacking and their eyes would be anywhere except on the camp's interior, or so Rawlings devoutly hoped.

Once inside, the truck had driven slowly along the main road, Rawlings and Curtis eyeing each of the buildings on either side for signs of life. The first few were obviously stores huts, locked and deserted. But halfway along they spotted the office complex with the two Gestapo guards standing at the doorway. "Bingo," Rawlings said softly and ordered Hawkins to stop the truck. Rawlings and Curtis exited the cab and moved round to the doorway. Half a dozen of the men in the truck jumped down to join them – Rowley, Sanderson, Garside, Pearson, Mitchell and one of the Russians – as they marched with a purposeful step to the doorway.

The guards halted them but Curtis barked: "Special orders to see the prisoner" and beckoned them forward with such authority that they obeyed without stopping to think why these men had approached from the wrong direction entirely. The document Curtis pulled from his tunic pocket looked official enough and by the time the guards were close enough to see that it was merely a fuel requisition form Rowley and Sanderson were close enough to grab them from behind; one hand over the mouth, the other driving a knife under the ribs to pierce the heart. Both guards died instantly without a sound.

The two sergeants propelled the lifeless bodies into the office while the rest of the party screened them from the gate and the road. But there were no eyes to see them and within ten seconds the guards' bodies were dumped out of sight in the reception area, Rowley and Mitchell had taken their posts – and Rawlings had run into the brick wall of Brandt's refusal to open the cell to anyone but Hoffman or Ziedler.

The truck stood, engine idling, as the minutes ticked by. Not only was Rawlings getting nowhere – some of the men could see he and Curtis arguing with the unseen jailer, through the large window of the reception area – but the time had passed for the partisans' attack to begin. "Come on," Walters said softly as he caressed the stock of his Schmeisser. "Let's be having you."

"Relax, son," Mayhew said. "It'll come soon enough. It always does." He stood up, head above the cab, to take another 360-degree sweep of the camp, and that was when he saw the German officers. They were walking down the road towards Vlasenin's cell. He leaned into the cab to warn Hawkins then stood up again, head just above the roof of the truck's cab, Schmeisser out of sight but at the ready. The officers were still advancing, getting nearer. There was no chance they could not have noticed the truck, but they did not appear to regard it as suspicious. A few more seconds and they would be close enough. "Jerries coming down the road, lads," he whispered. "Wait for it; if they just get closer, I can – damn it!"

It was the first time they had ever heard him swear, or even raise his voice. But there was good reason. Abruptly, and without warning, all five officers had dived for cover behind a stores hut. Ziedler had whispered to Hoffman and Dressler to keep moving but get ready. The message had been passed to the others in a second. They were all used to such situations and their step did not slow or falter. Then at a signal from Ziedler they had moved, gaining cover so swiftly that there was no chance for a shot.

"The truck?" Hoffman voiced everyone's thoughts.

"Of course. Why would any new arrival stop there and not head straight for the barracks area? Or join the ambush force? Why didn't I just crush those Greek bandits where they were? They'll start the first part of the attack and the rest of the garrison will head for the action." He gave a grim smile. "But not our boys." He turned to Dressler. "Double back to Sergeant Kobal. Tell him we have infiltrators. They're at Vlasenin's cell. One truck, six or eight men in it, probably more inside. I want his platoon and the Hermann Goering men in four trucks hitting it with everything they've got in sixty seconds." Dressler turned, poised for the quickest sprint of his life, but Ziedler caught him and added: "If those prisoners have arrived, kill them."

"The British?" Ciarelli whispered.

"It has to be," Ziedler replied. "Only SOE men could pass as Germans. Well, much good it will do them. Just as well your men follow orders, Klaus. In sixty seconds we'll have the whole damn lot. And we'll have the gate closed, too. Weiss, back to Unterbrecht's office and telephone them." Weiss nodded, but before he even had time to move all hell broke loose.

Veloutis' men did not have much heavy weaponry at their disposal, but they had brought every bit of it with them tonight. Four anti-tank rifles sent a shell each at the timbers holding the perimeter fence together and they detonated simultaneously with a great roar and a blast of white light. Three seconds later grenade clusters hit the wire all along its length. Some blasted the already sagging wire inside out; others sent up phosphorus and smoke to blind and stun the troops who were pouring from the barracks huts. Then, as half a dozen mortars pounded them, the main body charged, breaking from the tree cover like the Achaeans from the wooden horse. Rifles and submachine-guns from half a dozen nations spoke in accord, but they did not drown the wild yells of the *andartes* as they made for the wire. Three MG34 Spandaus and two Italian Breda 30 light machine-guns behind the tree line covered them, adding to the cacophony.

They were half-way to the wire when Ziedler's trap was sprung. A flare pistol shell arced into the night and exploded, bathing the killing ground in light. Raumann and Strasser had followed Ziedler's orders to the letter. A platoon in the trees at each end of the perimeter fence, assembled in silence without alerting anyone inside the camp or out of it. Now they cut loose, three heavy MG42s on each side hosing bullets into the *andartes*, cutting their number in half in a matter of seconds. As they began their slaughter the rest of the platoon moved into the trees, closing with the Greek machine-gunners even as they continued to support their doomed comrades.

Only two Greeks were running from the fight and that was because Amarazov was pushing them on, ordering them to guide him back to the vehicles. He knew as soon as the flare went up that Rawlings had tricked him. They would spring Vlasenin and he would take them to his papers while Amarazov died in the woods like a hunted animal. Well, he was not dead yet and the vehicles were not too far away. So he pushed his men onwards, away from the cries of slaughter behind them. They ran, jumping over fallen trees and through marshy gulleys. The clearing where they had left the truck was in sight when suddenly the air was full of gunshots as they ran right into a German patrol. One of the Russians went down, but the rest charged on, firing wildly, cutting Germans down left and right. Amarazov could see the Greeks too, keeping pace, howling savagely as they cut through the enemy, using the same short swords that the *evzones* of old had drawn against the hated Turk. Amarazov darted round a tree, straight into the last two Germans. He shot one in the head and closed with the other, drawing a knife from his belt and slashing it across the German's belly. The German screamed and sank to the ground, guts spilling out in front of him. Amarazov kicked him in the head as he lunged past, then they were at the truck.

It was a German truck and there were more German uniforms inside. With some luck they would be safe. The

Turkish border was an hour's drive away but Amarazov no more thought of that as a destination than he did the back of the moon. If Rawlings survived and got Vlasenin out, then the mission was still alive. Amarazov would pick up their trail. He had five men left, and he had done more than that with less in the past. He would find them and track them. When Vlasenin handed the papers over, he would be there. And then he would have his revenge. This was not to help Russia win this war, or the next. Nor was it to save him from the firing squad that Renkovich undoubtedly had ready should he return home empty-handed. No. This was revenge. Rawlings had tricked him. For that he and all his men would die.

Back at the camp it was almost over. Amazingly some of the *andartes* had almost made it to the wire. Spiro was one of the last to go down. He had been hit twice, but still he went on. He had seen Veloutis, Farzalis and Sergeant Evros go down but there were still other comrades standing, marching on. They were past the heavy machine-guns but now there were more Germans at the wire, coming out of cover to meet them. Achilles charged on, screaming, desperate for a sure kill, his first German, someone to pay for the suffering of his family and his country. Then a bullet hit him just below the knee, dropping him to the ground. He tried to rise, then another took him in the forehead. A few more isolated shots rang out. Then it was over. The Germans stood in silence for a moment. Then they heard the explosion at the main gate.

༄

For Rawlings and Curtis the attack had come at exactly the right moment. They had been getting nowhere with Brandt despite Curtis invoking his superior rank and playing the arrogant, peremptory Prussian to the hilt. "We have orders from Berlin, we were sent by Kommissar Hoffman. The prisoner must be moved," he shouted through the door for what felt like the fiftieth time.

"The Kommissar in person, or Oberst Ziedler. I open the door to no-one else."

"We have written orders," Curtis bluffed, despite Rawlings' warning look. Curtis held up the fuel request form with a shrug. Rawlings hastily scrawled a rough approximation of Hoffman's signature across the bottom.

There was a moment's pause, then Brandt's voice came again: "Let me see them!"

"How can we do that unless you let us in – oaf!"

Another pause. Rawlings cursed. Then the explosions and brilliant light of the partisans' ordnance hit their senses and Curtis got just the right note of panic in his voice. "Open up now! They're hitting us with everything! Hundreds of partisans. British and Russian paratroops too. The Kommissar could be dead by now. We must get Vlasenin out."

A key turned in the lock. Rawlings and Curtis rushed in, only to be confronted by the two guards levelling their Schmeissers at them, and Brandt with a pistol in one hand and the other held out. "Let's see the orders."

Curtis threw up his hands in frustration, but then proferred the fuel request form. Brandt moved closer to look at it – a fatal mistake. With one hand Curtis grabbed the Gestapo man's pistol arm and pulled him off-balance. With the other he drew his Luger and shot Brandt through the heart at point-blank range. The move put Brandt between the guards and the SOE team and Rawlings used their half-second unsighted to shoot both in the head.

The rest of the team rushed in, Amarazov's Russian in the lead. Garside saw movement to his left and turned, unleashing a two-second burst. Doctor Fleischer was slammed against the wall, then slid to the floor. One of the Gestapo guards twitched in a dying reflex. The Russian stepped forward and straddled both bodies with a two-second burst and Rawlings seized the opportunity, stepping behind and placing the barrel of his Mauser against the Russian's skull. As the noise of the last gunshot died away Rawlings turned to the chair and took his first look at Doctor Dimitri Vlasenin. He was covered in blood and looked near to death. But he was sitting bolt upright, looking at the scene of carnage with astonishment.

"Doctor Vlasenin? I'm Major Rawlings, SOE; the genuine article this time. We've come to get you out."

"But how did you know I was here?" Vlasenin croaked. "Where are you taking me?"

"No time for questions." Rawlings jerked round as heavy firing, followed by an explosion, came from just outside the jail. "If you don't come now, we're all dead."

"Well, since you put it like that," Vlasenin said with a flash of spirit as Pearson and Garside loosened his bonds and got him to his feet. He moved forward shakily, then picked up speed as the party moved out of the cell, through the reception area – and into a full-scale firefight.

∽

The attack had saved Vasily and Yelena too. They had been braced for the sudden light and noise. Their guards were not and it diverted their attention just long enough for the two Russians to move. Vasily's elbow swung back, catching his guard in the neck. As he staggered back, Vasily's huge hands swept the Schmeisser from his grasp then tightened round his throat.

Next to them Yelena clamped a hand over her guard's machine pistol, forcing it down and away from her as the guard hit the trigger. Using their forward momentum, Yelena tripped him and they fell to the ground together, Schmeisser spinning away. She tried to pin his arms down with her knees as they lay prone, while she aimed a killing blow at his throat. But the Brandenburger was well-trained, bigger and stronger. His forearm blocked the blow and with a heave of his whole body he threw her off him. He rose to his feet, drawing a pistol. But Yelena grabbed for his fallen Schmeisser and swung it into his midriff with all her strength. He dropped to his knees, winded and Vasily, his guard already dead, moved behind him and snapped his neck with one swift movement.

He pulled Yelena to her feet and they turned at the run, heading for the main gate where they knew Rawlings' party must be. But almost immediately they were forced to dive for safety as the first of the Brandenburg trucks rounded a bend, sped past them and turned sharp right onto the main thoroughfare.

There were two men with Schmeissers on either side of the truck's rear and another in the cab, ready for action. But the Britons were ready too. As soon as he had heard Mayhew's curse, Hawkins had turned the truck broadside, blocking the road and maximising the field of fire for the men in the back. They were crouched down, only the tops of their helmets presenting any target. The riflemen – Costas, Stavrakis, Jones and the second Russian – all put killing shots into the driver, causing the Brandenburg truck to swerve off the road towards one of the store huts. Mayhew and Walters poured Schmeisser fire into it as it smashed into the hut and a lucky shot hit the petrol tank. The explosion showered debris over them, but when they raised their heads again they saw the truck had formed a blazing roadblock.

The three trucks behind it braked to a halt and disgorged their loads – two dozen Brandenburgers and the survivors of Dorsch's Hermann Goering unit. They used the cover of the truck and the huts to get as close as they could and began pouring fire at the Britons. Then Ziedler, moving up to join them with the rest of the officers, saw the rescue party emerge from the jail. He spotted Vlasenin immediately and recognised Rawlings half a second later.

"Stop them!" he shouted and the front rank of Brandenburgers broke cover in a wild rush. While their comrades kept the truck detail's heads down they charged for Rawlings' party, firing from the hip. Pearson screamed and went down but Garside kept Vlasenin upright, almost carrying him the last few yards to the open tailgate of the truck and lifting him up and inside. The others were clambering aboard too. Garside turned and saw Pearson was still alive, trying to rise to his feet. "Jimmy!" Garside shouted and ran to help him. But he was cut down before he even got close.

Walters stood up in the truck, ignoring Rawlings' cries, and poured fire into the oncoming Germans, killing three and forcing the rest to duck for cover. "Come on, you bastards!" he yelled. Then Hawkins swung the truck round, heading for the gate and several pairs of hands dragged Walters down.

The truck built up speed, outpacing the Germans who charged after it on foot, heedless of the fire from the men at the tailgate. Then Rawlings shouted: "Slow down – look there on the left!" Vasily and Yelena had broken from the cover of the storerooms and were running towards the truck. The covering fire redoubled as Hawkins slowed down, gesturing frantically for them to climb into the cab. He flung the door open, slowing down as much as he dared, and the two Russians scrambled into the passenger seats.

They were almost at the gate. On seeing the battle break out it had been barred shut and now the guards opened fire on the truck. All their attention was focused there, so they had not seen O'Hare. He had slipped from the truck as soon as it had halted and worked his way to the last storeroom before the gate. Staying in cover, he had rigged a block of charges big enough to demolish the gate of a castle. Now he moved, sprinting for the truck and at the same time hurling the charges as far as he could. The fuse ran out just as they landed in front of the gate. The resulting explosion tore it in half, as the guards scattered for cover. Next moment O' Hare had jumped onto the side of the truck, willing hands hauling him inside as Hawkins gunned it up to sixty and it crashed through the remains of the gate.

"Jesus, that was close," Rawlings said as the truck

powered on into the forest. Then he turned to Walters: "That was bloody insane, what you did back there – but it probably got us clear."

Walters was calmer now but there was still a savage light in his eyes. "He was a mate. If you can't bring him back, send some with him."

"I wish we could have brought him back," Rawlings said, then listened hard. The noise of engines was already close behind. "Think you can do it again?"

Walters rammed a new magazine into his Schmeisser. "Just fucking watch me."

At the camp, the three remaining special forces trucks had cleared the roadblock and were streaming through the main gate. Behind them Strasser's partisan hunters had returned from the perimeter engagement and were clambering aboard three Hanomag armoured half-tracks. Unterbrecht was organising the loading of other vehicles. Several motorcycle combinations were already speeding towards the gate, as well as half a dozen Kubelwagens.

Ziedler ran over to Unterbrecht. "Get on the radio to every garrison and unit for fifty miles. All roads blocked and guarded, especially the ones into Turkey. Use the Bulgarians to the north too. My authority."

Unterbrecht nodded. Ziedler turned back to where Hoffman and the other officers stood by the entrance to the jail. He saw a Kubelwagen driven by the Brandenburg platoon sergeant, Kobal, heading towards them. He called to Dressler and Weiss to join him. Ciarelli ran up. "Give my men a vehicle," he shouted.

"Why not?" Ziedler replied. "This pursuit will need all the men we can get. Talk to Unterbrecht." He broke off as a stretcher party carried Pearson past. He signalled them to halt and ran over to look at the injured Briton. He had been shot in the stomach and was virtually unconscious with the pain, face pale and bathed in sweat. "Who are you?" Ziedler asked at last.

Pearson raised himself up on one elbow with some difficulty. "Your worst nightmare, squarehead – the bloody British Army."

He sank back on the stretcher. Ziedler turned to Hoffman. "Talk to him when they've got him in a bed. We need to know more about this team."

"I doubt he'll be able to tell us much." Hoffman replied. "Doesn't look like a big fish."

"Try, anyway – then shoot him." Ziedler saw Hoffman's look and said angrily: "Why not? He's in enemy uniform."

"Like all your boys were last night." Hoffman's voice was thick with contempt. "I'd like to see you do a dirty job like that once in a while, Herr Oberst."

"When we get back with Rawlings, you will." Ziedler jumped into the Kubelwagen and followed the rest of the hunters out.

∽

Rawlings was at the partition of the truck, talking to Hawkins as he steered the vehicle expertly along the twisting forest road, shouts and shots from the roadblock he had bulldozed aside echoing behind them. Rawlings had a large-scale map of the area in his hands. "We can't do anything until we get clear of this forest," Rawlings shouted above the roar of the engine. "There's only one road out and we're on it. Then it forks at the top of a hill. Side roads everywhere. Think you could lose them in that?"

"No bother." Hawkins glanced back as Rawlings held the map up, but his hands continued guiding the wheel around bends and over potholes in the road as though they had a life of their own. "Get the lads to chuck a few smoke grenades behind us, double back a few times, take the odd shortcut through the trees – easy as falling off a log. Provided they don't catch us first, of course."

He looked in his wing mirror and put his foot down. Rawlings looked back and saw the lights of the pursuit looming ever closer. "Nail those bastards!" he shouted. "I don't want to see anything closer than fifty yards."

"Better shut your eyes, then," Walters replied. "They're coming up like shit off a shovel."

"Well, you have my permission to discourage them, corporal. Go for the wheels. And I want two men with rifles up with him. You aim for the drivers. Rest of you watch the sides. Conor, can you lay down a little fog of war?"

"Already done." O'Hare, crouched down in the lee of the truck, near where Mayhew and Sanderson were forming a shield around Vlasenin, held up a cluster of grenades tied together. "Next time we get to a blind corner I'll give 'em a real London particular, with a dash of Fireworks Night."

"Good man yourself." Rawlings gave a reassuring smile to Vlasenin, who looked terrified, and took up station on the right hand side of the truck, Schmeisser at the ready. Walters already had his propped up against the tailboard, Rowley and the second Russian alongside him with their rifles. The first truck was close now, the

Brandenburgers firing from the cab and leaning over the rear at either side. They were aiming for the tyres, but the unreal light of the headlamps added little to the visibility and the tyres were black rubber on an unlit tarmac road. Coupled with the swift, unsteady motion of both vehicles it rendered a direct hit a matter of blind chance.

Rowley and the Russian had a far easier task. The headlights illuminated the cab and both men had killed from farther out than this. Their bullets hit the driver simultaneously. As his lifeless hands left the wheel the truck veered right, off the road and into the forest. As the second truck swerved to avoid it Walters took advantage of a clear shot broadside at one of the front wheels. He aimed downwards and his luck held. The rubber burst and metal screeched on the road, spinning the truck to the left this time, off the road and into the air as it sailed over a steep gulley to smash into the trees beyond. A second later it exploded in a gout of yellow flame.

There was only one truck left now, the one with Dorsch's Hermann Goering unit inside. But some of their comrades had taken one of the Kubelwagens too and now it moved up behind the truck, then past it, more off the road than on, taking a suicidal risk as the metal scraped against the tree trunks, threatening to spin the vehicle out of control. But the driver kept his head and then they were past the truck and clear.

The Kubelwagen was a lighter, faster vehicle than the three trucks and it gained on the Britons rapidly. Inside were six of the finest troops in the German army, thirsting for revenge on the dead of two engagements. There was a rear-mounted MG42 worked by a crew of two and everyone but the driver was firing small arms. Unlike the truck troops they had a clear field of fire and they poured a stream of bullets into the Britons' vehicle. Even Walters was forced to duck, and the German riflemen were starting to get close to the tyres. "Time for a change in the weather, Paddy," Walters shouted.

"It's coming, cobber," O'Hare said as he crawled towards the tailgate. He had seen a left-hand bend approaching and he timed his throw to perfection. The truck roared round the bend just as the Kubelwagen went over the grenade cluster at the moment of detonation. The blast flipped the scout car up into the air then back down onto the road, where it collided with the truck, sending both vehicles off the road.

But there were more Kubelwagens behind, as well as the motorcycle combinations. As the pursuing convoy rounded the bend they moved up to flank the scout cars, sending a field of fire that kept every head down in the truck. The combinations advanced, overtaking the scout cars, level with the truck now, aiming into the sides and at the cab and petrol tanks. A bullet shattered Hawkins' wing mirror. He cursed and sideswiped one combination off the road. The second, on the right-hand side, was almost level with the cab. The gunner tried to elevate his machine-gun to straddle the cab while the rider drew a pistol and fired shot after shot at Vasily and Yelena, forcing them to duck for cover. The machine-gun was almost on target, and one burst would have killed everyone in the cab. Then Curtis leaned over the side, one hand grabbing the bodywork to steady himself and got off two quick shots. Both were direct hits to the head. The combination careered off into the trees as Curtis ducked back into cover sharply. It was only later that

Rawlings realised Curtis had performed one of the best feats of pistol shooting he had ever seen.

But the firing from behind did not let up. Ricochets were everywhere. One came perilously close to Vlasenin. Another hit Sanderson on the left bicep. Walters tried to return fire but the fusillade kept his head down. Then the second Russian sighed and raised himself to his feet at the tailgate. He managed one snap shot before half a dozen bullets hit him. But it was a good shot, taking the lead Kubelwagen driver in the heart. It careered off the road, unsighting the vehicles behind, and in that few seconds respite the truck rounded another bend.

Instantly the Britons tried to help the Russian, placing dressings and sulfa powder on his multiple wounds. But to no avail. He gave a shuddering convulsion and lay still just as the German pursuit rounded the bend. The Britons rushed back to their stations, but once again a hail of tracer kept them down in the rear. There were four combinations left and behind them the Kubelwagens were veering left and right to make way for Strasser's Hanomags. The bikes moved in again, like wolves tearing at a deer's haunches. Walters blew two off the road before he took a bullet in the shoulder. Hawkins swiped the last two left and right. But they had hit a tyre. Metal screeched and suddenly Hawkins found himself driving a pneumatic drill with an anchor attached. "How much further?" he yelled to Rawlings.

"Another mile or so – but uphill."

Hawkins shook his head. "I'll keep her on the road – but we can't outrun them."

The lead Hanomag was almost level now, slamming its armoured snout against the truck's rear. The front mounted machine-gun could not traverse into the truck, otherwise every man would have been dead. But the troops in the rear were firing. One bullet took Costas in the forearm; another hit Jones between the eyes. He fell to the floor of the truck without a sound. As Stavrakis and Mitchell dived to help Costas the truck lurched to the right as the half-track slammed it again, metal scraping the trees, wheels skidding over the edge of the roadside bank. Hawkins, cursing, managed to keep her steady. The Germans moved in again. But then Hawkins braked sharply. The Hanomag kept going, open rear exposed, and as the troops inside ducked for cover. Conor took his cue. Another grenade cluster landed inside as the truck leapt forward, a split second before the Hanomag blew.

The second crashed into it, but the third simply bulldozed past and drew level, hitting the truck again and again like a shark at a lifeboat, keeping back to avoid its comrades' fate. The forward machine-gun was near to zeroing in on the truck's rear. Hawkins knew the last bend was coming up, and that the ground on either side was getting steeper. He did not slow down at all and the Hanomag driver, partly unsighted by the truck and too intent on his prey, did not notice the looming bend. At the last minute Hawkins threw the truck in a desperate right turn, only just keeping on the road. The Hanomag was not so lucky, careering over the lip of the slope and down in a mad descent, lurching off-balance and tumbling to destruction.

And they were clear. No pursuit close enough to catch them before the crossroads they could see ahead. "Where did you learn to drive like that, Private Hawkins?" Rawlings asked in grateful amazement.

"London Bridge on a Friday night, sir," Hawkins replied, but then the smile froze on his lips as a dozen sets of headlights were switched on. There were vehicles blocking every road. Trucks, scout cars, combinations, even an armoured car. Some were German, most Bulgarian. All had guns trained on the Britons' truck. Behind them the pursuit crested the hill, Ziedler's Kubelwagen in the lead now.

Ziedler stood up in the back as the pursuit halted. "A brave try, Major Rawlings, but it ends now. Throw down your weapons and send Vlasenin out first."

Rawlings looked at the sheer drop on either side, the drop which had claimed the Hanomag's driver and crew. Then he looked at Hawkins. "Think you can make it?"

"Only one way to find out." Rawlings clasped his shoulder in reply, then turned and looked at his riflemen. Only two left now, Rowley and Stavrakis, but both unwounded. "Get the lights of those boys in front; as many as you can." They took up position silently. The rest of the team were already taking a firm grip on the truck's sides. O' Hare had another grenade cluster ready.

"My patience is not limitless, major," Ziedler called. "Now!"

"You heard him" Rawlings said. "Now!"

Hawkins swung the wheel and pushed his foot to the floor as Conor threw the grenades at Ziedler's Kubelwagen and the riflemen shot out the headlights of the vehicles at the crossroads. Before the Germans could fire back the grenades had exploded, shrouding the road in smoke – and the truck was careering down the slope as Hawkins slammed back into first gear and swung the wheel desperately. Several times it nearly went over or hit the trees full-on. But at last the ground levelled out and it limped onto a dirt track. There was no sign of pursuit. Hawkins braked to a halt and patted the dashboard. "You tough old bitch."

༕

"You mean we're that close?" Rawlings could hardly believe it. But as Vlasenin looked at the map spread over the bonnet he pointed to a small town just across the border and barely twenty miles from the forested gulley where they now sheltered.

"Oh, yes. Professor Karkoszy has lived there for many years. He works at the University of Thrace in Edirne. But he is from Hungary originally. When I first met him he was still at Budapest University, head of their physics department. But then Horthy took over and he left. I kept in touch and when I heard he was in Turkey I thought this would be a safe place for the papers. When we were both guests at a conference in Lisbon in May last year I smuggled them out and gave them to him. I told him to keep them safe until I could get out. It's been a long while but he knows I couldn't even send a warning in advance for fear of discovery. He'll be ready for me."

"Not at the crack of dawn on a Monday, perhaps," Rawlings smiled. "But we need to get to him as soon as possible. Just as well Amarazov let us keep our civvies." He looked at the pile of clothing in the corner of the truck, then at the dishevelled, bloodstained German uniform which he, like the rest of the team gathered round him, still wore. "These will do until we're right at the border but once we're in Turkey we switch."

"The truck might look a bit conspicuous," Curtis pointed out.

"Can't be helped. We haven't got time to forage anything else, quite apart from the risk of going near the main roads. Anyway, she's brought us this far – reckon she's got one more ride left, Private Hawkins?"

Hawkins, bent double over the engine, working by the light of a hooded hurricane lamp, looked up. "Just about, sir." His eyes were red from fatigue in a face smeared with engine oil. He had been working ever since Rawlings had decided they were safe from pursuit and called a halt, replacing the tyre then trying to patch up the multiple scars inflicted during the chase. "If we're as close as you say, I'll get us there, but I wouldn't count on much further. I could do with a little longer to work on her, though."

"You'll have it," Rawlings said. "We've still got to bury Private Jones." The rest looked at the body, still in the back of the truck, but draped with a uniform jacket. "Then once we're back on the road, with the papers, we beg, steal or borrow a truck from somewhere. I'm sure Vasily knows all the wrong people. Then we radio Davies at the usual time and tell him to make sure that plane comes in to the airfield tonight. The transmitter's not too bashed up, is it, Conor?"

"Guarded it with me life, Alex," O'Hare said. "I can try to get through to Cairo now if you like."

Rawlings shook his head. "We're too close to the German garrisons – they might have monitoring equipment. Besides, might as well wait until we've got two pieces of good news to tell him. So, that's the plan. Sneak across the border just before first light, grab the papers, lay low until we get a replacement truck, then a drive along the back roads to get to the rendezvous point by nightfall." He looked at Vlasenin with concern. "That means a hard day's travelling for you, but there's nothing else for it. We can't afford to linger in Turkey too long."

Vlasenin managed a smile. "I've stood up to torture from the Germans and Amarazov for nearly a week now. I think I can cope with a journey along some country roads."

"Good man." He turned and helped the others to pick up Jones' body. The soil of the Dhadhia Forest was soft and they made short work of their task. When the last shovelful of earth was placed over him Rawlings stood back. "Anyone want to say anything?"

"He was a good man," Walters said. "So were the two blokes we left behind, and…"

He tailed off. Rawlings nodded and turned to Hawkins. Their driver's teeth shone white through a mask of engine oil as he gave a thumbs-up sign.

They clambered aboard and Hawkins slammed down the bonnet and retook his position in the driver's seat. There was a sickening moment when the engine refused to turn over at first ignition. But Hawkins tickled the clutch and said a silent prayer before trying again and this time the truck responded. "You fucking beauty," he shouted, then added in an embarrassed tone: "It's bloody unpatriotic, I know, sir, but I reckon a Bedford would be scrap iron by now."

"As long as she gets us there," Rawlings smiled. "Now let's move."

The house was set high on a wooded hillside, half a mile out of the town. A road snaked down the slope past it and on to the main road to Edirne. There was a patch of garden between the stone walls that marked the boundary and the house itself. An old Ford sedan was parked in the driveway. There was no sign of movement inside the house. Rawlings put down the binoculars and looked at his watch. 5.30 a.m. Earlier than expected. They had made good time, and there would still be an hour or so of darkness to cover their departure. "Right, let's get moving. Doctor Vlasenin, come with me to make the introductions. Rowley and Mayhew, you too; keep watch while we're inside just in case anything unexpected happens. The rest of you stay here. You see any movement on the road from either direction flash the lamp three times quickly. And I want one man to patrol the woods around, just in case there's any trouble from that quarter."

Hawkins' hand came straight up. "I'll keep an eye out, sir." Rawlings nodded.

"You think there'll be any trouble, skipper?" Walters' voice was sceptical.

"I always do. That's why I'm still alive." Then he was gone, Vlasenin with him and the two NCOs behind. The truck was parked on a dirt track, set back slightly from the hill road. The four men used every inch of cover and it took them almost to the driveway. Rawlings opened the wooden gate slowly and carefully, making no sound. Then he sprinted up to the doorway, Vlasenin following more slowly as Rowley and Mayhew took up station in the shadows on either side of the doorway. As Vlasenin reached the door Rawlings knocked twice. For several long moments they waited. But at last a light came on inside, then the door opened a fraction and a voice called in Turkish: "Who is it?"

"It's Vlasenin," Rawlings replied in the same language. "Let us in."

There was a sharp intake of breath but the door did not open. Then Vlasenin added in English: "It's true, Janos. I've come for the papers."

There was another pause, then the door was flung open and a small, slim man with greying dark hair and moustache stood before them, an expression of astonishment on his face. "Dimitri!" Then he laughed and said in English: "Jesus, it's good to see you. I heard you were dead – that the Reds had got you."

"Not quite," Vlasenin shrugged. "But it was a close thing."

"And it still could be," Rawlings broke in. "I'm afraid we don't have time for a scholarly reunion." He turned to Karkoszy. "Sorry to trouble you at this ungodly hour, professor, but you've got something belonging to the good doctor and we need it back – quickly."

"Why, yes, of course – come in, please." He led them down a long entrance hall, which gave onto a large living room-cum study. It was obvious that Professor Karkoszy was an academic, and a bachelor. Books and papers lay in untidy profusion everywhere. There was an atmosphere of dust and cigarette smoke. Cups and plates stood unwashed all around. But Karkoszy surveyed it with pride. "This place is the happiest I've ever been, Dimitri. You should have joined me years ago. The rest of Europe is run by the barbarians now."

"Yes, I'm sure you're right, Jani," Vlasenin said

nervously as he surveyed the chaos. "That's why it's so important my papers were kept safe."

"Of course, of course." Karkoszy looked at him, then at Rawlings, and gave a sly smile. "You think the old professor has let his wits wander, living up here with the goatherds, eh? Well, I haven't. I knew how precious they were to you, Dimitri, and I knew to keep them secure."

He walked to a wall at the far end of the room and took down an oil painting of the Budapest opera house. Behind it was a large, modern and obviously purpose-built safe. Karkoszy smiled again, then began turning the combination. After a few seconds the door sprang open and he removed a small leather briefcase. "I look at them now and again – it's tempting to use some of the theories in my lectures." Karkoszy's voice was wistful as he handed them over. "As ever you're far ahead of us all, Dimitri. All it needs now is a little work on the practical applications. But I'm sure there'll be plenty of people to help you with that." He cast a dubious glance at Rawlings.

Vlasenin had the briefcase open. There were scores of loose sheets inside; some with illustrations, diagrams and formulae, most simply text in a handwriting so small it seemed as though Vlasenin had strained to cram as much knowledge as he could onto every page. He snapped the briefcase shut suddenly and handed it to Rawlings. "My papers, major. Guard them well."

"Oh, we will, Doctor Vlasenin," said Ciarelli.

Chapter 6

Improvised Journeys

RAWLINGS SPUN ROUND. CIARELLI WAS framed in the doorway, Riva behind him. Both had drawn Beretta automatic pistols levelled at the three men by the safe. There was a crash of breaking glass and two more men appeared at the shattered windows on either side of the room. Like the officers they were in civilian clothes, but they too carried Italian Army weaponry; Beretta submachine-carbines.

"It's been a long time, *majore*," Ciarelli said as he advanced into the room. The English was good, but with the same heavy Tuscan accent Rawlings remembered from Spain.

"Not long enough," Rawlings replied as calmly as he could, trying to disguise his feeling of utter consternation. "Still, I might have known you'd be hanging on Ziedler's coat tails as usual."

Ciarelli's smile slipped a little. "You are mistaken, Major Rawlings. You will look in vain for our German allies this time." The smile returned to full beam. "I think Italy can claim sole credit for finally bringing Doctor Vlasenin and his papers together."

He turned to Vlasenin, who was standing dumbstruck, a look of utter terror on his face. Karkoszy looked scared too, but also angry. "What is going on here?" he shouted, taking a pace towards Ciarelli.

In reply Ciarelli shot him in the head. The Beretta had a silencer, so the only sound was a soft 'phut'. But the impact hurled Karkoszy against the wall. He slid lifeless down to the floor.

"Another traitor to his country and the Axis," Ciarelli said with contempt. "He's been on our files for years. So thank you for leading us to him also, Major Rawlings – an incidental bonus."

Rawlings looked at Karkoszy's body, then back to Ciarelli, eyes burning with anger. "And I suppose our reward for it is a dose of the same."

"Oh, no." Ciarelli shook his head in exaggerated dismay. "How wasteful do you think we are? Of course the good doctor here is coming with us. But so are you – and your men. Do not worry, they have not been harmed. Merely overpowered – with one exception." His smile vanished. "But the health of them all could change if you do not surrender Vlasenin and his papers to me – now!"

Rawlings sighed and turned to Vlasenin. "I'm sorry – you must go with them. Don't try to resist."

Vlasenin walked towards Ciarelli, moving like an old man in a dream. Rawlings followed him, the briefcase with the papers held out. Riva disarmed Rawlings as Ciarelli took the papers, then holstered his Beretta and took Rawlings' Mauser from Riva's hand. "A fine weapon, so I hear."

"It's served me well so far," Rawlings replied. "And it will again."

Ciarelli gave a humourless laugh. "I think not. Now move!"

He gestured for Rawlings and Vlasenin to leave first. The first thing Rawlings saw when he emerged into the driveway was Rowley and Mayhew with their hands tied, two more Italians standing guard on them. The rest of the team were there too, two more guards pointing carbines at them; so that was why Rowley and Mayhew had not been able to shout a warning. There was another German army truck parked by Karkoszy's Ford and as Rawlings watched their own truck drove slowly up the path and into the driveway. As it braked to a halt the body of Private Hawkins was thrown out. There was a gaping bullet hole in his chest. One of the Italians moved the body closer to the doorway, then placed a pistol into its hand. Ciarelli looked at him and smiled. "Riva is doing the same to the professor inside. The Turks will think some lone bandit tried to rob him but took on more than he bargained for. The open safe will help – we'll stick a few of your gold sovereigns in it." He laughed again.

Walters was at the wheel but one of Ciarelli's men had a pistol trained on him. Half a dozen other Italians, all armed with rifles or Beretta carbines, walked alongside the truck. The two who had covered the windows walked round to join them. Fifteen altogether, including the two officers. Not bad odds in a straight fight. And he could see from the faces of his men inside the truck as they looked at Hawkins' body being hauled around by the Italians, the body of the man who had saved them half a dozen times in the pursuit and died because he still wanted to keep an eye on that old cow of a truck, that they would be thirsting for revenge. But, as Rawlings reflected bitterly, such a prospect was unlikely in the extreme.

He cursed his inefficiency. Why hadn't he posted a full guard on the road, and in the forest? Or brought more men with him to the house? Because he had not wanted to attract undue attention. And he had not believed it possible that they would be followed. He turned to Ciarelli. "How did you find us?"

"Simple enough, *majore*. After your stunt on the hilltop, the *Tedeschi* were a little shell-shocked. They all stood around licking their wounds while we drove on. And of course Ziedler didn't notice that the little Italians weren't hanging on to his coat tails any more. There are many roads you could have taken, sure, but we looked at the map, figured out where you would have ended up, and then plotted a course that would take you over the border as quickly as possible – but using the little dirt roads, that wouldn't be a problem for a truck this size. We picked one, and got lucky. We saw you head past, and then we followed you right here. I admit I feared you would head for Turkey more quickly. What did you do? Stop to bury your dead?"

Rawlings did not reply. Ciarelli gave a contemptuous shake of his head. "Meanwhile, the *Tedeschi* will be trying to put men and vehicles on every road in Thrace," he continued. "But they haven't enough of either. That's their trouble. A problem comes up, they just throw more men, and tanks and planes, at it." He tapped his forehead. "Never use this."

"Well, much good it'll do you," Rawlings replied.

"You're hundreds of miles from the nearest Italian-occupied territory. You'll have to go through German or Bulgarian sectors, or Bulgaria itself, to get to safety. Either that or try Turkey, and I guarantee we'll not last much longer in these trucks without somebody getting suspicious. It's been a bad weekend for unwanted foreigners round these parts. If they catch us the chances are they'll intern us all and send Vlasenin back to Russia. Do you want that?"

"Of course not. But these trucks don't have to get us very far. You're quite right, Major Rawlings. If we had to get to safety by road we would have little hope. But why drive when you can fly?"

Rawlings nodded in reluctant admiration. "So you've found a private airfield nearby – bought some landing space and a lot of silence." He rubbed his thumb and forefinger together in the universal gesture.

Ciarelli's smile grew even wider. "Not a private one, *majore*; a full-size Turkish Air Force base. It's been running black market trips to every part of the Balkans since war broke out. Fruit, cotton, Scotch whisky – and people too, sometimes. The commander has a more sensible attitude to these matters than his government."

"That kind of thing takes more than one night to organise, though." Rawlings looked hard at him. "You had this planned long before we came along, didn't you?"

"Of course. Do you think we wanted to see the Germans take this man and his papers, when it was Italian intelligence that discovered his whereabouts? The original plan was to wait until Hoffman had beaten the location out of him, then try to separate the man or his papers from Ziedler during the last phase of the operation. That would not have been easy," he added reluctantly. "So you really have made this all much simpler for us, *majore*. My compliments and thanks." He looked up at the sky suddenly. The first streaks of dawn were beginning to appear. "But we waste time talking. Get in the truck."

A guard prodded Rawlings towards the truck with his rifle and Rawlings obeyed. Rowley and Mayhew were already aboard, looking as shamed and angry as the rest of the team. Vlasenin made to go with them but Ciarelli caught his arm and pushed him into the rear of the Ford. "You stay close to me from now on, *Signor Dottore*." He threw the car keys to Riva, who jumped into the front passenger seat and handed them to the driver. The engine turned over first time and within seconds all three vehicles were turning out of the driveway and leaving Professor Karkoszy's house behind.

"Well, that could have gone better," Rawlings said as he sat down in the back of the truck. Only Walters remained in the front cab, guard still watching him as he drove. Two more guards sat by the tailgate, machine-carbines trained on the SOE team. They were all looking towards Rawlings. Curtis, for one, had clearly expected a different reaction from his commanding officer.

"So what do we do now?" he asked.

"What else can we do?" Rawlings replied. "Play along but keep alert. Ciarelli wants us alive for some reason. My guess is he might want us to throw in with him in an emergency."

Curtis was aghast. "Why would he want us to do that?"

"Because he's out on a limb. They're taking a hell of

a risk cutting the Germans out of the loop like this. My guess is that when Ziedler finds out – if he hasn't already – he's going to come after Ciarelli with everything he's got. Ciarelli's only hope is to get Vlasenin and the papers back to Italy as soon as possible. But if Ziedler can locate the planes and force them to land in this part of Greece then Ciarelli's got a real job on his hands. The Italians hold a few of the islands, but that doesn't get them anywhere nearer to Italy. And to get to their sectors on the mainland they'd have to go through German or Bulgarian-occupied territory first. Too difficult. The only other option would be to land as close to the Yugoslav border as possible – Italy occupies the Macedonian sector there. But that's partisan country – and most of the Yugoslav partisans are Communist, even more so than the Greeks. They're going to be taking orders from Moscow on this job. If it came to a firefight he could well need us to help him out." He paused. "And we might have to."

"You'd help him? Fight alongside Italians?" Curtis was beginning to exhibit the same symptoms he had displayed over the shooting of Vasily. "Are you out of your mind? They're the enemy."

"Like I said back in Cairo, Captain Curtis; everyone's the enemy as far as we're concerned. The most important thing now is to stay alive and help keep Vlasenin alive and his papers safe. I'll throw in with the Devil himself if it helps us do all that. And I expect my team to follow me. Is that clear?"

He addressed the question to Curtis but his eyes scanned everyone as he waited for a reply. It was Mayhew who barked out "yessir!" in a parade ground tone. The rest nodded in agreement, even Curtis. "Good. So like

I said – stay alert. Don't start thinking like prisoners or we're done for."

There was silence for a while as the convoy wended its way along the Turkish back roads. Once or twice they passed traffic and received a backward glance but Ciarelli pressed on regardless. And the airbase was close. After less than an hour the hills gave way to a level plain. The base was clearly visible in the early morning winter sunshine and within a few minutes Ciarelli was being waved through by the gate guards, the convoy following. A tall, handsome Turkish Air Force officer with a perfectly trimmed moustache and a rakish gleam in his eye was waiting at the gate and after a brief conversation with Ciarelli jumped into the Ford, directing the convoy to a group of hangars. The doors on two of them were already open. A sudden roar of aero engines split the air and a Savoia Marchetti 82 transport plane taxied out of each of them. Ciarelli ordered the convoy to disembark and as their guards prodded the SOE team towards the planes Rawlings passed close by Ciarelli again. "Two, eh? That's a bit greedy."

Ciarelli shook his head. "Practical, *majore*. One to carry Vlasenin, one for the papers. And now that we have acquired a dozen SOE agents, a little more room for everyone. Two different flight paths, just in case Ziedler is on our tail, but one destination – the Otranto air base. In Italy. We'll be there in five hours."

"I wouldn't bet on it."

"You have nothing to bet with, *majore*. Except your lives – and I own them already. Now get aboard."

Rawlings obeyed and within five minutes the planes were airborne. The SM82 had originally been designed as a bomber and, despite the modifications, it was not built to take too many passengers. Rawlings and half his team, including Curtis, Vasily and Yelena were in one, together with Ciarelli, Vlasenin and five guards. The rest of the guards and the remainder of the SOE men were crammed into the other under the charge of Captain Riva, who was holding the papers to his chest like a dying child. As soon as the planes were in the air the Italians changed back into their uniforms but one guard kept a gun on the prisoners throughout.

The planes stayed together for a few miles, but then Riva's veered sharply off to the south. That one would skirt the Aegean islands, Rawlings guessed, then turn west just below the Gulf of Thessaloniki, and plot a course across the Italian-held sector of the mainland. The other kept heading due west, which would take it across Bulgarian-occupied Thrace to the border with the Yugoslav province of Macedonia, now in Italian hands. After that their options were limitless. They could change planes to throw the Germans off the scent, or do as Ciarelli had said and head straight for Italy. He knew that a fully-fuelled SM82 had sufficient range to get as far as Otranto, and beyond, in less than five hours at a push.

But first they had to overfly the German sector. Rawlings knew this was the time of maximum danger: one look at Ciarelli made it abundantly clear the Italian knew that too. He was in the cockpit constantly, muttering instructions to the pilot and keeping a close eye on the skies outside. It was unlikely that there was much in the way of radar equipment in such a far-flung corner of the Third Reich, virtually unreachable by Allied bombers and with no major targets to draw their attention anyway. But

Rawlings knew that whatever there was Ziedler would be using it by now.

So the tension increased as the plane ate up the miles. But after nearly an hour was up the pilot called Ciarelli into the cockpit and whispered something into his ear. Ciarelli's smile broadened and he pulled a Toscani cigar from his tunic pocket. The pilot looked at him sharply and after a moment Ciarelli replaced the cigar and pulled out a hip flask. "This calls for a celebration, Major Rawlings. We are clear of German-held territory and need not cross it again. I doubt the Bulgars have much need of radar to control a few leaderless Greek bandits." He proffered the flask to Rawlings.

"It's a bit early in the day for me – and too early for you to start celebrating, Eduardo. You've still got a long way to go and every mile brings you further into the Third Reich. There are still plenty of radar stations nearby – and plenty of Messerschmitt squadrons too."

"A lot of sky for them to cover, *majore*. And even if they catch us, what then? Shoot us from the skies? And see their best hope of victory die too? I think not. No, we shall be at Otranto by this afternoon. And there I am afraid our ways will part for a while. You have been useful to me so far, but on our passage to Rome you would be a hindrance. There is a camp near Otranto full of your comrades from North Africa and Greece. There you will have some time to reflect on your failure until we bring you in for interrogation." His smile broadened. "Perhaps we will give you back to Hoffman as part of the deal that Germany will strike with us? How would you like that, eh?"

Rawlings did not reply. Ciarelli gave a mirthless laugh and raised the flask to his lips. But at that moment the pilot called out: "Signor Colonel; come here please. Radio transmission."

Ciarelli sighed and replaced the flask. "What is it?" he asked as he entered the cockpit. "A message from Rome?"

"No, sir." The pilot gulped. "It is a Colonel Ziedler, of the German Abwehr."

"What?" Ciarelli barked. "Give me that." He grabbed the microphone from the radio operator, who relinquished his headphones with alacrity. "How did you get this frequency?"

"General Ame gave it to me." Ziedler's voice was muffled by the static but Ciarelli could still detect the calm, superior tone in it. "They seem rather displeased by your treachery, colonel."

"Treachery?" Ciarelli kept calm by a monumental effort. "We rescued something from last night's disaster. And you accuse me of treachery?"

"I can think of no better word for keeping two planes waiting in Turkey without disclosing the fact to me or my superiors. Or for mounting an independent mission for Vlasenin's papers without even informing me of your whereabouts."

"There wasn't the time." Hearing Ziedler outline precisely how tenuous his position was had calmed Ciarelli down somewhat. "We agreed in Berlin that if independent action was necessary and appropriate my team would be allowed to pursue it."

"And we are most grateful, Signor Colonel. But now the immediate danger has passed we would request that you bring both planes to land at an airfield of my designation."

"Impossible. All of Greece has a partisan resistance element, backed by British infiltrators. As does Yugoslavia. Italy is the safest destination and we can be there in a matter of hours. That is my decision."

"It is not your decision to make, Signor Colonel. The reason I have access to this frequency is that your General Ame and Minister Ciano have agreed to a request from Berlin for full co-operation. It seems Il Duce has a truer understanding of the word "alliance" than you do. So please let us have no more argument."

"And what if I refuse?"

"You will be shot down. I have the current location and anticipated flight path of both planes. Two Messerschmitt 109 squadrons have been mobilised and are on their way to intercept at this moment. If you try to escape they can outrun you. And when they catch you they will shoot you down."

Ciarelli thought frantically, wiping his brow to clear the sweat which had beaded suddenly. "You wouldn't dare. You would lose everything."

"So would the Allies. Everyone back to where they were seven days ago. Hardly ideal, Signor Colonel. Neither Berlin nor Rome will be very happy with either of us as it is. I allowed Vlasenin to be taken from my custody. You won him back. But then you violated every dictate of military co-operation, and simple common sense, out of greed. A greed which could result in total failure. I think the harsher judgement will fall on you. The alternative is to land your planes, and resume our earlier arrangement. This morning's events will be forgotten and you will be properly rewarded for your part in securing Vlasenin's papers. Then we will think of a better way to transport him to safety. If we can locate your little flying circus then I feel sure the British might be able to as well. Their fighters on Cyprus have the range. Be sensible, Eduardo. Bring your planes into land."

"I must check with Rome first. How do I know you have Ame's clearance?"

"The fact that I am talking to you on a Regia Aeronautica channel, for one thing. But check with your superiors by all means. They will tell you the same. I suggest you make it quick, though. The Messerschmitts will be intercepting you in around five minutes, by my reckoning. And if they see no signs of a deviation in either plane's course they will open fire."

The line went dead. Ciarelli scrambled through to the main passenger area and gestured for one of his men to hand the radio over. He dragged it back into the cockpit, closing the connecting door behind him as he switched it on and found the special frequency that patched him straight through to Ciano. "Good morning, Eduardo." His voice through the static sounded as unruffled as Ziedler's. "I presume you have just spoken to the Germans."

"Yes, and I don't believe what I heard." Ciarelli tried to keep his voice to a whisper but felt the anger rising. "Are we going to surrender everything we've won just because Ziedler wants it that way?"

"He has all the High Command behind him – right to the top. They told the Fuhrer, he spoke to Il Duce and… well, that's the way it must be."

"I don't believe them. They wouldn't shoot us down; it would mean they lose everything. I say we call their bluff."

"And I say we do not! As I told you before, Eduardo, I know them. They feel they have been insulted. To wipe that out, yes I do believe they would forfeit this man and his knowledge. There is no logic to it, but that is how they operate. And to keep Vlasenin alive we must do as they say."

"So I simply put down in some new Balkan cesspool and wait for them to come and take what I won?"

"Yes, Eduardo. I am ordering you to do so. Any variation from these orders will be regarded as an act of treason. Punishable by death." There was a long pause. "And if you attempt to hijack land transport and make for Yugoslavia our official response will be exactly the same. Do I make myself clear, Eduardo?

Ciarelli smiled. "Perfectly, Galeazzo."

∽

"So he's agreed to co-operate?" Hoffman asked.

"If you remove the comments about my family ancestry, then yes, that was the essence of his communication." Ziedler removed his headphones and sat back in his chair with a sigh. "For a while I thought the stubborn Tuscan son of a bitch was going to keep his course and damn the consequences."

"And what would you have done then?" Hoffman raised an eyebrow at Ziedler. It was the first time in their long acquaintance he had heard the Abwehr man swear. Ziedler shrugged.

"Radioed Berlin for final authorisation, then blown him out of the skies." He paused. "And resigned myself to spending the rest of the war on counter-terrorist duties in one of the more volatile sectors of the Reich." His laugh held no humour. "Maybe they'd keep me out here. It's the usual reward for that kind of failure."

They were in Unterbrecht's office, where they had been all night and morning. Ever since Ziedler had returned from the pursuit, bruised and shaken but otherwise unhurt, the radio on the desk in the corner had been humming with transmissions. Ziedler looked exhausted. His eyes were red-rimmed with fatigue and his normally immaculate uniform creased and bloodstained. Hoffman also looked tired. The interrogation of the wounded Englishman had yielded nothing. He had been too delirious with pain to say anything of import and had succumbed to his wounds before there had been a chance to execute him. But it had kept Hoffman and his remaining lieutenant, Schmidt, busy for most of the morning. He had only just rejoined Ziedler in the office. And now it seemed they were moving again.

"Yes, we would have been in the shit," Hoffman said. "But you especially," he could not help adding. "How long was it before you noticed the spaghetti-eaters hadn't reported back?"

"About the same time I realised your men had not contributed to the pursuit," Ziedler replied waspishly, "and had no intention of contributing to the search."

"That's not their job!"

"Ah, yes – now what was the Gestapo's job in this mission? To get Vlasenin to talk, and ensure his security in the meantime. I doubt you'll be getting an Iron Cross for this mission, Herr Kommissar, and…" he broke off with a wry laugh. "Anyway, pointless to argue. The main thing is we have another chance." Ziedler looked at the large-scale map of the Bulgarian sector spread on his desk. "Ciarelli should be landing at this airfield here in about fifteen minutes. It will take us a couple of hours to get there by road – flying would have been quicker, of course, but Unterbrecht tells me it will take most of the day to repair the mortar damage to the airstrip. The Bulgarians have promised to keep Ciarelli until we arrive, however. It's not far from the main town in the area, Xanthi, which has a sizeable garrison attached to it, and mountains all around. Vlasenin will be secure there while we decide the safest way to get him out of Greece."

"A convoy," Hoffman replied. "Using the back roads. Plenty of protection and decoys just in case the Tommies try a bomber raid to wipe him out. Once we've got him into the Salonika sector we're out of their aircraft range and back among our boys. Then what's the plan?"

"We get the man, the Italians get the papers. And we all go our separate ways." Ziedler's opinion of the arrangement was plain to see. "Another sop to the Italians. Ciarelli breaks faith, but to smooth things over we give the concessions."

Hoffman shrugged. "Not much we can do about it."

Ziedler looked at him, tired eyes suddenly gleaming. "Really? A convoy wending its way slowly along these treacherous mountain roads, vulnerable to a determined partisan attack… do you know, Klaus, I don't think all of us are going to make it."

The Gestapo man gave Ziedler a quizzical look. "You mean you're going to double-cross them?"

"It's no more than they did to us. Think of it, man. There are no other Italian troops for hundred of miles. There's bound to be some sort of partisan attack – you can't hide convoys that size in this country." He waved a dismissive hand. "And if there isn't one, I'll invent one.

Either way, by the time we get back to Salonika I fear that Colonel Ciarelli and all his men will have died a hero's death during a pitched battle in the Rhodope Mountains, keeping the greatest prize of war safe for the Axis. And we'll all be on a plane to Berlin, with Vlasenin and his papers on the same seat, before the Italians even have time to draft an official protest."

Hoffman was torn between admiration and caution. "You think Canaris and all the rest will be happy with that?"

"I'm certain of it. Besides, it will be a *fait accompli*. Once he's in Berlin he won't be going out again. Nor will his papers. It makes perfect sense. He'll be working with scientists who are as almost as advanced as he is. All Italy has left are second-rate assistants from Fermi's projects. Dividing the research is a nonsensical idea. No, Germany will have all of this victory, as is right and proper. I will give it to her. Don't you see, Klaus? If Ciarelli had not done what he did last night we would have no justification for this, but as it is… I'll show that jumped-up, swaggering Tuscan peasant who's the real spymaster around here."

"You know that if you do that they'll still crucify you afterwards? The spaghettis will want a sacrificial lamb. And I'm going to make damn sure everyone knows this was your idea."

"I would have it no other way, Klaus. They can post me to Outer Mongolia if they wish. As long as I know I have given the ultimate prize to my country and my people. Everything else is unimportant."

Hoffman looked at Ziedler as if he had just arrived from Mars. The Abwehr man did not seem to notice. He was smiling as he gathered up his cap and gloves from the desk and made for the door. Hoffman stepped back to allow him to exit first. "That's unusually courteous of you, Klaus," Ziedler said with some surprise.

"Courtesy's got nothing to do with it," the Gestapo man replied. "When I see a man walking up to a wolf pack wearing a coat made of raw steak, I always keep a few yards behind him."

∽

"Coming in to land now, Signor Colonel," the pilot called through the open door to the cockpit. Ciarelli nodded and signalled to his men. Then he turned to Rawlings: "When we get down, say nothing and keep close to me, *majore*. Understand?"

Rawlings nodded, puzzled by Ciarelli's unusually gnomic remark. After his rage had abated following the conversation with Ciano he had been quiet and withdrawn, occasionally engaging one of his men – a burly, ramrod-straight man with the universal look of the sergeant-major – in a whispered conversation. But in the last few minutes, as the plane had descended through the Rhodope Mountains, he had said nothing. Now he returned to the cockpit, looking out intently.

Abruptly the alpine backdrop of sheer peaks and pine forest, split by foaming streams, gave way to a fertile plain stretching for several miles, though still bordered to the north by the mountains. Through the window Rawlings could see a small airfield, twin to the one in Turkey from which they had taken off barely two hours ago. As the plane made its final descent he tensed himself for action. He could make no signal or communication to his men without being overheard. All he could do was hope an opportunity came. And keep his hand on the tiny Lilliput automatic in a hidden jacket pocket, the one which Riva's cursory search had missed.

The plane's wheels screeched as they hit the tarmac and it decelerated down the runway. Rawlings could see the main control tower, the only two-storey building on the base, looming ever nearer as they approached. A platoon of Bulgarian infantry, with a knot of army and air force officers in their midst, was drawn up in front of it. To the left and right were hangars with more groundcrew and guards around them. There were a couple of large transport planes parked near the hangars, but most of the aircraft were light, unarmed spotters. There was no sign of the plane which carried Riva and the papers. Rawlings guessed the main function of the base was for reconnaissance missions into the mountains, where both the Communist-dominated ELAS and British-backed EDES partisan groups were making inroads, mainly due to the Bulgarians' attempts to replace the Greek communities with Bulgarian settlers and 'Slavify' every aspect of day-to-day life. If they could escape they might well find groups, alerted by Davies, which could shelter and guide them. But that was one of the biggest 'if's of Rawlings' career to date.

As the plane taxied to a halt Ciarelli and his men pointed their weapons at the SOE team and signalled them to get up. They were herded down the steps to the runway, stretching their legs and gulping the cold, fresh air. Two guards kept an eye on them while Ciarelli strode towards the welcoming committee.

The Bulgarians came to meet him, stopping when

there were only a few yards between the two groups. A small, studious-looking young man with corporal's stripes advanced in front of the main party and addressed Ciarelli in faltering Italian.

"Signor Colonel, allow me to welcome you on behalf of Major Petrov of the Royal Bulgarian Air Force and Colonel Motev, commander of the garrison at Xanthi. We have instructions to make you as comfortable as possible until our German allies arrive."

Ciarelli looked at him. "What is your name, corporal?"

"Antonov, Signor Colonel. Simeon Antonov."

"Well, Corporal Simeon Antonov, I would like you to pass this message on to your colonel. And translate exactly, please." He paused, then said clearly: "I too have instructions for you, colonel – provide us with a staff car and two trucks immediately, plus spare army uniforms for my men and all these prisoners, and those in the other plane, which will be landing shortly." He paused, then pointed to Yelena and added: "and a nurse's uniform for the girl, of course."

Corporal Antonov had done as requested, despite the expression of amazement which had spread across his face as he did so. Rawlings could tell from the officers' reactions that the translation had been accurate. Colonel Motev looked dumbstruck for a moment, then fired off a volley in Bulgarian.

"Signor Colonel, he says…" Corporal Antonov looked very unhappy but continued after a nervous swallow. "He demands to know what the hell you are talking about and why the hell should he?"

Ciarelli drew Rawlings' Mauser suddenly and pointed it at Motev. "Tell him that I am on a mission vital to the

Axis victory and I have no time to wait for the Germans. I wish to be driving away from this airfield in half an hour. If he refuses I will shoot him."

Motev was frozen, pistol half-drawn. The other officers were in an attitude so similar it might have been comical – were it not for the forest of rifle barrels now trained on the Italian party, and the soldiers and airmen rushing in to surround them. Ciarelli's men all had their weapons up too. Every finger was on the trigger as Corporal Antonov finished his latest translation duty. Motev made no reply. "I want those weapons down," Ciarelli shouted. "Tell him that – now!"

Antonov hesitated, uncertain. At that moment Rawlings saw one of the officers move. Before his pistol had cleared leather Rawlings drew the Lilliput and shot him below the knee. The officer dropped to the ground with a cry. Motev turned to look at him and Ciarelli took a quick step forward, grabbing him by the collar and holding the Mauser to his temple before the troops could react.

"Tell them to keep calm!" Rawlings shouted to Antonov in Italian. "No-one needs to die here. Do as he says and we will leave you alone. This quarrel is between Germany and Italy alone. Do not interfere. Tell them that, corporal."

Antonov responded with alacrity. Major Petrov listened, looking uncertainly around, then at his brother officer, staggering to keep his balance in Ciarelli's hold, a look of terror on his face. He barked a sharp order and the troops lowered their weapons. "Come with me – all of you," Ciarelli said, pushing Motev towards the control tower. As Rawlings and the rest of the team moved up with the Italian guards Ciarelli whispered to him in English: "Good work, *majore*. I hadn't spotted that bastard going for his gun."

"We would have all died, too, *colonnello*. That's the only reason I did it. Just tell Riva to pay more attention next time he searches someone – for his own sake."

"I will, Major Rawlings. And I'll have you hand it over now, if you please."

They were inside the control tower now. All the Bulgarian troops had vacated it at a command from Petrov on their approach. Before Rawlings could do anything the Italian guards had trained their guns on him. He shrugged and handed the Lilliput to Ciarelli, butt first. "It's not much good past five yards anyway. And I think you'll need a bit more hardware than that when Ziedler catches up with you."

∾

"Damn that spaghetti-eating bastard to hell!" Hoffman kicked a chair across the room to punctuate his curse. They were in Petrov's office, the same room which Ciarelli had made his base until less than an hour ago, waiting for the delivery of the vehicles and uniforms. Ziedler sat at the main desk, Petrov having been given the same treatment as Unterbrecht with a side order of invective from Hoffman.

"He did react a little quicker than expected," Ziedler admitted.

"Is that all you can say?" Hoffman rounded on him. "He's driving up through the mountains like some damned Tuscan bourgeois on a motoring holiday. We've got to spot a Bulgarian Army convoy in a country teeming with the fucking things. And he's got less than a hundred miles to go before he's across the Yugoslav border."

"But to do that he has to go out of the Bulgarian sector," Ziedler replied. "Either he enters territory controlled by us, which he will want to avoid at all costs. Or he must traverse part of Bulgaria itself for the last stage of his journey. Remind me to congratulate whoever it was who drew up the administrative boundaries of this country. Giving us control of the Salonika region means no-one can pass between Greece and Yugoslavia without our knowing about it."

"We should have insisted the planes landed at Salonika in the first place."

"We tried – the Italians would not countenance it. They insisted on the Bulgarian sector because it was neutral ground. They knew we could not simply surround Ciarelli and force him to obey us as soon as he landed. Another concession for which we will make them pay. Yes, I think they have exhausted their credit with this little escapade. Ciano will deny that he encouraged Ciarelli to break faith again, but we all know better. Once we have Vlasenin and the papers back we will be fully entitled to custody of both."

"You think we're going to get him back just like that? Haven't you heard what I just said? Even if he has to go through Bulgaria he's wearing a fucking Bulgarian uniform, he and all his men. He can bluff his way past a border post with that. I don't trust these Bulgars to get the radio alert out in time. And there are a dozen posts along the border. How do you know which one he's going to use?"

"The one closest to Yugoslavia, I would assume. At least, I hope so. My plan depends upon it to a certain extent."

Hoffman gave him a suspicious look. "Plan? What plan?"

Ziedler waved a dismissive hand. "I knew Ciarelli would not simply wait here to hand his prizes over to us. Whether Ciano has sanctioned this escapade, or whether Ciarelli is simply being mutinous, I expected something like it all along. The only surprising element was the speed with which he got the Bulgarians to give him what he wanted. I had hoped we would be close enough to pick up his trail. But, as you say, there are now a dozen different routes he could be taking to get to the border country. Impossible to police them all, even if we had the resources. So I decided to target a specific area with my back-up force. Did you never wonder, Klaus, why we only brought ordinary troops with us as escort, not the Brandenburgers and Dorsch's men as well?"

"You told me you needed them to keep watch in case Ciarelli tried for Turkey again."

Ziedler gave an indulgent smile. "Why would he do that? The risk of internment is too great. If he had wanted to escape via a Turkish land route he would have done so this morning." He shook his head. "No, Leutnant Weiss will stay there just in case anything like that does happen. But Dressler and the rest of them are organising a little surprise for Colonel Ciarelli."

୰

"Border post coming up, Signor Colonel," Riva said. Ciarelli was instantly alert. He turned to Vlasenin, who sat beside them in the rear of the staff car, dressed as a major in the Bulgarian Army's medical corps. "This will be the hardest part. So you say nothing and do nothing. If you throw yourself on their mercy they'll throw you straight back to Ziedler and Hoffman. Understand?" Vlasenin did not reply. He merely sat hunched in his seat, looking as tired, beaten and dejected as he had done all throughout the journey. "And straighten up, dammit," Ciarelli added with some asperity. "Try to look like a soldier."

Vlasenin shot him a look of blank contempt. "You treat me like a caged animal, then dare to ask me to behave like a soldier. I am not a soldier. Neither am I your paid actor or performing dog. I will cause no trouble because I know all allies of Hitler are alike. I've no wish to end up in these people's hands, any more than I wish to be in yours. If I were you I'd save your bullying for these border guards."

Ciarelli frowned but said nothing. Instead he wound his window down for a better look at the post. It was small, functional and nondescript. There was a wooden barrier across the narrow forest road, a guardhouse next to it and a small barracks-cum-office next to that. It had a more permanent look than the two makeshift roadblocks they had successfully negotiated already in their flight from Xanthi. And Ciarelli knew that it might take more than a breezy manner and their cover story to get them into Bulgaria itself.

He had gambled on the recent influx of Italian troops from Yugoslavia to reinforce the garrison at Unterbrecht's camp to make their presence in a convoy less noteworthy. Plus he had a letter similar to Ziedler's, essentially commanding anyone allied to the Third Reich or within its dominions to grant him free passage. He had passed the party off as a joint force which had been engaged on a high-priority mission but was returning to Bulgaria (from whence the Italians would return to Yugoslavia) after taking casualties in a partisan engagement. The wounds suffered by four of Rawlings' men added credence to this and a couple of the Italians had used slings and bandages from the medical kits in the trucks to reinforce the charade. It also explained Vlasenin and Yelena's presence. It had worked so far but he knew that even if Ziedler had not managed to repair the radios he had carefully disabled before leaving Xanthi and broadcast an alert, this would be the hardest part. They could not have hoped to pass as Bulgarians – the request for uniforms for everyone had been a ruse to further complicate the pursuit, though the prisoners now wore them – and if the gate commander asked to speak to one of his countrymen then it would have to become a shooting match.

As the convoy halted before the barrier and an officer emerged from the guardhouse Ciarelli's worst fears were realised. He was of no more than medium height but strutted out onto the road with every inch of it held upright, casting an imperious glance at this latest unpleasant disruption to his routine. Despite the cold, his greatcoat was worn over his shoulders like a cape. It was a gloomy late November afternoon but he wore dark glasses in expensive tortoiseshell frames. Every buckle and button on his immaculately pressed captain's uniform shone. He was flanked by two corporals, cradling machine-carbines for show.

Ciarelli knew the type. He would keep them there for the rest of the day, and all night too, if he wished. For no better reason than to show them that he could. There was one like him at every border crossing in the world. Well, he's picked the wrong man this time, Ciarelli thought. He wanted to be in Yugoslavia by nightfall. The convoy was strung out along a narrow road, shielded partly by the forest but still vulnerable to air attack or ambush. Delay here was not an option. For a moment he thought of handling this himself rather than letting Riva present the Mussolini directive while he waited in the car. But that would be conceding territory. No, let the bureaucratic buffoon come to him, then he would learn that rank was not the only thing which gave a man authority. But as Riva got out of the car Ciarelli said to him: "Take no argument. That piece of paper gets us past every border post in the Balkans. Make sure he realises that."

Riva nodded and strode up to the officer, who greeted him with a broad smile and a handshake at first, comically exaggerating his difficulties with the language barrier and making the universal palm-out gesture almost as an afterthought. Riva handed over the document but the officer shrugged and spread his arms wide in a pantomime of incomprehension, making no signal to raise the barrier. Riva's voice rose and the officer's matched it. Then he waved Riva away and took a step back. The guards went with him, raising their carbines.

Ciarelli could hold back no longer. His adjutant was clearly unequal to the task, whereas he had bullied small-time bureaucrats into submission from Tripoli to Trieste. All it needed was a dash of real authority and you were on your way. He jerked a thumb at Vlasenin and barked: "Watch him" to the driver. Then he was out and striding towards the tableau at the checkpoint. It was nearly dark and the whole forest was a thing of shadows, but as

Ciarelli walked up the road he saw out of the corner of his eye that some of them were taking shape. Becoming figures. The figures of armed men, converging right and left. In that instant he realised just how great a mistake he had made.

In the next instant Riva died. Perhaps he had seen them too; perhaps he merely wanted to explain the hold-up to his commander. Whatever the reason he half-turned, taking his eyes from the officer, who responded by drawing a pistol and shooting him in the head. Before Riva's body hit the ground the officer had fired again. The staff car's windscreen shattered and the driver slumped lifeless at the wheel. Ciarelli drew the Mauser but before he could raise it two men were covering him from each side of the road. He could see more, a dozen at least, surrounding the convoy and holding the drivers at gunpoint.

"Drop the gun, Signor Colonel," the officer shouted. This time the Italian was perfect, but the German accent very pronounced. Ciarelli ignored him, his arm coming up ramrod straight to aim the Mauser at Vlasenin. "You drop yours – and your men too. Otherwise he dies."

The officer laughed. "Kill him. Then we kill you, take the papers and go on our way. Still we win. This way you live, Ciarelli; That's how Oberst Ziedler wants to play it."

Of course it was, Ciarelli thought. He loved to gloat as much as he hated to be duped. He would savour his moment of triumph, then let Hoffman loose. And no-one would lift a finger to stop him. Ciano had made clear his attempt to reach Yugoslavia would never be officially sanctioned even as he had tacitly endorsed it.

Ciarelli expected nothing less. He would have done the same. But what to do now? He could deprive everyone of Vlasenin and die like a soldier, not a tortured rat. But they were all still a long way from Germany. He shrugged and dropped the Mauser.

The officer smiled. "I thought you would see reason. No point in dying for nothing, eh? Tie him up and get his men out of the trucks." The ambush party obeyed. They too were in Bulgarian uniform but they carried German weaponry. Ciarelli thought he recognised one or two of them. He turned to face the officer, who was picking up the Mauser while the checkpoint guards covered him. As he straightened up and removed the dark glasses Ciarelli recognised him immediately.

"Topfer, isn't it? Dorsch's lackey from the SS?"

"Obersturmfuhrer Leopold Topfer, at your service, Signor Colonel."

"So they let you out on your own for a change, eh? Play a little dressing-up game, just like a real spy?"

Topfer's smile faded a little. "It convinced your second-in-command, Ciarelli."

The Italian looked past him at Riva's body, slumped shapelessly in the road, the bloody trail from his shattered skull seeping into the damp earth. "It shouldn't have. We were all together from Berlin to Unterbrecht's camp. That close he should have recognised you."

"Perhaps he couldn't believe we could have got here so quickly," Topfer said smugly.

"Another mistake," Ciarelli replied. "Always be ready for enemy action. So you took another route from the camp to get ahead of us. And Ziedler made a big show of driving to Xanthi to pick me up, thinking that I'd reckon he had all his little lieutenants with him as usual."

Topfer gave a sarcastic gesture of applause. "Well deduced, Signor Colonel. We arrived in the German sector two hours ago. Hauptsturmfuhrer Dorsch is stationed at the Yugoslav border there, but Oberst Ziedler felt you might take the easier route. And this is the closest crossing to Yugoslavia. So we radioed the commander and asked him to borrow a few uniforms temporarily." Topfer's voice hardened. "And do you know, Signor Colonel, I was a real spy once. In Sofia last year, after the Bulgars joined us. Helping them to hunt down elements in the government critical of Tsar Boris' decision. It really is such a beautiful city – and three months there gave me a reasonable command of the language. But you're right – Captain Riva should still have recognised me."

Ciarelli looked at his adjutant's corpse again. He had always been prone to mistakes – failing to spot the lady's gun while searching Rawlings, for instance – and his most serious error had been his last. But he had always done his duty and never shirked action. Ciarelli resolved that when he had won back his freedom from this SS popinjay and Vlasenin was safe on Italian soil, he would recommend Riva for a medal. Write it up as some heroic action in North Africa; give his wife a pension and his children a new toy at least.

Ten yards behind them the main force, Brandenburgers supervised by Leutnant Dressler, were herding the Italians and the SOE team out of the two trucks, while a third appeared from round a bend beyond the checkpoint. Topfer motioned Ciarelli to join them, then strode across to where Rawlings was standing.

"Major Rawlings – a pleasure to meet you at last," he

said in English. "Oberst Ziedler has spoken much about you. If only the circumstances could be more pleasant. As it is, this is merely an exchange of jailers. Oberst Ziedler feels that you can still tell him much about the legendary SOE, as can the rest of your men. And your Tsarist contacts will be useful too." He walked past Rawlings and stood in front of Yelena, running his eyes up the length of her body. "What is it about a nurse's uniform that makes every woman more attractive – even when she is beautiful to start with?"

Yelena held his gaze with a look of pure hatred. Rawlings said softly: "If you touch her, I'll kill you. I swear it."

Topfer appeared on the point of pursuing the matter, then he looked into Rawlings' eyes and contented himself with a dismissive laugh. Then he moved on to Vasily. "And the talkative Tsarist who gave us all that information. Still, it enabled us to wipe out more Red scum. No doubt you will appreciate that."

Vasily spat at his feet. "Any help it gave you was by accident, German."

"Just so," Topfer replied. "And any good that comes to you from now on will be by accident, *untermensch*." He punched Vasily hard in the stomach. The Russian was jolted back but kept his feet. He looked Topfer in the eye and said: "If you had not treated all my people like this when you invaded my country, then perhaps we might have helped."

Topfer laughed in his face, then turned as Leutnant Dressler marched up at the double and saluted. "All the British are on board one truck, Herr Obersturmfuhrer, as you ordered. And all the Italians in the other – with two exceptions, of course."

He looked at Riva's body and his distaste was plain to see. Topfer held his gaze and said: "He was on the point of making for his weapon. I had no other choice." Topfer looked downwards as he added: "And the driver might well have escaped with Vlasenin still on board."

Dressler kept calm with an effort. "The Italian High Command might well question both of those assumptions, Herr Obersturmfuhrer."

"I hardly think they are in any position to lecture us about loyalty and co-operation." Topfer's voice was rising, but he controlled it. "We waste time. Let's get these vehicles moving and give the Bulgars their checkpoint back."

He raised his arm in the Nazi salute. Dressler gave him a punctilious military salute in return, then turned on his heel and marched back to the second truck, motioning Vasily, Yelena and Rawlings to follow him. Within seconds they had been reunited with the rest of the team, who were now bound hand and foot with two guards watching them. Dressler gave a wordless gesture of apology and motioned one of the guards to bind the three new arrivals. He drew a Luger and watched all three intently until they were tied up, as did the second guard. Rawlings reflected that being with captors who gave absolutely no opportunity to escape was becoming depressingly familiar.

Ten yards ahead Topfer was gesturing Ciarelli towards the first truck as he occupied the Italian's seat beside Vlasenin and Bauer, the sergeant of the Hermann Goering platoon, cleared the shattered glass from the windscreen and took up position in the driver's seat.

The two disguised guards, both Hermann Goering men, joined Topfer in the rear. "You and your men are not being tied up, Signor Colonel," Topfer said, "for the sole reason that if we encounter partisan activity I will expect you to do your duty as soldiers of the Axis. There is a chest of arms in their truck, but I can assure you it is being watched very closely. For myself I would as soon shoot you all down, but Oberst Ziedler has other ideas." He smiled. "And perhaps he is right. A bullet is too good a death for traitors who connive against the Axis. I suspect my government will request a noose for each and every one of you. And your government will acquiesce. Perhaps our Captain Riva was luckier than he realised."

Ciarelli turned to him. "Don't sell a wolf's hide before you've skinned it, *Tedeschi*."

Topfer laughed in his face. "I think we're talking more of disobedient curs than wolves – *macaroni*."

⁓

Topfer pushed the convoy hard through the twisting mountain roads, as evening came and then yielded to night. Rawlings expected him to find a safe garrison as soon as possible and bed down there before travelling on to Xanthi in the relative safety of daylight. But he could understand Ziedler wanting Vlasenin back under his wing as soon as possible. And Topfer evidently felt that two dozen of the finest German and Italian troops were more than a match for any band of brigands, should they even materialise.

And it seemed as if he was right. There was no sign of any life in the still forests on either side of the road and the guards were beginning to droop with night duty fatigue when the huge pine trunk smashed down in front of them, a voice called in English "get your heads down!" and the air became alive with bullets. Bauer braked sharply, just managing to avoid a head-on collision with the tree. A rifle shot to the head was his sole reward. Topfer grabbed Vlasenin and dragged him to the floor of the car. But then he realised that most of the fire was being directed at the trucks. The two guards in the rear were unhurt too. "Into the trees – now!" Topfer shouted to them. Then he drew the Mauser and held it to Vlasenin's temple while his free hand grabbed the briefcase of papers. Shoving the door open, he launched himself at the trees in a diving run.

Rawlings and his team had dropped to the floor as soon as they heard the English warning. Dressler understood it too, and dropped a fraction of a second quicker than the guards. They died as a burst of automatic fire shredded the truck's tarpaulin. But Dressler dropped to his knees, one hand still holding the Luger, the other gripping the truck's steel bench for balance. The driver tried to reverse back, into the trees and out of the line of fire. All he succeeded in doing, before a rifle bullet took him, was colliding with the truck behind. The impact knocked Dressler off-balance, Luger spinning away. Rawlings seized his chance. He swung his whole body round, legs up, two booted feet connecting with Dressler's right temple. The German groaned and fell to the floor of the truck. For a second he was flat on his back. Before he could recover Rawlings raised his legs again and brought both heels down on Dressler's windpipe. There was a hideous cracking sound. Dressler gave one choked cry, then lay still.

The firing continued, and Rawlings could hear that the Germans were beginning to fire back. He crawled to one of the guards' bodies and managed to work his bayonet loose from its scabbard. Holding it clumsily in his bound hands he managed to cut them free, then his feet. He grabbed Dressler's Luger and turned to Curtis, cutting him free in seconds. "The same for everyone else, then keep your heads down, and get those Bulgar uniforms off. Sounds like they know who we are but I'm taking no chances. Anyone comes along before I get back, use all the English and Greek you know to stay alive."

"Where are you going, sir?" Curtis asked.

"To get Vlasenin, of course – where else?"

Then he was gone, kicking down the tailgate and sliding over the edge before crawling to the trees at the road's edge, from where he looked along the length of the convoy. Their truck had been the middle of the three and it was drawing the least fire. But the other two, and the staff car, had been riddled. Tyres blown out, glass shattered, engines steaming as they haemmorhaged water and petrol. The few remaining Germans and Italians were clustered round the outsides, returning fire. But the trucks only gave cover on one side and as Rawlings watched the last few began to be picked off and the rest broke, running for the trees even as the partisans moved down to the roadside to finish them.

Not wishing to join them, Rawlings looked up the road for cover. That was when he saw Topfer. He was crouched behind two large boulders that lay at right angles, giving the one piece of cover from both sides of the ambush. He had two men with him, Schmeissers at the ready, and Vlasenin. They had their backs to Rawlings and, as he watched, Topfer gave hand signals to his men and they braced themselves for a run to the trees.

Rawlings raised his Luger. It was easy killing range and the noise of firing was so great that Topfer would never hear one more shot. But there was a chance that when he saw his men go down he would have time to shoot Vlasenin. Of course the man himself was expendable now they had the papers. Davies had made that quite clear. And a briefcase was easier to conceal, easier to transport safely. He could shoot Vlasenin himself and no-one would know or care. Instead he took the biggest gamble of his life.

He ran forward at the crouch, making little attempt at concealment or silence. When he was five yards from the Germans he fired. The bullet blew the first guard's skull in. As his comrade turned he took the second bullet full in the chest. Then Rawlings threw himself at Topfer, screaming to Vlasenin: "Run!"

Topfer had the Mauser out, bringing it to bear on Rawlings. But neither man had time for a shot before the collision that drove nearly all the breath from their bodies. Half a second later the impact as they crashed into the boulder took what was left. The Mauser spun from Topfer's hand but Rawlings hung on to the Luger for grim death as Topfer pulled him round, trying for a judo trip, dragging both men out of cover and onto the road. Rawlings aimed a blow with the pistol at the SS man's head. Topfer's left arm came up instinctively and the heavy pistol hit it just above the elbow. Something broke. The German fell back with a cry of agony and his hold loosened. But he lashed out with his left boot, catching Rawlings in the groin. Rawlings doubled over as Topfer scrabbled for the fallen Mauser, grabbing it in his good hand.

Rawlings raised the Luger. Topfer's finger was not even on the trigger. He had time to take aim, make the kill certain. But the next second he was crashing onto the road as the chest-shot guard grabbed him from behind. The effort took what little of the guard's strength remained and Rawlings pushed him away, then grabbed him by the collar, Luger barrel touching his tunic as he shot him three times. The guard fell away, blown open. Rawlings turned, beginning to rise – and saw Topfer standing over him, Mauser levelled at Rawlings' head. Rawlings raised the Luger in one last futile gesture, Topfer's finger whitened on the trigger – and a deafening burst of gunfire crackled in Rawlings' ears. He dived and rolled away automatically but from the corner of his eye he saw blood spurting from a dozen wounds as Vlasenin emptied one of the guards' Schmeissers into the SS man.

The force of the bullets spun Topfer round and more hits took him in the chest, punching him back against the staff car's bodywork. Rawlings kept his head down until he heard the click of a trigger on an empty chamber and saw Topfer's lifeless body slide to the ground. Then Rawlings stood up, propping himself against the staff car. He was in full view of the ambushers but he was too tired to care. In any case the firing had died away to almost nothing.

Vlasenin was crouched between the bodies of the two guards, the Schmeisser now hanging limply from one hand. He rose up and staggered towards Rawlings, still holding the gun. He looked at Topfer's body. "That's the first time I've ever killed a man that close."

"It's not pretty," Rawlings told him, "but under the circumstances I'm glad you could bring yourself. *Spassibo*."

Vlasenin looked at him and a flash of spirit came to his tired eyes. "Perhaps now all you bastards will stop treating me like a piece of cargo."

"It's a deal," Rawlings said – then grabbed Vlasenin and threw him off the road again as the first truck roared to life behind them and Ciarelli gunned it forward. The bare metal under the shot-out tyres juddered and shrieked in protest. But the three-ton dinosaur still steamrollered over the spot where Rawlings and Vlasenin had stood seconds ago. Bulldozing the staff car aside it rammed up against the tree trunk. It was too heavy to move but Ciarelli shifted gear and the truck revved up and over it, wheels hitting the ground on the other side with a huge thud.

Ciarelli accelerated up again – but by then Rawlings was up and sprinting for the running board, oblivious to the bullets that now targeted the escaping prey. He did not know how Ciarelli had managed to slip his guards and get behind the wheel, or get the riddled truck to work, but he did know that the Italian wasn't getting away if he could help it. With the last of his strength Rawlings leapt onto the running board and yanked the passenger door open. As Ciarelli turned, his face a mask of astonishment, Rawlings put a fist into it.

The Italian slammed against the driver's door. The driverless truck, building up speed, veered right towards the trees. Rawlings grabbed the wheel with both hands, trying to pull it back on to the road – and Ciarelli sprang back at him. A fist in the belly, then another in the face, winding Rawlings and flinging him across the passenger seat and against the half-open door. He grabbed at the handle to keep himself from falling and Ciarelli flung it to its utmost, slamming Rawlings against the side of the bonnet. Rawlings made one last effort to clamber in as the door swung back. But Ciarelli's boot lashed out, catching him solidly in the chest and flinging him down to the roadside.

Ciarelli's eyes turned back to the road – and saw only the trees that flanked a sharp bend to the left. As the truck careered through them and down the slope he fought to gain control but the truck gained speed and momentum as the slope became steeper.

It rocked on to its side then turned right over, once, twice, again and again, before it hit the bottom of the slope with a huge explosion. Rawlings stood at the top of the slope, searching for a sign of Ciarelli, until the heat from the burning pines forced him back. Then he turned and limped back towards where he had left Vlasenin.

He was still there, surrounded by armed men in a motley of camouflage gear, scraps of uniform and civilian clothing. A few of them raised their weapons as Rawlings approached but a tall, bearded figure stepped in front of them. He was wearing a green tunic with crossed ammunition bandoliers, grey corduroy breeches and scuffed black riding boots. He carried a Sten gun cradled in a shoulder sling. It was pointing at Rawlings but his finger was off the trigger. There was a Webley revolver in a holster at his hip, a Walther automatic in another at his shoulder and a hunting knife stuck in his belt. A long scar ran from his right temple to the bridge of his nose.

He stopped dead in front of Rawlings, looked him up and down and then said in a voice that would not have sounded out of place in an Oxford common room: "Davenport's the name, Major Rawlings – Lieutenant William Davenport. Sorry we couldn't get all this sorted out sooner."

Chapter 7

Alpine Interlude

"*BELIEVE ME, SIR, CAIRO IS* dying to hear from you."

"I believe you." Rawlings was facing Davenport across a smokeless fire in a cave high in the Rhodope Mountains. Outside the sun was rising on a crisp, cold winter's day. The day was Tuesday, November 24th, 1942. It was exactly a week since Vlasenin had been intercepted and taken to Istanbul; at the same time Rawlings had been making his escape from the cell in Toulouse. He felt he had lived several lifetimes since then – and used up his store of luck for all of them.

"Yes, there were a lot of very panicky signals being sent yesterday," Davenport continued, while he used his hunting knife to carve another slice of the goat's haunch that was forming their breakfast from the skewer over the fire. "They didn't tell us much, as usual. Just that some very top-secret op near the Turkish border had gone wrong and we were to keep eyes and ears open for any unusual traffic on the roads. Well, that was no problem

– it's pretty much all I've been doing since they sent me here in September. It's a bit out of my bailiwick – the main HQ for the band is in the hills beyond Xanthi, much further north and east than we are at the moment. Chap in command there is a Colonel Thraxos. Real tough old bird; twenty years in the Greek Army, cut his teeth fighting Ataturk at Sakarya, that sort of thing.

"He's developed about the best intelligence-gathering service in the whole of Thrace. It's his home turf, of course, which helps; came back here after the surrender in '41 and tried to live a quiet life. But then the Germans let the Bulgars come in and administer the place and every ethnic Greek in the sector found themselves being persecuted. Most of them fled to Salonika or the German sector near the border. The rest just put their heads down and tried to survive. Thraxos didn't want to do either; he got a band together and took to the hills. But he kept a lot of sympathisers in Xanthi and all the surrounding area. Nothing happens but that he knows about it. So when he heard that there'd been this disturbance at the airfield, and that a convoy of Eyeties were heading north with Allied prisoners dressed up in Bulgar uniform for some reason he reckoned it was worth looking into.

"Fortunately I was in the area with this bunch plotting some general mischief. So we started radioing the other groups to try to get a fix on you. And I took the boys down from the hills to rig an ambush if we hit the main border road ahead of you.

"Meanwhile, of course, Cairo's broadcast back saying yes, by God, get the buggers back. But your trail was a little on the cold side, to be honest, and by dusk I'd pretty much given up hope. Reckoned you'd be in Bulgaria by then and that really is uncharted territory as far as we're concerned. But we'd alerted the group nearest the border and they radioed back about seven last night to say there'd been reports of a bit of shooting at a checkpoint and that a convoy was heading south again. I don't mind admitting I was thoroughly confused by then, but all's well that ends well. There's only one road back into Xanthi through the mountains – not unless you really know the lay of the land – and we were on it. So I picked my spot and rigged up a little surprise. Just got it finished in time for your arrival, too." He paused and shook his head. "I tell you, if I'd known taking Greek at Oxford and coming here for a dig in '38 would mean letting myself in for all this I'd have taken that bloody job with the old man's firm instead."

He gave a wry laugh and took a bite from the chunk of goat's meat on the end of his knife. Rawlings looked at him. Close up you could see that despite the scar and beard it was a young face, clear-eyed and open, with a shy, ironic smile never far from it. Rawlings had met so many like him in the SOE – men barely out of their teens, whose knowledge or enthusiasm for a particular race or country had resulted in them being parachuted into its wildest spots with instructions to make the mountains their home and turn the local resistance into a co-ordinated fifth column striking terror into the hearts of the occupiers. And be bloody quick about it. The reason why the Germans were finding their newly-won empire such an intractable beast was because so many of the SOE's inexperienced young aesthetes sent forth into the world and told to perform miracles had done precisely that. Without him they would probably be on their way to Berlin by now. And even if they had managed to escape, the radio which was their only link with the SOE network was down in the Dhadhia Forest, with his booby-trapped briefcase, hidden in the ancient Lancia Yelena had used to tail them to Greece.

"Well, I'm glad you didn't," Rawlings said. "Having a bit of local liaison will be a godsend while we try to figure out exactly what we do next."

"Yes, Cairo has some ideas on that too. They said they'd reply as soon as they got your broadcast." Davenport pointed with his knife to the entrance of the cave. "Looks like your man's got the signal at last, so I'll leave you to that. Don't worry – I won't pinch all the breakfast."

Rawlings smiled and stood up. The cave was high enough for that, and for another man to stand on his shoulders. And it was deep and long, offering plenty of room to shelter all of his party and the two dozen men under Davenport's command. Two of them were patrolling the mountain slopes below while the rest ate, slept or cleaned their impressive array of weapons – everything from ancient muzzle-loading muskets and ornate Turkish daggers to Mauser sniper's rifles and silenced Sten guns. Rawlings' team had been re-equipped from their stocks while two medical orderlies tended the four wounded men from an equally impressive medicine chest. And there was a 1500 series radio transmitter too, for O' Hare to make the team's first contact with Davies in three days.

Rawlings handed the coded message to O'Hare: *Lords calling Headingley. Much activity from red and blue teams. Foul play was prevalent and no communication possible with the pavilion. Blue team tried to steal star player from grey team and us with him. But now star player, and his contract, have been retrieved and we are amongst friendly supporters. But many of team are injured. Return to pavilion will take several days at least. Request information on future tour schedule, and any news on how grey team obtained inside information.*

Conor's hands were aching by the time he had finished, but Rawlings had found no way to make the communication more succinct and still convey all the complications of the previous two days. And they did not have long to wait before an even more succinct reply: *Make way to original ground as best you can. Start of play at usual time. Keep us informed of progress and location but feel free to use own initiative. No news on grey team's scout as yet, but still looking.*

"Use our own initiative, eh?" Rawlings smiled grimly at O'Hare. "Not that we've got much choice. So that's it, Conor me boy; original pick-up time and place, so back to Turkey quick as we can."

"That'll be a tall order, Alex," O'Hare replied. "Especially with so many of our blokes crocked."

"You're telling me. He didn't give a deadline, but they're not going to keep the plane landing in Turkey every night for the next month just on the off-chance. Especially now the police, army and Emniyet all know our faces – not to mention the Topkapi museum guards." He gave a short, sour laugh. "I'd try to avoid the place altogether if it weren't for the fact that there's no Allied territory for five hundred miles and no other neutral country for a thousand. We'll just have to take the high roads and rely on Davenport and his men to get us through. And I think we could be in worse hands as far as that goes."

"Well, of course we'll help out as much as we can," Davenport said uncertainly when Rawlings told him the news. "Obviously the first step is to get you back to Colonel Thraxos' main base. We'll go there tonight. But after that… it's a hell of a long way, sir, through some pretty rough terrain."

"We're all used to that," Rawlings replied. "And it looks like your boys are too."

"Oh, they're not really my boys, sir. They just take orders from me because Thraxos tells them to. They fight for him, and for Greece." He lowered his voice before continuing. "To be honest, sir, I've lived with these people for two months now, twenty-four hours a day, and the more I get to know them the more I realise I don't know the first bloody thing. Blood feuds, personal power-broking between the local bandit chiefs, racial grievances going back centuries – it's hard to get them worked up about a crusade against Fascism when a lot of them see all this as just the latest one of the Balkan Wars. I mean, Thrace belonged to Bulgaria until the last war, rightly or wrongly. We'll be going through some areas where there are more Bulgars than Greeks – and others where there are more Turks than either. So we won't always be able to count on the local populations sheltering us.

"And on top of that, sir, there's… well, the plain fact is that the Communists, ELAS, are much stronger in these parts than us. This lot are the best bunch of fighters I've ever come across and I'd be happy to count any of them as a friend. But the organisation they belong to, EDES, the one we're throwing all our weight behind, just isn't as co-ordinated. Once you get past the level of local groups like this there's no central organisation, or even a clear sense of what they want if they ever manage to kick all their occupiers out. The leader, Napoleon Zervas, was a general in the Venizelos days and a lot of them want a republic again, not us bringing the king back. But there are some monarchists in among them too, and others who even seem to want some bloody dictator like Metaxas again. You know the kind of thing; to make Greece strong again, take back everything that's hers, right the way to Constantinople… I tell you, it's a shambles.

"No such trouble with ELAS, of course. Well, you were here last year, so you know. Their leaders have got them singing from the same hymn sheet: national liberation, no return to the bad old days, definitely no king. So that's not a side we favour, in general – and, I gather, for this mission in particular."

"That's right," Rawlings replied emphatically. "I can't tell you too much about our mission, lieutenant, and I'm sure you don't really want to know. But contact or co-operation with any organisation that has Communist links, or sympathies with the Russians, is absolutely out of the question."

"Well, you won't get any argument about that from these chaps, sir. Most of them hate the Communists. But EDES is out on a limb here – the north-west's their power base. The only reason we've a few groups here is because Thraxos knew Zervas in the old days. But most of Thrace is ELAS-dominated, particularly down in the German sector. They've got some very big, well-organised groups there."

"I know." Rawlings' reply was even more emphatic this time.

"So you'll also know that it's going to be the Devil's own job getting you to Turkey without some unfriendly elements getting wind of our presence. But if anyone can do it Thraxos can. We'll get you to his HQ, then decide the best way to proceed. But it's really not the ideal situation."

"It's a better situation than the one we were in this time yesterday, lieutenant, I can assure you. Don't be too hard on yourself. SOE owes you a huge debt of gratitude."

Davenport gave his ironic smile again, but his face did not look so young as he replied. "I'd prefer some more guns and dynamite. Plus some blokes to help me out. You know, if we could get EDES and ELAS really working together we'd have the best bloody resistance movement in Europe out here. They've both got more than their share of good fighters and they both want to see Greece free again. It's just that…"

"I know." Rawlings patted him on the shoulder. "They've got different ideas about what she should be once she is free. That's for others to worry about. The priority now is to get us back to Turkey. And I don't mind if I don't get a warm welcome in every village. I've been in more occupied countries than you've had hot dinners, Lieutenant Davenport, and I know that expecting a warm welcome is a sure way to get killed."

ಌ

A warm welcome was the last thing Ziedler and Hoffman were expecting at that moment. They were enjoying considerably more comfort than Rawlings, sitting in an anteroom at Salonika City Hall. But their mood was much less optimistic. After discovering the fate of Topfer and Dressler's rescue mission the previous night and informing Berlin they had received a curt message from Canaris by way of reply. It said that a meeting with representatives of the SIM to "salvage the situation" was to be held there at 9 a.m sharp. It had also made abundantly clear that failure to attend was not an option.

So a transport plane had flown them to Greece's second city, the bustling trading post of the Ottoman Empire now turned into the northern HQ of the occupation. Of course its former status meant that, in Hoffman's words, it stank of Jew. He had noticed evidence of the once-thriving community throughout the drive from the airfield. An article in one of the occupation newspapers on the coffee table in the anteroom recounted with pride the mass labour registration which had taken place in July, when ten thousand of them had been made to stand hatless in the sun for a whole Saturday, then perform physical drill until they dropped. But the Gestapo man still found it hard to disguise his distaste at the scourge's proximity.

Today, however, all they could see from the window was early morning bustle along the squares and boulevards that were the rival of any in Europe, and the sun shining on the clear waters of Thermaikos Gulf. It was a carefree prospect compared to the thoughts running through Hoffman's mind at least. "It's the Russian Front for both of us. I know it," he whispered.

"Rawlings is still far from safety," Ziedler replied calmly. "This is obviously just to remind us that we must work more closely with the Italians in the future."

Hoffman shrugged. "Wonder which of the spaghetti-eaters we're meeting today, then?"

It was clear that neither of them expected it to be the man who rose to greet them as they entered. General Cesare Ame, head of the SIM, himself. His uniform was immaculate and only the eyes in that scholarly white-bearded face, lacking some of their usual sparkle, hinted at a long journey and a delicate brief. Hoffman tried to mask his amazement with little success. He looked at Ziedler, who gave a millimetric raising of his eyebrows. "Signor General," he said in Italian, "it is something of a surprise to see you here."

"I thought it wise to take a personal hand at this stage," Ame replied with a disarming smile and in fluent German. "Though I have been in regular contact with Berlin ever since this operation began. And more so recently. There has been an unfortunate lack of communication and co-operation in this matter so far."

Starting from the moment you stole our prisoner, Hoffman thought bitterly, but a sideways glance at Ziedler convinced him that silence was the preferred response for the moment. Ame continued: "Your superiors feel, and I heartily agree, that the best way to proceed now is to forget what differences we have had in the past and direct our combined resources to the main task – rescuing Dr Vlasenin and his papers."

"I could not agree more." Ziedler's calm, optimistic tone was almost a mimicry of Ame's. "The Allies must not be allowed a victory by default."

"Indeed." If Ame had expected a different response he gave no hint of it. "Now, to the particulars. Vlasenin and the SOE agents are almost certainly somewhere in this area." He moved to a large-scale map of north-eastern Greece on the wall behind the desk and pointed to the stretch of the Rhodope Mountains due east of Xanthi. "To attempt to search such a vast and inhospitable area would be impossible, even with the extra resources which I am happy to say the occupying forces are placing at our disposal. When you leave this city, gentlemen, you will be followed by a convoy containing three companies each of the finest Italian and German troops in Greece.

"They will be invaluable, I believe, in the final capture and safe conduct of Dr Vlasenin, but even with the co-operation of the local Bulgarian forces, they could not hope to mount a search and destroy mission against any group in those mountains. They are too well-organised and well-informed. Our movements would perforce attract attention and the British agents would be able to stay one step ahead of us constantly."

"So what do you suggest we do, Signor General?" Ziedler asked with interest.

"Turn occupied Greece into an armed camp," was Ame's blunt reply. "Seal and guard all the exits and wait for them to make a move. They must try for Turkey – it is the only non-hostile country for hundreds of miles. We will station troops all along the border. And we will throw a naval cordon across the Gulf of Samothrakis." His hand swept down the map. "I think that will be their preferred option. The resistance regularly ferry escaped prisoners and refugees across to Smyrna from this maze of coves and inlets on the Thracian coast. Again, it would be futile to search them all. But the distance between Samothrakis island and the Turkish coast is barely twenty miles. Every Axis warship and patrol boat in the Mediterranean is currently making its way to the area. The blockade will be so tight that even the smallest fishing *caique* could not get through without being spotted and searched.

"So, gentlemen, you can see that through co-operation we will render their position untenable. They cannot stay in the mountains forever; they must attempt a border crossing. That is when we will strike. Or rather you will, gentlemen – aided by my subordinate, of course."

"Subordinate?" Ziedler sounded puzzled for once. "I assumed from your presence, Signor General, that you were taking charge of the Italian element of the operation."

"Oh, no." Ame gave him an indulgent smile. "I have many other matters to attend to back in Rome – which is where Vlasenin will be taken to initially, by the way; Berlin has agreed to this. But I have brought some… er, reinforcements, from the SIM as well as the regular army. And their commander, the man you will work with, has proven experience and prior knowledge of this operation." He pressed an intercom buzzer on the desk. A small door in the left-hand corner of the room opened and Ciarelli walked in.

Hoffman simply gaped, dumbfounded, and even Ziedler looked surprised as Ciarelli walked towards them. Or rather, limped. His whole body seemed stiff, as if the starch in the immaculate new colonel's uniform had seeped into the flesh below. His right leg dragged noticeably and he leaned heavily on a long ebony cane. A livid scar ran from his left temple to his jaw and his face was pale and drawn. But his eyes were bright and defiant as ever as he looked at all three men in turn.

"Fortunately, Colonel Ciarelli survived the partisan

ambush," Ame continued smoothly, barely seeming to notice the Germans' reactions. "He was thrown clear when the vehicle in which he had attempted to escape crashed. The Bulgarian army patrol which discovered the ambush found him and took him to the nearest garrison hospital. We would have told you earlier, but we did not know until a few hours ago whether he would be fit enough to fly down and join us."

"We're not working with him!" Hoffman could contain himself no longer. "Not after..."

"Yes, we are." Ziedler cut in with a voice like iron. "As General Ame has pointed out, the past is behind us and our main priority is to recapture Vlasenin using our joint resources. I shall be grateful – we shall be grateful – for anything Colonel Ciarelli can contribute to this operation in the future. And may I congratulate him for demonstrating once again his remarkable capacity for survival."

Ciarelli looked deeply suspicious, but gave a polite nod of acknowledgement. Ame beamed like a benevolent uncle on Christmas morning. "Excellent! Now the next step is for all three of you gentlemen to proceed to the airfield. Your cars are waiting. Some of the troops are ready to fly out at this moment; you will travel with them. The rest will journey by road, and be in the Bulgarian sector within twenty-four hours. Tsar Boris has assured us that his occupying force will continue to render you every assistance. I look forward to regular progress reports – and good news very soon."

He pressed the intercom buzzer again and the main door swung open. Two German and two Italian soldiers with slung carbines stood in the doorway.

Ziedler indicated that Ciarelli lead the way and, after a moment's hesitation, the Italian limped to the doorway. The Germans followed him out, guards filing to their left and right. Ciarelli and Hoffman glared at each other as they descended the stairs, but did not speak. Ziedler walked a little way ahead, admiring the architecture and the artworks on the walls, whistling softly to himself and seemingly unaware of any tension.

It was not until they were outside and in front of the two cars that would take them to the airfield – a Lancia and a Mercedes, each with a uniformed driver from their respective armies – that Ciarelli broke the silence. "No tricks, Ziedler – we both know what's gone before, what we all tried to do. I'll have just as many men out there as you, and we've got just as many spies among the locals. Try anything and we'll know. Together again, eh – it's the best way."

There was an almost pleading note to his voice and Ziedler gave him a reassuring pat on the shoulder. "None of us is *persona grata* with our superiors at the moment. We won't be until we give them Vlasenin, the papers – and Rawlings' head on a platter. If we work together we can give them all three by the end of the week."

Ciarelli looked relieved. He eased himself into the Lancia's rear seat with some difficulty while the Germans entered their Mercedes. Ziedler nodded and the two cars set off, Mercedes in the lead. That was when Hoffman exploded. "What the hell's got into you? I've never seen you take so much shit from anyone. At least you could have refused to work with that double-crossing bastard again."

"He's experienced and he knows a lot about this

operation; Ame was right." Ziedler's face and voice were absolutely neutral. "If we have to work with the Italians again – and it's just been made abundantly clear that we do – then I can't think of anyone better."

Hoffman gave a contemptuous laugh. "Yesterday you as good as swore to kill him."

"So what should I have done back there, Klaus – pulled out my pistol and shot him down? What precisely would that have achieved? At the moment it suits us well to have Ciarelli – and Ame, and Ciano – think they got away with their little stunt yesterday. So we'll work with Ciarelli – you'll work with him, and like it – until we catch Vlasenin. Then we can think about who keeps him."

Hoffman looked into the Abwehr man's eyes. That light was back in them. "You notice how Ame mentioned so casually that Vlasenin is bound for Rome once he is recaptured. He will stay there, if they have anything to do with it. And we and all our colleagues will fall gallantly in battle with Rawlings' men, I'll warrant. Courtesy of those SIM reinforcements so generously provided by General Ame. Well, not if I have anything to do with it. Vlasenin goes to Berlin – by the shortest possible route. Out of Greece, which is crawling with Italians and too close to the *verdammt* country itself, and into Bulgaria. Tsar Boris may be co-operating with us both, but he knows it's Germany that will guarantee all those disputed territories his people have wanted for centuries. That's the only reason he joined the Axis in the first place. No, I think we can slip Colonel Ciarelli's leash easily enough should the need arise – you know, Klaus, I don't think he's as fast on his feet as he used to be."

He gave a beautiful smile and Hoffman responded with a malevolent grin. "The game's afoot," Ziedler quoted, then gave Hoffman a patronising look. "Though I suppose you never had much time for Sherlock Holmes in your days in Hamburg?"

"I'm not stupid, Ziedler – us *Kripos* can read, you know, and I like a good detective story as much as any man. But that stuck-up English milord wouldn't have lasted a day of Reeperbahn duty. He didn't know enough dirty tricks."

"Indeed – and Colonel Ciarelli is about to realise that the only ones allowed on this operation are mine."

ω

"I'm dreadfully sorry, sir, but that's the way it is." Davenport's face was a picture of contrition. "It really is tight as a duck's arse down there."

He seemed to regard the situation as personal failing on his part and Rawlings was moved to give him a reassuring pat on the shoulder. "I didn't expect anything less. If nothing else, I'm sure this has convinced you how valuable our boy is. I'm just glad you kept yourself safe down there."

They were seated in another cave, but this one was even larger, and it was flanked by two brothers that together could give shelter to nearly a hundred and fifty men and women, though less than half that number were there at the moment. But it still represented the main concentration of force for Colonel Thraxos. The man himself sat across the fire from them, with his two sons (and chief lieutenants), George and Yannis, at his side.

The firelight, together with the gloom of the cave and the fading winter sun, threw his hawkish features into even sharper relief. He reminded Rawlings of an ageing Greek hero, an Odysseus still condemned to wander a cold and hostile earth.

But his intelligence-gathering operation was modern enough. An SOE-provided transmitter, twin to Conor O'Hare's, had maintained the link to Cairo and an equally powerful ex-Greek Army radio set had kept him in close contact with the other EDES groups in the area throughout the two days they had been there. Their news, and the reports back from the other half of his force, spread out in patrols down into the lowlands, had all painted the same depressing picture.

"They really have got everybody out, major," Davenport continued. "Germans, Italians, Bulgarians, local police, the Security Battalions and the rest of the right-wing militias – even chaps with clubs and pitchforks. Every road out of the mountains is being guarded like the crown jewels. From Xanthi down to the coast there's more troops than we've ever seen in Thrace. And the German sector's even worse."

"Well, going overland isn't the only option," Rawlings replied. "I was hoping if you could get us to some quiet spot on the coast Cairo could arrange a fishing *caique* to come in and sail us into Turkish waters. That can't be much of a distance. And your boys have done it a time or two before, so I'm told."

"Oh, yes, sir – that wouldn't be the problem," Davenport replied. "Obviously it would be harder now to get you down to the coast unnoticed, but once we got there we'd still have plenty of places to hide out and wait for the boat. The tricky bit would be getting a boat through, and sailing it to Turkey afterwards. The navies have been busy as well, and the stretch between Samothrakis and the coast is like the bloody Spithead Review. Battleships, destroyers, cruisers of all three flags strung out like the old Persian boat bridge; every kind of MTB and patrol launch zipping in and out of the gaps and a full-scale wolf pack of U-boats swimming underneath just in case we try bringing one of our subs in. I bet even a rowing skiff couldn't breach that little blockade."

"So what do we do?" Curtis, sitting at Rawlings' side with Emerson and Mitchell, asked gloomily. "Just sit up here and let them sit down there…"

"…'till famine and the ague eat them up," Davenport quoted. He had seen Curtis on stage before the war and had taken every opportunity to slip a Shakespearean reference into their conversation. "Well no, sir, of course that wouldn't do any good. For one thing, the flyboys are just as busy as everyone else. We're well hidden up here but a spotter plane could still get lucky and if they spot this camp then the chances of being tracked down on foot would be doubled. However, the colonel thinks he has an answer."

Thraxos nodded and leaned over, placing a map of the area in front of Rawlings. The firelight gave the worn, heavy paper the look of a medieval manuscript. But it was modern, with every road and rail line clearly marked. "The guard is heaviest to the south and east of here." His voice was a deep, rich baritone, the English good if heavily accented. "Between Xanthi and the island of Thassos is where they start to guard every road and every village. And from there to the border is the same story. But to the north is the mountains. No garrisons, no patrols. And in winter the weather is bad even for planes." He spread his hands wide. "They do not watch them for they think; who can travel through them in this weather? Especially with a man who is not used to the mountain way of life."

He lowered his voice as he looked at Vlasenin, who sat a little apart with the rest of the SOE team. But the Russian turned to him and replied in English: "I was born and raised a country boy, colonel, and I want to get to freedom. Wherever Major Rawlings wants me to go, I go."

Thraxos smiled at him and lifted a finger to his Greek Army sidecap in salute, then turned back to Rawlings. "I know the other groups. I can arrange for them to take you all the way through the mountains."

"That's good," Rawlings replied. "But that still leaves a stretch of low ground between the foot of the mountains and the border. Even at the narrowest point it's the best part of twenty-five miles to Turkey. And that's where the enemy will be thickest. I can't see how we can get across there."

"There is only one way," George put in. "Our group there have some good smugglers and bandits among them. They drive between the farms in trucks with hollowed-out bottoms for taking black market goods in and out of Turkey. Sometimes they have smuggled people too. They can put you in and take you to Turkey by back roads."

Rawlings shook his head. "Too risky. Every road in that area will be watched. If they've as many men as you say they have then everything bigger than a handcart will be stopped and searched."

"They have never been caught yet," George said defensively.

"Maybe, but this time it will be more than a bunch of bored garrison troops looking for contraband. It will be…" he broke off as he looked at the faces around him. "It will be a slim chance – but it's our only one. So we thank you once again, Colonel Thraxos, and ask you to help us once again."

"I will contact the other groups," Thraxos replied.

"Don't worry, sir," Davenport said. "If anyone can get you through, these boys can. Unfortunately," he added almost reluctantly, "the opposition do know who they're looking out for. Show him, Yannis," he said. In response Thraxos' son pulled a long sheet of rolled-up paper from inside his battledress tunic and spread it in front of the fire.

Rawlings cursed. It was a wanted poster. Obviously printed in a hurry and of poor quality. But Vlasenin's likeness above the lines of script in German, Greek and Bulgarian, was unmistakeable. As was the price in large print at the bottom. Ten million drachmas. Even in a currency blighted by the economic chaos arising from the Germans' strip mine approach to occupation it was still a handsome reward. And it was in gold.

"They've got ones of you and Captain Curtis too," Davenport said.

Rawlings nodded. "And anyone else who has an Abwehr or SD file with a picture attached by now, I bet. Still, I suppose that was inevitable once Ziedler knew who was in our team. Damn, I'd like to know who tipped them off to raid the camp in Turkey."

"Well, I can assure you there's no traitors in the ranks

here, sir." Davenport tried to sound reassuring, but it didn't quite come off. "And I've worked with all the other groups in the Rhodope. Even the border smugglers won't betray Greece. I promise you, they're as sound as a bell."

"I'm sure they are, lieutenant. But posters like that have a tendency to bring all sorts of people out of the woodwork. And the kind of price we've got on our heads could test anybody's loyalties."

༶

"Nothing at all? Are you sure?" Ziedler could not help a trace of frustration creeping into his voice.

"Quite sure, Herr Oberst." Leutnant Weiss stood rigidly to attention in front of Ziedler's desk. He had made his office in Xanthi's town hall on their return from Salonika two days ago, usurping the Bulgarian's chief administrator as smoothly as he had done with Unterbrecht. A mass of maps and papers were spread out across the desk, to which Weiss had just added a thick sheaf of intelligence reports. "No reports of partisan activity or movement at all. And no indication as to where the fugitives might be hiding."

"What the fuck are they doing out there?" Hoffman, seated to one side of the desk, looked at the young Abwehr lieutenant with suspicion. "Are you sure they know how serious this is?"

"I am indeed, Herr Kommissar." Weiss looked uncertainly at Ziedler, waiting for his nod before replying. "The searches undertaken by units of all three nationalities have been extensive. And we have used every available intelligence contact operated by the Bulgarians, as well as our own and those of the SIM."

He looked at Ciarelli, seated opposite Hoffman, who shrugged. "We've got a few men out here. But not many. We never needed them; this part of Greece has always been a backwater."

"Not any more it isn't," Ziedler snapped. "And if we don't dredge up something soon, Berlin – and Rome – will start asking why."

"They should try looking in those damned mountains for themselves," Hoffman grunted. "As godforsaken a chunk of rocks as I've ever come across."

"I don't see much snow on your boots, Hoffman," Ciarelli sneered. "Why don't you…?"

"Yes, well, that will be all, Herr Leutnant," Ziedler cut in smoothly. Weiss gave a crisp military salute, turned on his heel sharply and went out. Ziedler sighed. Dressler had been by far the more promising apprentice. He might have suggested some ideas as to why the most extensive search ever mounted in occupied Europe had failed to yield any sign of a group of foreigners in country where they should have stood out like beacons. All Weiss did – had done – was diligently bring in all the testaments to failure that made up the pile of waste paper on the desk. Ziedler began to skim through the latest batch, then tossed them aside.

"Rawlings is up to something – something unexpected," he mused.

"*Naturlich,*" Hoffman responded. "But what? He can't have come down from the mountains, or they'd have spotted him. And he's got to do that sometime, whichever option he's decided on."

"It won't be by sea," Ziedler said. "If he tries that, and

we get on his tail, there's nowhere he can run to."

"Then seal the border," Ciarelli replied. "Put every available man guarding every route into Turkey. End this pissing about in the mountains. There's too much space for them to hide up there. But Hoffman' right," he added grudgingly, "the bastard has to come down sometime."

"I know," Ziedler said. "But what if we're missing something?" He stared intently at the map in front of him, then looked up. "I'm going to deploy more troops to the north, right at the highest points along the Bulgarian frontier."

Hoffman gave a dismissive grunt. "Not that again. It's the fucking Alps up there. They're just a few Tommies and a half-dead Russian civilian, not an Olympic skiing team. Anyway, you've already sent some of our *Gebirgsjager* mountain boys up there – to sit on their backsides and pick fights with the Bulgars."

"Well, then let's send some more to keep them company," Ziedler replied, refusing to rise to the bait. "And even the odds for the next fight."

"I'm against it," said Ciarelli. "I want all my men to stay near the border."

"They can." Ziedler tried not to let his relief become too obvious. "The nearest troops are German –it will be much more simple from a logistics point of view to redeploy them."

Ciarelli bristled instantly. "I wish to be kept informed. If you are right, then any capture operation must be a joint effort."

"I would not have it any other way, Signor Colonel," Ziedler replied. Hoffman put his hand over his mouth to disguise the smirk that crept unbidden to his face, then said to Ziedler: "Makes no difference. Rawlings won't turn up there – and Berlin will roast your arse for diverting men from a key area."

"Oh, I don't think we need bother them too much with such mundane details," Ziedler replied airily. "All they care about is whether I get Rawlings and Vlasenin. I'll make damn sure of that. One way or another."

ღ

The sun was at its highest point, beaming down from a clear blue sky through the pines to dapple light on the forest floor. The day was cold but crisp, an afternoon like so many Rawlings had known in his boyhood, where the woods and hills of Northumbria would become anything his imagination wished them to be – the wild lands of Arthur's kingdom, the Indian territory of a James Fenimore Cooper tale – in days of adventure that lasted until a tired suppertime. Even the countryside was reminiscent of those days; dark woods with the scent of bracken everywhere, countless dells and gulleys strewn with bushes and boulders, narrow paths which followed sparkling streams down to a slow, quiet river.

It was good country for a camp, too, and he had felt more secure in these few days at Thraxos' hideout than he had at any time since the start of the mission. But that time was drawing to an end. Tomorrow, Saturday November 28th, 1942, they would begin the first leg of their journey to the border. That would initiate the endgame, one way or another. He had been grateful for these few days. All the wounded were recovering well, though Costas' arm was still in a sling. Everyone was rested and alert. And they would need to be. They were about to undertake the most dangerous part of the mission so far.

This was why Vasily and Yelena were staying behind. The fewer people who had to be concealed from spotter planes or patrols, and crammed into the trucks' false bottoms for the final run, the better. And all the SOE men had experience of staying alive and hidden behind enemy lines. The two Russians did not. They had performed wonders at the German camp but it was unfair to ask them to do it again. It would be safer for them to return to Turkey once the mission was over and the border had returned to a less heightened state of security.

They had agreed with some reluctance, seeing the logic but conscious of the bond that had grown with the SOE men. For Rawlings it was more than that. He was glad that Yelena would not be in the thick of the action once again. But he wanted to see her alone at least once before they parted.

There was no logic to it. He was aware that he had known her for less than a week, and had been no closer to her than anyone else in his team in all that time. He had expressed nothing of his feelings, besides that one comment to Topfer. That had been no more than any of his men, any man with a shred of decency, would have said. And had Topfer decided to indulge his desires Rawlings knew that in practice all he could have done was watch at gunpoint.

So why did he feel that he had to see her? Why was he walking down to the river, where he knew she was washing, risking not only the spotter planes, but Thraxos' old-style Greek sense of propriety and possibly a lowering in his men's estimation? It was selfish and unprofessional, he knew, the pointless indulgence of a love-struck swain. And he had to do it. Because she had touched him as no woman – not even Angela – had ever done before.

He saw the two guards, standing at a respectable distance from the river, and signalled to them. They waved in response, then gestured him on as he pointed down the path. They gave a knowing look apiece as he walked past, but said nothing. He hesitated, nervous as he had been before his first village hall dance, and peered through the trees. She was kneeling by the river's edge, dressed in the clothes she had borrowed from one of the women members of Thraxos' group. Her hair was still wet, glistening like ebony in the sun, and she rubbed it with a coarse towel before taking a tiny comb that lay spread on another towel close by, next to a cake of soap and a Luger pistol, and running it through the strands. She looked intently into a tiny, cracked mirror balanced on a rock as she did so. She was so incongruously, captivatingly feminine in those surroundings that Rawlings' heart leapt to see her.

He moved towards her almost without realising it. Yelena heard and whirled round, grabbing the pistol. But she smiled and lowered it as soon as she saw him. "Major Rawlings – you startled me."

"I didn't mean to. I wanted to look – I mean, I wanted to keep an eye on you. I didn't want you straying too far."

"I only came down to wash my hair – at last. I know we are still in danger. I am used to staying hidden." There was a note of anger in her voice, but then she saw his eyes and smiled. "But you are kind to think of me."

"I have to think of everyone on this mission – it's

my job. God knows, you've proved you can look after yourself."

She shrugged. "We did what had to be done – Vasily and I. But now you face the greater danger. We will think of you when you are gone – and pray for you."

"I'll think of you too. It's no picnic what you're going back to. All your group is destroyed – because of us. You'll have to build it again from scratch."

"We are used to that. The Reds destroyed everything I had – everything I loved."

She was silent for a moment. "Your husband?" Rawlings asked gently.

She looked up at him. "And my child." She hesitated, then began to talk; slowly at first, then more quickly and easily, as if it were a relief to let it out at last. "I was six months pregnant when they arrested Sergei. The only reason I escaped was because another teacher at the school where I worked had a brother in his unit. She risked her life by telling me, but I don't know what happened to her. I left the school that day and never went home. I knew they would be waiting for me. So I ran. I found the Tsarists and they smuggled me into Turkey. But the journey killed my baby. A son, they said at the hospital. We had thought to name a boy Misha."

Tears welled in her eyes. Rawlings reached for her hand and she took his and gripped it hard. "I wanted to give up then. But I did not. If I do that, they win." She wiped the tears away with her other hand and again that smile came unbidden. "And Vasily helped so much. He took it on himself to look after me. He was kind, and never asked for anything. It was as well. I could feel nothing for any man then. I have felt nothing – until now."

Rawlings could hardly dare to hope. He looked into her eyes. "Do you mean that? Believe me, I didn't come here to force anything from you. I just wanted to see you – before tomorrow."

She cupped his face in her hands. "I wanted you to come. So much. But I knew if you did not, I would say nothing." She was still smiling, but her eyes were sad now. "Why do people meet when there is no chance for them ever to be together?"

"What do you mean – why can't we be together? Once all this is over – the mission, the war, everything – I'll come back for you. Why not? You'll have your group working better than ever by then, if I know you and Vasily. He can keep running it, but you can come back with me. To London. I don't have much," he laughed, "but I've never wanted to share it with anyone more than you."

"You are kind, Major Rawlings…"

"I think you can call me Alex now," Rawlings laughed again. "I don't think I'm technically your commander."

She laughed back. "All right – Alexei". Love surged inside him to hear his name said like that. He made to kiss her, but she drew back. "You are kind. And strong, a good man. But it cannot be. I have my life. It is not yours."

"Why not? You can still do the same work in London. We need people with your talents."

"To do what? Sit in some office translating all day, then come home and cook and clean for you? And be patronised by your friends? And maybe go to some Russian café once in a while, to listen to more lonely exiles singing of the old days over their cheap vodka?" She shook her head. "Vasily needs me more. Our work here is too important."

"Then I'll join you. I'll get a posting in Istanbul – God knows they owe me a quiet desk job. We can be together, Yelena. That's all that matters."

"Not in a war, Alexei. Some things matter more then. You have your work, I have mine. We have both chosen a path of danger. Why must we think of the future when neither of us may live to see it? And if we do, why not accept that we met in the wrong time, but be glad that we met at all?"

"Because we could make each other happy. For the rest of our lives. It doesn't have to end here."

"Yes, it does. Here, but not now. We have until tomorrow."

Then she reached for him, her lips meeting his. They were as sweet as the river water, as soft as the earth that yielded to their bodies.

∽

They left at dusk the next day, after transmitting to Cairo that they were on their way. They were escorted by two dozen picked men, including Davenport and Yannis. First down from the camp, through the steep passes to the same tiny dirt road they had reached on the night after the rescue. Two guides were waiting there for the next stage. Nicos and Lapkaris, from the group they would be passed on to. They were cut from the same cloth as Thraxos' men – short, but broad and powerful with weather-beaten faces and beautifully cultivated moustaches. They smiled at Davenport and Yannis, exchanging hearty greetings, but their eyes remained hard as flint. There was a reassuring air of competence about them. Whatever problems might lie ahead, Rawlings reflected, getting lost was unlikely to be one.

Vasily had come down to the trucks with them. He had insisted, and now he waited to return to the camp with two more of Thraxos' men. Yelena had stayed behind. No-one had commented on the events of yesterday afternoon, and Rawlings had not pressed the matter. As he had left the camp she had kissed him on the cheek and briefly held his hand in hers. Now Rawlings took Vasily's hand and the Russian clapped him on the shoulder. "Safe journey, major."

"And to you, my friend. We owe you so much – all of you."

"Repay us by keeping him safe." He gestured to Vlasenin. He looked slight and frail, wrapped in layers of winter clothing much too big for him. But he squared his shoulders, shifting the light pack on them for better balance, and laughed with the rest as Walters loudly complained that his fucking boots didn't fit properly and if he lost his toes from frostbite he would sue the bloody War Office. "He is a good man," Vasily said. "He has suffered much."

"I know – worked over by Amarazov and Hoffman. It's a wonder he survived that double dose."

"I did not mean that." Vasily looked at Rawlings almost sorrowfully. "I mean in the past. I know something of this man's story. The Reds honoured him. Raised him to their highest ranks. They must have done something truly terrible to make him turn against them."

Rawlings shrugged. "We don't know much about him, except what's on the official record. He's always been critical of some aspects of the system. This is just the logical next step."

Vasily shook his head. "Many men speak out. Not all act. If the right time comes, ask him. You may be the first to learn his secret. Such knowledge might help to save him. And I think he will want to tell you."

Rawlings gave him a quizzical look, but at that moment Davenport came up and saluted. "Ready to move out when you are, sir."

"Thank you, lieutenant. But try to remember that Greek mountain men don't tend to give military salutes to each other, as a rule."

Davenport blushed. "Sorry, sir. I still forget sometimes."

Rawlings gave an indulgent smile. "You've done a grand job, son, and by tomorrow we'll be out of your hair. Just keep it up until then. Right, you lot," he said as he moved to the head of his men, "a nice little nature ramble to round it all off. Hope you've all got your long johns on."

There was a general laugh and they set off. Thraxos' guides motioned to Vasily to start back to the camp. As they moved into the trees the Russian took a look back. The column had already vanished into the forest. A shiver came on him, but he shrugged it away and turned to follow Thraxos' men back to the camp.

*

"Rawlings is on the move," Ziedler said. It was Saturday evening and he was still at the desk in the office they had occupied for almost a week. The pile of intelligence reports on the desk was even thicker but still contained not a single sighting or piece of evidence that could lead them closer to the SOE team.

"That's impossible," Ciarelli scoffed. "The security is as tight as it's ever been. Nothing could move in those mountains without us knowing it."

"A rash statement, Signor Colonel," Ziedler replied. "We don't know this area, and the Bulgarians don't know it as well as they claim. For all their talk of this being their land, they're still invaders and plenty of the local population don't like them. I don't think every road in this accursed place is marked on our maps. Rawlings has used one of them. He's getting closer to Turkey now – I can sense it."

"You couldn't put a map reference to that, I suppose," Hoffman inquired innocently. Ziedler was on the point of finally losing his temper with the Gestapo man when Leutnant Weiss burst in. He had not even bothered to knock and Ziedler was about to issue a mild rebuke when he saw the look on the youngster's face. "What is it, Herr Leutnant?" he asked calmly.

"A message, Herr Oberst." Weiss could hardly contain his excitement, trembling and stuttering out the words. "The caller said the British have moved from a camp in the mountains, escorted by partisans, and they will contact us again when they have further information on the group that will shelter them next."

"Is that all?" Ciarelli's voice was thick with scorn. "It's not the first time we've heard rumours like that. We've sent men on wild goose chases three times already after telephone tip-offs. It's the Greeks laying a smokescreen.

Come back when you've something better, boy."

"This one was different, Herr Oberst." Weiss pointedly ignored the Italian. "I am sorry, I should have made myself clearer. This was not a telephone message but a radio one. On an Abwehr frequency and using a recognised SOE cipher."

Weiss reflected later that he was probably the first man in the Abwehr, and perhaps the entire German Army, to have seen Oberst Ulrich Ziedler with his mouth wide open.

∽

"It will be a good journey, major. We will be there early. Hot dog!" Rawlings was finding it hard to get used to Major Eroglu's incongruous Americanisms. As he had informed them on the first night they met he had lived "five years in Chicago! Goddamn sonofabitch, good life. Best butcher on the South Side. Capone comes to no-one else. But I miss the mountains and the old farm. So I come back, yessirree. Then the war. Kraut bastards, eh? Worse than Bulgars, even. But I keep you safe from them. They never catch me. No goddamn way!"

His English was disconcerting but his command of his group, and their obvious knowledge of the most secret mountain paths, was as impressive as Thraxos' had been. Davenport and Yannis had said farewell when the guides had brought them to the shepherd's hut that marked the initial rendezvous with Eroglu's four-strong advance party late on Saturday night. Eroglu's men had satchels full of cured meat and goatskin canteens full of water and strong *raki* for their guests. They had briefly supped, then Davenport and Yannis turned their escort detail around and begun the journey back to their own camp while Eroglu's six men allowed only the briefest of rests before the first long night march.

It had been hard going, lasting until dawn on Sunday, but it had brought them safely to Eroglu's main camp, a series of bunkers dug into the banks of a small valley just below the treeline. Smokeless fires had banished the cold and damp from them and Eroglu had prepared a feast of exquisitely baked and seasoned goat's meat pasties for a breakfast as good as any Rawlings had eaten in his life. Some real coffee and much *raki* had followed as Eroglu recounted his colourful life story. But he became businesslike and his voice was sober as he pulled out a large map heavily marked with secret trails.

"We start early tonight. I take you myself, with ten of my best men. Four days to get to the next group. Captain Loporos is in charge. Good man – for a half-Bulgar. We meet him here, Adraxos Pass, at dawn on Thursday. From there, he will take you another three days' march. Then the last group will take you across the border." He waved the ornate dagger he had been using as his sole item of cutlery at Rawlings and his voice was grave as he said: "Watch them. Mikos' group are black market boys. Some say they deal with the Germans and the Bulgars. Smuggle coffee and cigarettes in for them and get left alone in return. Fucking gangsters." He shrugged. "But I deal with them sometimes. They never double cross me. You pay them enough they get you across OK. Otherwise they know they got me to deal with. Goddamn right!"

Rawlings felt that dealing with Eroglu, a barrel-chested bear of a man whose scarred face (dominated by a splendidly waxed moustache) and ornate dagger stuck into his black velvet cummerbund presented the image of the mountain *condottieri* cutthroat of comic opera, would be enough to dissuade most men from sharp practice. But it was still worrying to be reminded again how much the success of the mission depended upon trusting strangers. He said as much to Eroglu, who laughed.

"Your job is all work with strangers, seems to me. But we will not be strangers by the end of our journey, major. And then you will have no strangers. All who fight the invaders here are brothers. Me, Loporos, Mikos – even the ELAS, goddamn Red bastards. I know we have to stay clear of them, and they never find me neither. But they fight the same enemy. And we keep you safe from them, also, major. Goddamn right!

☙

At that precise moment Davenport and the rest of the escort were finishing the long climb uphill to the camp. It had been a hard journey back from the exchange point, but Yannis had pushed them hard. He did not like to leave the camp under-garrisoned. Davenport could see his logic. Whatever became of Rawlings and his party the Germans would not rest until they had found every Greek who might have helped them. And because of Vlasenin they would know it must be the EDES who had aided them. They could look forward to nothing from this winter, or the spring beyond, but more hiding and fighting.

But it would not be their first hard winter. Davenport knew they would endure and repay with interest any violence and cruelty done to them. So he was in good spirits as he and Yannis led the column up that last steep path through the forest. They had seen no enemy patrols in all their travels. And now they were near to what had become their home.

Yet they were still alert for any danger and waited behind the final bend until the scouts returned and waved them on. As they rounded the bend they saw the slight figure of Takis, one of the youngest of the band, waving them forward. As they began to move out of the tree cover, Davenport noticed that the boy did not have his father's old hunting rifle slung around his shoulder as always. A jolt of fear spasmed through him but before he could move or shout a warning Takis did both, jumping from cover and sprinting towards them, his shout turning into a scream as the machine-guns opened up.

Half of the column went down in that first terrible scything burst. Davenport, alerted a split second early, dropped to the floor as the bullets cracked overhead, cutting into his comrades from both sides. All about him men were diving for cover in the trees, only to be pounced upon by camouflaged figures, appearing from the shadows like silent devils. As Davenport rolled under the cover of a clump of bracken he saw Yannis draw his Browning pistol as three men closed with him. One went down with a scream as Yannis gutshot him, the other with a grunt as the pistol smashed into the bridge of his nose. But the third grabbed Yannis from behind as more rushed in. A rifle but slammed into his stomach then across his skull and he sank to the ground with a groan.

Davenport saw all this as he lay stock-still in the bracken while around him the killing continued. Knives flashed, garottes tightened, stray shots rang out. Slowly and silently, Davenport began to crawl back down the slope, away from the camp, eyes constantly scanning their limited vision field for danger. At first there were many men moving around him, but gradually their footfalls died down and then disappeared completely. He reached a gap in the trees, looked around quickly then rose on one hand and knee, half-turning around, poised to sprint across to the next cover.

As soon as he rose to his feet they moved on him, materialising out of the trees as quick and quiet as all the rest had done. They covered him front and back, guns trained on him. Three of them; tall and broad, dressed in camouflage gear. There was camouflage cream on their faces too, the faces that were split in mocking smiles. Davenport sighed and stood up. "Leaving so soon, Englishman?" the tallest of them asked in Greek. Then he rammed the stock of his Schmeisser into Davenport's face. Unconsciousness came like a door slammed behind his brain.

When he woke up he was lying bound and gagged in the centre of the camp. A fire had been lit and his captors were grouped around it. Thraxos, his sons, Vasily and Yelena were lying in a row beside Davenport, all similarly helpless. A shaven-headed, black-bearded giant of a man moved out of the ring of captors into the firelight. He was not dressed in camouflage gear and, as Davenport's eyes adjusted to the light, he could see that many of the others were not either. They wore no uniform that he could identify, just scraps of clothing from half a dozen sources, like Thraxos' men. The only single item that they had in common was their red star armbands. The giant who moved towards Davenport now had one sewn into his sidecap too. He was obviously their leader. Davenport swallowed hard and tried not to let his fear show.

But the leader ignored him and bent over Thraxos, tearing the gag from his mouth. Thraxos spat at his feet. "Are there no invaders left in Thrace that you make war on your brothers, Communist?"

"You are not our brothers, colonel," a voice spoke from inside the circle. Davenport looked to identify the speaker but could only see shadows. "The only brothers these men have are their fellow workers. Comrades in the struggle to rid the world of all oppressors – German, Bulgar or Greek." The voice was different to those Davenport had become used to. The Greek was excellent but the accent hard to place. "Why should they not make war on a rabble who follow their Napoleon like sheep and would see their worthless king, or a dictator like Metaxas, rule Greece again; who form alliance with the Fascist invaders to kill the true defenders of liberty."

"You lie!" Thraxos shouted. "My soldiers have never done that. They will never. If you can speak no word that is not a lie, then kill me as you have killed them and be on your way."

"Not yet, colonel." The speaker moved from the shadows to join the leader. He was much smaller, of no more than medium height, but Davenport could tell he was far more senior than the giant who towered above him. And far more dangerous. "Your men died through this man's mistakes, colonel – those and those of his government." He turned to Davenport, cold, fierce eyes burning below a black beret with a red star in the centre and amazed him by speaking the next words in

English. "The SOE has picked the wrong side, Lieutenant Davenport, and Major Rawlings has deserted you – as I knew he would. Your only chance to save yourself – and your friends – from much suffering is to tell me where he is."

Davenport did not reply. Amarazov stepped back and drew a long, slender-bladed knife from his belt. Then he walked slowly along the line of prisoners. "To begin with you will watch, lieutenant. Now who shall I pick first?" He knelt beside Thraxos. "Your beloved colonel? Or the sons who have accepted you like a brother?" He stood up and continued down the line. "Or shall it be this one?" He looked down on Vasily and whispered in Russian: "I should have made sure of you, Tsarist – this time I will."

Vasily lashed out at him with his bound feet. Amarazov stepped back and his eyes fixed on Yelena. He knelt beside her and with a swift but almost gentle movement used the knife to remove her gag. The motion caused the blade to brush her left cheek, though it did not draw blood. Amarazov moved it down her cheek, then under her chin and along the curve of her neck. "When I was trained, one of my instructors showed me how to skin a body completely," he said in English. "He proved it could be done, too – and that the subject could stay conscious for the whole time."

Davenport screamed against the gag, writhing in impotent fury. The leader moved to take it off. Amarazov turned in triumph but Yelena shouted in English: "Tell him nothing, lieutenant! You must be strong. You must give Rawlings time. We all must. I can take anything this filthy Red can do to me." She looked up at Amarazov and said in Russian: "I will tell you nothing."

Amarazov smiled and replied in the same language: "We shall see." He turned to the fire, and began to heat the blade in the flames.

∽

The wind howled against the stone walls of the shepherd's hut, knifing through every gap to blast the men inside, huddling together for warmth. All of Rawlings' team were there, including Vlasenin. Eroglu and his men were outside, camped in a nearby cave. Rawlings had offered to make room for them too, but Eroglu had insisted. "Too cramped. We spend the whole day tripping over each other and farting in your faces. No fucking way! Besides, who keeps watch then, goddammit?"

Rawlings had to admit he had a point. The hut was barely big enough for the dozen men in his party. But they were packed together so tightly that their bodies generated a communal heat to add to the smokeless fire in the hearth. It helped, but not much. In the last two days they had become used to the biting cold of the Rhodope Mountains, a cold that never went quite away. The night marches chilled them to the bones, and even the watery sun that came with the dawn did little to warm them, because that was when they had to shelter from the spotter planes. They tried to rest, while Eroglu's men took it in turns to stand watch (and Rawlings insisted that his men take their turn on sentry-go, too) but even in sleep the cold insinuated itself back into their bodies, forcing them back awake at least half a dozen times a day.

Vlasenin was suffering most, of course. He had borne up well during the first two marches. But as the afternoon of Tuesday December 1st, the seventh day since Davenport's ambush, dragged on Rawlings could see he was dreading another. He had barely slept all day and now, as Conor made the 5 p.m 'sked' transmission informing Cairo of the next phase of their itinerary and the rest of the team stirred from semi-wakefulness to the real thing, he sat up, shivering, and lit another cigarette.

Rawlings walked over to him with a thermos of raki-laced coffee. "Drink this, doctor," he said gently. "It'll help you get through the night. Eroglu says tonight's march isn't so bad. Only eight cigarettes."

There was a hoot of scornful laughter from his men. In their two days on the trail Rawlings had come to realise (though Curtis and Walters had forewarned him) that in the Balkans in general, and Greece in particular, distances on foot were invariably measured in cigarettes. And, as Curtis had pointed out, it was "a method which is invariably a hundred per cent wrong".

Vlasenin did not join in the laughter. "It's not the marching I mind. It's the waiting. All day, cooped up like a prisoner. Every moment I imagine I can hear them coming for me."

"They're not coming, doctor. And even if they were Eroglu's men would hear them long before they got near us. Then he'd bore them to death telling them about the goddamn old days in Chicago, hot dog!"

Vlasenin managed a weary smile. "I know you are right, major. But fear knows no logic. It was like this before I made the break for Turkey. No matter how much they reassured me, those last few days were the worst of my life. I used to dream of the NKVD scouring the whole country for me, then getting to my door and sniffing at it like wolves, scenting me, then…" he broke off with a sour laugh. "And of course they didn't need to do anything of the sort. They just waited until I was out in the open and got me then."

"What made you go through all that?" Rawlings asked gently. He remembered Vasily's words. The more he knew about his prize the better the chance of learning something that might help to save them all. Added to that was simple curiosity. Vlasenin was the most hunted man in the world; his power and knowledge had made him so. But he was still just a man. Rawlings hesitated, then asked: "What made you turn against your own people?"

For a moment it seemed Vlasenin might not answer him. He looked Rawlings in the eye for a long moment, then said: "It took me most of my life to learn that they were truly not my people, major. I have no people."

"No family?"

Vlasenin gave Rawlings a look almost of contempt, then replied slowly. "I am a scientist, Major Rawlings. My definitions are precise. I have no people. Stalin killed them all. In their millions. When this war is over I hope Britain and America look a little closer at how their glorious ally became what it was. To make Russia into the first Communist state Lenin, then Comrade Stalin after him, decreed that all the land of Russia should be turned over to great factories and great farms, the twin pillars of Marxist endeavour. The only problem was that the land already had owners."

"The kulaks," Rawlings said softly.

"The kulaks," Vlasenin repeated. "The small farmers. The peasant landowners. The agricultural bourgeoisie. They, even more than the great landlords, were the enemy of the proletariat, so Comrade Lenin taught. But Comrade Stalin hated them even more. He was the one who decided to really paint them out of the picture." He gave a bitter laugh. "You know, gentlemen, my country is truly a marvel. Every time a part of her population has displeased her, she has simply got rid of it."

"The British Empire's done a pretty good job of that a time or two, as well," Walters said. Vlasenin looked at him for a long time before replying. "I know what you speak of, and it is nothing any country should remember with pride. So many countries have a story like that in their past. But compared to what Stalin did to the kulaks…" he shook his head. "Maybe you're right. Maybe a wrong is a wrong, and the scale is unimportant.

"All I know is he wiped them out. Took their land, burned their homes, killed their livestock – dear God, killed all the animals; cattle, pigs, chickens, everything. Animals that could have stocked his new farms, fed the workers in his new factories. But no, they had to die too. And lie there and rot. Because they were kulak animals. Some of the kulaks killed their own animals, because they thought it would save them. They thought it might make Comrade Stalin stop.

"But he had no intention of stopping. There were only three alternatives for a kulak; deportation, a camp, or death. For most it was the third. And the second usually meant the third. Not many subsets in that equation, gentlemen. Personally I never heard of any deportations. So let's just say they all died. Millions of them. No-one knows how many. No-one will ever know. The kulaks. My people. My family.

"And he got what he wanted. He got his new factories

and farms. His new Russia. Maybe he was right. The old Russia could never have fought Germany for this long. And Hitler's evil must be fought. I don't know which is worse – to wipe out a people because you have a mad hatred of them or simply because they are in your way. Perhaps one day we scientists will find out which element in the human mind is the more corrosive, which one carries the greater negative charge.

"For now, all I know is that I could never work for a system that does such things. The western allies may all be flawed and culpable in many ways, but they have never done anything on such a scale. Life still seems to have some value for them. Maybe I'm wrong, but sometimes a choice has to be made. To refuse something when it is demanded, and to give when it is unasked." He gave a bitter smile. "And my father always said a man's work was his most precious gift."

"But why did you work for them at all?" Curtis asked. "And how did they ever accept a man from your class?"

Vlasenin's smile vanished. "Because, my friend, there was a time when, for all my fine speeches just now, I hated the kulaks as much as anyone. I hated my people. And I was glad to work for anyone who seemed to be what they were not." There was a long pause. "Does that surprise you?" he continued. "It should not. To feel pity for a people – or a family – is not to deny that they had faults. I was raised to be a farmer. Nothing else. To tend my father's land. Raise new litters of livestock. And marry a girl from the same class as me, one who could put food on the table and give me sons to tend the farm when I was dead. And she could dust the one row of books in the best room, and sit beside me in the pony cart as we rode to church. Every week."

He looked at them almost pleadingly and Rawlings looked back with something like understanding at last. "You wanted to escape." It was a statement, not a question.

Vlasenin nodded. "I hated that life. I loved the world of the mind, not the hands. I pestered my school teachers for books on everything – physics, mathematics, politics, literature. When my parents found out they took me from the school. So I went back and stole the books. Then my father found them and burnt them. He said reading and thinking were what a man did when his day's work was over. And the teachers agreed with him. They all thought I was getting above my station. I hated them. I hated him. I hated their world.

"So when the first war came I joined up, just to get away. They brought me back. Because I was too young and because they needed someone to work the farm. That was more important than the country or the Tsar, than right or wrong. That fucking farm, to work it until I died and make sure I had a son to work it after me. I knew if I stayed I would be a farmer, a kulak, all my life. So I ran away again and this time I made sure they did not find me."

"And you joined the army?" Walters asked. "Bet they gave you plenty of time to read and think, mate."

The laughter from all the soldiers in the hut even drowned out the wind. And Vlasenin laughed too. "Maybe I would have that part different if I could do it all again, my friend. But I would still have run. If there had been no war I'd have headed for the nearest city with a university. But joining up seemed the right thing to do at the time. Until I saw how terrible war was, and how brutally the army kept its men under control. Cossacks hunted down deserters while generals ate caviar miles from the front line. I couldn't stand to kill after my first battle, so I trained as a medical orderly, then became a doctor – of sorts. There were no medical schools at the front, of course. We were all like that at the hospital. But there were some who saw the injustices too, who were from backgrounds like me, who wanted something different for themselves, and for every Russian. People like Valery, Pyotr – and Raisa."

"Your first wife?" Rawlings asked.

Vlasenin nodded. "All my life that's on your files – on anyone's – began there. She was a nurse, and a Party member. So were the other two. They became my closest friends. Taught me all about the new world that the revolution could offer. I knew about the Bolsheviks of course, and I couldn't wait to join. If there had been no Bolsheviks at that hospital I'd have gone looking for them. I believed so deeply. And I knew many of the men did too. All the ones we sent back to their units carried instructions on how to mutiny. So did all the staff at the hospital. And on October 25th, 1917, that's just what we did. The Bolshevik Revolution. The most glorious day of my life. Apart from my wedding day, two months later."

"It had to happen," Walters said. "It needed to. But it went wrong bloody quick."

"Not straight away," Vlasenin said. "The first days were glorious. We were united against everybody – first those traitors in the Provisional Government who wanted to keep us in the war, or so the Party told us. Then the Whites, and the Mensheviks and all the forces from the rest of the world who came to destroy us. You can't imagine the sense of rightness we felt, the sense of freedom and power. Not that I did any fighting. We were heroes of the Revolution and we could choose our destinies. We wanted to be true doctors, all of us. So we went to the university in Moscow. And I discovered a new world. Not just medicine, but physics and mathematics, mineralogy. A world of systems that brought order and truth to the universe like the Revolution would bring order to Russia. A world that could sweep aside religion and superstition, the things that had kept us enslaved for so long. I knew that, even more than being a doctor, I wanted to be a scientist.

"And the new Soviet Union needed scientists. That's what Comrade Lenin said when he pinned that worthless medal on me. I was encouraged to take more courses even as I completed my medical degree. And then soon after I was invited by the new Soviet Academy of Sciences to join Professor Kulik's expedition to Tunguska. That was where I first saw what the power of pure, concentrated energy could do, and I first began to…"

"Don't say any more about that, doctor," Rawlings broke in gently but firmly. "The less any of us know about it, the better."

Vlasenin shrugged. "You are right. In any case, my strongest memory of that first trip now is that I was away when the typhus took Raisa. When I came back it was everywhere. She caught it caring for sufferers in her first job as a doctor. Then there was the famine. That was how Valery died. He gave up his share of food to keep his patients alive. To no avail. And the Whites killed Pyotr, out east somewhere. He was doctor to a special cavalry unit. He never talked about that much, and we never had a chance to say goodbye properly.

"So within a year my closest friends were dead. The war had killed them all, in its way. I wanted so much to make sure that no-one ever had to suffer through war again. And I began to wonder if a weapon could be made that would stop countries ever daring to make war again."

"How?" Mayhew asked. Like all the rest he was looking intently at Vlasenin.

"That's classified information," Rawlings broke in again, his voice hard as flint this time. "I think you've said enough, doctor."

"I've said nothing, major!" Vlasenin bit back with the same spirit shown in the ambush. "But I will say no more of my work. Anyway, the last chapter of my story begins now. For years I continued with… my work. And gradually I began to realise that I might be on the verge of a breakthrough, something that none of the others had considered.

"This was in the early Thirties, and by that time we had started to hear about the 'kulak problem' and how it was vital to solve it. You heard it at social functions, in the newspapers. But of course that was all about how necessary it was, how any trouble that resulted was a case of the peasants being stubborn, or sabotaging the state like the counter-revolutionaries we'd always known they were.

"But I knew my parents were not like that, or anyone of my village. They would have obeyed anyone in authority. That was when I began to suspect that it was all a lie. And I discovered the truth courtesy of my NKVD liaison man. Comrade Stalin was not so interested in science, not like Lenin. Scientists like me worked in the world of theories and possibilities. That would not build his factories or conjure grain for his starving people out of thin air. So I had little dealings with the upper echelons. They selected a drunken time-server to keep an eye on me, visit me once in a while and report back to his bosses, who told a Central Committee who couldn't care less that Comrade Doctor Vlasenin was doing interesting and valuable, but very complicated work.

"One night our meeting ran late and he invited me to share a bottle of vodka before dinner with him. That bottle turned into three. What did I care? I had no-one waiting in my little apartment near the university to welcome me home. I had to be careful not to say too much to an NKVD man, even a minor oaf like this one. But I need not have worried. He did all the talking, boasting about how Tchekists like him were the real power in Russia now. The bosses might make the decisions, but they enacted them. They were the archangels, sent forth to scourge a sinful world. And they were scourging the kulaks, oh yes. Every last one of those bastards would die. *Pravda*'s not telling you the half of it, comrade, this time the tree's not bending in the fucking storm. This time we uproot it. Then we burn it.

"I decided then and there what I had to do. I had to reach my family again. I had to try to save them. I knew it was suicide. I knew I could never explain it. As far as anyone knew my family were good Russian workers – landless farmhands who had died at the start of the war. Vlasenin is not even my real name, you know. My old one might have linked me to my class. At one time

I wanted to forget my old name, for reasons that had nothing to do with security. Now that it was more vital than ever I wanted the world to truly know where I was from, what I was.

"I asked my NKVD man about my home area. It was a long way from Moscow, and I phrased it so it seemed like professional Party curiosity. Have they really got that far already? Oh yes, comrade, just starting but those boys don't hang around once they start a job. Damn, I wish I was with them, but this work is important, too, eh, keeping an eye on you scientist chaps. When are we going to hear more about this great weapon of yours, then? I don't know much about science but that sounds like it could really wipe the fuckers out."

His voice had grown hoarse. He paused, and Walters passed him a flask of *raki*. Vlasenin drank deep and lit a cigarette before continuing. "I wanted to go the very next day. But that would have been too suspicious. I had leave coming up, so I had it pushed forward a little. I said I wanted to visit a colleague in Minsk. And I did. But I made sure I had to change trains on the way, at the town near our farm.

"I got there too late. When I asked the station master he was proud to tell me that he had informed on every stinking kulak in the district. It was the same in the tavern, and at local Party HQ. Nobody remembered me – I'd been a boy with another name when I ran away. And the local Party boss had been drafted in from elsewhere. He was very impressed when he saw my papers, though. So impressed that he laid on a car for me when I asked to see the farms for myself.

"Mine was just like the others. Gone. Not even ruins.

They had burnt everything to the ground. The grain had been confiscated and the livestock slaughtered. The owner had resisted so the NKVD had shot them and buried them in unmarked graves. It had been done not so long ago. The ashes were still warm. If I had gone straight away – if I had not been a coward who cared more for his reputation than his family – I would have been in time."

"To do what?" Rawlings said. "Expose your lies and get yourself arrested? Make sure the NKVD killed you and gave your work to someone who would have hidden nothing from them?"

"I know – but try telling that to a man whose first sight of his home in twenty years is to see it burned to the ground. I paid for my tardiness, anyway. Soon after I resumed my journey, they stopped us. Because there was an NKVD armoured train on the line ahead, waiting while its occupants continued their work. They ordered us all out of the train to watch.

"It was only one dacha out of God knows how many millions. But I dare say it was like all the rest. Like my home. First they ransacked it for the grain. Then they put all the animals into the barn and set it ablaze. They screamed like no screams I had heard before, not even in the field hospital. They made the family watch that. Then they shot them one by one. The youngest was a girl of eight. They left her until last. Said she had a right to more life than the rest of them.

"So that was the kulak problem solved right in front of my eyes. To Comrade Stalin it may have been a practical necessity. But he knew that every bully and sadist in uniform would play his own little variation on the theme. And Russia has thousands of them. Those

NKVD men made us watch to check that none of us showed any emotion except the appropriate Soviet ones. And to remind us that what they had just done they could do to any of us. Then they put their train into a siding, smiled and waved us on.

"As soon as I got back to Moscow I slowed my work down as much as I dared. I had seen how wrong it had all become. People should not be exterminated for what they are, or what they represent. For faults and human frailties – if that is all that condemns a man you might as well execute the whole world. So I kept back as much as I dared. Luckily there was no-one in the Soviet Union who knew enough to realise what I was doing. Some of my colleagues elsewhere in Europe – men like Karkoszy – suspected, and whenever I met them outside of Russia I told as much as I dared about what I had discovered, what I was discovering.

"It helped that I had married Ekaterina by then. She was an administrator at the university. Party through and through. And she loved me so much. Enough for it not to matter that I never loved her. But she died in a car crash in '37. That was when the bad years truly began. That was the year I acquired my first shadow. He wasn't very good – I spotted him, for God's sake. But it made me realise they were watching me. There was a war coming and I might be able to provide them with a weapon. After that it was just a question of whether they found out and killed me before I could escape." He took another pull on his cigarette before adding with surprise: "1937 – that was the year I won the Nobel Prize."

At that moment the door opened and Eroglu stepped in, bringing a fresh blast of icy wind with him. It was only then they realised darkness had fallen. "Ready, eh?" he asked, looking with concern at Vlasenin.

The Russian stood up and squared his shoulders. "I'm ready."

∾

There was an air of expectancy in Ziedler's office. All were present; Hoffman, Ciarelli, even Dorsch. Since his return from guarding the Yugoslav border against Ciarelli's escape Ziedler had kept him busy – and away from the decision-making – by assigning him to take charge of the many special patrols that had followed up rumours and tip-offs about the location of Rawlings' group. He and the seven men left from his Hermann Goering platoon had spent ten very cold days gaining an intimate knowledge of the foothills of the Rhodope Mountains and regretfully reporting back to Xanthi that their information had been unfounded.

Then had come the call message in the SOE cipher. It was mystifying. Neither Abwehr or the SD had penetrated SOE, or any of the other major British intelligence services. But someone was obviously tipping them off. The news about the Tsarist camp in Turkey had come from an SD contact among the Tsarists in Istanbul, and they were notoriously loose-tongued. But since Ciarelli's attempted coup had deposited the British in Greece, nothing. Until that call. And since then, nothing. Until today.

The side door opened and Ziedler strode in, Weiss at his heels as usual. He looked extremely pleased with himself. "Good morning, gentlemen. I have excellent news for you," he said as he sat at his desk. "As you remember, we received information from a… very valuable source on Saturday evening that Major Rawlings and his party were on the move. That was four days ago. Since then we have redoubled our efforts to pick up the trail. Without success. Unfortunately this source is most selective with their information. They have given no precise geographical location. Until now."

He paused for effect. The others were almost straining their heads to listen. "A radio transmission has been made to an Abwehr frequency using a recognised SOE cipher. It said that Rawlings' party are due to make a rendezvous with another EDES partisan group at dawn tomorrow. Here." He stood up and rammed a finger against the wall map. "Adraxos Pass, which lies half way between the towns of Organi and Smigada. They have promised a precise map reference tomorrow." He turned back to face the others. "I believe this represents the best opportunity we have had yet of capturing these men. I have selected a special force from units of all three countries. We shall proceed to Organi this morning where we shall establish an operations centre. Then, when we hear from our source again, we will strike. Any questions?"

"What's the catch?" said Hoffman. "We know this boy isn't one of ours. So why is he telling us all this?"

"That thought had occurred to me," Ziedler agreed. "It may be that he is so senior within the SOE ranks – which is plausible, as only a select few would know of this mission – that Berlin have not disclosed his identity even to us. But I think this unlikely; it would be taking inter-service rivalry to a ludicrous extent." He glanced briefly at Dorsch before continuing. "The other alternative is that the source is a relatively low-ranking SOE member in Cairo or London – a cipher clerk or radio operator – who has gained access to this information and wishes to sell it for a price. Unlikely, as they have made no mention of money."

"The third, and most plausible, explanation is that SOE has a Russian agent in its ranks. They wish to see Vlasenin returned to the Soviet Union and have been trying to engineer this all along. You remember, Hauptmann Dorsch, that I raised this possibility when we received the location of Rawlings' camp in Turkey."

"Indeed, Herr Oberst," Dorsch replied. "I admitted the possibility. But I would remind you again that the information came from the SD, obtained from a reliable contact within the Tsarist network in Istanbul."

"Ziedler nodded. "Yes – planted there by the GRU, on information received from their agent in SOE. At that stage they were still keen to keep us in the dark. But now they have no option. I think they are using us to eliminate Rawlings, leaving them free to recapture Vlasenin. Obviously their intention is to intercept the EDES group at the pass and eliminate them, taking Vlasenin for themselves and escaping before we arrive, conveniently late, to pick up either the bodies or the living persons of Major Rawlings and his team."

Hoffman smiled. "And I presume we're not going to do that?"

Ziedler smiled back. "Only half of it. We take a large force to the map reference they give us. I shall lead it in person, to convince them we simply think our source is motivated by money or preference. After all, if Rawlings is alive, we will need a reasonably strong escort to deliver him to you, Klaus." Hoffman licked his lips as Ziedler went on. "Meanwhile we shall post troops at every known road or pass down from the mountains into Turkey. The Russians will count on us neglecting this, because we assume the source is a German agent in SOE who wishes to keep their identity secret for security's sake, and genuinely wishes us to take everything in one fell swoop. They will try to get to Turkey as quickly as possible, but this will be their undoing. If we arrive at the pass quicker than they expect there is a good chance we will pick up their trail and, in any case, we have our back-up force waiting. Either way, I predict Vlasenin will be ours by the end of tomorrow. Any more questions?"

"Just one, Herr Oberst," Dorsch said. "If we are to cover all eventualities, should the roads into Bulgaria not be covered too? There is a strong Communist resistance developing there also since Tsar Boris came over to our side – as Obersturmfuhrer Topfer could have attested."

Ziedler relished the sadness and bitterness in Dorsch's voice at the mention of the only other officer to weigh in on Dorsch's side in these councils, since the other SD lieutenant whose name he could not remember had got himself killed on the first day. "I hardly think that a likely eventuality, Herr Hauptmann," Ziedler said with a patronising smile. "It would, after all, be in entirely the wrong direction." Ziedler held up a hand as the rest laughed. "Turkey is the safest destination for any group not allied to us. But you have reminded us of the necessity to cover all options. So we will detail a guard on all the roads into Bulgaria which lie in that area – and if you would care to take command of that detail I would be most grateful."

He really does walk into these traps, Ziedler thought as he saw the SD man's cheeks colour an even deeper red and his eyes burn as they held his superior's mocking gaze. You can watch the back door, young man, while the glory is grabbed elsewhere. "Well, gentlemen, if that is all I suggest we leave for Organi – which, I very much hope, will be our last port of call in this accursed country."

༄

"Good journey, major. We will be there early. Hot dog!" After four days on the trail, Rawlings was beginning to get used to Eroglu's Americanisms. And he was getting better at gauging distances. For this last uphill climb he had won a bet with Curtis by exactly doubling the ten cigarettes the partisan chief had confidently stated would get them to Adraxos Pass.

The journey had taken it out of all his men, especially Vlasenin. But they were still going, and soon they would be able to rest again. In a dry cave at the head of the pass where Eroglu had assured them Captain Loporos and his men would be waiting. It sounded a step down from the shepherd's hut where Vlasenin had told his story, but an improvement on the temporary shelter Eroglu's men had rigged for the first camp, or the day just past when they had simply found some sparse tree cover, then swaddled themselves in their bedrolls and packed close together for warmth.

The cold had been intense, but so far snow had held off. And the low cloud had limited the effectiveness of the spotter planes. They had seen no evidence of any enemy patrols; as Eroglu had said: "Too goddamn high for them. Goddamn pansies!" Rawlings felt it more likely that they were simply waiting for the team's inevitable descent. But he had no wish to argue the matter.

And despite the EDES leader's eccentric volubility Rawlings would be sorry to say goodbye to him. He had organised and commanded his men just as efficiently as Thraxos had done. Their approach to the rendezvous had used every scrap of cover and two men had gone ahead to make initial contact. Now Eroglu scanned the bend with his binoculars from the safety of the trees by the path and only motioned his men forward when he had seen one of the scouts wave him on.

They moved up the path swiftly to the pass itself, a natural funnel formed by two rock falls, perhaps ten yards wide. The party filed through in small groups, Rawlings among the last. He saw a half a dozen partisans taking guard at the pass. An equal number escorted their group into the cave as Eroglu embraced a lean, ascetic-looking man with dark Balkan features. Eroglu turned and beckoned Rawlings on.

"Major – meet Captain Loporos."

"We're glad to see you," Rawlings said.

"And I am glad to see you, Major Rawlings," Amarazov's voice came from behind. Rawlings whirled round just as the partisans raised and cocked their weapons, covering his men and Eroglu's. Amarazov had another half-dozen at his back and, as Rawlings watched in amazement, another eight or nine emerged from around a bend beyond the cave. Loporos stepped back from Eroglu's embrace with a look of sorrow and pain. "I'm sorry, Christos – they said they would kill all my men if I did not co-operate."

"And do you think they will not, anyway – fool?" Loporos bowed his head. Eroglu lunged towards him but half a dozen gun barrels swiveled towards him as their owners' fingers tightened on the triggers. Eroglu stopped in his tracks and his shoulders slumped.

Amarazov moved through the pass, Tokarev automatic pointed at Rawlings' heart. "Thought you were dead, Comrade Major," Rawlings said.

"I am happy to disappoint you." He certainly sounded it. "No doubt you thought you had seen the last of me after that pre-arranged ambush at the German camp."

Rawlings felt a sick dread rise within him. "How did you find out about that?"

"I began to suspect the moment the machine-guns began cutting my men down. The rest I learned from the two Tsarist traitors who were stupid enough to trust you. It took a long time to get them to talk, I admit. The girl lasted longer than the big ape; that surprised me, I confess. Still, perhaps she enjoyed some of the things I did to her."

Rawlings went for him then, all thought of the mission wiped from his mind by black hatred and the desire to kill. He got half-way before a Schmeisser butt dropped him to his knees and another partisan kicked him in the face, sprawling him on his back. "Tie him up and get him on his feet," Amarazov ordered. Within seconds Rawlings was face to face with the Russian but unable to do anything but spit in his face.

"I should have specified a gag." Amarazov smiled as he wiped his cheek. "But since that is all the revenge you will ever take for her, I suppose I can allow it. If it makes you feel any better, that young English pup and the rest of the EDES rabble had a quicker end. They told us about your rendezvous with little persuasion." He lowered his voice. "And Captain Leonidas is regrettably squeamish about torturing fellow Greeks, even if they fight under a flag of Fascism." He jerked his head in the direction of the black-bearded giant who stood at the head of the partisans guarding Rawlings' men.

"Yes, well he hasn't had your training," Rawlings gasped. As he looked at Amarazov his eyes burned with hate but he kept his voice level with a supreme effort. "Still, that's another few dozen men that the Germans won't have to worry about. I wonder how many of his cadre felt guilty about killing comrades in arms."

Amarazov looked at him with contempt. "Greater needs drive out lesser, major. There is an international brotherhood, of true comrades, that is above the petty squabbles of the capitalist nations. It has helped me to this victory. And its work is only just beginning."

"Save the speech for when they pin the Order of Stalin on you. You've still a long way to go yet."

"Only as far as Turkey – and you have kindly brought our prize part of the way already." He moved past Rawlings, guards following him, and advanced on Vlasenin, who was looking at him as a rabbit looks at a snake. "We meet again, Comrade Doctor," he said in Russian. "I have looked forward to resuming our discussion."

"I have nothing to say to you."

"Not yet, perhaps. In any case, the principal purpose behind it has now been resolved." He gestured to one of the ELAS men, who had pulled Rawlings' rucksack from his back as he disarmed him. The partisan threw it to Amarazov, who fished around in it briefly before producing the briefcase with Vlasenin's papers. "Together at last. But there are still many things I would like to discuss with you, Comrade Doctor. All in good time, however. First I must prevail on you to do a little more walking. But after that it will be a short journey by truck down from the mountains, then a rather longer one by train – goods train, I'm afraid – over the Turkish border."

Rawlings was dazed by the guard's blow and his brain was reeling, trying to shut out the image of Yelena dead by torture. But at Amarazov's last comment he forced himself to focus. He turned to look the Russian in the eye again. "Your boys have been giving you some duff intelligence, Yevgeny. There's only one railway line in these parts. It begins on the coast a long way south of here, and hugs the border all the way up to Edirne. Ziedler will have troops turning everything that comes up it inside out. You'll never get through."

Amarazov nodded. "True – if we were to follow the course you have outlined. But who said anything about Greece, major? We are crossing the border into Bulgaria first. The brotherhood is equally well-established there, and they are not so closely watched as our Greek comrades. We will be over the border by dusk, on a train before midnight and in Turkey by tomorrow morning."

"You'll still have to cross into Bulgaria. It's Axis territory, and Ziedler will be sure to have somebody watching the border passes."

"True. But not so closely. Especially as we have been feeding information as to your whereabouts. Since you will be dead within hours I see no harm in telling you this now, Rawlings. We have an agent at the highest level in SOE. He has been monitoring your progress and relaying the information back to me, as well as telling the Germans what we feel it is useful for them to know, under the pretence of being a German agent.

"At this very moment he is making a radio transmission to Ziedler's headquarters in Organi. Within a matter of hours you will have troops from three armies swarming all over this pass. They will be expecting to surprise you while you rest for the day. And they will get what they want – with two vital exceptions."

He held up the briefcase, then turned and pushed Vlasenin towards the waiting partisans. Half of the group were already poised to move on. The remaining dozen were shepherding Rawlings' team and Eroglu's men into the cave. "Your guards will leave as soon as they hear Ziedler's force approaching, major. But they will leave you bound and gagged, of course." He laughed out loud. "The look on that arrogant bastard's face when he realises he has been duped; it might almost be worth remaining just to see it. Still, I'm sure Hoffman will be pleased to meet you all again – especially you, major."

Amarazov turned to Leonidas and barked a string of orders in Greek. Two of Amarazov's guards pushed Rawlings up to join his men in the cave, then rejoined the escort detail preparing to set off, Amarazov at its head. The Russian gave the order to march. Vlasenin hesitated. One of the guards struck him across the shoulders with a rifle butt. Several of Rawlings' men cried out and moved to help him, but were halted by a dozen levelled guns. "Leave it," Rawlings said, then called to Vlasenin. "Do what they say – and stay alive! We'll come for you."

Vlasenin forced a smile, straightened his shoulders

and began to march. Rawlings turned to his men. "Not yet, lads. No point in dying for nothing."

"But you will, major," Amarazov said. "By the gun now, or later at the hands of the Gestapo. This way will be quicker, and certainly less painful."

"Game's not over until the final whistle, Yevgeny."

"Your gift for cliché has not deserted you, I see, Rawlings. We play soccer in Russia too, and I think we have a few goals' advantage. But I forget; rugby is your game, is it not? The game for thugs played by gentlemen." He gave a vulpine smile. "Not unlike our own. But whatever the metaphor, the end result will be the same. You dead, Ziedler beaten and Vlasenin back where he belongs. You know, I think the Order of Stalin is the least I can expect for this. Goodbye, Major Rawlings."

And then they were gone, lost from sight as they marched around the next bend in the pass. Leonidas gestured for the rest of them to go inside. Then, as two partisans stood guard, the others bound the SOE men hand and foot (apart from the injured Costas, who simply had his feet tied), then did the same to Eroglu's escort. There was little room for so many in such a confined space, but the ELAS men gave no opportunity for a surprise attack, or any resistance whatsoever. "How the hell do we get out of this one, sir?" Curtis whispered as he was shoved in the corner next to his commander.

"I've got a few ideas, captain." Rawlings looked out of the cave as a cold, grey dawn emerged. "For what he's done, this is the last day of his life. And I'll get the name of the traitor in SOE before I kill him."

"Got them, Herr Oberst." Weiss almost fell into the tent, such was his eagerness. Ziedler looked up from the trestle table around which his command was grouped: Hoffman and Ciarelli; Oberst Mauritz, leader of the tripartite force assembled for the mission; Captain Bertolli, head of the Italian detachment; and Major Czarny, commander of the local Bulgarian garrison.

They had all been on standby for twenty-four hours, ever since arriving at Organi and setting up camp on the outskirts, and there was a palpable sense of excitement as Weiss composed himself, saluted and stood to attention, then handed the signal flimsy to Ziedler. "Transmission received five minutes ago. Again using the same code word and a recognised SOE cipher. It was a brief broadcast, Herr Oberst, but as you can see it gave a map reference for Rawlings' party, and said they would be resting there all day."

Ziedler passed the flimsy to Czarny. "You know this location?"

Czarny nodded. "It is not far from here. Just above the treeline. An hour's hard march, maybe more."

"Oh, I think we can make it under an hour for this particular expedition. Not so, Oberst Mauritz?"

Mauritz, a lean, tall *Gebirgsjager* colonel with a weather-beaten face, gave an appropriately wintry smile. "It'll be good exercise for the boys. If they know there's a fight at the end of it they'll be there in half an hour."

"Not much of a fight if we take them by surprise. But I'm sure I can rely on your men to do that." Ziedler clapped him on the shoulder. "Well, I think we should all make this trip, gentlemen. It is a historic day for Germany – and Italy, of course." He gestured to Ciarelli, who nodded in acknowledgement.

"A great day for all the Axis, Ziedler," he said. "I'd like my men to be as close to the action as possible. After all, they've had experience of this kind of work."

Ziedler returned his disingenuous smile. "I would not wish it any other way. It is only right and proper that the SIM should be there – at the death."

∾

Leutnant Ernst Fischer heard the siren as he was dressing in his tent, a considerably smaller one than that in which Ziedler's command group had heard the good news. It was just large enough for the folding chair in which he sat and the camp bed on which he had laid out his equipment. The Schmeisser and Luger were polished and ready, but it was a long time since they had been fired in anger. That would soon change though, he thought, and swallowed hard.

He was still not at all sure why the hell they had selected his platoon for this mission. True enough, the unit had seen service in some hot spots – France in '40 and Crete last year, plus that dirty little business with the Czech partisans in between. But for the past few months they'd been sitting on the Turkish border hunting smugglers and Jewish refugees. And that suited him fine. He'd heard all the horror stories about Russia, and North Africa sounded no picnic, either. A quiet life in the arse-end of the Third Reich until everybody saw sense and negotiated a peace, that was the way to make sure Mama Fischer's little boy got back home safe and sound.

But then this big flap came up, and still nobody really

knew what it was about. All he knew was that a week or so ago, there'd been a general mobilisation and every unit in the German sector had been told to either hot-foot it to some supply base in the Dhadhia Forest to guard a VIP prisoner, or stand guard on the border in case enemy agents tried to get him back.

Fischer was lucky – his unit was put on border watch and they had duly sat on their thumbs for two days. And it was there that they had heard the sensational news; there'd been a big battle at the supply base. Greek partisan attack, hundreds dead on both sides and the prisoner sprung. Some said it was the British, some the Russians; some said it was both. But the upshot was he was missing. And he had stayed missing ever since.

Fischer's unit, like nearly every German unit in the sector, had found itself hopping over into Bulgar territory to help look for him. Well, that was no surprise. Everyone knew the Bulgars couldn't find a spare prick at a wedding; they'd only thrown in with the Axis to win back a few acres of swamp and rock that everyone else in the Balkans had spent the last fifty years taking from them. Wouldn't even send troops to Russia, the arrogant bastards. Not that Fischer blamed them for wanting to steer clear of all that – but, for God's sake, what was the point of having allies who didn't fight?

Seeing the Italians join the search, now that WAS a surprise. They hadn't come this far east since the Greeks had surrendered. The extra manpower was needed, so the official explanation went. But everyone knew there was more to it than that. Then the rumours really started to fly. The favourite at the moment was that the prisoner was an Italian agent with news of a plan by Musso to sue for a separate peace. He'd been meeting Russian and British spies in Istanbul to sound them out but German agents had grabbed him and whisked him over the border. Now the Allies wanted him back and the Italians wanted to silence him.

Fischer wasn't convinced by that one. He reckoned the first rumour had been nearer the truth; the prisoner was a Turk, a high-ranking official in Ankara who'd discovered that Turkey was going to give the Russians and the British passage through to invade Thrace and Bulgaria simultaneously. He'd crossed the border to try to sell his information but Churchill and Stalin had sent a special team in to bring him back.

But whatever the truth of all that was, the fact remained that the prisoner was missing. And the boys who had him were good. They'd sprung him in the first place, from a secret location under the noses of every soldier in Thrace. Then they'd taken him up into the mountains and linked up with the partisans. Now they were heading back to Turkey and, until yesterday, nobody had a clue where the hell they were. They'd already wiped out a special Italian unit that had been sent after them, and a German one too, some said. The most wanted men in all of Europe. And the most dangerous.

And Fischer's platoon was going to go up there and get them. He swallowed again. Why him, for God's sake? His men weren't mountain troops, like the Gebirgs and the Italian *Alpini* unit that were going up as well. And they didn't know the terrain, like the Bulgar platoon that completed the set. He reckoned it was just Colonel Edel's way of getting him killed. *He's never liked me. Thinks I'm a rich boy playing at being a soldier. Well, I wasn't* playing when that Anzac stuck a bayonet in my ribs. And I don't recall seeing the Herr Oberst with us in the ditch when the Czech partisans sprung the ambush in the High Tatra. We were all lucky to come out of that one alive. And now we've got to do it all over again.

Still, that was the soldier's lot. And this Ziedler fellow who was in charge had promised everyone involved in this mission a medal and a choice of posting afterwards. Well, the medal would impress the ladies and as for the posting… Thrace wasn't too bad, despite the occasional unpleasantness with the bandits in the mountains (he wasn't looking forward to renewing acquaintance with those mad bastards, either), but if this invasion came it would be as hot as anywhere he'd ever been. No, a staff posting back home would be the safest bet of all. Just a case of surviving this one last show – and maybe they were right; maybe it would be just a case of surprising them while they slept, then dragging them back down to the camp – and making sure his men did too.

They were waiting for him as he finished dressing and emerged from his tent. Drawn up in two lines as though they were back on the parade ground. Sergeant Zimmerman saluted him, radiating efficiency as always. God knows where I'd be if I hadn't had him beside me for the last two years. But he could say the same of them all. He'd try to keep them safe today. That was the main thing. And after that, who knew? Medals, promotion, a safe posting. That would show Oberst Edel what he was made of. And the bastards who kicked me out of accountancy school, and dear Papa who'd used that as an excuse to cut me out of the inheritance. Jesus, it's been a long road here. But I could end today as Hauptmann

Fischer, hero of the Reich. Yes, why the hell not?

"All right, lads. You know why we're here. Keep your heads down and your eyes open. Let's show those Gebirg peacocks, and all the rest, what the Bremen Grenadiers can do. And don't forget – if the bullets start flying, fall back to where I am."

It still got a laugh, even after all these times. A nervous, forced, thin laugh, true. But a laugh nonetheless. He nodded to Zimmerman and they marched off to join the rest of Ziedler's force.

∽

And far to the north Hauptsturmfuhrer Dorsch looked upon another platoon from the Bremen Grenadiers. Ziedler had generously allocated him three, one each for all of the major crossings into Bulgaria. The plan had been to divide his Hermann Goering force into three also, so there were specialists in each detail.

But Dorsch had left two of the platoons to fend for themselves and kept all seven Hermann Goering troops with him. This was the crossing they would take, he felt certain. Whether it was Rawlings, or the Russians, or both. He did not share Ziedler's reading of the situation, but whatever the truth was, if the men who had Vlasenin and his papers tried to enter Bulgaria they would use this pass. It was remote, with good cover all around. The overhanging rocks gave good shelter from spotter planes. But they also made it easy for snipers to get above the pass and command it from excellent cover. Two of the Hermann Goering men were up there now. The rest would close with the enemy before they had a chance to kill Vlasenin or throw his papers into the ravine that plunged to the river far below. Then back down into Bulgaria and radio from the nearest garrison that the prize was theirs. He could even use the truck radio to give Ziedler the good news straight away. But perhaps better to wait until the prize was absolutely secure. Besides, why not let the Herr Abwehr Oberst get some more snow on those fine, shiny boots of his?

And if Ziedler was right, it would not matter how he disposed his forces because the enemy would head straight for Turkey. But Dorsch felt sure he was wrong. And if he was, then this would be the ideal opportunity to wrest the glory from the Abwehr. Schellenberg had told him he expected no less, and if Dorsch wanted to rise further in the SD ranks he had to deliver no less. He had born Ziedler's sarcasm and upbraidings for too long. Today would see the much-needed shift in the balance of power. It had been coming for a long time. But the Canarises and Ziedlers of the world still wanted to play their gentlemanly Weimar spying games. Today would acquaint them with reality.

Always assuming anyone came this way, of course.

∾

It had been over an hour since Amarazov had left. And the vigilance of the guards had not wavered in the slightest. Leonidas and his dozen men had never taken their eyes, or their guns, off the prisoners for a moment of that time. Soon the lookout would come back and tell them the Germans were on their way. Then the gags would go on and they would disappear as quickly and efficiently as they had done everything else, Rawlings reflected bitterly. If something was to happen, it had to be now.

The rest of his men were silent too. All except Costas. For most of the hour he had been in a fitful doze. But now he was writhing and sweating in his blanket, blood seeping from the bandage on his arm. Suddenly he gave a massive convulsion and rolled out of his blanket. He raised his head and called to the guards in Greek: "Water! Give me a drink! I'm burning up. I need water!"

The guards looked at Leonidas, who showed no emotion and made no movement. "If you don't help him he could start screaming," Rawlings said, also in Greek, as he looked at Leonidas. "That might let the Germans know where we are a little too early, eh? How would your Russian comrade like that?"

Leonidas held his gaze for an instant, then gestured to one of the guards. "Give him a drink. Then gag him." The guard slung his Sten gun and pulled a canteen from his belt. With the other he drew a Luger pistol. He bent over Costas' writhing frame – then fell forward in agony as Costas jacknifed both knees into his groin. He fell on top of Costas, who shrugged the sling off and grabbed with both hands for the German stick grenade at the guard's belt. The rest of the ELAS men charged forward, weapons up.

But they could not shoot Costas without killing their comrade too. As they hesitated Costas heaved the guard clear. And raised the grenade he now held in both hands. "Come any closer and I blow us all to Hell!" he cried as his fingers found the lanyard.

Leonidas, poised at the head of his men, revolver

out and pointing at Costas, said the last thing Rawlings wanted to hear: "Go ahead! It will kill some of us. Not all. The rest will make you pay – Turk."

"Even if I throw it in the explosives – Greek?" Costas replied, jerking his head towards the pile where the team's rucksacks had been stacked. The partisans had looked inside O'Hare's satchel, seen the dynamite, nitroglycerine, gelignite and detonators, and set it down very carefully, a long way from the fire. Now they looked at it again. "I'll throw myself on it, Captain Leonidas. Believe me, I will. If we are to die today, then every one of you Red bastards dies too. *Inshallah*. Tell your men to drop their guns and stand back. Or I blow this cave off the fucking mountain."

After the barest hesitation Leonidas shouted: "Do as he says." The guards dropped their guns. Rawlings held his tied hands up and gestured to the youngest guard, the one they called Micky, a boy whose face would not have looked out of place in a school photograph until you saw the eyes. He looked uncertainly at Leonidas, who merely nodded. Micky came up to Rawlings and drew his knife, a long-bladed, wide-pomelled dagger that looked like the poniard of a Borgia assassin. As Rawlings turned he cut the wrist thongs. Next second the knife was in Rawlings' hand and under the boy's chin. "Now untie my feet – and no tricks." As soon as they were free Rawlings plucked a Walther pistol from Micky's belt and gestured for him to move back. At the same time he tossed the knife to Curtis. "Free yourself, then the rest."

"Yes, sir," Curtis said with relief, adding as he began: "Another plan you decided to keep secret from the rest of us?"

Rawlings gave a grim smile. "I'd have trusted you to act surprised, Captain Curtis, but not the others. I mentioned it to Costas during a quiet moment when Thraxos' men first took us under their wing. Just in case we were ever left to the tender mercies of ELAS. You might have some rivals in your first season back after the war."

"Not me, sir," Costas said in English with a relieved smile. "Just hope I didn't leave it too late to start. But I reckoned too soon after they tied us up would look suspicious, maybe."

"You did all right, son. Just keep a tight grip on that grenade until you're freed. Then keep an even tighter one. And you lot," he said to the partisans, "stay very still."

They needed no second bidding. In any case all the SOE men were free now and each partisan had his own guard. Curtis led the rest in freeing Eroglu and his men. Eroglu grabbed his dagger and advanced on Leonidas, murder in his eyes. But Rawlings came between them, pistol up. "I decide who lives and dies today."

Eroglu held his gaze for a moment, then stepped back, still glaring at Leonidas. "Why not let him kill me?" the ELAS leader asked.

"Because I don't need to. And because you can help us."

"Help you?" Leonidas' tone matched his look of utter bewilderment. "How? And why?"

Rawlings turned to Costas. "You translate this for me. And make sure he realises I'm serious."

Costas nodded and Rawlings began to speak. "Why they should help us is simple: survival. The Germans could still pick up the trail. Once Ziedler realises he's been duped he won't just sit about feeling sorry for himself. He'll either kill us on the spot, or send us down the mountain with a few guards, and take the rest after Amarazov. He's bound to have mountain troops with him, Alpine specialists. There's a good chance he'll find your comrades and catch up with them.

"That's how you can help us. Give us time." He turned to Eroglu. "I'm asking that of your group too. My men can catch up with Amarazov but there'll be no point if the Germans are five minutes behind us. We need more time, to cover our tracks and put some distance between us and them. I'm asking you to work together, ELAS and EDES, against a common enemy.

"You've got a natural defence position here – only one narrow approach, plenty of cover. Twenty-three men could hold an army at bay for days. We'd be content with one. If you can keep them here until sundown, then slip away under cover of dark, we'll be far enough away and they won't know the country well enough to follow us." He shrugged. "Even a few hours could be enough. If it gets too bad, save yourselves. Just give us some time."

He looked at the three partisan officers. There was hope again in Loporos' eyes and Eroglu was beaming at the prospect of a fight. But Leonidas still looked suspicious. "You have told us why you need help, Englishman," he said at last. "Not why we should help you. Let your lapdogs stay and die for you if they wish. But you are not my master."

Rawlings waited until Costas had translated before he replied. "That is true. But more men will buy more time. If the Germans catch us – or Amarazov – with the prisoner that will be the end of the war. Believe me, if they take Vlasenin, and his papers, they will win. The Fascists. The Germans and Italians, and all their allies. They will rule your country, and the rest of the world, for your lifetime and God knows how many after. If we keep him, or Amarazov does, they will lose.

"I'm not saying we won't try to take him back, by force. And the Russian will try to keep him, with your comrades' help. A straight fight, and whoever wins will have a chance to get him to safety. But only if you keep the Germans here." He shrugged. "I can't force you – I can't force any man here."

"I can!" Eroglu shouted. "But I don't need to, goddammit. All my men are with you, major. Your lapdogs will hold them." He looked at Leonidas with contempt. "With or without a pack of Red curs!"

Rawlings turned to the ELAS leader. "If you don't fight I'll leave you bound and gagged. Eroglu can do what he wants with you – kill you or leave you for the Germans. Either way, your deaths will be of no purpose. Just as ours would have been of no purpose had you left us. But if you stay and fight your deaths, or your lives, will have a purpose. To beat the Fascists. They are the greater enemy. Any man who is not blind can see that. Help us to beat them. Or die with your hands tied. Your choice. Choose quickly."

Costas finished translating. Then, as if to underscore the point, Leonidas' lookout ran into the cave. "Germans. Over the…" he broke off as he saw the prisoners free, but before he could do anything more Rowley and Sanderson had him disarmed with a knife at his throat. Rawlings signalled to let him go. He looked around in confusion, but Leonidas said calmly: "It's OK. Speak."

"The Germans are over the next ridge. Coming through the valley to the pass. Maybe two miles away. The scouts are closer."

"How many?" Rawlings asked. The lookout hesitated, but Leonidas nodded again. "A hundred at least, maybe more. Mountain troops in front. Bulgars and Italians too. Big trouble."

Rawlings turned to Leonidas, who looked him in the eye as he spoke. "For myself, I would care not if you killed me now. You are an enemy to my cause as much as any Fascist. And the Russian ordered me to stop you. But I have failed. I must die for it, and better to die fighting an enemy than be shot by one to no purpose.

"So I will fight. But I cannot speak for my men. No man should do that for another in the matter of his death. That is how I see it, though the Party says we must obey in all things. If they wish to fight I will lead them, as their *kapetan*, not the Zervas man. If they do not, let them go. That is all I ask."

Rawlings thought for a moment, then said: "Agreed. Take your weapons."

Leonidas stooped and picked up his Thompson gun. The Britons and Eroglu's men tensed. Leonidas saw their reaction and gave a wolfish smile. Then, slowly and deliberately, he slid the safety catch on. Then he bent again to pick up his knife and pistol. The rest of them followed suit, lining up beside him. Micky was last. As he slung his Lee-Enfield rifle Rawlings whistled to him. As he looked round Rawlings tossed the Walther pistol and the dagger to him with a smile. The boy did not return the smile, merely caught them, stuck them in his belt and moved to join his comrades.

Rawlings shrugged, took the Mauser pistol as Curtis handed it to him, then turned to Eroglu. He was already directing his men to take up defensive positions. Loporos picked up a Sten gun and made to join them, but Rawlings shook his head. "You're coming with us. We need a guide, and this is your territory now."

"I let them take my men. I know now they are dead. I should be dead too. I'll die here, and see these ELAS bastards die too."

"Then your death has no purpose either. We need you alive, Loporos. Get your revenge by helping us."

Loporos looked to Eroglu, who shrugged. "He is right. There are enough here to kill many Germans. One more makes little difference. I will make sure our Red friends do not run." Loporos still hesitated and Eroglu clapped him on the shoulder. "Such is war. No blame on you, my friend. Now go – time is short."

Loporos smiled and clasped Eroglu's hand, then turned and picked up his back pack. Eroglu was scanning the land before the pass. He frowned and passed the binoculars to Rawlings. The pass was bare of cover and fell away steeply at the junction with the track Rawlings' men had used, down to the valley floor, perhaps five hundred yards below. Scrub pines and boulders lined the valley. At the far end he could see troops moving among them. Half a dozen or so, well spread out, wearing snow smocks and the white peaked caps of the German Alpine Corps. The *Gebirgsjager*. Some of the finest mountain troops in the world. Rawlings felt a chill that was more than the morning air.

"Skirmishers," Eroglu said. "They will have them in the slopes to our flanks too. No matter – we have sent men up there. They will have a little surprise for them. Hot dog!" He took the binoculars again. "But you must go now – and quick."

Rawlings gripped his hand tightly. "Go with God. We can never repay you, and I wish with all my heart we did not have to leave you like this."

Eroglu waved a dismissive hand. "It is we who should talk of repayment. We led you into a trap. They caught us like children, and your men freed us. And you still have an evil road ahead." He hesitated, then fished in his pocket and brought out a handful of the dried currants he had eaten throughout their marches. "In the bad days of the famine last year they said these would save you from Charon the ferryman." He pressed them into Rawlings' hand and shook his head, as if to clear the superstition from it. Then he looked up again, eyes gleaming. "But some Germans will meet him before today is out. Goddamn right!"

"Just the Germans," Rawlings said. "Fight, then live." Then he was gone, Loporos leading him and his men out of sight in double time. Eroglu shrugged and turned back to the mouth of the pass. Two of his men had set up a Browning automatic rifle on its tripod on one side of the natural rock funnel. Two ELAS men had done the same with a Bren gun on the other side. Four sharpshooters, Micky among them, were already in the rocks above. They would be the first in action, dealing with the *Gebirgsjager* skirmishers. The rest were lined up in firing positions along the mouth of the pass, spare magazines and rifle clips laid alongside them. Leonidas had three spare drums for his Thompson and as he saw Eroglu take position opposite he slid the safety catch off.

"So are we curs still, EDES lapdog?" he shouted across.

"I have not seen you fight yet. Ask again in an hour's time. How are you called, Red?"

"Comrade Leonidas. The Lion."

"A Spartan king, too. He held a pass against the invaders. Did they teach you that in school? I doubt it – you Reds are all illiterate peasants."

"We know how to fight."

Eroglu nodded sagely. "I have heard that Comrade Lion's cadre is a legend in ELAS – for cowardice. Today we show you how real men fight."

Leonidas replied with an obscenity, ripe and biological even by Greek standards. As his men laughed, he continued: "When you babies cry for your mothers at the first Fascist gunshot we will put you to bed, then carry on the fight."

"What good is a bed without a woman?"

"Little enough – but you have your fist." Leonidas clenched his in the Communist salute, then pumped it up and down with vigour.

Eroglu and his men joined in the laughter. "Now that is a salute I can answer. Good hunting, Comrade Lion."

"And you." Leonidas turned to face the front as the Germans reached the edge of the trees.

Rawlings and his team were over a mile from the camp when the firing began, but they still heard it clearly. A few looked back, then turned again and carried on.

∽

Leutnant Bernd Adler's *Gebirgsjager* detachment never

knew what hit them. They had advanced cautiously to the treeline, then checked the slopes above before moving into open space. Even if the enemy were sleeping, he had known there would be a lookout. And sure enough there he was, on the slopes above the pass. Adler had sent two of his best men to deal with him. Now when he looked up there they were, waving him on with the pre-arranged signal.

So they moved, still keeping to the sides of the pass, using the few stunted shrubs and bushes as cover. Two men up ahead on either side, eight more strung out in single file behind. Half-way up already. They could be at the mouth of the pass inside a minute. Sentries there probably, but only one or two. Then the rest in the bag and home again.

They were within a hundred yards of the mouth of the pass when the trap was sprung. Four rifle shots cut through the morning air and his front-rank skirmishers fell dead. Then two machine-gun bursts swept across the pass, cutting down four more men and stripping the cover from the rest. They fell back firing, then turned and ran as the small arms joined in, taking two more in a merciless fusillade. Adler blew a futile blast on his whistle, then ran with the rest of them, diving behind a boulder as they found the treeline again.

The firing ceased. The silence that followed seemed unnatural, broken only by the startled cawing of a few crows disturbed at roost. And the cries of agony from the one man left on the slopes who was still alive. As Adler watched he tried to crawl back to safety, dragging his shattered leg behind him. A single rifle shot snuffed out his life. Then there was silence again. A few of his men began to return fire. "Save your ammo!" he shouted. "Wait until you can see something to aim at."

He unslung his binoculars and looked out at the scene. Ten men dead. Not a single glint of a weapon or helmet raised too far above the rocks to indicate where the enemy were. Except that they were up there, in force and ready. The hot breath of exertion in his throat was the taste of defeat itself as he turned and looked at the remainder of his platoon and the rest of the assault force beyond it. At their head was Oberst Mauritz and the Abwehr man with the film star looks who had sent them up here.

"Why have you not taken the position, Herr Leutnant?" the Abwehr man asked softly. For a moment Adler thought he must be going out of his mind, then said with as much calm and dignity as he could muster. "Beg to report, Herr Oberst, they were waiting for us."

"Impossible," Ziedler replied. "They should all have been neutralised, by the Russians. I presume you took care of any lookouts?"

"Of course, Herr Oberst. I sent two of my best men up there. I saw them give the signal, and…"

He paused as he saw the Abwehr man's expression and his shoulders slumped. "You saw two men in hooded snow smocks give a signal," Ziedler said with a calm irritation that was more wounding than any outburst. "No doubt they saw one of your men give it when you first moved beyond the treeline."

Adler felt his cheeks burn, but still managed to reply. "With respect, Herr Oberst, such resistance does not indicate a rapid deployment. That was a trap laid out well in advance."

"We were early – we should have taken them all by surprise, British or Russian," Ziedler said, as much to himself as to Adler.

"Are you sure this source is trustworthy?" Ciarelli asked. "He could have led us here for nothing."

"It was our best lead – our only lead," Ziedler replied impatiently. "More than anything your intelligence has ever yielded. We had to follow it up."

"And if it was all a plot to lead us here for nothing, surely we'd have found nothing," Weiss put in, emboldened by his superiors' obvious discomfiture. "Was it a trap to try and wipe us all out?"

Ziedler shook his head. "That would need more men than the entire resistance in these parts can boast."

"So it was to lead us on, then leave us?" Ciarelli still sounded doubtful. "In that case, why open fire?"

"I suspect the best people to answer these questions are the men up there," Ziedler said, keeping his patience with some effort. "So we will just have to go and ask them."

"With the Herr Oberst's permission," Adler said hesitantly. "A major frontal assault on such a position will require more troops than I currently have at my disposal, plus heavy weapons support."

"Yes, of course, whatever you require. Oberst Mauritz, if we are to abandon the rapier for the bludgeon perhaps this is where some of the… less elite units could be deployed."

And thus it was that Leutnant Fischer received the call of duty in the second phase of the battle of Adraxos Pass. He had heard the firing and seen the edelweiss-pickers come running back; this had simply confirmed his view that they were fighting a combination of cut-throat espionage agents and mad Greek bandits, a combination designed to ensure that this would be no 'easy kill'. As he ordered Zimmerman to line the men up he fingered the 'Gott Mit Uns' motto on his belt buckle. "*Und mit mir,*" he whispered. "He'd fucking better be."

༺

Amarazov was too far away to hear the firing begin. But he was certainly not as far away from the cave, or as close to the Bulgarian border, as he would have liked. It had begun to snow – a thin, narrow fall blowing down from the highest peaks past them and on to the lower slopes where Rawlings and his men strode in pursuit. But Amarazov's team were not striding, and had not been for some time, even before the snow. They were walking at a snail's pace, these ELAS veterans who had taken him to the ambush point half a day ahead of Rawlings. He knew they could go much faster. But their pace was being dictated by Vlasenin.

He had been slow from the outset, constantly staggering and out of breath, complaining of hunger, fatigue and cold. His condition had forced half a dozen halts already. Now, as the icy wind drove the snow into their faces, he seemed to shrivel inside himself, coughing and spluttering as he slipped and dropped to one knee. The two partisans constantly at his side grabbed an arm apiece to stop him from falling. And once again the entire column halted.

Amarazov cursed and strode to where Vlasenin was being helped to his feet. "This is beyond a joke, Comrade

Doctor. We must reach the border in good time, especially with this change in the weather. For that we need more speed."

"I can go no faster. I am tired and you have used me ill. I must be allowed to rest."

"You rest when I say you can rest. And you speed up when I say 'speed up'. You made good enough time with the British."

"Perhaps that is because they treated me like a human being."

"Your treatment now is as nothing to how I could treat you – as I think you are well aware. If you do not make better time now you will regret it later. Please believe me. Now move!"

He pulled him free of the partisans and pushed him forward. As Vlasenin squared his shoulders and marched on Amarazov said to his guards: "See he keeps the pace up. If not, it will be the worse for you." He pulled a hip flask from his tunic and took a long swallow before moving back to the head of the column, oblivious to the expressions on the partisans' faces.

But his threats worked. Despite the snowfall, which increased as the day wore on, they made good time. By the middle of the afternoon they were above the long, steep gulley which led down to the road. It was the first thing deserving such a name which Amarazov had seen in days, but it barely deserved it. A narrow, serpentine length of hard-packed earth which the new snow was bound to make even more treacherous. But to Amarazov it was a superhighway and the battered pre-war truck parked on the stretch of flat ground at its head was a limousine, ready to bear him in triumph past the border post that his Bulgarian contacts had bribed in advance.

They were sheltering in the truck, but they emerged and waved him on when they saw his signal. Two of them, in dress and looks identical to the Greek partisans. Thirty years ago their fathers would have been at each other's throats but now they were united, joining forces to deliver the greatest prize of the war to Russia – and cement Amarazov's reputation for good. Let Renkovich try to keep Grigorin's desk from him now. And let him watch his own. To think how different it had all been just a week or so before. He smiled to himself in triumph and signalled his men to bring Vlasenin down.

They obeyed with alacrity. Once this fool's errand was over the Russian would be out of their hair. They didn't like working for him, no matter what Comrade Leonidas had told them, and only the hotheads had enjoyed killing the EDES men. They had never trusted Russians. And they would keep their hands on their money while they met the Bulgars too. Still it was what their leaders had ordered and after this they could get back to the real business – driving the invaders out.

Amarazov was out of the cover of the trees now, walking across the bare patch of ground to the truck, Vlasenin and his guards behind. He was half-way to the truck when the first bullet hit him. High on the back, between the shoulder blades, pushing him forwards. At first he thought one of the partisans had barged into him and he was about to turn and ream them out when the pain hit him. He had known that pain before – there was no other like it – and he knew in an instant that they were in trouble.

Then the second hit him. From in front this time, in

the chest, and now he saw the bloody hole plucked in his tunic at the same time as he felt the sledgehammer impact that knocked him to the ground. Sniper's bullet, from high above. Not quite a killing shot, probably unsighted by the snow, he thought in a dull, absent manner as his body hit the cold, damp earth.

Bodies were falling around him. Vlasenin's two guards, hitting the ground as their prisoner ran for cover. The men at the truck, identical expressions of amazement on their faces. Then, when the sharpshooters had taken out the key targets, the submachine-guns opened up. Within ten seconds not one of the partisans was left standing. But Amarazov tried to. With two bullets in him he should have stayed down until they came to finish him. But from somewhere came the strength to rise. Part of it was instinct, part a dogged, illogical belief that because he had come so close to winning, he still could. He'd been back from the dead once, after all.

So he rose, slowly and painfully, on to one knee, then two feet. And they shot him again. A pistol shot this time. They were coming in for the kill. A shot on the run, too hasty, because it missed his heart by a long way, hitting his left shoulder instead. He staggered back but did not fall this time. Instead he reeled around drunkenly, drawing the Tokarev with his right hand, looking around for his killers. He could not see them. But he saw Vlasenin, running for the trees. Amarazov brought the Tokarev to bear dead centre on his back. A useless gesture, he knew. They would still get the papers. But it might take them more time, give good Soviet scientists a chance to catch up. And he wanted to see the little bastard dead.

A second pistol shot shattered his right forearm, and

the Tokarev spun from his grasp. Then he began to run too. Hopelessly, without direction, in the sluggish panic of the truly doomed. He got barely five yards before the third pistol bullet slammed into his right calf, dropping him to his knees. This time he did not get up. Instead he began to crawl towards the Tokarev. Perhaps to try again, perhaps to end it himself. His mind was so numb with pain he could not even tell any more. Before he even got half-way to it a booted foot loomed into his field of vision and kicked it away.

Amarazov stopped dead and rolled onto his back. After a while he looked up. He had expected to see Rawlings. Instead he saw half a dozen German soldiers. In paratroop uniform. Hermann Goering Division. He recognised the insignia and he vaguely remembered seeing some of them at the camp on the night of the attack. They were levelling Schmeissers and Luger pistols at him, looking down with faces devoid of pity. Then they parted as the man who had kicked the pistol away approached. He bent over Amarazov. He too was in a paratroop camouflage tunic, but the breeches and boots below were immaculately tailored and polished. Under the officer's sidecap close-cropped blond hair gleamed as the snowclouds briefly parted, bathing the killing ground in sunshine.

"Major Amarazov," Dorsch said. "A pleasure to meet you," he added in Russian as he drew his pistol. It was a special issue Walther, Amarazov noticed. Its wide, blue-metal barrel filled his vision as Dorsch straightened up and took aim.

This was the worst, Fischer thought as he scrambled back into the cover of the trees. The last few survivors of his platoon were alongside him. Two dozen of their comrades were dead and God knows how many *Gebirgsjager*, Italians and Bulgars alongside them, strewn up and down the slopes of that infernal killing ground. He remembered the night the *maquis* had machine-gunned the German officers' café; the street-fighting in Heraklion when the Anzac unit had held every house to the last man; and that ambush in the High Tatra, where the Czechs had attacked six times and tortured the wounded prisoners between each one. All bad, as bad as bad could get. But this was the worst.

There was only one way to take that position and that was to advance up the path until you got close enough to make a dash for the rocks. Simple enough, but they hadn't managed it yet. Because every time you stuck your head out from the cover of the trees a couple of dozen guns started trying to blow it off. They had at least one MG up there, plus a dozen SMGs and a few sharpshooters on high for good measure. Every attack had to go in front of them and keep going, further and further up, closer and closer to the dragon's mouth. All the while the firing became more intense, the ground got narrower and the cover became thinner until it was non-existent. Then you were just walking into the arms of Death himself. And that was when you broke.

They had broken four times now. The first time was just after the mountain boys had tipped over the hornet's nest and the Abwehr man, Ziedler, had called up the cannon fodder. Fischer's platoon had gone up there alone and half of them had not come back. And Ziedler and

Oberst Mauritz and the boss Italian and the Gestapo man, looking so out of place with the snow smock over his civilian clothes, had looked up from their coffee and schnapps and tutted with disapproval. The Bulgars next, the poor bastards who'd been sitting around on garrison duty until a day ago. Up they went and back they came – well, some of them, anyway.

The Italian, Ciarelli, had cursed them for cowards and their lieutenant, Janosz, had almost come to blows with him. And Ziedler had said why didn't the new Roman legions show what they were made of. So the *Alpini* had been next, with exactly the same result. And the last rush had been all of them together. No thought of military tactics at all, just a blind rush relying on sheer weight of numbers. Their fathers would have recognised it all too well.

But it had come close, damn it. Right to the brink, close enough to see their enemy at last. Even to kill a few. Right in the mouth of the funnel, packed so close that you had to step over bodies to advance and the rocks were all around, so even the bullet that missed could ricochet back to have another try. And in the midst of all that they had broken again, running all the way back down to the trees, the territory they had gained a domain of corpses once more.

Behind them Ziedler was almost lost for words, a sheer dumbfounded fury threatening to break free at last. He struggled to keep his voice even as Adler relayed the bad news once again. "How can it be so difficult for trained, regular troops to take a position against irregular forces, Herr Leutnant? I was led to believe your men, and all the others, were the cream of the troops at my disposal. Yet here you are being held at bay by a handful of Greek brigands."

Adler was struggling to stay calm also. "With all due respect, Herr Oberst, it is a perfect defensive position. They have an uninhibited field of fire and we have to cover several hundred yards without a scrap of cover."

"It is a soldier's job to advance upon defensive positions, under fire and without cover, Herr Leutnant. It is a soldier's duty to be a soldier and not to make excuses. Now go and do your duty."

"Same again, lads," Adler reported back to his fellow subalterns. "The usual tactics, I suppose."

"What tactics?" Fischer asked gloomily. "Go up that hill until we die, then report back?"

"We'll never do it like this," Janosz said in halting German as he looked back up the slope. "The only thing that'll stop those bastards is running out of ammo."

"We need to get above and around them." Brega, the *Alpini* lieutenant's German was even worse than Janosz's, but his tone was equally morose. "My boys are climbers, not footsoldiers. We do that, it will be easy. Either that or call in the planes."

"We tried climbing after the second attack, remember," Adler replied. "Half a dozen of my lads trying to get up a sheer face where a fucking chamois couldn't go. The sharpshooters nailed them the second they hammered the first piton in."

"And we tried for the planes after that." Fischer managed a bitter smile at the memory. "And the Luftwaffe boy back in Salonika said they couldn't fly in shit like this and he didn't care how much authority the Herr Abwehr Oberst had, he wasn't sending his planes up just to crash into a mountainside." He spread his hands in the age-old gesture. "So it's down to us – as always."

The others shrugged and went to rouse their men. Fischer's were sheltering from the snow under a thick group of pines. Sergeant Zimmerman; Voss, the pianist from the Bremen Symphony; Volk, the black market specialist; Kramer the handball player; Bartelski the half-Pole; Kleber, who was rumoured to be a Socialist and a quarter-Jew and never bothered to deny either. All veterans and all probably doomed to die on a poxy Greek mountain hundreds of miles from a proper fight. He'd lied to them, and himself. Here was no glory and medals and passports to safe postings. Here was only blood, pain and death.

The whistles blew. The two-inch mortars, worked by some of the men from the Bulgar reserve platoon, began their low, insistent coughing, to try to keep the enemy's heads down. Then the heavy MG42s opened up, their high insane chattering matching the war cries of the attackers, men from all four platoons and some of the reserves this time. They spilled out from the trees again, clambering and dodging up the slopes, throwing grenades to try to blast a way through those natural barricades. The fusillade lessened a little then, as it always did. But it was still a devil's storm. And still they braved it. Trying for the gap. For victory.

And far below Ziedler listened to the shots and the screams with a heavy heart. They would take the position eventually. But how far away would the prize be by then? Whoever had Vlasenin would be halfway to Turkey now. Well, the units in the lowlands were still on full alert, and Dorsch's men at the Bulgarian border. That was something. But he had wanted Rawlings quickly, to tell him which way the Russians had taken Vlasenin. Then they could have picked up the trail within minutes, and had the prize within the hour. But chance had robbed him, and the simple logic of geography and weather. The snow was heavy now. And they had brought no tents or other shelter. Well, he would just have to get wet.

ॐ

The snow worried Rawlings too, but for other reasons. They had been making good time. Gaining on Amarazov, he was sure. But the snow made the trail harder to follow. And they were nearing the border, Loporos said. That was where Amarazov had let slip that there was a vehicle waiting, and Loporos had confimed that the road started there. Rawlings could only hope they would decide – or Vlasenin's condition would persuade them – to halt for a while before continuing. It was unlikely, but if they were too late, then it would be a case of alerting all SOE and other intelligence contacts in Bulgaria and trying to find transport to get them to Turkey first.

But they would find out soon, for they were approaching the head of the valley that led to the road. Loporos had gone ahead to scout the way, along with Mayhew and Stavrakis, while the rest waited in the tree cover. After a few minutes Mayhew came back. "Better take a look up ahead, sir." This time his tone lacked its usual air of calm authority and, after a second's pause, he added: "I think we'd better all get up there – at the double."

"Very well." Rawlings motioned the rest of them

forward and they came to head of the valley. As soon as he came up level with the two Greeks Rawlings could see what had happened. "Oh, shit," he cursed under his breath and started down the path, signalling the team to follow. They followed him, looking in amazement as they saw the field of corpses, pausing now and again to check for signs of life among the ELAS men. There were none.

Rawlings found Amarazov at the edge of the road. The last bullet had been at close range, blowing his face clean off. But the beret with the red star still rested above the shattered skull. "A better death than I'd have given you," he whispered, then straightened up as Mayhew marched up to deliver a report. "All the ELAS men are dead, sir. Captain Loporos and Private Stavrakis are checking the road further down to see what more they can learn." He cleared his throat. "No sign of Doctor Vlasenin, or his papers."

"You do surprise me," Rawling said. "So the Germans were waiting for them after all that. I knew he was risking too much, trying a run in broad daylight."

"Looks like it was professionals too, sir," Mayhew said almost apologetically. "Not a single German casualty. And the shell casings are from the latest snipers' rifles and special issue pistols."

"So Ziedler watched the back doors too. And they guessed the right one." He turned as Loporos and Stavrakis ran up. "Please tell me you've got some good news."

Stavrakis shrugged. "Could be worse, major. There was one truck up here, but they must have taken it and used a couple more. Three sets of truck tyres, we think. Two German at least. And a staff car too. The ground is still warm where they passed, snow melting on the road, not lying. Maybe only half an hour since they left."

"Still a good head start on us," Rawlings replied. "Unless they've kindly left us a spare truck."

Loporos shook his head, but he was smiling. "No such luck, major. But I know this road. It is slow and treacherous. A long way down to the valley, especially with this snow. There is a quicker way."

"The mountain goats' path?" Rawlings asked. Loporos had mentioned it at the start of the journey but he had moved it to the back of his mind, still focused then on catching Amarazov before he reached the road. "OK – where is it?"

"Here." Loporos led him to the very edge of the ravine. Fringed by bushes and scrub was a narrow path. Rawlings looked over the edge. It continued into tree-fringed blackness. Narrow, unfenced and treacherous as hell. But still a path. He looked up into the darkening sky. Dusk was only a matter of minutes away. Part of his brain screamed 'no' but his voice said to Loporos: "How long to get down, and can you guide us?"

"Thirty minutes if we rush. To get as low down will take vehicles at least an hour. And I will guide you – but we must be careful."

"No kidding." Rawlings looked at his men, who wore expressions that mirrored his own of seconds before. "OK, lads. We need to do this before dusk comes in. So double time down but watch your step. Jettison everything in your packs – except you, Conor. Your bag of tricks will come in handy again."

"Why did I know you were going to say that, Alex?"

"Because I'm an English bastard, of course. Leave

everything else here. We'll take food and ammo from the Germans once we've wiped 'em out and got the doctor back."

Walters looked over the edge as he emptied his pack. "I suppose you know that path's bloody suicide, sir?"

"I wouldn't do it if we had any other choice, corporal. Would you rather sit up here and wait for Christmas to come?"

"Suits me. But you Poms never win a fight without us givin' you a hand." The Australian smiled as he slung his Sten gun round his shoulder. "Jesus, this little bugger's taking too much rescuing for my liking."

"Come on, corp," Curtis said. "Where would Errol Flynn be if he thought like that? He's an Aussie too, so I hear."

"Tasmanian," Walters corrected him stiffly. "And they're all mad bastards, as well."

☙

Up again. Jesus, we can't do it. This time there's a bullet for me. The thoughts repeated in Fischer's mind like an endless funeral procession. It had been some time since the last attack had failed. And when they had retreated back into the pines that time Ziedler had merely looked at them in dejection and turned away. He had not issued the usual order to go back up again, had said nothing at all in fact, despite the bemused looks of Oberst Mauritz and the rest of them.

So the soldiers had huddled in the shelter of the trees against the snow that fell even more strongly now, opening their packs of field rations and swigging from canteen and thermos against the cold, as the afternoon wore on. Then Ziedler seemed to notice them again and suddenly demanded another assault.

And as Fischer put on his helmet and loaded his Schmeisser once again, looking round to see only Zimmerman and Volk left from his platoon, the thoughts had begun. It had to happen this time. And so close. An hour or so more and it would be dark enough for the bastards to slip away. Time for three or four more attacks before that, though. Ziedler had had foresight enough to bring four reserve platoons with him. They had waited with the trucks at the road but now he had called them up. Men enough and time for as many attacks as he wanted. And one was all it took. Pitcher to the well, Fischer thought, you can't keep being lucky all the time. Survival or death. The soldier's life had never been as purely distilled as on this day. But this time it would be death. Of that he was certain.

Perhaps he would have felt more optimistic if he could have seen the defenders of Adraxos Pass. From the original twenty-three, there were now just half a dozen left. And none of them were unwounded. That last charge had come close to breaking them. The bravery of the Germans and Italians had stunned them. Even the Bulgars had won grudging admiration. The defenders had been ready to break and run, but the enemy had broken first.

They had thought of trying to make their escape then, especially since no attack had come for so long afterwards. But the truth was that none of them were fit enough to make it now. Eroglu had a shattered leg; Leonidas had taken one in the gut; Micky was lying at the entrance to the cave, unconscious after a shot of morphine had relieved the agonies of his chest wound. Mani and Stathi, the Bren gun team, had wounds to head and arm but were still fit enough to fight, as was Drakos the sharpshooter, last of Eroglu's men. He had been called down from above two attacks ago and had exchanged his looted Mauser sniper's rifle for a Sten gun, which he was looking at with resigned distaste. He too had taken one in the leg in the last attack.

Eroglu looked at them all and saw the exhaustion and the resignation in their faces. One more attack would finish them, that much was clear. Then he looked up at the sky. Dusk was gathering but it would be some while yet before it was dark enough to make an escape. The snow was not enough, especially as they were all cripples now. And who would carry the ELAS boy? But he remembered Rawlings' words; fight, then live. No-one could deny they had fought. So he called across to Leonidas: "This could be our last chance, Comrade Lion. Do we make the retreat now?"

Leonidas turned a white, pain-racked face to him and spoke with some difficulty. "You have lost your stomach for the fight already, Zervas man? If all of your stamp give up so swiftly, then truly Greece shall never be free."

Eroglu smiled, also with some difficulty. "By the saints, you Reds are fearsome. We have killed more Fascists today than in all our huntings before. But to hunt another day we must go now, or I fear the hounds will take us."

"A wolf cannot hunt with a broken leg, nor a hole in its guts," Leonidas replied. "We are all shot to pieces. Even blind and fumbling hounds like these would catch us easily if we ran. And they would have little mercy for us having so denied and inconvenienced them."

"Think you they will have mercy if we stay?"

"No, by Saint Spiridon – and I expect nor desire none. But if we stay we can hold them off a little longer. Give my Russian comrade – or your English major – more time to get away. And we will add more Fascists to our tally. I ask for no more now. But go now – and with honour – if you or your men wish it."

"My man, you should say," Eroglu smiled grimly.

"And he does not wish it!" Drakos shouted. "A fine sight the two of us would make, hopping up the mountain with one set of legs between us. No, my major, let us stay and fight, I beg you. Do not leave these Reds to hold on to a position. They have not the sense to hold on to their wedding tackle in a butcher's yard."

Eroglu laughed with him, then turned back to Leonidas: "You have your answer, Comrade Lion. Never let it be said we left the fight to you."

The ELAS man shrugged. "Such a fight as is left."

They all fell silent then, listening. The cough of the mortars came first, as always. The blasts were absorbed by the high rocks all around, but they served as a signal to make ready. Eroglu snuggled his shoulder into the stock of the Browning. Right hand on the trigger, left touching the three pans of ammunition beside him. His loader had died in the previous attack. The Browning's rate of fire would be slower this time. Yes, this would be the last attack. Drakos propped his Sten against the rocks; Leonidas hauled himself up to a kneeling position with some effort and slammed another drum into his Thompson. Mani and Stathi looked at each other and gave strained smiles, then made the Bren ready.

And the enemy came. German, Italians and Bulgars all together once more. Out of the pines. Dodging or jumping over the bodies that strewed their path. Throwing grenades, firing from the hip. And screaming. Fischer was right at the front, charging ahead of Volk and Zimmerman, firing his Schmeisser wildly. Men fell all around him, but he charged on. Then he was hit. Left arm, high up. Just a flesh wound, but it stopped him in his tracks. As the rest rushed past him, Adler shouted: "Get back down, to the medics."

Fischer looked up at him. "Not now." He tore a strip of his tunic away to bind the wound then carried on, catching up with the front-runners as he drew his Luger and began firing. Next to him a Bulgarian threw his grenade, and this time he got lucky. It was close enough and high enough to clear the rocks and land between Mani and Stathi just as the fuse ran out. The blast killed both instantly and knocked Leonidas onto his back.

Eroglu switched his field of fire to cover the right side of the slopes. But now the fusillade had halved and the enemy scented victory. They came on. Moving faster, firing more intensely. Now they were doing the pinning down. Eroglu rose half out of cover, Browning in both hands, firing wildly, sweeping across the whole mouth of the pass. To his left, Drakos did the same. For a moment the enemy wavered again. Then Eroglu's breech jammed. Cursing, he bent to clear it. Drakos traversed right to cover his leader. But in doing so part of his body broke cover. A Schmeisser burst caught him in the left shoulder, throwing him clear of the rocks. Another took him full in the chest. Eroglu looked round as Drakos fell and a rifle bullet hit him in the neck, killing him instantly.

And there was silence. The enemy paused on the very lip of the pass. The pass they had fought so hard to win. But now they hesitated. Perhaps from caution, perhaps out of sheer disbelief. Then two *Gebirgsjager* men edged their way around the mouth of the funnel – and died in a burst from Leonidas' Thompson. Fischer, just behind them, dived prone behind a rock and got off one snap shot. It took Leonidas in the heart. He grunted once, fell back and lay still.

Fischer rose to his feet and moved forward hesitantly. He was alive. Volk was there too, and Zimmerman. Adler and Brega were rallying their men. There was no sign of Janosz, but some of the Bulgarian troops were there at the mouth of the pass too, gazing in disbelief at the small patch of corpses that had made the forest below. Drakos stirred and one of Brega's men stood over him and put a rifle bullet in his brain. The shot sounded unnaturally loud.

Fischer walked on, then noticed the boy lying by the mouth of the cave, still and silent. Poor little bastard, Fischer thought. About the same age as my kid brother. Jesus, Horst will be old enough to join all this soon. Suddenly his exultation at being alive turned to weariness and pain. He lowered his pistol.

The boy's eyes flickered open and he threw his knife at the nearest target. Fischer jerked back and looked down in surprise at the blade embedded in his chest. "Oh, shit," he said and sank to his knees. Micky was struggling to throw off his blankets and reach his rifle when Adler and Brega ran up, emptying their pistols into him.

Fischer was still on his knees as Micky died. He

looked up as Adler and Brega ran to him, then coughed up a huge gout of blood and fell to the ground. Volk and Zimmerman got to him first and looked at him. Zimmerman turned to the officers and shook his head.

Adler rubbed a weary hand across his brow, then beckoned his own sergeant, Dorff, to him. "Go back down and tell the Abwehr man he can come up now – if he has the stomach for it."

All the senior officers were up within a matter of minutes. Ziedler looked around glumly. "So few to keep us here so long," he said to no-one in particular as they waited for Adler's scouts to return with news of their quarry. He had cast a brief glance around for Rawlings or Vlasenin, but did not really need Weiss' earnest report that there was no sign of any of the SOE team to confirm his worst fears. After that he simply sat with Mauritz and Ciarelli at the mouth of the cave, apparently oblivious to the looks that every surviving soldier directed at him. Hoffman stood apart, taking frequent pulls at a hip flask and watching Ziedler very closely.

The scouts returned after five minutes. The news was as expected, with one major variation. Two sets of tracks, one older than the other, but both leading further up into the mountains. In the direction of the Bulgarian border.

"We can radio our positions on the border to be on the lookout," Mauritz ventured when Ziedler responded to the news with only silence. "Then we can reinforce them in the morning, once we have returned to the camp."

Return to the camp?" Ziedler looked up at him as though he were mad. "Let me make one thing clear, Oberst Mauritz. We do not leave these mountains until we have what we came for. It has been denied us once. It will not be again." He turned to Adler as Hoffman and Ciarelli regarded him with gazes equally questioning of his own sanity. "Have your men ready to begin the pursuit within five minutes. We have how many men left? Seventy – eighty? Half will secure the roads to the east, the rest will follow me to the Bulgarian border. We will march through the night. We will catch them. You go with the Turkish force," he said to Ciarelli, "and find out as much as you can about any partisan groups in the lowland areas. If Rawlings continues to elude us he will make contact with them at some stage. Klaus, you stay with me. When we catch them, we may need to make them talk, and you can have Rawlings anyway." He stood up and surveyed all his officers and men who were standing still as statues. "Do you hear me? We go on. We eat on the move and sleep when we have found them. But find them we will."

∾

Rawlings realised, with a certain degree of surprise, that he had never been so scared in his life. The team was careering down a slope that was almost perpendicular, hanging on for grim death to the rope that Loporos and Costas, the advance party, had lashed to boulders and trees at each stage of the descent. Their boots churned the snow-covered ground to mud as they went, constantly throwing them off-balance and perilously close to the sheer drop onto jagged rocks that lay within feet of the path. It was not the creeping dread of the wait for action or the intense, raw terror of action itself but a constant sense of balancing on a knife edge that tore at the nerves as much as the descent tore at the muscles. And it seemed to have gone on for hours.

But he knew it was only minutes. He knew they were making better time down the mountain than any vehicle could. Especially now the snow was almost a blizzard, reducing visibility to a matter of yards. Of course, that did not matter when the only way was down and you only had to look at where your feet found purchase. God alone knew how Costas and Loporos found their way down to belay the ropes in the first place – or how Stavrakis managed to keep his balance as he undid the ropes and brought up the rear, relying only on his sense of balance. Rawlings' admiration for the two Greek mountain men in the team had always been high but now it knew no bounds.

At last the slope eased, then abruptly levelled off into an almost flat stretch of wooded valley. This continued for a few hundred yards until it ended in a heather and boulder-strewn patch of bare ground preceding a ditch and then a road. The road was packed earth only, but it was smooth and wide enough for a convoy of trucks to pass along in single file. Another wide stretch of flat ground followed, giving ample room for traffic to pass on both sides, then came another sharp, thickly forested slope.

The snow on the road looked undisturbed but he sent Loporos and Costas forward to confirm. Within seconds they were back. "No sign of any tracks, major," Loporos said with a rare smile. "We made it!"

"Good work, everybody. But they can't be far away. We don't know the enemy's exact numbers, but from the evidence up above it's two truckloads at least, maybe more. So we're looking at platoon strength. And some of them will be specialists – probably the boys we came up against in Turkey, or something like them. They wiped out Amarazov's men without taking a single casualty, remember."

"And we gave them the right-about-face in Turkey, major – remember that?" Rowley grinned. The rest murmured in agreement and Rawlings felt a swell of pride.

"OK – let's see if we can do it again, then. Conor, we need to put the trucks out of action but not destroy them. Vlasenin could be in any one of them. Think you can do that."

"Just watch me, Alex." He was already rummaging inside his satchel. "One set of charges to straddle the cab of the first truck. That'll wreck it and give us half our roadblock at one go. Then another set by that big tree near the bend to block the back way and they're sitting ducks."

"Good man. Then the snipers blast every tyre on every vehicle. We'll have two on each side. Rowley and Stavrakis this side, Sanderson and Costas in those trees beyond. Then when they're stuck fast and we've whittled down the odds two groups go in at close quarters. Curtis, you take Mitchell and Walters from this side; I'll have Captain Loporos and Mayhew in the trees on the far side. Emerson provides cover for your group and O'Hare does the same for mine, along with the snipers. We get in close, to where Vlasenin and his papers are, then whichever group gets there first separates him from his guards and gets him into tree cover. The second group helps out by killing everything in a German uniform. Questions?"

"Just one, skipper." Walters sounded unusually hesitant. "What if they look like getting away with him, and we can't stop them all, but one of us gets a clear shot?"

Rawlings swallowed hard. "Take it. We can't afford to lose Vlasenin or the papers. But a bullet won't destroy a briefcase full of documents. If it's that kind of choice, then Vlasenin's expendable. But let's try to make sure it's a choice none of us has to make."

They murmured agreement again. "All right, then – let's get cracking!" They set to with an energy and efficiency Rawlings could not have dared hope for after the grueling descent, added to all the day's other travails. But it was as well they did, for Dorsch's convoy was there within minutes. Three trucks boxing in a Mercedes staff car. The tarpaulins were up against the snow, but from a quick sweep of the cabs and the rear Rawlings could see they were manned by ordinary Wehrmacht troops, probably a platoon in all, but with one of the Hermann Goering specialists alongside the driver of each. The rest – five in all – took up every seat but one in the staff car. The last place was occupied by Vlasenin, looking cold and frightened, casting frequent glances at the briefcase in the lap of the officer next to him. Rawlings recognised the shock of blond hair from their previous encounter and he knew that, after rescuing Vlasenin, finally removing that danger would be the action's number one priority.

All this was registered in the few seconds between the convoy rounding the bend and the lead truck hitting the first of Conor's booby-traps. The charge blasted the front half to scrap metal, killing every man in the cab and sending it careering off the road to smash into a pine tree, half of the body straddling the road. Behind it the staff car swerved round the newly-created roadblock and accelerated to clear the ambush. At that moment Rowley and Stavrakis blew out both the near-side tyres and it lurched to the right, slamming into a huge boulder. The second truck braked to a halt and the third tried to reverse round the bend. But Conor had already pressed the plunger on his next charge and the roar of the explosion was followed by a screaming crash as a pine tree landed across the road. The truck slammed into it and stopped dead.

Then the killing began. Sanderson and Stavrakis, firing from both sides of the road, took the driver and paratroop sergeant in the cab of the rear truck, then blasted its tyres out. Meanwhile O'Hare and Emerson were sweeping it and the second with submachine-gun fire, shredding the tarpaulin even as the occupants dived out for cover. Half a dozen men never made it out of the truck; two more went down as they scrambled for cover behind the vehicles' bodies. They began to return fire, but their backs were exposed and Rowley and Stavrakis began to pick them off one by one.

The story was the same at the front of the ambush. The two assault groups had been positioned as close to the centre of the killing ground as possible. Now Rawlings could see that Curtis' group, slightly further down, were better placed to keep the troops in the first truck busy while his men went for the staff car. They had already killed half a dozen of the truck detail as they scrambled for safety. But now the Germans had found a good defensive position in the crooked reverse 'L' shape formed by the two crashed vehicles and were beginning to return fire.

Rawlings signalled to Curtis to keep the Wehrmacht troops' heads down, then turned to his own men. "We go round the corner to the staff car – shooting. I'll nail the officer, then grab Vlasenin and the briefcase. Loporos, you take the driver; Mayhew, get the other three. Right – let's go!" He led them out of the pines, Mauser at the ready. But just as they broke cover Dorsch made his move too. He had spent roughly half a second cursing the sudden surprise reversal of fortune. The rest of the interim had been spent devising a plan to get his prize into tree cover and communicating it to his men. Now, at his signal, the covering fire from the six or seven survivors of the first truck intensified and his party dashed out from behind the staff car.

Two men with Schmeissers blasted the pines on either side, while Dorsch led the other two to a gap just to the right of where Rawlings' men were poised. The SD man had the briefcase in one hand and his Walther pistol in the other. As soon as he saw Rawlings' men emerge he began firing. Rawlings ducked and the first bullet cracked harmlessly overhead. The second caught Loporos in the shoulder, spinning him round and to the floor. Dorsch ran on, aiming for the gap. The two other Hermann Goering men went with him, shielding and guiding Vlasenin. One hand of each held him and propelled him on, the other fired pistol shot after pistol shot into the trees, adding to the hail of fire that kept the SOE team's heads down. Only Costas, perched in the lee of a pine, ten feet above the ground and ten yards back from the road, had a clear shot. He traversed away from the second truck and shot the Schmeisser man nearest to him in the head. Without breaking stride Dorsch's eyes flicked right, his pistol arm came up and a single shot took Costas in the heart. The Greek cried out and fell to the ground. Then Dorsch was in tree cover, the two men guarding Vlasenin with him. The last Schmeisser man ran to join them, spraying right to keep Curtis' group busy. But now Rawlings was on his feet again with a clear shot and half a second to take it. He did.

Rawlings looked round and saw Loporos nursing his shoulder. Mayhew was firing at the first truck, giving cover to Curtis' group as they ran to join Rawlings. "We need to catch those bastards – quick!" Rawlings gasped. "Curtis, Walters and Mitchell come with me. Mayhew, you link up with the others on this side. Make sure nobody else gets through. Best way to do that is wiping them all out, I'd say."

Mayhew nodded grimly and turned back to the road. Rawlings moved deeper into the pines, the other three at his heels. "They won't have time to cover their tracks so we should be able to follow them," Rawlings said as they broke into a run. "We stay on the same side and as soon as we're level start shooting. No time for finesse – you three nail Vlasenin's bodyguards. I'll take the officer with the briefcase. Clear?"

They nodded. After that there was silence. Just the soft flutter of bracken and leaves as they brushed past, quick but quiet. The men in front were quick too. It was several minutes before they caught up and the draining light of day in the dense tree cover made the scene almost as dark as night. But they saw a flash of gun metal, and heard a snapping of twigs as Vlasenin stumbled again. He was slowing up his captors once more, but this time there was no conscious thought of sabotage. He was simply exhausted.

Dorsch turned round to urge them on and that was when he saw Mitchell, less experienced than the rest, his pale face not completely behind cover. Dorsch made no outward sign of his discovery. But as he walked to the bodyguards he made a brief, almost imperceptible hand signal. Both men saw it and acknowledged it only with their eyes. But it meant that when the Britons broke cover again they were ready.

Dorsch whirled, firing an aimed shot that took Mitchell between the eyes. Then he dived back into the trees to give one of the bodyguards a clear shot at Rawlings. But he was already diving for cover. So was Curtis but as he dived he fired and as he rolled he fired again. Both were killing shots. The bodyguard cried out and spun back, releasing his hold on Vlasenin.

The second guard was alone, officer nowhere to be seen, an unknown number of enemies upon him. He hesitated, then remembered Dorsch's prime order. With no attempt to take cover he forced Vlasenin to his knees and brought his pistol against the Russian's skull.

Rawlings and Curtis were on the floor and unsighted. But Walters was not. He fired once, aiming for the gun arm. But his aim was out. It took the German in the left shoulder, punching him back. But he stayed on his feet. Vlasenin tried to scramble for cover. But now the German was looking for him again. He found him and the pistol was brought to bear once more. Then Walters broke cover, firing wildly. The bullets missed but the German turned and aimed his pistol at the greater danger.

The two shots blended as one, then the two men collided together, tearing at each other as they fell to the ground.

Curtis and Rawlings were on their feet now. "Help Walters, and keep Vlasenin safe," Rawlings cried. "I'll get the briefcase." Then he was gone, into the trees, black rage in his heart. He should never have risked Mitchell. Too many people had died already for his mistakes. But he knew he could not afford to make another. So this time he used all his training to keep close to his quarry, without presenting a target. It paid off. Dorsch knew he was being followed but could not get a clear sight of his pursuer. So he risked a shot when he thought he caught a glimpse. It chipped the bark from the tree an inch above Rawlings' head. Rawlings did not bother to fire back. It might give away his position. And the German taking a risk meant he was not so far ahead that he could not afford to try and discourage his pursuer. He might as well have tried to discourage a tidal wave.

Rawlings quartered round far to the left of the direction of the shot, crouching low and moving fast. He had not been able to get a clear sight of the German when he fired, but he hoped to be able to gauge his position, move ahead and take him where he least expected it, from in front and on his blind side. He moved as he had been trained but also as he had loved to do in his childhood. Hide and seek had always been his favourite game and the woods of Northumbria offered a thousand hiding places. But Rawlings had always preferred to be a seeker. The target this time was a different proposition from little Billy Monkhouse and the rest but the principle was the same. And the lack of mercy for the quarry.

Then Rawlings saw him. Ten yards to the right and

about two behind. Heading almost directly towards him. But Rawlings was hidden by a thick clump of bracken and now he dropped to his knees behind it, offering no sight or sign of his presence. He could have tried a shot, but if it missed… he was in a bad position for a clean kill. Besides, if he took him alive he might be able to find out if there were any more troops nearby before he killed him. He had got close to this one in Turkey, but let him go. This time there would be no mistake, He was close now. Five yards. Three, two…

Rawlings moved, fast and deadly. One hand chopped the Walther from Dorsch's grasp, the other tightened round his throat as Rawlings brought a knee up into the German's groin. Dorsch turned a thigh to block it, but he was still off balance. Rawlings swung him round and slammed his whole body against a tree trunk. The arm carrying the briefcase went limp and it dropped to the floor. Dorsch's knees buckled but then he righted himself, using the tree for support, and punched Rawlings in the stomach with his gun hand. Rawlings' throat grip loosened and Dorsch tore free, falling to the ground. He groped for his gun but Rawlings kicked it away as he drew his Mauser. Dorsch kicked upwards, catching Rawlings in the stomach. Rawlings fell back but was up again in a second, finger on the trigger. No answers, then. Only death.

But the clearing was deserted. There was no sign of the German. Rawlings' made a full 360-degree turn, alert for any sign of danger. But Dorsch was nowhere to be seen. A sudden spasm of panic seized Rawlings and he looked down for the briefcase. There it was. With a sigh of relief Rawlings picked it up. Then he scanned the perimeter of the clearing and saw the German's Walther. Scooping it up hurriedly he tucked it into his jacket pocket.

A sudden noise made him whirl round. But it was only Curtis, moving into the clearing with both hands in view. One hand held his smoking revolver. "Just me, sir."

"Did you get a shot at him?"

Curtis shook his head. "Didn't see a sign of him." He looked at his gun. "This is still fresh from back there. Do we go after him, sir?"

"No – too late." Rawlings looked up at the sky, which was now full dark, then at the dark mass of wood before them. "We'd never find him in this – and we've got what we came for."

"Yes, we have, sir," Curtis said with a note in his voice Rawlings could not immediately place. "Doctor Vlasenin is safe and well," he added as they began to walk back to the road.

"Good work," Rawlings said with a smile. "I knew I could rely on you – I'll have to talk to Walters, though. Mad Aussie taking risks again. He should have waited – but it's just as well he didn't."

Curtis turned to him. "He never will again, sir." It was then that Rawlings saw the look in his eyes and recognised the note in his voice. They were back at the site of the last gunfight now. Vlasenin was sitting in the clearing, Mayhew alongside him. The Russian was weeping uncontrollably. Five yards away, next to the body of the German he had killed, was Corporal Walters. He was lying on his side, hunched in the odd shapelessness that Rawlings had seen so many times. The bleeding had stopped, but the bullet hole in his chest was clear. An identical one was to be found in the German, and his face was the blue of the strangulation victim. Walters had made sure even when they were both dead.

Rawlings hung his head and wiped a grimy sleeve across his eyes. Then he straightened himself. "Let's get back to the road."

Mayhew and Curtis helped Vlasenin to his feet. The Russian looked at Walters again. "He was a good man," he said softly.

"A brave one," Rawlings agreed. And he had died a long way from home and there was no time to bury him. "Any more casualties?" he asked Mayhew.

"Just one, sir – Second-Lieutenant Emerson. Caught a bullet from one of the men behind the trucks. Their lieutenant managed to organise them to make a break. We had to go in close to try and stop them. Managed to account for most, including the lieutenant, but a few got away."

They were at the roadside now, the rest of the team coming to meet them. Emerson lay on his back, a few yards away from Costas. The light of the burning trucks gave a clear view of all of the corpses. Emerson had taken a head shot. A pool of blood and brains lay alongside him. He had probably died at the same time as his old college friend. The wound he had taken in the team's first combat was still not quite healed.

Rawlings sighed and turned to Mayhew. "I expected more from you, Sarn't-Major. With Emerson dead you were in command. This operation wasn't supposed to leave a single survivor."

Vlasenin looked at him in disgust. "Hasn't there been enough killing here today?"

"No, doctor, there hasn't." Rawlings turned to him. "Those men who we left alive will probably be in the mountains again tomorrow, hunting for us. And if there are any other troops nearby to see these trucks burning they could be on our tail by the end of the night, with however many survivors of this to bolster their ranks. I'm afraid keeping you and your papers safe demands that I think like that. Now, Captain Loporos, can you get us back onto our original route by the end of tonight?"

Loporos looked at him gravely. "Yes, there are other, safer paths back up into the mountains nearby. We can get nearly as far tonight as I had originally planned."

"Good, because we've a rendezvous with Mikos in three days' time and we can't be late. So salvage what food and ammo you can from the trucks, lads, and let's be off."

"No rest, sir?" Curtis asked cautiously.

Rawlings turned to him. "We've just had our day of rest, captain."

༄

So they climbed, back into the mountains. Loporos guided them unerringly, despite the obvious pain of his wounded shoulder. By dawn they were back on the Greek side of the mountains, as far along the trail as intended, but some way from their original first stage camp. This was exactly as Rawlings wanted it; as he explained to his men, and to Davies in the transmission he sent before they bedded down in a gulley just below the treeline: "Whoever knew where we were going yesterday never will again."

It was the same the next day. And the next. They kept to their schedule, drawing ever closer to the rendezvous point with Mikos' group, but never using the same camp for their day's shelter as Loporos had intended. Instead they made him find other shelters, usually more bare and remote than the ones he had planned. And on the second day they radioed Mikos to change the rendezvous itself, so that no-one outside of the two groups knew exactly where they would be meeting. And there had been no broadcasts to Davies in all that time, despite a series of increasingly terse demands for "*some sort of progress report at least*".

So it was that as dawn broke on Sunday December 5th, 1942, Rawlings was leading his group up an almost identical path to an almost identical pass in the Rhodope Mountains. The only differences were that they were much more cold, hungry and weary than they had been three days ago; there were only nine men in the group, including Loporos and Vlasenin; and Rawlings was convinced that, whoever the traitor in SOE was, they had no possible way of knowing the group's precise whereabouts.

But Rawlings was still alert for danger, especially after all Eroglu had told him of Mikos' reputation. Loporos had confirmed this. "He will not be in the mountains, major. His headquarters is in a disused tobacco factory on the outskirts of a village down in the valley. But he has sent two of his men to guide us there."

"Do you know them by sight?"

"Yes – Vasilis and Latsis." He shook his head. "I taught them when I was their village schoolmaster, many years ago. I knew they would end up as bandits. But they know the country between here and Turkey like the wild beasts do."

"Good enough," Rawlings said. "Lead on. But be ready for anything," he said to the whole group, and as they moved on he dropped back down the line, past O'Hare and Mayhew to Curtis, the last man before the two sergeants and Stavrakis, who guarded their rear. Curtis was looking after Vlasenin, while Rawlings held the briefcase in one hand. "If anything goes wrong and I can't make it take the lads over the edge and don't stop running until you get to Turkey."

Curtis looked at him. "You think there'll be another double-cross?"

"Maybe, maybe not. I'm learning belatedly not to trust anyone on this op."

They paused at the last bend, still in cover. Loporos called out for Mikos' men to show themselves. Two faces appeared at the head of the pass; dark, unshaven, villainous faces below knitted woolen caps. But Loporos hailed them with relief. "It's them, major."

"Last time it was you," Rawlings reminded him grimly. "You and me go up first, and we check everything before we wave the rest on."

Loporos nodded and they emerged from cover, walking up the pass slowly. One of the men walked down the pass to meet them, smiling in welcome as he saw Loporos. "Teacher – remember me; little Latsi." He made to embrace him but Loporos gave no returning smile. Latsis frowned and turned to Rawlings: "Where are the rest?" he asked in Greek

"Soon," Rawlings replied in the same language. "We just want to make sure no tricks first."

Latsis looked hurt. "Tricks – no man in Thrace thinks we can make an honest deal." He turned to Loporos. "And you taught us all about trust, eh, teacher?"

"That was a long time ago, Latsi. Just take us behind the rocks so we can be sure it's only you two. Then all our friends will join us."

Latsis shrugged. "Sure – my old teacher, sensible like always." He beckoned them on, up to the head of the pass. There was no cave this time, only a smokeless fire over which Vasilis squatted like a disgruntled gnome. Rawlings, pistol out, looked around every inch of the pass and the surrounding terrain, then far up the path, oblivious to the hostile gazes of Mikos' men, before pronouncing himself satisfied and waving his team on.

As they moved up towards the pass, Latsis and Vasilis began to move towards the first bend. But as they did Loporos looked at them and said suddenly: "You have no packs."

They stopped and turned: "They are at the cave – where we will spend the day," Latsis said.

Loporos looked at them and his voice was cold. "So you left them unguarded. No partisan does that – even from a band like Mikos'. You have none because you are going nowhere today, except to your new paymasters. Major, tell your men to run!"

Rawlings was already moving, running to the mouth of the pass, a warning on his lips. But it was drowned in the noise of a dozen rifles and submachine-guns opening fire. O'Hare hesitated, and took a bullet in the heart as the rest dived left and right. Stavrakis, Rowley and Sanderson at the rear went over the edge, careering down the steep, wooded slope. Ahead of them, Curtis and Mayhew did the same, an arm apiece round Vlasenin. But the Russian's foot slipped on a snow-wetted stone and he fell heavily to one side, dragging the Britons with him. Before they could recover troops were surging from a dozen hiding places around the pass onto the path, covering them before they could rise again.

Rawlings turned. Vasilis and Latsis, frozen by Loporos' discovery, moved now, drawing pistols from their belts. But their old schoolteacher moved first, Sten coming up to cut them both down. Rawlings moved to join him but a rifle shot from above took Loporos in the side of the head. He fell to the ground without a cry. More troops were emerging from all sides, closing on Rawlings. He shot two men who appeared in front of him as he raced to the edge of the gorge and made to throw the briefcase away. Then a rifle butt slammed into the small of his back, knocking him to his knees. Another blow to the head laid him flat on his back.

As he tried to rise two carbine barrels were thrust in his face and voices in German and Italian ordered him to keep still. He looked round. Men in uniform were everywhere; German mountain troops, Wehrmacht, Italian *Alpini*, Bulgarians. As he was hauled to his feet he saw them escorting Curtis, Mayhew and Vlasenin up the pass. Behind them others were searching the body of Conor O'Hare. They handled his bag of tricks carefully and did the same with the radio transmitter, carrying them straight past Rawlings and picking up Vlasenin's briefcase on the way, to present in triumph to the man who now walked around the bend to join the troops whose three days in the mountains had finally yielded victory. Oberst Ulrich Ziedler was unshaven and his uniform was in the shabbiest state Rawlings had ever seen it. But the dazzling smile was still there as he looked down the pass.

"Good morning, Major Rawlings," he said.

Chapter 8

Fast Train to Berlin

"*GOOD EVENING, MAJOR RAWLINGS.*" *ZIEDLER* was looking much more his usual self now. He was clean-shaven, chestnut hair washed and combed. His Transport Corps uniform had been cleaned and pressed, every button and medal gleaming. He was seated at a fully-laid silver service dining table.

The sight was the latest in a series of surreal tableaux Rawlings had experienced that day. Starting with the ambush on the mountain, where he had been confronted by all his nemeses – Ziedler, Ciarelli and Hoffman – looking very much the worse for their weekend in the mountains. But Ciarelli had barely time to gloat, and Hoffman to retrieve his Mauser then deal Rawlings a vicious blow to the head with it, before Ziedler had ordered the entire task force (with the exception of a *Gebirgsjager* detachment under Leutnant Adler, detailed to pursue the three escapees) back down into the lowlands.

A hard morning's march had brought them to

Organi, where Rawlings had seen a sleepy Thracian town transformed into the biggest armed camp he had ever encountered. Hundreds of German, Italian and Bulgarian troops had swelled the guard around the four prisoners while Ziedler organised a convoy to, as Hoffman put it, "get us out of this shithole as soon as possible".

It had materialised in double time, and the rest of the day had been spent on the road – first the earthen tracks of the Rhodope, then the tarmaced narrow carriageways of central Thrace, and finally the broad, well-mettled expanse of the main coast highway. Their journey had ended in late afternoon, at Alexandroupoli, last major port in Greece, barely ten miles from the Turkish border and one of the larger garrisons of the German sector. The entire journey had yielded not one opportunity for escape, and the convoy was so large that an attack by every partisan group in Thrace would have yielded nothing but a massacre. The sense of helplessness was exacerbated when they entered the town, to see it turned into a fortress-cum-prison. Checkpoints guarded every road, there were patrols throughout the streets and the main square had been cordoned off with barbed wire.

The prisoners were taken the local command HQ, a converted hotel. Rawlings was separated from the others and taken to what had obviously been one of the better rooms. The guard instructed him to make himself comfortable, avail himself of the clean civilian clothes on the bed and be ready for dinner at seven sharp. Rawlings had not been quite sure if he had translated the guard's German correctly; but in any case he washed, changed, shaved and passed the time to the appointed hour alternately dozing and staring out of the window (under which a guard patrolled, twin to the man behind the locked door) at the Turkish coast. The neutral territory looked close enough for him to have emulated Leander and swam there, but Rawlings knew that from an escapee's point of view it might as well have been the back of the moon.

As his antique bedside clock chimed the first stroke of seven, the key turned in the lock and there was his guard, gesturing out into the corridor with the barrel of his Schmeisser. A short walk brought them to a larger, more elegant version of Rawlings' room. It was obviously Ziedler's office and personal quarters for the duration and it was dominated by the dining table where Ziedler sat as he welcomed Rawlings, alternately eyeing him as he sat down and supervising the Wehrmacht orderly who brought in a basket of bread and then poured Rawlings a glass of white wine from one of the superior German vineyards.

"I thought you might welcome a change from *retsina* and *raki*," Ziedler smiled as Rawlings looked at his glass in astonishment. "And I am sure you will find the food to your taste also."

It was only then that Rawlings noticed a typewritten card at his place setting. It read:

Grilled sole with béarnaise sauce
Roast lamb with seasonal vegetables
Treacle pudding with custard
Coffee and mints
Wines: Kirschner Riesling 1937, Chateau Rabaud Burgundy 1935
Twelve-year-old Glenfiddich single malt

"Your file was unusually informative about your preferred dining choices, Major Rawlings," Ziedler continued as he signalled the orderly to leave. "And I think we have managed well at short notice. The treacle pudding was especially difficult – and I do not think it stretched the garrison cook's talents as much as he would have liked. And the 'seasonal vegetables' are rice and peppers. The Greeks are regrettably unused to cultivating what the civilised world regards as the perfect accompaniment to good meat."

"Well, I've always been partial to everything on here," Rawlings replied as he put the card down and reached for his wine glass. "And I've always found that a Kirschner '37 has a very distinctive bouquet." He sniffed the glass for a very long time and studied the colour intently, but did not drink. Ziedler laughed and beckoned him to hand the glass over. When Rawlings had done so, he took a long draught and sighed with admiration. "A fine choice, major, and a wise precaution – but you need not worry. This is not the age of the Borgias. I am happy to do the same for every item of food and drink which appears in front of you but I hope you will take my good faith on trust. Besides," he added with an edge of steel, "if I had wanted you dead tonight there are far more direct methods available to me than poison."

"Or *poisson*," Rawlings said as the orderly brought the sole to the table and the first bite gave a sharp reminder of how ravenous the past weeks had made him.

Ziedler smiled at the joke. "Very good, major. I have looked forward to the opportunity for an evening such as this for many years. Our previous encounters have been too fleeting."

"Toulouse dragged a bit for me, I'm afraid. And the accommodation was a disgrace compared to this. That's why I left early."

"Without even a note." Ziedler returned his ironic smile. "But I understand."

Rawlings' smile vanished. "And that's why I'm not taken in by any of this bollocks. If all this is to soften me up before Hoffman gets to work I'll still be ready for him and I'll not tell him a damn thing. And if this is a diversion while Vlasenin and my men get the treatment I'll find out – and I'll pay you all back in kind."

"You wrong me to think so, major." Ziedler looked genuinely shocked. "You, and all your men, have made an excellent attempt at performing an impossible task. No-one else could have eluded me for so long – and eliminated so many of my subordinates. But now it is over. You have lost. That does not mean you should not be afforded the courtesies befitting a prisoner of war."

Rawlings almost choked on his food with laughter. He took a long draught of wine to clear his throat. "Well, if all our lads get the same as this when they go in the bag from now on, perhaps you might just win the war. But that's the only way." He looked at Ziedler and there was no laughter in his voice now. "You really believe all that rubbish, don't you? You've tried every dirty trick in the book in your career, Ulrich. Set your SS and Gestapo dogs on me and people like me whenever we've fallen into your hands – and yet you still think those hands are clean. All that Great War brotherhood of officers and gentlemen bullshit died when your lot let Hitler into power.

"Him and his crew rule Germany now. And the

whole bloody world if we don't stop them. You're not working for the *Junkers* now, you know, Ulrich – and I think they'd have regarded you as a bit too much of a *kleindeutsch*, anyway. You're working for men like Hoffman. Monsters." He gave a bitter laugh. "But at least they're honest about it."

"Kommissar Hoffman is my subordinate," Ziedler replied coldly. "Not my master. A dedicated servant of the Reich, and my subordinate."

"He's an evil, vicious bastard and if there's any justice he'll get as nasty a death as the deaths him and his kind have given too many men – and women. And all his bosses, and yours, right up to old Adolf himself, will get the same."

"Well, that looks somewhat unlikely now, does it not?" Ziedler's voice was heavy with scorn. "Since I have secured for Germany all that she needs for ultimate victory; Vlasenin and his papers – with three of His Majesty's top secret agents as a bonus."

"Ciarelli said something similar when he trumped you a week or so back. He found that getting us and keeping us are different matters."

"Perhaps that is because you have not yet been kept by me, and me alone. Rest assured, major, you will not be ill-treated here. But neither will you be afforded any chance to escape. The same goes for Doctor Vlasenin, as well as Captain Curtis and Sergeant-Major Mayhew. It may interest you to know that at this moment each of them is being served a meal very much like this one – and I hope they are accepting theirs with better grace. I suggest you eat well tonight, major. Because tomorrow a long train journey begins. It will end in Berlin and I suspect its dining car will be less well-equipped than the kitchens here."

"Train, eh?" Rawlings mused. "Yes, there is only one main line in this part of Greece, I suppose. And it skirts the Turkish border up to Bulgaria, as I recall. Are we taking that route, or back to Salonika?"

For a moment it seemed Ziedler would not answer, but then he said: "We go on, major. To Sofia, then Belgrade, Vienna, Prague and Berlin. Not that you will see much of any of them."

"Shame – just when the Christmas market season's beginning. Is Ciarelli joining us?"

"Regrettably, no." Ziedler permitted himself a smile, but there was a bitter edge to his voice. "He will be returning to Italy via Salonika and Albania – with the papers. It has been decided to divide the spoils in that manner. His train will also provide a decoy. Salonika is a more logical first destination, as the British have demonstrated by bombing every road and airbase in the area over the past five days, and strafing every convoy of any size that has attempted to reach it. They have obviously despaired of the legendary SOE's ability to influence Doctor Vlasenin's travel plans.

"Of course, this means also that in the very unlikely event of you managing to set Vlasenin at liberty again your victory will only be partial. Not that this eventuality will arise, major. For the next three days I will have you where I want you at last, and I do not intend to take my eyes off you."

"Very touching. So this is the modern version of being dragged behind the chariot, then? And all services to Berlin may be subject to delays until we get there. Your countrymen won't be happy with you for that, Ulrich. You know how they like their trains to run on time."

"I think they will forgive me when they learn the reason."

"And wouldn't a plane be quicker?" Rawlings added with genuine curiosity. "Safer, too."

"Not really. For one thing, as I said, every airbase and landing strip within range has been bombed to oblivion this past week. Even if we were to take off safely, a good deal of our flight path would be within range of RAF fighters, either from Egypt or Britain, or your carriers in the Mediterranean. Mr Churchill might consider a suicide mission worth it for the chance to shoot us down. It would be typical of the British mentality to decide that if they cannot have Vlasenin and his knowledge then no-one shall. Not to mention the Soviet air force – even less of a danger, but a nation even more capable of vindictive spite."

"They just can't understand when a nice, friendly spy game is over, can they? Is that all this is to you? A game? Does winning just boost your ego, and losing hurt your pride?"

"Do not think yourself above me, major. Can you honestly say you have always believed your country to be right in everything she has made you do? Or your superiors men of absolutely pure motives? Of course not; no-one in our profession does. So why then do we pursue this profession? Why do we not give it up, as logic dictates we should. No-one should serve that which is not worth serving. No, major, we do it because it is not a game – it is THE game. The finest of them all. The stakes and rewards the destiny of nations – of the world, even. The penalty for failure, death – one's own, or that of thousands of others. For the thrill of that game we do it. You, me, Ciarelli, Amarazov…"

"And the SOE traitor who helped you track us?"

"What SOE traitor?" Ziedler gave him a disingenuous look. "I caught you using my own skill – and the perfidy of the Greeks, that age-old and seemingly inexhaustible commodity. I needed no traitor."

Rawlings shrugged. He had expected no less. "Have it your own way. So we get to Berlin, after half a dozen train changes to throw SOE off the scent. Then Vlasenin goes to the research labs and us three get the cellars at Gestapo HQ. Then, when they've realised we're not going to tell anyone a thing or do your dirty work, we're legitimately shot as spies and buried in an unmarked grave on a bomb site. Fair enough, I suppose."

He fixed his eyes on the Abwehr man's. "Except we're not going quietly, Ulrich. For the first leg of this train ride we're going to be less than ten miles from the Turkish border. If we can get free we could be on neutral territory within the hour. And we'll get free. Even if we can't manage it from inside, you haven't caught all of us."

"Ah, yes, the sergeants and Private Stavrakis. Two lower-ranking British NCOs and a Greek common soldier." He waved a dismissive hand. "Hardly the types to hatch a grand rescue plan, I think."

"They've managed to stay free so far – otherwise you'd be parading them in front of me now."

"They have not been found yet," Ziedler admitted. "But they will be. They are no threat."

"A man at large is always a threat, Ulrich. In this game, at least. And there are still plenty of people up in those mountains who'll help them. Every minute they stay at large they're more of a worry to you, and Canaris and the rest. You don't beat the SOE, or Britain, or any of the forces that want to see you destroyed, just by capturing me. If I thought that I'd be as much an egomaniac as you are. I hope they come out of the mountains with an army. I hope that train has to fight every yard of the way to Berlin. I hope you're watching your back for…"

Ziedler stood up abruptly, marched to his desk and pressed an intercom buzzer. "I am weary of this, major. If you cannot honour good food with pleasant conversation you may return to your quarters." The door opened and two guards stood in the threshold, Schmeissers levelled at Rawlings. "Take him," Ziedler ordered.

Rawlings grabbed a hurried gulp of food and a mouthful of wine as they advanced. "I think we've run out of small talk anyway, Ulrich. I don't think we'll ever start a beautiful friendship." He wiped his mouth on one of the snow-white napkins. "Compliments to the chef, though."

After they were gone, Ziedler retook his seat at the dining table and picked up his wine glass. He sat in thought for a long time before taking a drink.

∽

Rowley woke up freezing cold, with every bone in his body aching. Stavrakis had gently rubbed his shoulder to wake him and now he looked down on him with an apologetic smile. "It is time to move, sergeant. The Germans will not be far away."

"I know," Rowley agreed ruefully as he stood up and

stretched his tired muscles. The Germans had never been far away in the last twenty-four hours. The three of them had barely finished their mad, scree-running descent of that suicidal slope when they heard the noise of pursuit. After a second's pause to confirm that, by a minor miracle, none of them had broken or sprained anything they had set off at a run, nothing to guide them except one of the maps Captain Loporos had provided and Stavrakis' vague familiarity with the area from his travels at the tail-end of the Greek campaign.

It was little on which to base a flight from determined pursuers and they had struggled to shake them off throughout the day. Every time they thought they had come across an unknown trail and covered their tracks onto it, they would snatch a few moments' rest. Then the sound of boots would be heard, or the sight of a snow-camouflaged helmet glimpsed among the trees, and they would be off again. All day it had gone on, as they first tried to move further up, back into the mountains, then doubled back when they saw their pursuers above them. They had no real destination, though they tried to move away from the main roads and in the vague direction of the Turkish border. The main objective had simply been to shake off the Germans.

But they had kept coming, kept following. And they did not stop at nightfall. The hooded torchbeams made them easier to spot, but they signalled that the pursuit would not end until the quarry was brought to bay. The three men had kept ahead of them, and finally lost them. They risked a few hours' sleep but they knew the respite would be only temporary. And as Rowley looked at Sanderson, ready for the off but clearly as cold and weary as his fellow sergeant, he wondered how long they could keep this up.

"North and east again today then, lads," Sanderson half-asked, half-ordered. He was senior to Rowley by length of service, but every decision had been agreed with the other two; with Stavrakis because his local knowledge was obviously superior; and with Rowley because, after all this time, the idea of pulling rank on him seemed unnatural.

"I think so, Colour-Sergeant Sanderson," Rowley replied with a parade ground formality he could still not quite shake off. "Unless Private Stavrakis advises against it."

Stavrakis shrugged. "It is closer to the border, and further from the enemy. And we might run into other EDES groups if we pass through Mikos' area." His normally saturnine face darkened even further. "Then we can pay him back for what he did."

Sanderson shook his head. "If we get away from this lot, the first priority is try to rescue the major and Doctor Vlasenin. That's what he said we had to do if any of us were left free – and we're going to do it."

"Wherever they are," Rowley began in his customary morose tone, but then caught sight of the look in Sanderson's eyes. "Wherever they are we'll find them. But like you say, we need to get away from this lot first."

Stavrakis nodded, looking intently at the sky. "Better weather, at least. I think it will not snow today."

"That'll mean better visibility for the squareheads," Sanderson replied. "I'd lie up here for the day if I didn't think they'd find us. But a good day's march could get us to the border, and a chance of meeting friendlies. Then we can really start thinking about helping the major."

"Knowing him, he'll have got free and found them before us," Rowley smiled. "We'll probably get a bollocking for being late."

Sanderson and Stavrakis smiled back and the three set off. They had been on the move less than an hour when the ambush came. It had been sheer good luck that they had avoided Leutnant Adler's ten-man section as it passed in front of them in a forced night march. And sheer bad luck that Adler himself was the first to catch a glimpse of them. One of his NCOs might have been too eager, blown a whistle or shouted a command to bring the rest of the detail running.

But Adler was determined to make no mistakes. So he doubled back quickly to Sergeant Dorff and whispered instructions. Then he got back on the trail and stayed on it. He knew the perfect ambush spot was just ahead and he trusted his men to lay the trap perfectly. He had picked them himself; each was a veteran of countless pursuits like this in Russia, Czechoslovakia and Greece itself. They would have no trouble taking three tired men unused to mountain work. For a moment he felt a pang of sympathy for the fugitives. Then he remembered his duty – and the many men whose deaths this operation had caused already. Now was the time to finish it.

Sixty seconds later the two sergeants were poised on the edge of a strip of open ground between two thick belts of pine trees. On the other side Stavrakis waved them on. When they were half-way across the trap was sprung. Two men in front, covering Stavrakis, two behind, blocking the retreat back into cover. And two on each side, moving in, rifles and Schmeissers raised.

As the three men stood, heads hung in the bitterness of defeat, a voice from the trees said in English: "Drop your weapons!" Sanderson looked at the other two for an instant, then at the eight guns levelled on them, and reluctantly unslung his Sten and placed it on the ground. The others followed suit. From the trees to the right a tall, dark-haired man, flanked by two others, advanced towards them. Like the rest of them he was dressed in alpine gear. But he carried a pair of binoculars round his neck and a Luger pistol in his right hand. He waved it at each of the three in turn and said, again in English: "A good try – but it ends now. Come with me, please."

They began walking towards him. Then a rifle shot rang out and Adler staggered back with a bloody hole dead centre in his forehead. He gave a strangled cry and fell. Other shots rang out, then a burst of submachine-gun fire. The SOE men dived to the ground as Adler's section fell dead around them. One man made for cover but was cut down on the edge of the trees. Only Dorff was left standing. He turned his Schmeisser toward the men on the ground – but Sanderson had already dived full-length to grab his Sten and give Dorff a three-second burst full in the chest. Adler's sergeant was dead before he hit the ground.

Sanderson rolled over to him and checked, though. Then he looked round at the other two. They were kneeling, weapons at the ready, covering both sides of the clearing. As they looked on in bewilderment a dozen or so men in white sheepskin coats and leggings emerged from the trees. They were armed to the teeth and looked very dangerous. A blond giant with a snow hood was at their head. They looked down on the three SOE men, silent and unsmiling. "Anyone speak English?" Sanderson asked hesitantly.

"With a bit of an accent, but yes," the blond man replied in a cultivated Edinburgh brogue. "Watson's the name – Captain Alan Watson, SOE Cairo. Looks like we found you fellows just in time."

Sanderson was dumbfounded. "How did you…?"

Watson smiled as he replied, but there was an edge of tension in his voice. "No time for questions at the moment, old chap. We think these are the only Huns on the mountain at the moment, but we could be wrong. You're Public Enemies number One, Two and Three at the moment, so the sooner we get you absolutely safe the better."

When he later reflected on that morning, Sanderson could never quite believe how they kept going. Their rescuers set a punishing pace, one the SOE men would not have believed they could match after the events of the previous day. But match it they did, as the party pushed on into the mountains. Then, just before noon, they came to the head of a crag and there, hidden by the trees and rocks all around, was a long, winding path down, almost twin to the one that Loporos had taken them down a few days before. It was hard and treacherous, but there was less of the muscle-tearing strain of an uphill climb. And when they reached the bottom they found themselves in thick pine forest once again. But the land was level and the air warmer. There was no time for rest even then, though. Watson and Katsoulis, the senior man among the Greeks, kept pushing them on until at last, in mid-afternoon, they entered a clearing with a huge derelict building in the centre. The party dashed across the open ground and inside.

It had obviously been a factory or workshop of some kind once, but now it was gutted, the interior given over entirely to boxes, cartons and sacks of varying sizes, and clusters of bedrolls where a dozen or so men sat smoking, reading or cleaning their weapons, of which there was a diversity that the two sergeants were coming to regard as very familiar. At a shout from Katsoulis a man sitting at a desk in what remained of an office rose from his seat and walked towards them, smiling broadly. He wore a knitted cap of the type which seemed standard issue to the partisans of Thrace, but underneath was a pinstripe suit jacket and a white vest. Below that a pair of cavalry twill trousers with a pistol and knife stuck in the belt and a set of embroidered top boots. "Gentlemen, meet Mikos Andreas," Watson said.

Stavrakis' hand darted to the pistol at his belt. Katsoulis and two other men grabbed him as Sanderson turned to Watson, disbelief yielding to a sick fear. "He betrayed us – do you know that?"

"Actually, he didn't." Watson held up a calming hand. "Should have explained this sooner, chaps, but time was of the essence, and I wondered if you'd have come with us had you known. Mikos entrusted two of his men to come and collect you, but they proved to be not as trustworthy as we would have liked."

Mikos spat into the ground. "They betrayed me, too. Took the Germans' money. They had no honour."

"And you do?" Stavrakis' question was followed by a Greek epithet that made even Mikos' men blush. Watson winced and said: "I can understand your reaction, old boy, but you have to believe me. After all, if we were working with the Germans too, would we have killed ten of our own men and taken you as far away from the nearest garrison as you can get? I think not."

Rowley still looked suspicious. Sanderson's head was reeling. "But why weren't you there yesterday? We would have trusted you."

"We only arrived yesterday – sorry, we being Sergeant Jennings and I." He gestured to a small, gipsy-dark figure in British battledress standing among Mikos' men. "When Colonel Davies heard that you were on the last stretch but maintaining radio silence for... various reasons, he decided you might need a little help on the home furlong. So he found a couple of spare Greek specialists who knew the territory – though we've been on ops over in Epirus lately; just arrived back in Cairo last week – and told us to get back in pronto. Gave us contact details for Mikos' group and told us to make sure they kept up their end of the bargain." He looked across at Mikos. "Which they will."

Mikos shrugged. "A deal is a deal, and you British pay good money. I wanted to welcome you yesterday. The transport was ready, and so were your friends."

Watson nodded. "We were expecting a radio transmission to say you'd made contact safely, so when it never came Mikos detailed his… adjutant and me to take a few chaps and look for you. Well, when we got to the pass we felt like the Big Bad Wolf at the turnip patch – too bloody late. We could see that his men had done a deal – probably been caught by the Huns on the way and decided to collaborate to save their lives. Much good it did them; your major must have nailed him before he was caught. And we could see someone had escaped and the Jerries were after them. So we radioed back to Mikos, he relocated his HQ to another of these rather handy old factories, just in case they'd told the Huns where to find him too, and we decided to track you down and get you here safe."

"We know the major's a prisoner," Sanderson said. "And the doctor, and two more of our team. We saw them get taken. We lost everything we were supposed to keep safe."

Watson smiled and put a hand on his shoulder. "You did all you could, sergeant. You kept yourself and your men alive. That's the main thing."

Sanderson looked at him. "Thank you, sir. But now we've got to rescue them."

Watson nodded. "Well, of course. But not on your own. We've been finding out a lot about the German plans, thanks to Mikos' contacts. They've taken them to Alexandroupoli, which is right down on the coast, and every German soldier in Thrace is watching them. No hope of getting in there. But they're being taken back to Germany by train. It sets off tomorrow afternoon and there's a point not far from here where the line passes within a few miles of the Turkish border. We've got a plan to get onboard and get them off. Mikos and his men have agreed to help – for a little extra commission on their fee – but we'll need your help too. Think you can do that? I know you've been through a hell of a lot, and we'll need men in the party that stays near the train and takes them over the border afterwards. You can join them if you like."

Sanderson looked at Rowley and Stavrakis. Both were shaking their heads. "We've done this kind of thing before," Sanderson said. "These lads haven't. We'll get on that train and we'll get them out." Even as he spoke he knew that no-one would have thought any less of them for staying in the back-up party. But he knew that after all he had been through with Rawlings and the rest he could not have stayed in the rear. It was their duty. He remembered what Rawlings had said at their first briefing. "Come back with your shield or on it." He had not really understood at the time but now he realised. And that was how he'd lived his life as a soldier, anyway.

Watson smiled with relief. "Well, I'm not denying it'll be good to have you along. But there's time before then for a hot meal, and some sleep."

Sanderson looked at the other two, and said: "Anything you say, sir."

∽

Ziedler was not in a particularly good mood. The memory of last night's unprofitable conversation with Rawlings was still fresh in his mind, the fugitives were still at large and he had spent most of the day in frustrating discussions with Berlin and the local military authorities. The trains were still not ready to run. Certain modifications had to be made, Canaris and Himmler had both insisted that more security was needed and the time-serving incompetent in charge of the area was dragging his heels over bringing more men in from their chicken-guarding duties.

At least they would all be German this time, however. The Bulgarians had been thanked for their help and told to remain on guard in their sector; the Italians to return to theirs. The sole presence which Il Duce's new Roman legions had in Alexandroupoli was the dozen-strong SIM detachment which Ame had brought to Salonika to replace Ciarelli's original team. They had been accoutred as *Alpini* for the Adraxos Pass operation and now languished in some corner of the local barracks with their commander.

And after tomorrow that would be the last Ziedler would see of him, he sincerely hoped for the duration of the war. So his mood was worsened even further when a knock on the door and his curt "enter" revealed none other than Colonel Eduardo Ciarelli himself.

"What do you want?" Ziedler asked wearily; he was finding it hard to feign civility now everything had been arranged, and his orderly had already begun preparing dinner.

"It's about the train trip," Ciarelli said as he took a chair in front of Ziedler and helped himself to brandy from the decanter on the desk.

"I thought we had arranged all that. Your train leaves for Salonika at noon tomorrow, just before ours sets off for Sofia. I am sorry it could not be any earlier, but for security reasons…"

"I know all that." Ciarelli waved him to silence. "This is about your train, not mine."

"I fail to see what concern that is of yours, since you won't be on it."

"No," Ciarelli agreed, smiling broadly. "And neither will Vlasenin."

Ziedler sighed. "If this is a joke, Signor Colonel, I can assure you I am not in the mood."

"No joke, Ziedler. When my men and I leave, we

take the doctor and his papers."

"I see." Ziedler's tone was absolutely neutral. "Do you think that is fair – or that my superiors will allow it."

"Your superiors will not know until it is too late. And if you ask me what I think is fair, you piece of Prussian pigshit," the smile was gone as Ciarelli leaned forward, eyes blazing, "I think it fair that after all Italy has done to get this man and keep him safe, after her soldiers died in that bloodbath two days ago, that she should take all the rewards; Vlasenin, his papers – and the three Englishmen."

"Naturally." Ziedler's face and voice still registered no emotion. "It makes your coup so much the more complete. And to arrive in Berlin with a trio of minor SOE agents instead of ultimate victory would be worse than arriving with nothing at all."

Ciarelli eyed him with suspicion. "You mean you'll let me have them?"

"Well, I presume you have a threat poised which will be so terrible as to override all my natural – and reasonable – objections. So please tell me. But first let me tell you," now he too leaned forward and his voice was cold, "it had better be a good one."

Ciarelli sat back, smiling again. "Oh, it is. What do you imagine the reaction would be if half a dozen bombs went off tomorrow, throughout Italy? Say, for instance, in Il Duce's palace in Rome; St Mark's Square in Venice; the Uffizi Gallery in Florence; in Milan and Naples too; and in the heart of the Vatican. Not really Italy, I know, but still a place held dear by my countrymen. And what do you imagine my countrymen would think if, after these atrocities, evidence was found linking them to German intelligence? Of a plot to bully Italy into handing over a high-profile prisoner of war and his vital secrets?"

Ziedler was silent for a long moment. Then he spoke slowly and calmly, only the film of sweat on his brow and the trembling of his hands on the desk betraying his thoughts. "It would arouse the hatred of every Italian soldier and civilian. Mussolini would have every right to dissolve the Axis. There would be violence wherever German and Italian troops were stationed side by side."

"And we would have justification for taking our prisoner back – or ensuring he never reaches Berlin," Ciarelli said softly. "This may be extreme range for the British and Russian air forces, Ziedler, but not ours. That train would never reach Sofia, let alone Berlin."

Ziedler did not seem to have heard him. "The rest of the civilised world would be outraged. The Vatican bomb would set every Catholic country against us. Spain would be lost forever as a potential ally, her Blue Division in Russia would probably mutiny. As would our Croat and Hungarian allies. Maybe even our own men, from the Catholic provinces. And of course Italy would be justified in pulling out of the war. No more support for our troops in North Africa, no passage for them from the Italian mainland. Half of our Balkan conquests would have to be re-garrisoned – or abandoned."

"Too terrible to even think about, eh?" Ciarelli gloated. "With Vlasenin you may have reason to think the war is won. If those bombs go off tomorrow you will certainly lose. You would go under too quickly for his knowledge to be of use. Even assuming you could get him to Germany."

"And you would risk all that?" For the first time since

Ciarelli had known him, Ziedler seemed completely dumbfounded. "Destroy your own country's heritage, shed your countrymen's blood? Have you higher authority?"

"Oh, yes," Ciarelli exulted. "My superiors know of my plan and have approved it. Not in writing, of course. And the explosions will be staged so that the damage will be minimal and casualties almost non-existent. But we will make it look convincing enough for the newsreels. The Axis will be destroyed but we will survive. We came into this war on a whim and we have nowhere near as much blood on our hands as you. We will be able to negotiate a peace; you will not. The western allies will forgive us; we have been a small part of the attack on Russia and America we have hardly encountered at all. Britain will fall into line to avoid further complications. They will allow Il Duce to remain. If they can condone Franco they can condone him. They did for eighteen years. They will probably honour him for helping to bring Germany down.

"For we will, Ziedler." He leaned forward again. "Make no mistake, we will. Unless I get my way. And truly, where is the harm in it? We have the papers already, you agreed that. If we take the man as well you will have the fruits of his knowledge – in due course. An Axis victory, as was always intended, or a German defeat. The choice is yours."

Ziedler steadied his hands on the desk. "It seems I have no choice. Very well, I accept. When do you want him handed over?"

"Midnight tonight. At the town hall. Neutral ground. My men take him – with the English – and head straight to the train station. Our train is to be ready to go the minute we arrive. Any tricks, any attempt to contact Berlin, and those bombs go off. Clear?"

"Perfectly," Ziedler said, then sank back in his chair. He seemed to shrivel in upon himself, incapable of movement or speech. After a few moments Ciarelli stood up and raised his brandy glass. "To partnership, then – and victory."

☙

"Move, Englishman, on your feet." The light in Rawlings' quarters flicked on, blinding him. Soldiers were all around him, jostling him out of the bed and throwing his clothes at him. "Get dressed," a voice ordered in the same English. He looked round. Leutnant Weiss was standing by the doorway, pistol out. The four guards with him stood back as Rawlings finished dressing, Schmeissers levelled at him the whole time. "Come – now," Weiss ordered as he tied his boots and stood up. Immediately a pair of handcuffs was slapped on his wrists, then the whole procession moved out and down the corridor in double time.

Well, this is it, Rawlings thought. A few hours' torture to try to get something out of us, then a bullet one way or the other. He had spent most of the preceding day lying on his bed weighing up Ziedler's options. The Abwehr man had obviously realised how dangerous having three British agents on the train with Vlasenin would be. So Hoffman gets the chance he's been waiting for and then… he tried not to think of the 'then'. There was no point. The train would roll with three fewer passengers and any hope for the mission would lie with the sergeants and Stavrakis. He could see the logic in Ziedler's actions. He would have done the same.

He looked at his watch. Quarter to midnight. A good time. He had been asleep for nearly two hours, sufficiently deep sleep for him still to be disoriented. The other two would no doubt be the same. He forced himself to wake up and focus. If he was to resist Hoffman he needed to be strong and alert. For all the good it would do in the end.

They were at the main door now, out into the street where an Opel truck stood, tarpaulin up and motor running. Weiss joined the driver in the cab as the four guards bundled Rawlings into the back. Another dozen or so German soldiers were already in the rear. With them was Ziedler, as well as Mayhew, Curtis and Vlasenin. All the prisoners were handcuffed. All looked as puzzled as Rawlings felt. He turned to Ziedler. "Keep quiet and do as you're told, major," the Abwehr man said. "And don't bother to ask any questions."

He banged his fist twice on the partition of the truck's cab and they set off. Ziedler and the rest of the Germans stayed silent for the duration of the trip, which was a matter of a few minutes. As the truck halted Ziedler gave a wordless signal and four men gestured for the prisoners to disembark then followed them out of the truck like second shadows, close enough to ensure escape was impossible, far enough away to ensure resistance was equally so. These were the last of the Brandenburgers, Rawlings guessed. He knew better than to try anything. The cuffs rendered resistance suicidal and he had not even thought of escape. This was not the prelude to torture, he guessed; no sign of Hoffman for one thing. He had no idea what it might be, but a part of him was curious to find out.

They were in front of a tall, ornate building, lit only by the occasional moonlight glinting through the clouds. Despite that Rawlings recognised it as the town hall. They had passed by it on the way in yesterday morning. He was still puzzled. Then he saw the Italian army truck that had been with them, now parked outside, and his mind began working at last.

Two guards led the way up the steps to the main entrance, two behind prodding the prisoners on with their Schmeisser barrels. Ziedler and Weiss brought up the rear of the procession. As the guards opened the large oaken double doors and moved in Rawlings whispered to the other three: "I think this is some sort of trade-off. When the shooting starts, drop to the floor and stay there until it's over."

"You think there'll be shooting?" Curtis asked in a whisper.

"I'd bet good money on it – if I thought I could find someone to bet against. But I think both sides still want to keep us all alive, and…" his guard cut him short with a gun barrel jab to the ribs. Rawlings took the hint and kept quiet as Ziedler and Weiss moved through the doorway, closing the doors behind them.

They were in the main entrance hall now, a high-ceilinged, marble-floored eminence with stairways leading up to galleries on either side, running the length of the hall. The only light came from two hooded lanterns on the floor before them, and every window had heavy blackout curtains over it, casting the galleries into gloom and giving the whole scene a sepulchral glow. But there was still enough light to make out the figure of Ciarelli, smiling in welcome as he puffed on the inevitable Toscani. He too was flanked by four of his SIM guards in *Alpini* uniforms, Beretta machine-carbines levelled at the German party.

"Did you bring everything I asked?" Ciarelli called.

"As you can see," Ziedler replied.

The Italian nodded in satisfaction. "Send them to me – slowly."

"Any minute now," Rawlings whispered as the guards motioned them forward. They began to move. Ciarelli and his men were perhaps ten yards away. When the prisoners had covered half that distance Ziedler suddenly asked: "What guarantee do I have that those bombs won't go off, anyway?"

The prisoners stopped dead. Ciarelli's smile broadened as he replied: "The best guarantee in the world, Ziedler; they don't exist."

If he had expected shock or fear to appear on the German's face he was disappointed. Instead Ziedler laughed and pointed a finger at him, like one American vaudeville comedian to another. "Trust you, Eduardo," he said with affection. "Or rather, don't. But I'm sorry to spoil your surprise, Signor Colonel – I already found that out."

Ciarelli's smile vanished. "What do you mean?"

"You said no contact with Berlin – you never said anything about Rome, or the Vatican City. You know the Abwehr has some real agents working there, too, not just the ones in your faked evidence. I must admit that our penetration there is not as good as it should be. But after your coup in finding Vlasenin's whereabouts we decided to cultivate the man who obviously supplies you with information from the Vatican – and their Soviet contacts. I forget his real name but I believe you know him as 'Rodrigo'.

Ciarelli's mouth gaped in astonishment. "He's ours, damn it. SIM. Always has been."

Ziedler shook his head. "Until now. We gave a financial incentive to switch horses. You really should pay your men better, Eduardo, especially ones as good as him. Two senior contacts in Soviet intelligence as well as scores of others. He had been told nothing of any bomb. And if the Vatican one was a bluff I deduced that the others must be too. I had suspected it from the start. 'Rodrigo' confirmed it. So I'll have my prisoners back, please."

Ciarelli's gaze darted up to the balconies. Ziedler shook his head again. "I'm afraid your sharpshooters aren't up there any more. Well, they are, but not in any state to help you. Mine, on the other hand…"

Two men on each balcony moved out of the shadows. The rest of the Brandenburgers, Rawlings guessed. Each had a Mauser sniper's rifle with telescopic sight trained on the Italian party. Ciarelli's shoulders slumped as Ziedler continued. "As soon as you left, I had my men take up position here. They were waiting when you sent yours up. You should have double-checked before we arrived, Eduardo. But you were so pleased with yourself that you forgot basic security; so convinced you had trumped me at last. Perhaps you even thought I would be so desperate to keep Vlasenin that I would try to resist and your men could shoot me down. You could no doubt invent some tale of betrayal that had left you no choice, to satisfy your superiors and mine. But did you never think that Hoffman and Dorsch might have other ideas? Do you even know where they are now?"

Ciarelli made no reply. His head was shaking like that of an automaton. Ziedler continued: "They are at your quarters, disarming the rest of your men – I hope with the minimum of violence – and acquiring Vlasenin's papers." Ziedler sighed. "If you had been content to return to Italy with them, I would have reluctantly let you. But you had to try to trick us one last time. You failed. Once I inform Berlin, and Rome, of what you have done there will be no possible objection raised to my taking everything back with me, since the SIM clearly cannot be trusted. Ame, Ciano, Il Duce himself – they will have to accede. But I do not wish to antagonise them more than is necessary. So drop your gun, Eduardo. All of your men, too. We will put you under guard until our train leaves. After that you can return to Rome. What they will do with you, I know not. But here I give you my word; put down your guns and you can live."

The prisoners dropped to the floor. Ciarelli gave one last wild look around and drew his pistol, diving to the right as he did so. The movement ensured the sniper assigned to him did not make a clean kill. The bullet took him high on the chest, not in the heart. But it still lifted him off his feet and flung him five yards backwards. He hit the marble floor hard, pistol spinning from his grasp. The four guards hit the floor with him, but they were all dead. Three from sniper fire, one from a Schmeisser burst by the guard nearest to Rawlings. The other three moved up, Ziedler and Weiss behind, shielding the prisoners.

As they watched in amazement, Ciarelli rose to his

feet. His knees buckled as the blood poured from his chest, but he stayed upright. He saw his pistol and made a move to pick it up. This time the sniper's shot was straight through the heart. Ciarelli fell to the ground without a cry and lay still. Weiss moved cautiously towards him at a nod from Ziedler, knelt beside him and turned him over. After a moment he looked up and round at Ziedler. "He's dead, Herr Oberst."

"Well, there's a surprise," Rawlings said as he scrambled awkwardly to his feet. "And it couldn't have happened to a nicer person."

"Be quiet," Ziedler said irritably as his snipers moved down from the galleries and the guards hauled the other three to their feet. The Abwehr man was standing over Ciarelli's body, looking down intently.

"I thought you'd be happier, now you've finally got rid of him."

"There will be others like him," Ziedler said as he turned round. "All full of comic opera bravado and petulant resentment at Germany's status and power. And his death will cause all kinds of recriminations, at diplomatic and operational level. This whole charade was an unnecessary complication and a dangerous waste of time. Vlasenin could easily have taken a bullet – so might any of you."

"I'm touched by your concern," Rawlings replied and Ziedler allowed himself a thin smile. "I suppose it does mean I will never have to smell those vile cigars of his again. And if Hoffman and Dorsch have done their job we will leave Greece with more than we expected – the papers."

"You always need something to read on a long train

journey, don't you?" Rawlings said as the guards opened the doors and gestured for the prisoners to start walking again. "So the man, the papers and us – all on the same train. I suppose you know the old English saying about putting all your eggs in one basket."

"I do indeed, major." Ziedler's smile vanished. "And I believe Mark Twain had the best answer to it: 'Put all your eggs in one basket – and watch that basket'!"

∽

The Brandenburger detail was surrounding the prisoners again twelve hours later as they emerged from the German HQ. Ziedler walked ahead, with Weiss and Hoffman flanking him. Dorsch had been assigned the task of checking security along the route; Hoffman's second Gestapo adjutant, a burly tough named Schmidt who had somehow squeezed his boxer's bulk into a captain's uniform, was the fourth officer, ensuring that each prisoner had a personal guard. The detail was preceded by a platoon of picked troops from the local garrison. Two more platoons waited in a fleet of trucks, Kubelwagens and armoured cars that would escort the prisoners to the train station. Two staff cars had been placed dead centre in it. Rawlings found himself in one with Vlasenin, Ziedler, Weiss and two guards. Hoffman had the papers in the second, with Schmidt and two more guards watching Curtis and Mayhew.

"Be careful," Ziedler said to the Gestapo man as they boarded the cars. Hoffman looked at him with contempt. "They'll be all right now. After you nearly fucked things up in the mountains, both our heads would have been on the block. So I'll keep all of them safe – and when we get to Berlin I'll make the SOE boys share a few secrets with us, too." He threw himself into his seat and slammed the door on Ziedler.

There were troops lining every street around them, snipers on every balcony and rooftop around. Planes circled overhead and as they drove past the harbour area Rawlings could see a flotilla of E-boats, destroyers and cruisers spread out across the bay. As the convoy pulled to a halt inside the station, Rawlings saw a huge armoured train, of the type used on the Russian Front, being boarded by four men wearing identical clothes to the prisoners. The prisoners themselves were ushered to a smaller platform, where stood an ordinary passenger train, and the troops began to board. Rawlings found himself next to the other three again as Ziedler led them to a well-appointed carriage in the centre. As they walked on Curtis whispered: "I hope this doesn't sound like a cracked record, sir, but how the hell do we get out of this one?"

Rawlings looked at him. "At the moment, I haven't the faintest idea."

༄

Three hours later, he was forced to admit, his response would have been exactly the same. They were making slow but steady progress up through the forests and hills that marked the very easternmost limits of Greece. The setting sun was sparking fire on the snow-capped tips of the Rhodope in the distance. It seemed inconceivable that just a few days ago they had been moving through those mountains as free men. And equally incredible that it had been over two weeks since they had first entered Greece with Amarazov. To Rawlings that time seemed both an instant and a lifetime away.

But now it was late afternoon on Tuesday, December 8th, 1942. Ziedler, seated opposite Rawlings at the end of one of two long, velvet-upholstered rows of seats that faced each other, was leafing through a copy of the Wehrmacht magazine *Signal*. Reading between the lines, he could tell that Stalingrad was going badly and that Alamein had truly been the death blow for Rommel's men in North Africa. But he knew he had that in his possession which would render those reversals immaterial.

Vlasenin's papers were in the briefcase between his feet, and the man himself was seated next to Rawlings, under Hoffman's watchful eye. Schmidt and Weiss discharged the same duty on Curtis and Mayhew. There were two more guards stationed at the door of the carriage, and a further two patrolling the corridor. Two men manned each of the platforms connecting their carriage to the ones in front and behind. They regularly climbed up to the roofs to check for intruders, despite the fact that the curved metal allowed virtually no purchase. There were sentries at each tunnel, and every tunnel had been checked in advance for explosives. Fighter planes circled overhead and convoys shadowed the train wherever a road ran parallel. Dorsch, now waiting to join them at the Bulgarian border, had done his job well.

Yet it was impossible to have an escort for all of the journey, and at the moment the train was twisting slowly along a steep stretch, encountering frequent tunnels blasted through the rock. At the entrance to one they were waved through by the four-man detail and the train passed by too quickly in the gathering dusk to notice the faces under the helmets, or the bodies of the real detail dumped in a nearby ditch with their throats slashed. All along the tunnel other men lay in wait; Mikos' men.

Rawlings knew nothing of this, but he guessed that if any rescue were to come it must come soon. Darkness was almost upon them and the train was as far from any German back-up as it would ever get. So he asked to use the toilet once the train had cleared the tunnel. The routine had never varied on any of the previous occasions and it did not now. One of the guards on the door checked the corridor outside before nodding in satisfaction. The other drew a pistol and motioned Rawlings out of the carriage. Once outside the guard checked that each sentry was in position at either end of the corridor before motioning Rawlings forward. Rawlings had no idea what he could do, but rendering himself free would at least be a start.

The WC was at the rear end of the carriage, just before the door that gave access to the platform and the two troop cars beyond that made up the end of the train. The guard kept a safe distance behind Rawlings all the way, pistol pointing at the centre of his spine. As they reached the door, the guard gestured Rawlings to stay back while he opened and checked inside, pistol still on his charge despite the sentries' presence. Satisfied, he moved back into the corridor, one hand reaching for the handcuff keys. As he produced them from his pocket the sentry behind lunged forward and looped a garrotte around his neck.

The guard's face contorted and his nerveless fingers relaxed their grip on gun and keys. The sound of their hitting the floor was drowned by the roar and rattle of the train. Rawlings scooped up the keys and quickly freed his hands. Then he grabbed the pistol, whirling round at a sound from behind. The other sentry was standing over him, but his Schmeisser was shouldered and he had both hands out in front of him, palms open. Behind them the guard's struggles ended. The sentry released him and stepped forward. "Sorry we took so long, sir."

"I'll forgive you, Colour-Sergeant Sanderson. Are the other two all right?"

"Indeed they are, Major Rawlings," the second sentry surprised him by speaking in English. "Colour-Sergeant Rowley is in the locomotive, making sure we keep chugging along for the moment. And Private Stavrakis – well, let's bring him in."

He gestured to the two German troops on the rear platform of the carriage. They moved in quickly, taking off their helmets. One of them was indeed Stavrakis, the other a lean, tough-looking Greek with a broad scar running down his left cheek. "This is Katsoulis, second-in-command to Major Mikos," the second sentry said. Rawlings started and the pistol came up, but Sanderson put a hand on his arm. "It's all right, sir – a long story, but they're on our side."

"And they've pretty much taken the train over for you, major, so cut them a bit of slack," the second sentry said. "I'm Captain Watson, and I'm…"

"…a helping hand from Davies." Rawlings finished the sentence with a smile. "Well, I won't say you're not welcome. Right – so the plan is to get the lads out of the carriage without a sound, then jump for it?"

"Yes, sir," Watson replied. "Meanwhile we uncouple

everything behind it. Send the rear carriages back down the slope while the men in the loco get the front lot far enough away from us, then ditch them too. Unless you want to play it different?"

Rawlings shook his head. "Better than anything I've managed to dream up," he said sincerely. "But we need to move fast. They'll get suspicious any second now. Watson, you and Sanderson come with me. Have you got silenced pistols?" Each man drew one, then Watson produced another from his tunic and handed it to Rawlings, who nodded in satisfaction. "Stavrakis, you and Scarface here keep the men in position at either end of the carriage. You see anyone but us coming from anywhere, shoot them. Clear?"

Both Greeks nodded and took up position. "There's a guard on the door, plus four officers in the carriage – all armed and dangerous. Watson, you're the same build as my guard; get me through the doorway, then we take the other one. Sanderson, you follow me in and cover them."

They were at the door now. Rawlings looped the handcuffs over his wrist and signalled to Watson to knock three times. The second guard opened the door. He looked at Rawlings, then Watson and his eyes widened. Rawlings smashed the handcuffs into his face, the momentum carrying them into the carriage. Watson and Sanderson followed him in, silenced pistols out to cover the startled Germans as Rawlings looped the handcuffs round the guard's neck like a garrotte. There was a brief struggle, then he went limp.

Rawlings released the body and drew his pistol, pointing it at Ziedler, who was leaning back in his seat, hands obscured by his dropped magazine. "Think I didn't spot the buzzer in the seat arm, Ulrich?" Rawlings said in a conversational tone. "Less obvious than pulling the cord, I grant you. Move away from it, and let's see your hands in plain sight. That goes for the rest of you. Not a sound, and not a move. Curtis, let's get everyone free."

Curtis was ahead of him, clumsily yanking the keys from Schmidt's pocket while Sanderson covered him. Once he was free, he worked more quickly, setting Vlasenin and Mayhew at liberty within seconds. "Right, let's have every non-Nazi bastard out of the carriage," said Rawlings. Then he turned back to Ziedler. "And I'll have that briefcase too."

Ziedler had made no movement to obey Rawlings' instructions. Now he looked him in the eye, calm as ever. "No."

"I'll kill you all if you don't do as I say – now!"

"You wouldn't do that, major. Not in cold blood."

"Try me."

Ziedler held his gaze for a moment, then said: "Very well." His hands moved down to the briefcase. There was a muted clicking sound and when his hands came up a sleeve cable had launched a tiny automatic into his right palm. He got off one shot that took Watson between the eyes, then he was diving at Curtis, his other hand slamming into the buzzer.

Rawlings tried to get a bead on him, but Hoffman launched himself across the carriage, under Rawlings' gun arm. The impact slammed them both against the carriage wall as a mad melee broke out. Weiss dived for Sanderson but the sergeant was still on his feet with time to aim. Weiss took the bullet straight in the heart but he unsighted Sanderson long enough for Schmidt to grab his legs and send him crashing to the floor. He was up again straight away, grabbing the Gestapo man and slamming him against the rear of the seats.

Curtis pushed Vlasenin to the ground, then turned as Ziedler sprang on him. The automatic was a single-shot but Ziedler used it as a knuckle-duster, hitting Curtis square on the temple. Curtis groaned and fell to his knees. Ziedler tried to draw his Luger but Sanderson saw him from the corner of his eye. Killing Schmidt with one blow to the throat he grabbed Ziedler from behind, twisting his arm to make him drop the Luger, then swinging him round and grabbing his throat with the other. The struggle between the two giants was brief. Ziedler broke the throat hold with his free hand, but Sanderson rammed an elbow under his neck and slammed his head against the carriage wall. Once. Twice. On the third, Ziedler groaned and went limp.

Rawlings saw all this as Hoffman grabbed his gun arm with his left hand and clasped Rawlings' throat with his metal one. Rawlings felt a terrible pressure as the Gestapo man squeezed. He almost blacked out but at that moment Mayhew grabbed Hoffman's coat and hauled him off. As the two men fell into the corridor a blade gleamed in Hoffman's left hand. Hoffman rose to his feet, pushing Mayhew away. Mayhew stayed down. Rawlings looked down as he stumbled from the carriage, and saw the huge crimson stain on Mayhew's chest. Black rage in his heart, he went after Hoffman.

There was firing outside, from both directions along the train. Katsoulis was down, and Mikos' other two men had been shot from the platform connecting to the rear of the train. At the other end Stavrakis turned from his post as he saw the brawl spill out from the carriage. He tried to draw a bead on Hoffman as he rose, but Rawlings blocked his aim as he chased Hoffman. Stavrakis turned back – and took a bullet in the chest as the German troops, alerted by the buzzer like their comrades. charged up from the front carriages. They were at the door now, Rawlings in their sights. But as they took aim Curtis dived from the compartment, under their gun sights, rolling and firing prone. He squeezed off an entire clip of Ziedler's Luger, killing two men and forcing the rest back into cover. Then Sanderson joined in, standing over him, firing his Schmeisser, covering Rawlings as he caught up with Hoffman.

The German was almost on the platform, but he turned as he heard Rawlings charge up behind him. He swung the knife in a wide, vicious stroke, but Rawlings got under it, grabbing the knife arm in one hand, blocking Hoffman's metal hand with the other. Rawlings smashed the arm through the window. Hoffman cried out and the knife span away into the darkness. Rawlings tried to work the wrist onto the shattered glass, aiming to sever the artery. But Hoffman managed to land a breath-robbing gut punch, winding Rawlings. The Gestapo man grabbed Rawlings' jacket and slammed him against the wall, then threw him out onto the platform.

Rawlings hit the metal railing with an impact that drove what little breath he had left out of his body. His knees buckled but he kept upright as Hoffman advanced, black coat billowing behind him in the wind, eyes ablaze with the desire to kill. He got in one perfect right cross that knocked Rawlings to the floor, head and upper body over the edge of the platform as the ground streamed by just a few feet away. Hoffman raised a foot to stamp down on him, but Rawlings got a hand to it and pushed him back to the other platform edge. Hoffman used his metal arm to grab the railing for balance and fumbled in his coat pocket, drawing the Mauser he had taken back from Rawlings.

With the last of his strength Rawlings kicked out and up, catching Hoffman in the groin. As he doubled over, dropping the pistol, Rawlings had one precious second to rise to his feet. Then he simply charged at Hoffman, left shoulder first, elbows out. Hoffman looked up in amazement, then Rawlings' left elbow connected full in his face, every ounce of his weight behind it. The impact flung Hoffman from the platform, tearing the metal arm from its socket and the railing as his final scream vanished behind him into the night.

Rawlings almost followed him over, but he grabbed at the rail for support and flung himself back onto the platform. He fell to the floor but forced himself to rise up again. There were Germans at the window of the next carriage. They had been unsighted by Hoffman but now they took aim. Grabbing the Mauser, Rawlings loosed off four quick shots, forcing them to duck for cover. He dived back into the corridor. Slamming the connecting door behind him, he saw Curtis and Sanderson still holding the Germans at bay at the door of Ziedler's compartment, Vlasenin next to them.

He shouted to Curtis: "Move, I'll cover you!", then squeezed off shot after shot at the doorway to the front carriage. There were no targets but he prayed it would keep their heads down. Sanderson came out first, firing his

Schmeisser from the hip, shielding Curtis and Vlasenin as they ran up the corridor to the platform.

Curtis opened the connecting door carefully, body shielding Vlasenin – and the air was instantly alive with bullets from the troops in the rear carriage. Rawlings whirled round and joined him, firing the rest of the Mauser's clip off, forcing them into cover. But neutralising that danger left Sanderson exposed. As he neared the door one of the Germans from the front carriage rolled in a smoke grenade. The blast impact knocked Sanderson off his feet and as he rose again a German soldier dived into the carriage and fired a Schmeisser burst from the prone position. It caught Sanderson full in the chest. As Curtis screamed "No!" and turned back, killing the German and two more who had tried to follow him into the carriage, Sanderson rolled over and tried to rise. Then he fell back to the floor and lay still.

The carriage was full of smoke, blinding friend and foe alike, Rawlings slammed in a new clip, loosed off two more snap shots at the rear carriage then bent double over Sanderson. He looked up at Curtis and shook his head. Curtis had his pistol levelled but there were no targets and no firing for the moment. Rawlings saw that the smoke was billowing out onto the platform, blinding the Germans in the rear carriage. He looked at Curtis, who nodded and took Vlasenin's free hand in his. Rawlings grabbed the other. Rawlings shouted to Vlasenin above the roar of the speeding train: "We jump – now! And for God's sake don't break your neck!"

"Not after all this," the Russian replied, face fearful but set in determination. Rawlings nodded. "Right – one-two-three!" The three of them ran on to the platform, jumped together, hit an embankment hard, then rolled down a long slope. By the time they got to their feet the train was far in the distance. But Rawlings still scanned the darkness for any sign of the enemy. "Surely nobody else would have jumped, sir," Curtis said as he helped a winded Vlasenin to his feet. "I'm amazed we're still in one piece."

"Not from the train, maybe. But there'll be patrols all around here, and they'll get a message to the escort." A noise in the trees made him whirl round. A group of half a dozen men were in front of him, led by a small, dark figure in British battledress. "Sergeant Jennings, sir – I came in with Captain Watson. We were supposed to meet you further down the line, but we heard the firing. Are you all right?"

Rawlings nodded wearily. "Yes, Sarn't – but Watson's dead, and the rest of the men who were with him. The plan didn't work out. If there's a guide among you who can get us to Turkey then put him on the scent straight away."

Jennings nodded and turned to the leader of the partisan section. As Rawlings moved to join them, Curtis asked: "What about Rowley, sir? And the rest of the men on the train?"

In the darkness it was impossible to see the expression on Rawlings' face. "They have to take their chances. Get the train as far as possible from us, then uncouple it – those were the orders, and I know Rowley will follow them to the letter. I just hope he gets clear and makes for the border too. But we've got a mission to finish, and we're going to do it. So let's get moving."

Rowley knew things had gone wrong when he heard the firing break out. Then the partisans started jumping from the platforms of the front carriages. He looked at Gerasimos, the only other man in the engine cabin. There had been two more in the party that had taken the cab, but they had died as the German guards, and the driver and fireman, had fought in vain for their lives. Gerasimos had taken a wound to the shoulder, and he winced as he forced the throttle ever further open and the train sped on and on. He was a plump, middle-aged man, the only one of Mikos' group who knew how to drive a train. He looked very scared.

"I don't know what's going on," Rowley said. "I hope the major's got everyone clear. But I can't be sure. The orders were to keep her going until we saw a signal. But… they wanted us to get further away from the ambush point. I know it. If it's failed, then it doesn't matter, anyway, I suppose. But if they're on the run we've got to keep this train going, otherwise all the boys on board can get after them."

Gerasimos nodded. "It is a level stretch. The train might just stop dead – no crash, no bang. And if we jump, they have time to bring her under control."

"Then we keep her going."

The Greek shrugged. "Then we will die. They will be coming for us even now."

Rowley unslung his Sten. "They might not try climbing over the coal, and that's the only way onto here. I'll hear them a mile off. If I can keep them away until we hit a steep stretch…" he tailed off as he saw the fear in Gerasimos' eyes. "But I can't make you do it. I've never given a civilian an order in my life. If you want to jump now, jump. Just show me how to keep her going first."

Gerasimos looked a him for a long time, then sighed. "That is a job for a railwayman, not a soldier. You just keep feeding her." He gestured to the shovel by the furnace and smiled a sad smile. Rowley smiled back and grabbed the shovel.

It was a few minutes before the Germans tried anything and Rowley did indeed hear them long before they were any threat. It was impossible to climb over the coal stack in silence, even with the engine roar at its height. Rowley kept stoking until the last moment then jumped back, grabbing the Sten. He raked a long burst across the top of the stack and four Germans fell screaming over the sides to left and right. Rowley looked at Gerasimos, nodded in satisfaction, then got back to stoking.

But there had been five Germans on the stack. Hans Bartel, an ordinary private from the Alexandroupoli garrison, had ducked down flat as his comrades died. Now he did not know what to do. The corporal in charge had died too, and was not from his unit anyway. Until a few days ago, he had been resting with his comrades from a tour in Russia. Train guard duty was the last thing he had expected. But he had been mentioned in dispatches once or twice and that had been enough to select him. Now all he knew was that the prisoners must be loose and, unless they got control of the locomotive, they could not be tracked down.

He knew the Greek bandits below would hear him if he tried stealth again. So he simply grabbed his Schmeisser and launched himself at the lip of the stack, firing wildly. The first burst caught Gerasimos full in the back. He fell over the controls, and died instantly. Bartel jumped down onto the platform as Rowley sprang back, grabbing for the Sten. Bartel had landed badly, on his knees, but as Rowley turned he got off another burst, riding up from stomach to chest. Rowley was slammed back against the boiler but he kept firing, killing Bartel and punching him off the platform into the night.

The boiler scorched against Rowley's back and he fell to the floor. He tried to rise, but his body failed him at last. He looked across at Gerasimos, still straddling the levers. The train was still going fast. But then it hit a gradient and came to a stop, then slid back down, gathering speed again. Rowley simply lay there and waited, the smell and taste of smoke reminding him of childhood journeys. And he died just before the crash that killed so many more in the unknowing ranks, who died because of a man they had never known and whose knowledge they could never understand.

Vlasenin heard the crash, and the explosion, along with Rawlings and the rest as they moved further into the hills. "Maybe they jumped clear," Curtis said.

"Then they know where the rendezvous is, and the deadline for getting there," Rawlings replied in a neutral tone. But inside he thought bitterly: another one for the VC, posthumous. Sanderson should get one too, and every man who took that train and held it for us. Mikos' men, the black marketeers, the ones they had trusted the least. And the ones who were left had done their job well, too. There were German patrols everywhere, heading for the railway line, but Jennings' group had avoided them all, finding this secret path and driving on and up at a punishing pace. But now they were slowing down.

Rawlings looked round and saw that Jennings and the two scouts patrolling wide on each side had come in to join the main group. Some of the others were even shouldering their guns. "What's all this?" he shouted to Jennings.

Jennings turned to him with an apologetic look. "Sorry, sir, you're right, there's still danger, of course. But I meant to tell you – that last push got us across the border. For the past half a mile we've been in Turkey."

☙

By late evening the group was well inside Turkish territory. But there was to be no rest that night. As Jennings explained, and Rawlings remembered from his entry with Amarazov just a few miles south, this was wild country; sparsely populated and hostile. It had not been unknown for German forces to pursue fugitives far beyond the frontier, citing the lack of clear border points, for much less pressing reasons than Rawlings and his party afforded. So it was a relief when they reached the rendezvous point on a stretch of rough road near a remote village. Here a battered pre-war truck supplied by another of the SOE's contact groups in Turkey, mobilised by Watson and Jennings on their way through, was waiting.

The SOE team said goodbye to their partisan escort there. They would wait until the German activity on the border had died down, Jennings explained, and make their way back in secret. No doubt with a truckload of black market produce, Rawlings reflected. But they had fulfilled their part of the bargain, he had to admit, and their immediate future – several days of lying low at one of Mikos' safe houses in the village – looked much more attractive than his.

For the danger was still prevalent. Although the truck was taking them further and further into Turkey, beyond the point at which the Germans could risk a pursuit by uniformed troops, Rawlings knew that the SD and Abwehr had extensive networks along the border. And whether Ziedler was alive or not, someone would set them in motion. It was those networks that had planted the rumour about Rawlings and his party on their arrival in Turkey, he felt sure. And the complications arising from that had rendered any thought of approaching the Turkish authorities out of the question.

So the answer, as Davies explained when Rawlings used the radio transmitter in the back of the truck to broadcast to Cairo, was to get out of Turkey as quickly and legitimately as possible. To that end SOE in Istanbul had arranged for a private charter flight out of an airfield near Edirne the next night. In the meantime, hotel rooms had been booked for Vlasenin and the three SOE men in a small town nearby. They would lie low all day and at dusk a car would come to pick them up and take them to the airfield.

"In the meantime, sir, there's not much to do except wait," Jennings said as they dumped their belongings onto the four beds in the bare but functional room on the top floor of the shabby *pensione* that de Chastelain had selected. Like the other three, Jennings was now wearing ordinary civilian clothes, another treasure that the truck had yielded. They were authentically shabby travelling suits and made the quartet look as inconspicuous as any obviously European men could in such surroundings. Fortunately, the towns on the outskirts of old Adrianople still had a more cosmopolitan feel than the rest of Balkan Turkey. But Rawlings still felt unduly exposed. "Isn't there any way we could get out of Turkey quicker?" he asked as he hid Vlasenin's briefcase under a prised-up floorboard. "And where we wouldn't stand out so much?"

"Sorry, sir – orders from Cairo," Jennings replied. "Normally we'd whistle you down to a *caique* on the coast – the Turkish navy's pretty lax when it comes to letting our boys in and out – but the Jerries have still got everything that can float posted all the way down the Aegean. Just outside of territorial waters but close enough to spot us and bag us two minutes later. We'd have to run a gauntlet all the way down to Cyprus. This way you'll be in Cairo by tomorrow morning. Meantime, why not get some sleep? I'll keep a close eye out. Besides, even if they find us, there's a limit to what they can try in a neutral country."

"That's probably what the little piggies thought in their houses of wood and straw, Sergeant Jennings. Believe me, the men who want what we've got won't worry about blowing this little lot down."

~

As the buzzer sounded in the anteroom to Admiral Canaris' office in Tirpitz Ufer, Ziedler got to his feet unsteadily and opened the door with some difficulty. His right arm was in a sling and his left severely bruised. Multiple cuts and lacerations crisscrossed his body. His broken left ankle dragged and he leaned heavily on his cane as he limped into his superior's office. It hurt like hell every time he moved and yet he knew he had been lucky.

Most of the men on that train had not survived. He would not have if some of the escort troops, rushing in on hearing the crash, had not pulled him from the wreckage of his carriage just before fire consumed it. They had taken him to the nearest garrison town, where he had made the most humiliating telephone call of his entire career. A sleepless night and a flight back to Berlin in the morning, the first one out from Unterbrecht's hastily-repaired supply base since the bombing raids, had ensued. And now here he was, walking up to the Admiral's desk. Bormann and Himmler flanked Canaris in high-backed chairs. All three wore identical expressions, like a trio of presiding magistrates surveying the village malefactor. Ziedler gave the Nazi salute with the wrong arm and lowered himself slowly into the chair in front of the desk.

Each of the three had a copy of his report, typed the previous evening and couriered with him to Berlin. Himmler held up his copy. "We have been studying this closely while we waited to summon you, Herr Oberst," he said in his dry, level tone. "I for one have been trying to find some explanation or mitigating circumstance for this catalogue of incompetence. I confess I can find none."

He set the report down, then took off his pince-nez and rubbed his eyes. "I did my duty as I saw fit, Herr Reichsfuhrer," Ziedler replied. "I made every effort to secure Doctor Vlasenin."

"If wars were won by effort – and good intentions –

Germany would have prevailed long ago without need of Vlasenin," Bormann said. "We required more of you, Herr Oberst. We were led to believe you could provide it." He looked at Canaris. "And we were proved wrong."

"I think it only fair to say that Oberst Ziedler was hampered throughout by the actions of Colonel Ciarelli and the SIM in general," Canaris replied.

"And he killed Colonel Ciarelli because of it!" Bormann snapped back. "And absconded with the papers we had promised to Italy. I can understand his actions in that respect; if he had brought both safely back here, nothing more would need to be said. As it is… the diplomatic repercussions and the implications of our future relations with Il Duce can only be guessed at. That episode is not to be mentioned again, for reward or punishment."

Ziedler had the uncomfortable feeling that they had forgotten he was there – and that the meeting was merely the prelude to a death sentence. "I accept that I have failed you all badly," he said. "But I believe it is not too late. I have received intelligence from Abwehr sources in Turkey as to their whereabouts and I believe if I could go there and take charge of…"

He tailed off. All three were looking at him as though he were mad. "I hardly think that would be appropriate, Herr Oberst," Bormann said. "Or practical, given your physical condition. Rest assured, intelligence has been received from many sources regarding the fugitives. The most concrete has come from an SD contact. We have dispatched Hauptsturmfuhrer Dorsch to attempt to salvage something, he being the only other surviving officer from the original team. We can only hope that he can achieve some success with the limited time and resources at his disposal. Frankly, Herr Oberst, any success of any kind now will be despite your actions, not because of them. In the circumstances I am sure you cannot question the justness of that conclusion."

For a moment Ziedler felt the insane urge to argue with them. To ask if they could have done any better; if they could have sprung Vlasenin from the consulate, or trumped Ciarelli's run, or found Rawlings in the mountains. Any of those would have been the making of a lesser man's career. But it all counted for nothing set against his last failure. They had insisted on the trains, and on the extra precautions that had wasted a day and given the SOE time. He began to open his mouth – then saw the look on the Admiral's face. This had already been a body blow to the Abwehr's standing. The Admiral did not deserve for it to be made worse. So he merely said: "I accept your censure, and apologise once again. I will also accept whatever punishment you deem appropriate, Herr Reichsleiter."

"We considered several alternatives," Bormann said nonchalantly. "But the Herr Admiral has given a most eloquent plea in your defence, citing an admittedly exemplary past record. So we feel that a long period of leave to heal your wounds is in order, followed by a posting suitable to your particular skills – head of counter-terrorism in one of the occupied capitals seems eminently suitable to me. We will inform you of the specifics in due course."

So that was it, Ziedler thought. A policeman's job with a thousand men trying to kill me day and night. Danger without honour. Better than a firing squad, but not much. "Thank you, Herr Reichsleiter."

If Bormann caught the faint trace of sarcasm he gave no indication. "You will report back to the Herr Admiral when you are fully recovered. In the meantime you will play no further part in this operation or any other arising from it. And you will tell no-one of your role in it. Otherwise we will not be so merciful next time. Dismissed."

Ziedler got up and staggered towards the door. He felt dead inside. All over. He would never get another chance like this. He had failed his country and his parents. All of his career from now on would be a shuffling from one inglorious post to the next. And first he would have to bear months of Ilse's scorn – the affairs would become more open now, he knew that – and Manfred's touching but diffident love. Would that even last now that he could see him every day, broken and ruined?

The only consolation was that he was still alive, and somewhere Rawlings was too. He would survive this operation also, no matter what the upstart Dorsch thought he could do to stop him. And some day, before the war ended, perhaps, he and Rawlings would come face to face again. Rawlings the author of his pain and disgrace. Rawlings who would now be the motive power of his life. Rawlings, and the revenge that I will take on him.

As he walked back down the stairs to his car and driver – how much longer will that last, he wondered – a striking dark-haired man in Wehrmacht uniform caught his eye. Not only because his so obviously Slavic looks seemed incongruous in such a setting, but because he looked as miserable as Ziedler felt.

As he passed by, Petar looked back at the tall officer whose face was so scarred. It must once have been very handsome, you could tell. The war had made so many like that, especially here in Berlin. A city of scarred and lonely people. Like him. They had barely thanked him for what he had done, the information he had given. Judging by the rumours the mission to get the man Grigorin had been so keen to keep a secret – Vladimirin, was it? – had not gone well. Was that his fault? He had deserved better in return than this job, as lowly and demeaning as the food ministry. And he was sick of the taunts – Ivan, Ruski, *untermensch* and worse. He missed Russia but he knew he could never go back. Had it been worth it? Well, worth it or not, it was his life now. He squared his shoulders and continued on his way.

༄

At that same moment, General Ame and Count Ciano sat opposite each other at the ornate desk in Ciano's office. Each wore identical expressions, which would have been familiar to both Ziedler and Petar.

"So he's determined, then?" Ame asked.

"Absolutely. No further action from SIM in this matter. No operatives to be sent into Turkey unless specifically requested by Berlin. We follow their orders from now on."

For the first time in their acquaintance, Ame swore. "And in all other matters it will be the same. I predict it," the SIM head continued. "What can have possessed him to back down so meekly?"

"Justifiable German anger at Ciarelli's last little

escapade." Ciano's voice was rueful. "It's the old story – if Ciarelli had succeeded he, and we, would be heroes. As it is, we are bad boys who have put him out of favour with the Fuhrer." He rubbed his forehead wearily. "That was one of the worst meetings I've ever had with him. We will not be allowed such freedom of action again."

"We were so close." Ame's knuckles whitened. "When I find that traitor who told the Germans…"

"If Ciarelli had not set up that ludicrous charade of a midnight meeting, but simply demanded Vlasenin straight away, Ziedler would not have had time to make use of traitors."

Ame sighed. "He always did have a melodramatic streak. A drawback in our profession. Damn him!"

Ciano nodded but said nothing. And so the epitaph was pronounced on Eduardo Ciarelli as his body was unloaded from a plane at the Otranto air base and his wife made arrangements for the funeral. It would be with full regimental honours, of course, as befitted a hero of the North African campaign. And in the heart of the Vatican 'Rodrigo' entered his office and locked the door behind him. Once at his desk he opened the sealed envelope delivered to the *poste restante* box just outside the limits of the Pope's city.

The contents were a coded message confirming that the operation had been a success. His information had been acted upon and the only source that could trace the leak back to him had been eliminated. Suspicion would be sown incriminating lowlier members of the SIM in Rome. And the money had been deposited with his Swiss account that very morning.

He would check, of course, but there was no reason

to believe that the Germans would not be good and prompt payers. Everyone else was, for the good reason that he always gave good information. And he knew that the power of the SIM would only decline the more Germany took the ascendant in the Axis. Ciarelli had been insufficiently aware of that. And to try to involve the Vatican in his ludicrous subterfuge, without consulting him. The courtesy of one radio message, and 'Rodrigo' would naturally have backed up his story – for a little extra consideration, of course.

No, a little more distance from the SIM would be no bad thing. If both Germany and Italy lost, the Vatican's neutrality would be placed under severe scrutiny. And there were plenty of British and American agents in Rome equally eager to employ his services. Balance and fairness, that would be the key from now on, to encourage the proper degree of harmony in his world. And the appropriate level of reward, naturally. He threw the letter onto the fire and sat back in his seat as the bells of St Peter's chimed three on a crisp, cold winter's day.

∽

It was even colder in Moscow. The gravediggers in the small cemetery near the Kremlin had to work hard to chisel away enough earth to accommodate the coffin of Major Yevgeny Amarazov. The wind cut through Renkovich as he watched them lower the plain wooden box down, hands almost slipping on the snow-wetted rope. It wasn't much but it was more ceremony than Grigorin had received. No senior members of the GRU had been present when his neck-shot body had been dumped into the pit.

And if Amarazov had managed to get Vlasenin back before getting himself killed there would have been a hero's funeral. Red Guards by the hearse, a flag draped over the coffin, Ilya Ehrenburg reading the eulogy… and Amarazov would have been the luckiest man present, for not having to listen to it.

Renkovich gave a grim smile. You're lucky really, Yevgeny Petrovich. You got a quicker death than most of your enemies – and a better one than most of the rest of us. Still, if you'd had any sense you'd have vanished into Istanbul and opened a spies' bazaar. That would have been freedom, of a sort.

A cold hand rested on his shoulder. He turned and looked into the eyes of the two hard-faced men in thick overcoats and Homburg hats who had been waiting for him to pay his respects before the long journey began. Renkovich shivered. Failure was failure, whether at policy or operational level, and death was death, whether… he steeled himself, deliberately squaring his shoulders as they led him to the car. Such thoughts took away your strength and he would need all his strength in the years that lay ahead.

From a window above the minister's secretary watched them go. A sad loss. Renkovich was an able man, and a less blinkered ideologue than many. Of course, to have put in a plea on his behalf would have been utter folly. They had found their scapegoats and it was in everyone's best interests to be content with that. The cold eye had passed over him, and Vladimir, then moved on, thank God.

But there would be no more games of chess for a

while. Better to let events take their course and see how they played out. If all ended happily – from the point of view of a good and loyal Soviet servant, of course – there would be no need for any further raking over of coals. The GRU and NKVD were co-operating to an unheard of extent to try to find Vlasenin before the British could get him out of Turkey. And even if he was lost to them, there was a lot of talk about a new scientific genius, this young man from the Energetics Institute. A star at Moscow University and an unquestioningly loyal Party member. What was his name, again? Ah, yes, that was it; Sakharov.

∞

Rawlings had been awake for hours now. Curtis had just woken from a light doze. Vlasenin had been asleep for most of the day and looked considerably refreshed. Jennings looked more tired than any of them, but he had been on duty all day, either standing guard at the door or liaising with the two guards downstairs. But now it was dark and he was starting to look more relaxed.

They were all ready to go, suit jackets buttoned over the guns at their belts, hats on. Rawlings had the briefcase in his left hand; the other two carried identical ones. Jennings at the door said: "We've arranged a signal; two short knocks, one long. The chap in the car knows that, too."

As if in response, they came. Jennings shouted for the password in Greek. A muffled reply came and he nodded in satisfaction, opening the door. The next second he was falling back into the room, a red hole in his forehead, as the blond German from the ambushes moved inside, slamming the door behind him. He was in civilian clothes now, but carried a still-smoking silenced Luger, gesturing with it at Rawlings and Curtis to drop their guns. They obeyed. The German smiled.

"You know, I don't think we've been formally introduced, Major Rawlings," he said in perfect English. "Despite our two interesting previous meetings. Hauptsturmfuhrer Gerhard Dorsch, Sicherheitsdienst."

"Well, you have the advantage of me, then, because I've never heard of you. But I must admit I'm surprised to see you here."

"You're not dealing with Ziedler any more. The SD have a better network in Turkey than those Prussian dilettantes at the Abwehr. We knew within hours that there were four new arrivals at this hotel, with descriptions. When the SD has information it acts, and nothing stands in its way."

"So I suppose you killed Jennings' guards downstairs?" Dorsch nodded. "Promised one his life in return for the password?" A smile to accompany the nod this time. "And the family who run this place?"

This time Dorsch laughed. "I don't kill people I don't need to. I just locked them in their office. They won't get in the way, either."

"And what way is that, exactly?" Rawlings knew he had to keep him talking. *For some reason he wants all three of us alive. That's the only reason for not simply giving Curtis and me the same as Jennings, then walking out with everything.* "It's a long way back to Greece and we'll have everyone looking for you when I don't make that plane. You won't get ten miles down the road before every SOE man in Turkey's on your tail. You'll need to keep an eye out for the Russians too. Unless you've got an army to back you up I don't fancy your chances when Amarazov's replacement turns up with half the Turkish Communist Party behind him."

"I have no army to back me up, major. I once had a platoon, but you killed them all. So now I must be content with the SD's local man. Not quite Hermann Goering Division calibre, I admit. But good enough to keep watch downstairs and perform simple guard duty. That is all I require. I have not seen much evidence of any SOE legions in these parts so far. As for the Russians, they are floundering blind, as usual. It is no matter, anyway. For I am not going ten miles down the road. More like ten minutes, I think – to your plane."

Rawlings laughed out loud. "And what makes you think they'll let you on?"

"Because you will be with me, major. We will take the courier's car when it comes and my colleague will drive. You will introduce me as Sergeant Jennings, then explain my presence to the pilot. I am sure that if he is being paid enough he will not care who he flies – or where to."

Rawlings nodded. "I see – we can get you out of Turkey the quickest way possible, in return for our lives. Not a bad idea. Except it won't work."

"And why not, precisely?"

Rawlings gestured to Vlasenin. "Because we're not giving him up – not to you, not after all the men who've died to keep him safe. You've killed more of my team than everyone else I've encountered on this lousy mission put together. Do you think I'll do anything to help you?"

"Yes, major, I do." Dorsch was growing impatient

but the Luger, flicking from Rawlings to Curtis with metronomic precision, was steady as a rock. "Because the alternative is for me to put a bullet in the right kneecap of you and the boy here, and then to shoot Dr Vlasenin to pieces slowly. He will still be alive and in no position to resist when I take him and his papers, with all the money I can find in this room to buy the pilot off. Then the Turks can intern you, or the Russians kill you, whoever arrives first. Do what I say and everyone is spared further suffering, especially the doctor here. I think that will appeal to your strange kind of morality."

Rawlings felt sick with defeat. He could find no answer. Dorsch gave a mocking smile. Then, to both men's surprise, Curtis began to speak. "And suppose we try to stop you?" The question was delivered in a strange faraway tone. There was fear in his voice, but courage too, and sadness.

"Stop me?" Dorsch gave a scornful laugh. "How? I can kill you both now?"

"If we both move at the same time? Those guns aren't far away. You should have kicked them clear. Risky to get so close to us to do it, but as it is..." he shrugged. "Who do you choose to shoot first? You've seen us both in action. Tough choice, I'd say." He paused, then added in German: "How good do you think you are, Nazi?"

"No, Curtis!" Rawlings shouted. He knew he wasn't bluffing. "Don't do it. That's an order!"

"Quiet!" Dorsch commanded. He looked at them both. "You wouldn't dare – whoever moved first would know he was a dead man."

Neither Curtis nor Rawlings moved. The smile returned to Dorsch's face but Curtis matched and eclipsed it. His smile was that of a Stratford Hamlet, ready for the final scene. "Ah, yes, the survival instinct. And no-one can fight that." He spoke in German again. "Big mistake."

Then he moved, diving for the gun, fast as ever. But to pull a trigger takes an instant. Dorsch's bullet took him in the heart, punching him back onto the bed. In one movement Rawlings dived right, barged Vlasenin to the floor, and scooped up the Mauser. A bullet cracked over their heads as they hit the ground. Rawlings got off one unaimed shot lying prone. He was up again in a moment but he knew if the first had not connected there would be no time for a second.

It had connected. Dorsch was staggering back towards the door. The bullet had hit him low on the right side of the chest. Bad, but not fatal. He was off-balance, but regaining it, gun arm starting to aim again. Rawlings fired again, double tap, chest and heart. Dorsch was slammed against the door, gun falling to the ground. Rawlings had not had time to aim properly and they had not quite been killing shots. Dorsch turned, scrambling to open the door and escape. Rawlings' fourth bullet was dead centre in his spine, punching him through the door as it burst open. He collided with the wall and tried to stay upright, but his knees buckled and he fell to the floor.

Rawlings came on through the doorway, still firing, again and again. Then he was standing over the body, aiming one last shot at the head. The hammer clicked on an empty magazine. Rawlings jettisoned it and fed in a new one. Then he saw, as if for the first time, what was lying beneath him. Suddenly he felt very tired.

A noise to his right made him whirl round, Mauser coming up. Dorsch's back-up, unsighted by the gloom of the stairwell, but bringing his pistol to bear. Rawlings shot him in the right shoulder, following him as he tumbled back down the stairs. The bodies of Jennings' guards lay in the lobby. The SD man stumbled over them, trying to retrieve his pistol, then stopping as he saw Rawlings above him. He looked up, waiting for the axe to fall. He was fat and unshaven, a middle-aged man with a vaguely Bulgar cast to his features. He looked terrified.

"Go home," Rawlings said in Turkish. "And find some better work." He kept the pistol on the SD man as he stumbled through the door, babbling gratefully. Rawlings looked around the room and wiped his sleeve across his face. "Big mistake," he said in German. Then he checked the rest of the downstairs rooms and outside in case Dorsch had been lying once again. Just as he finished a car pulled into the forecourt at speed and a man in a shabby suit and Homburg hat jumped out, pistol at the ready.

"Major Rawlings? I'm Carson, the courier. Jennings sent for me. I heard the shooting as I came in. Where the hell is Jennings, and the local guards?"

"Dead. And Captain Curtis too. The Germans tried for Vlasenin one last time. Don't worry, they're... neutralised. And Vlasenin's fine. Keep the engine running. We'll be down in thirty seconds."

He walked back into the room. Vlasenin was kneeling over Curtis' body. He looked round as Rawlings entered, tears in his eyes. "He's dead."

"I know," Rawlings replied. "No professional misses a killing shot from that range. I don't know why you even bothered to look."

Vlasenin said angrily: "That was the bravest thing I

have ever seen."

Rawlings looked thoughtful, seeming to analyse the statement before saying at last: "Yes, me too. I didn't think he had it in him. I even thought he might be a traitor at one time. But I certainly didn't think he had it in him." He paused. "I didn't think any of them had it in them. But they saved you and me more times than I can remember. They saved us, but not themselves. Mayhew, the sergeants, Walters, all of them." He shook his head and looked at Vlasenin. "Is what you know really worth all this?"

Vlasenin lowered his head. "I cannot say. Truly."

"Of course you can't." Rawlings seemed to come to himself then, looking for the briefcase and picking it up. "None of us can. Only history can, I suppose. But that's for the future. For now, I have a job to finish. Let's get going."

He held out a hand. Vlasenin took it gratefully, rising to his feet, then they both went down to the waiting car.

༄

Of course, it still wasn't over. The ride to the airfield was nerve-wracking – Rawlings was still wary in case Dorsch had been lying about back-up, or the nearness of the Russians – and the pilot was suspicious at the absence of two of his passengers, demanding that he be paid full fare for them anyway. He almost cried off, but Rawlings' prominent display of his pistol, with the safety catch still off, carried the day.

And all through the flight Rawlings expected to hear the approaching drone of a Messerschmitt squadron.

To deprive everyone of Vlasenin and his knowledge for good might be worth incurring the wrath of the Turks. And the anxiety increased as they left Turkish airspace for the final leg of the journey to Cyprus. There were fighter aircraft on Crete and Rhodes, and he knew that a seek and destroy mission with them as the target would have absolute priority in the Third Reich that night. He only began to relax when they had touched down in Cyprus and he knew they could transfer to any one of a dozen aircraft bound for destinations throughout the Middle East.

Rawlings had expected a transfer to Cairo, but the SOE link man at the airfield, a young flight lieutenant named Peters, had new orders. Davies had left for London and Rawlings was to follow him, with Vlasenin and an armed escort, immediately. Within the hour they were on a Dakota bound for Malta. The same irascible Scots RN Commander who had assisted Rawlings' passage from Barcelona was still there and still impatient to get such troublesome supercargo off his hands. Within another hour they were on another Dakota – final destination RAF Northolt.

They arrived there just before 8 p.m on the evening of Thursday, December 10th, 1942. It was less than twenty-four hours since Rawlings' final confrontation with Dorsch. It was twenty-two days since Vlasenin's capture in Turkey, and twenty since Rawlings had escaped from France. Rawlings could not speak for the Russian but he felt he had lived through a century of living rough and fighting hard since then. He could barely stay awake to shake Davies' hand at the airfield, and register Vlasenin being escorted to a staff car by several hard-faced men in civilian clothes. Another car was waiting for him, with instructions to take him to overnight quarters at the airfield and then convey him to Baker Street the next morning for a formal debrief.

The meeting was at 11 a.m sharp, which gave Rawlings a chance to have a good night's sleep and take a hot bath in the morning. A uniform for a major in the Durham Light Infantry was pressed and ready for him in his quarters and he was still adjusting to the unusual feeling of being officially a soldier again when he knocked on Davies' door.

The office looked exactly the same as it had done when Davies sent him off to France – oak-panelled, thickly-carpeted and with a roaring fire. He noticed a decanter of whisky and two glasses on the desk as Davies rose to greet him and invite him to take a seat. "Well, I think this calls for a celebration, Alex," he said, removing the cut-glass stopper and pouring himself a generous measure. But Rawlings put his hand over his glass.

"It's a bit early in the day for me, Hugh. And to be honest I don't feel like celebrating the fact that I got all my team killed." He hesitated. "And all the contact group."

Davies nodded. "They were good men, all of them. Not to mention, ... er, Miss Artova, of course. But they helped you do what was needed. Both Viscount Selborne and I extend you, and them, our profoundest gratitude. It's obvious that we, and your country, owe you a great deal."

Rawlings leaned back in his chair and sighed. "Well, I won't call in the debt just yet. But if the country really wants to show its appreciation it can give me that month's leave in the Caribbean and…" suddenly he didn't feel like joking "… and it can hand out some medals. VCs for Curtis, Mayhew, the two sergeants and Walters; Military Crosses at least for all the rest. And the George Cross for Vasily Stolnikov and Yelena Artova. I owe them that much, at least. They were the real heroes of the mission. If Vlasenin's here it's because of them, not me."

Davies shifted in his seat and chose his next words very carefully. "You know, that's really not on, Alex; it would draw too much attention to a very… delicate operation."

"Then make something up!" Rawlings said savagely. "Say they all died at Alamein, or blowing up a bridge somewhere. They deserve those medals – and the soldiers' widows can hock them when the Army pension runs out."

"Sarcasm ill-becomes you, major. If we honour any of those involved in any way, it might be wrongly interpreted."

"By who?"

Davies looked even more uncomfortable. "The Russians."

Rawlings kept his temper with a supreme effort. "And why exactly should we be so concerned about their feelings? In fact, I'll forgo the pleasure of a holiday if you put me straight on to finding out exactly who in SOE was tipping them off all this time. Whoever it was must be high up, and they were obviously working hand-in-hand with the traitor in SIS who got Vlasenin captured. There's a nest of them, Hugh, and anything else we do that involves any crossover will go the same way unless you let me flush it out."

"That is out of the question, major. Relations are

strained enough, and the orders from above are to do nothing to exacerbate that. We are officially allies, and that alliance must be maintained. We already have indications from diplomatic level that they are willing to let the matter rest, as long as we take no further 'unfriendly' action. Let it drop, Alex. I can't see a situation like this arising again until after the war's over. Then we'll have plenty of time to root them out. For now, the priority is to beat the Germans – and you've just brought that a damn sight nearer."

"So you're telling me that Stalin and his boys will be quite happy for Vlasenin to go down to the Cavendish Laboratory – which I presume is where they took him last night – and start work on a weapon that will make Britain the most powerful country in the world. Sorry, Hugh, I can't see them taking that lying down."

"That is why Dr Vlasenin will not be based in England." Davies looked intently at the rubber stamp on his desk. "He is currently en route to America, where his work will be done under their supervision."

Rawlings looked at him in disgust. "So that's what all this means in the end? That's what my men died for? We hand him over to the Yanks because the Russians aren't so annoyed at them. That's why they kept out of the picture, isn't it? Because they knew – and you did, too – that there'd be some dirty little compromise like this. And what does Britain get out of it? Nothing."

Davies looked up again now, angry too. "We get victory over the Nazis. That's what this war's about. Yes, it's a dirty little compromise, Alex – and it's one that keeps our two main allies happy. And it may have escaped your notice, but without either of them, Britain is finished."

"Britain is finished if she allows something like this to happen. So he'll join this Manhattan Project that all the talk's about?"

"Yes – as an anonymous member, naturally."

"Naturally. So the boys who took him away last night were Wild Bill Donovan's lot – the OSS?" Davies merely nodded. "Thought they looked too well-dressed to be our lads." Rawlings gave a mirthless smile. "You didn't think it worth telling me that, obviously." He shrugged. "Probably just as well – not that I'd have been in any fit state to stop them, of course. So another long journey for the poor sod, then. Still, he's tough enough to take it. They'd just better treat him right." Rawlings looked at the ceiling. "He's a good man. Saved my life out there once, you know – yes, of course you do, I told you in the transmission, didn't I? And I'd mention it in the report if any of this were ever to go down on paper. Yes, I'd set it all out, and add a little appendix – I'm going to find the Red in SOE and make him regret the day he joined the Party."

Davies looked him in the eye. "You heard what I said, Major Rawlings. No action to be taken in that respect. That's an order."

Rawlings shook his head. "He'll do it again, Hugh. Him and the rest like him in SOE, and SIS. God knows how many there are. At least let me find a name, so we can bribe him to back off, or try to turn him."

"Absolutely not, major. That's an order."

"OK." Rawlings stood up suddenly. "Then I resign."

For a moment Davies was speechless. As Rawlings made for the door, he stuttered: "You can't do that."

"Can't I? You just try making me work, Hugh."

"You can't resign from SOE. Nobody's ever resigned."

Rawlings turned back to him. "Like you keep saying, Hugh, you've never had an officer like me in SOE before. If you let traitors stay in the ranks you can't expect me to fall in alongside them. I'll not work for you – and I'll make sure everyone knows why."

"By doing what?" Davies shouted scornfully. "Going to the newspapers? We'd slap a D Notice on them before you even got there. And where's your proof? Nothing on paper, everything deniable and everyone who could corroborate your story dead. Don't forget the Official Secrets Act, either – it was a long time ago when you first signed, but you're still bound by it."

"You think that scares me? A British prison's the only one I've not seen the inside of yet."

"You won't do it, Alex. Deep down you know we're right. It's shabby, it's a compromise, but it got the job done and it keeps the status quo. Once the war's over we'll hunt them all down. But for now you shut up and get back in line."

Rawlings held his gaze. "I won't work for you."

"So what will you do? Refuse to fight? Join the rest of the conchies filling out forms in the food stores? Or drop out of sight? And do what? Can't see you as a black marketeer, somehow, Alex."

"Then give me some decent soldiering." Rawlings' voice was cold. "Send me to North Africa, or put me in the Commandos. Just don't tell me to sit by while a traitor who got my boys killed works in the same organisation as me."

"That's the way we're playing it, Alex. That's the game

– and you can't just opt out of it. For one thing, you'd never be happy doing anything else. Fine, we can put you back in the DLI. But you'd still have to keep your nose out of our business. Be an ordinary officer, or do the thing you're best at. Your choice."

"I'm leaving." Rawlings turned again, almost at the door now.

"Fine. I think this meeting is over, anyway. But you'll be back."

"Don't bet on it," Rawlings said as he slammed the door behind him.

"I won't," Davies replied softly to himself. "I'm not a betting man. But you will come back."

As Rawlings left the man entrance and turned towards Marylebone Road he stopped at a news vendor's and bought a pack of Players and a box of matches. The thought of smoking the entire pack seemed the most enticing prospect in the world at that moment. And perhaps it wasn't too early for a whisky now, either. Both were, he reflected, pretty low on his list of vices at the moment. As he walked on the wind gathered force, biting into him, and a thin but steady rain began. He put his cap on and began to button his coat.

But the weather was not deterring a Salvation Army band and a group of carol singers gathered near the Tube station. Surely that was weeks away, he thought, and if they think they can make me feel festive...

God rest ye merry, gentlemen

... but it was well into December now – he'd lost track of time, recently, with one thing or another... and ...

Let nothing you dismay

... you had to admire their persistence in this weather. So he put the remainder of his change in their collecting tin as he passed. "Thank you, sir," said the old man conducting

For Jesus Christ our Saviour
Was born on Christmas Day
To save us all from Satan's power
When we were gone astray
Oh, tidings of comfort and joy...

As Rawlings turned the corner into Marylebone Road the wind and rain stung his eyes. He wiped them clean, turned his collar up and walked on into the grey morning.

EPILOGUE

February 12th, 1943

WELL, THAT WAS IT, CAPTAIN Nikolai Danko reflected as he locked up the now-deserted office building of the little airfield that had been their home for – three years, was it? On many occasions, it had seemed much longer. But now the time had finally come he felt he might miss it a little.

It certainly seemed preferable to the Central Asian shithole whose name he couldn't even pronounce that would be the next stage on his *via dolorosa*. His previous experiences there had not been good. The locals had been downright unfriendly and ungrateful. How he was going to co-ordinate supply airlifts to the Chinese in a land where they still thought aeroplanes were flying demons was beyond him. Added to that the small fact that they've been fighting us for centuries and they've only just stopped. Didn't they realise that it was all for their benefit, that taking their land was part of the process of turning them into good, civilised Russians? Hadn't worked, anyway. At least the locals here had made some pretence at Christianity before the Party outlawed God.

Still, at least it was further from Stalingrad. He grudgingly admitted that things did seem to be going well there. But the Fritzies would hit back. They wouldn't surrender a city – and an army – just like that. No, they'd throw some real heavy ordnance at the whole Caucasus very soon and Nikolai didn't mind being halfway across the world when that happened.

Ostensibly that was the reason why the airfield was being closed. But he knew better than that. It was all to do with the business of the weapons officer. They wanted to make damn sure that no-one who'd been there that night talked too much about it, to each other or anyone else. If this had been about Stalingrad, they'd have been transferred together to some new airfield nearer the fighting. But the rest had been scattered to the four winds weeks ago. Kaminski was down in the Crimea somewhere, the ground crew had been sent to Leningrad and the guards – well, God alone knew what use had been found for them. Put out to graze, perhaps, or sent to clear a minefield by walking over it in heavy boots, more like.

And he was heading on the Golden Road to Samarkand. Hurrah. Well, that would probably kill him one way or the other. If the locals didn't take a dislike to his face, then take a knife to it, he would find a good supply of the only stuff that made life bearable out there and smoke himself into oblivion.

He certainly wouldn't talk. He'd never had any intention of talking. One look at that NKVD bastard had seen to that. He wondered what had happened to the weapons officer, as he locked the main gate. Usually a cover-up like this meant it hadn't gone too well. That thought gave him a grim, secret satisfaction. He pulled a hip flask from his coat pocket and raised it in a brief salute before turning away, taking a swig as he headed for the car that would take him to the train. Here's luck to you, Comrade Weapons Officer. Let's hope you and your balls are still sleeping in the same room. In this world us little men need all the luck we can get.

September 14th, 1944

Group Captain Roderick Anson could not remember a busier time in his entire SIS career. He had thought that a posting to Istanbul would be relatively safe and relaxed. But lately the problems seemed to mount up daily. Even the time a couple of years back when there had been that unfortunate Vlasenin business had not been so relentlessly demanding.

To be honest, he felt that the shock waves from that little escapade had never really stopped rippling in Istanbul. It had been the Devil's own job to calm the Turks down after that damned shooting match at the Soviet Consulate and the planted bodies in British uniform. They had bleated about infringement of neutrality, disregarding diplomatic conventions – some of them had even spouted some nonsense about British deserters planning to rob the Topkapi Palace, of all things.

It had meant that a lot of the good credit built up by chaps like dear old Percy Loraine at the embassy in Ankara over so many years had been spent overnight. So getting information about what the Germans and

Russians and everybody else was up to was twice as difficult. It wasn't just a case of swanning into Rejans every night and tipping the right waiter any more. And, of course, the Czech exiles had stopped paying visits to the Blue Mosque.

Added to that was the complication of Greece. The poor bastards who passed through Turkey on their way into and out of that bloody cauldron all said the same thing. The Huns were going to leave a wasteland behind them when they finally got out. All the efforts of the SOE teams – and these new Yanks types from the OSS – were just finger in the dyke stuff. Unless there was a full-scale invasion to keep some order when the Germans went there would be nothing to keep the ELAS and EDES from each other's throats. And no-one was taking bets on the EDES – unless we really did decide to prop them up by force.

Well, we would if it looked like the Russians were going to move in, of course. And that seemed more than likely; not just in Greece, either. Bulgaria was in turmoil; Hungary and Romania too. It looked more than probable that the Communist partisans in all three would get together and offer Uncle Joe their countries on a platter. But we were still their allies, and after the Vlasenin business no-one was rocking that particular boat.

So he and the SOE chap de Chastelain were trying to keep it all in order. But the Russians were getting more audacious. Shot down poor old Vrushkov as he was coming out of Rejans not two months ago. Another thing they couldn't be touched for. And there was as much activity the other way. More and more defectors sticking their heads above the parapet, some with a lot of information to trade for safe passage. He would have to make more efforts to get some of them on side, at least. Especially since Section IX in London, the boys that dealt with espionage against Russia, seemed to be taking more interest in Turkey. But the section head certainly seemed to know his stuff. Very keen to get more involved. Forster had been too much of a cold fish but this new chap was a good laugh. And a fellow Cambridge hand, too. Yes, Anson had met a lot worse in the service than Kim Philby.

July 16, 1945
05:29:45

Vlasenin could not believe the light. It filled his vision, and everyone's. His knees began to tremble as he saw the light dissipate, and what came after it. And heard that deep, almost subterranean, rumble. Of course, they had all calculated to the minutest detail exactly what would happen when they tested it. He had spent nearly three years – and some of the men around him much longer – calculating that. But they could not know, truly, until it happened. And now it had.

He looked around at the others; Fermi, whom he had become closest to, through their similar histories. And Oppenehimer, the director. He was looking directly at the sight, his mouth forming words Vlasenin could not understand.

All the generals were looking too. Some dumbfounded, some unbelieving, some afraid. But none exultant. That surprised him. Had they not delivered exactly what they wanted? Then he too looked back at Ground Zero, that carefully selected patch of nothingness in the middle of the Jornada Del Muerte desert. And he knew, also, that this was not a moment to exult.

They watched for a while. Then the military police put them back in the convoy that would return them to Los Alamos. And later in the day, when it was safe, they would go back and see what this test – the one Oppenheimer had codenamed Trinity – had really done.

The intense heat of a New Mexico morning was already drawing the sweat from Vlasenin's body. After two years he was still not used to it, it still drained him even when he wore his lightweight linen suit. He took off his hat to fan himself, and wound down the rear window of the car that carried him back. Because of that he heard the shouting before some of the others. Then they all heard it. And saw the tiny, dilapidated truck which had crashed into a dry wash near the road along which they travelled. A smaller road, even rougher and more primitive, snaked off into the hills. The truck driver had obviously been travelling along it when the blast had occurred.

He was far enough away to be safe. But he was lucky not to have been hurt in the crash. He limped slightly and looked shaken as he ran haltingly up to the convoy, which had now stopped dead. The military police were out of the trucks and forming a guard round the car as half a dozen of them walked up to intercept the truck driver.

The lieutenant in charge said something to him. Vlasenin did not hear him but the truck driver's reply was much louder. "Sure I'll get back. But what you goin' to do now? The sun's blowed up."

He repeated that a few times while the lieutenant

tried to calm him down. Eventually he succeeded and walked back to the convoy, detailing one truck and its occupants to help "drag the old boy's biscuit box out of that wash. Then send him on his way and tell him to keep his mouth shut."

He waved the convoy on and Vlasenin's car moved away. Vlasenin looked behind as it did so, looking at the old farmer walking back to his truck, still shaking his head, still asking the soldiers what they were going to do, now that the sun had blowed up.